Irish Kings

Cillian

The Leader

By Katie Broussard

Acknowledgements:

Cover created by SelfPubBookCovers.com/Joetherasakdhi

Irish Kings

Cillian

The Leader

Chapter 1: A Little Sassy

Biting into a piece of bacon, Chloe Guidry shared a grin with her dad while they listened to her mom recite her list for the third time. David and Angela were leaving after breakfast to go on an Alaskan cruise to see the glaciers. They'd been planning the trip for months.

After David retired from the Marines, he'd opened a high-end sporting goods store that quickly grew into a large chain of stores across Louisiana and parts of Southeast Texas.

Chloe had only been home for a few days. She attended school in Manhattan where she was studying for her Master's degree in art history. She'd just completed her first year in the Master's program. Which meant that this time next year, she'd begin her career, and carefree lazy summers would be a thing of the past. So, in just a few hours, she and her friends were heading to Panama City Beach for the week. An entire week of sunshine, cocktails and no responsibilities. She couldn't wait.

"Potato chips, clothespins, jelly beans."

"Chloe!" Angela complained with a giggle.

"What? No jelly beans? You've got to have jelly beans." Chloe attempted to hold a straight face.

"Smart aleck." As usual, Angela's excitement was getting the best of her. She made lists. It's what she did. And Chloe teased her relentlessly.

"What time are you leaving for the beach, kiddo?" David stole a piece of bacon off of his daughter's plate.

"Hey, watch it old man." Chloe giggled and snatched a piece of toast from his plate in retaliation. She loved these times with her parents. The kitchen table was their gathering place. It's where they usually started and ended each day. She wanted to soak up every second because she missed them so much when she was away at school.

She had always dreamed of going to art school. But not just any art school. No, it had to be the best. Everyone said it was a long shot, but she didn't care. She'd never wanted to do anything else, so she's busted her ass to get accepted. The school only took thirty new students a year, and she'd been determined to be one of them.

When she painted, she brought the people and places in her head to life on canvas. Mostly she painted for the sheer joy of it, but sometimes, she did it because she needed to. As far back as she could remember, she'd felt most at peace with a brush in her hand. She supposed it was her coping mechanism. Because, when she was angry or frustrated, she painted. And her art teachers were impressed with the level of detail she could create.

Chloe knew herself well. She was the type of person who had to stay active. She was competitive by nature, and being the daughter of a retired Marine came with certain expectations. Expectations she was only too happy to meet.

Some would call her an over achiever and she was ok with that. From an early age, she'd trained in martial arts at her father's insistence. She'd made the Varsity softball team as a high school freshman and had earned a spot on the All-State Team three years in a row. She'd been co-captain of the volleyball team her senior year and won several awards in track because she was seriously fast. She'd always been a good athlete and loved a challenge. But now that she was in college, she was happy to just focus on her art.

David scowled at her. "Do you hear that, Angie? Old man she says!"

"Chloe, no old man jokes today." Angela threw into the items she was reciting from her list without missing a beat. Proving that not only did her mom have eyes in the back of her head, but she could multi task like a boss.

"Because she's about to get that Master's degree she thinks she's all grown up and can be a little sassy." David winked at his beautiful daughter. Chloe was their saving grace. He and Angela had always planned on having a big family. So, a year after their son Brock was born, they were ready to try again. But to their disappointment, it wasn't meant to be. The doctors couldn't find a medical reason why Angela wasn't getting pregnant and eventually they resigned themselves to being the parents of an only child. Then, ten years later that changed. Chloe came into the world kicking and screaming. He smiled to himself as he remembered the doctors placing her little body into his large hands. She'd been so tiny. When he'd spoken softly to her, welcoming her into the world, she'd immediately stopped screaming and locked eyes with him and stolen his heart.

Chloe was as beautiful as her mother. No one could ever dispute that. Although a petite five-three, she had the same white blond hair, classic bone structure and sparkling blue eyes of her mother's Nordic heritage that was only enhanced by the long dark lashes she'd gotten from him. When

2

strangers see her for the first time, their immediate response is always the same; she should be on a runway in Millan. But thanks to his Angela, Chloe took those comments with a grain of salt. She knew she looked just like her mother, and her mother put little emphasis on physical beauty. Angela was special that way. She'd taught Chloe very early in life that appearances changed easily, but what was deep inside the soul of a person didn't. She said that was where you found true beauty.

Chloe was no different. But as delicate as she appeared, Chloe was also a force to be reckoned with. At twenty-four, she was ready to set the world on fire. She'd accomplished everything she set her mind to so far. And despite everything she'd been through, he was confident she would continue to do so.

Chloe was only twelve when they'd lost Brock. He'd been in his sixth year as a Navy Seal when the accident happened. He and his team were infiltrating a terrorist camp over in the Middle East, when the building they were searching exploded. And there'd been nothing left. No remains for the families to bury. Nothing.

Chloe had worshiped Brock, and he had adored his little "Chloe Bell." He'd called her that because she reminded him of Tinker Bell. She was such a tiny little sprite with big blue eyes and sheets of white blonde hair and Brock swore she was a dead ringer for the little fairy.

He'd doted on his baby sister. Teaching her how to read, to count and as she grew older, to his mother's consternation, how to wrestle. He'd made sure she knew how to break a hold by fighting dirty. He told his mom one day when she was giving him grief about it that Chloe was too small to fight fairly.

But when they lost him, Chloe lost a piece of herself. She'd fallen into a deep state of depression. And he and Angela were so grief stricken themselves, that it had taken a few months to realize their baby girl was barely functioning. That's when he'd taken her to her first Krav Maga lesson. The instructor was a Marine buddy of his who understood that Chloe needed an outlet for her grief and anger. Those lessons brought her out of her shell, and she finally started living again.

Angela set her list aside and glanced at her watch. "My goodness, where did the time go? David, we better get going. Chloe honey, what time are you leaving?"

"Sid and I are meeting up with everyone at the coffee shop around 11:00. We should hit Panama before dark."

"I spoke to Sara last night. She said to tell you to call her if anything happens during your trip. I think she's worried Sidney will get a little crazy at the beach."

"Sidney's always crazy. That's not news. But she's responsible, too. Remember, we spent our entire gap year in France all by ourselves without a single incident. So, I'm pretty sure we can handle Panama City." Chloe rubbed her sock covered toes over her white German Shepard Juneau's belly under the table. Juneau was her baby. She'd gotten him a few months after Brock died.

"Angie, sweetheart, they can handle themselves. Hell, you and Sara have had those girls schlepping across the world every summer since they were thirteen years old." David winked at her.

Angela glanced at her watch again and frowned. "We better get going. We have to drop off Juneau to Sara and Bill. We should probably bring them back something special from our trip to repay them for watching him while we're all out of town."

"Something special? Are you kidding? Sara's gonna spoil that dog while we're gone. It'll take weeks to retrain him. Isn't that right, boy?" David patted his knees, and Juneau immediately put his paws on them and stood on his hind legs for a brisk pet.

"I think you're the one who spoils him, dad." Chloe picked up her plate and grabbed her fathers on the way to the sink to rinse and load them into the dishwasher. When she finished, her mom pulled her in for a tight hug.

"We'll only be gone ten days, sweetheart. Have fun at the beach."

"I will."

"And good luck on your fist day at the gallery. We'll come by and see what they have you doing as soon as we get back."

"It's an internship so I doubt if I'll be doing anything special, but I'm excited about it." Chloe held on tight to her mom. Big hugs comforted Angela, so Chloe gave them to her every chance she could. Then she turned and hugged her dad just as tightly.

"Be careful, kiddo." David whispered into her ear as he held her.

"You two have a good time."

"Set the alarm when we leave." David kissed Chloe's forehead, then snapped the leash onto Juneau's collar.

Chloe dropped to the floor and hugged Juneau. She grabbed his face and put her forehead to his like she's done every day before leaving the house since he'd been a puppy. "You behave yourself. Don't cause too much trouble. I'll miss you, boy." Juneau nuzzled her neck, then licked her cheek.

Chloe rushed back inside after seeing her parents off, stopping only long enough to lock the door and set the alarm. She ran up to her room to get dressed and finish her last-minute packing. She was just pulling her cut off jean shorts up over her bikini bottoms when her cell rang.

"Yo, Chica, you ready?"

"Almost. Did mom and dad leave your house yet?"

"Yep. And I got to snuggle with your pooch, but now I'm ready for margaritas on the beach!"

"I know, right? Do you want to go grab a coffee and pant over 'Hot Glazed Hank' before we meet up with the girls?" Chloe couldn't help but giggle. Hank was the owner of the local doughnut shop and he was totally hot. Sidney saw him first when they were seniors in high school and had dubbed him 'Hot Glazed Hank' and the name stuck. It had been their official hang out spot ever since. They went there every chance they could, just hoping to catch a glimpse of the sexy owner.

"Hey, don't be perving on my man! You know he's mine."

"Yea, yea. I know. You saw him first." Chloe's phone beeped with an incoming call, making her glance at the screen. "Hang on a sec, someone from the gallery is calling on the other line." Chloe quickly clicked over to answer the other call.

"Hello?"

"Chloe?"

"Ms. Diane?"

"Chloe, thank goodness I caught you before you left."

Diane sounded a little frantic. Not at all like the poised, polished manager of the gallery.

"Is something wrong?"

"Chloe dear, I know you're not supposed to start at the gallery until next week, but my assistant Marcel's father had a heart attack this morning!"

"That's terrible! I'm so sorry to hear that."

"Yes, it was so sudden. But now I'm completely shorthanded for the showing this weekend. I need your help."

Her summer internship at the gallery was extremely important. It was a requirement for her Master's program, and it had taken her months to secure the position. "I'm happy to help. What do you need me to do? I've been to dozens of art shows, but I've never worked one before."

"Bless you, Chloe! There's no secret to it. All you have to do is greet the customers, guide them toward the exhibits and provide details about the work and the artists. I'll send the packet for the show to your email so you'll have a chance to study it before tonight. It starts at 6:00, so please be here at 5:00. I'll also need you for tomorrow for the last viewing from 1:00 to 5:00. Can you do that?"

"Sure, I'll be there."

"Chloe, you're a gem. I'm sorry to spring this on you last minute."

"Please don't worry about it."

"Thank you, Chloe. I'll see you in a few hours. Don't forget to check your email for the packet and study as much about the pieces and artists as you can before the show."

"I won't. I'll see you at 5:00."

"Bye dear."

Chloe clicked over to the other line and sighed heavily.

"What? That sigh doesn't sound good."

"It's not. Diane's assistant's father had a heart attack this morning. She needs my help for the art show this weekend."

"No way! Chlo lo, we're leaving in two hours!"

"I know Sid, but this internship is really important."

"Shitake Freaking Mushrooms!"

"Come on Sid. Don't be like that." Sidney had a way of cursing without actually cursing. She felt that people who cursed did it because their vocabulary was lacking.

"I know, I know. I'm sorry. It's just that the timing sucks."

"I have to do this."

"Ugh. Alright. So, what's the plan?"

That's why she loved Sidney so much. She understood her. She was her partner in crime and always had her back. "I'll work the event then head to Panama City before the butt-crack of dawn Monday morning."

"Alright, come pick me up and drop me off at the coffee shop. I'll ride to Panama with Sofia and Julie, then ride back with you."

"See, this is why I love you! Now, help me figure out what to wear."

Chapter 2: Sparring with the Devil

Cillian (Kil-e-an) O'Donnell headed for the bar in the corner of the crowded art gallery with his cousin, his bodyguard, Finn fast on his heels.

"Bushmills, neat." Cillian held up two fingers to the eager bar tender.

"That didn't take long. Do you think he was followed?" Finn scanned the crowd for any possible threat. His job was to keep his cousin and best friend alive. Cillian was too important to the people of their clan to let anything happen to him. Especially on US soil.

"Probably. He was sweating like a fuckin' pig. Something's up."

The microchip hidden in the pen Finn had just picked up off the floor several yards back contained the vital piece Cillian needed to complete GhostStorm47, his latest software program. GhostStorm47, once complete will have the ability to bring entire countries to their knees. This latest technology was sleek and far too sophisticated to be traced by the best hackers.

As the leader of the O'Donnell Clan, Cillian's genius brought to life another more lucrative way of survival. His family made their wealth the old-fashioned way. They took it. Generations of powerful men leading his Clan into prosperity by amassing a fortune through international arms deals, the whiskey trade and horse flesh. His great grandfather and his father before him lead by fear and intimidation. They were legends in Ireland. The whisper of the O'Donnell name brought fear to the most hardened criminals.

His father was no slouch, either. He did his duty by following traditions and leading his people with strength and confidence. He inspired loyalty and respect from the people he called his own. His power and intellect made for a formidable enemy.

However, that changed twelve years ago when the mantle of leadership passed to Cillian at the tender age of eighteen. He'd always been extremely intelligent. A child prodigy whose analytical mind fascinated his professors. He was already well on his way to completing his Master's Degree in Micro Intelligence and Bio-Tech Software Development when the news came that his father's plane had gone down over the Pacific. He'd lost his parents, his aunt and uncle and his grandparents on that terrible day, leaving Cillian and Finn the last of the O'Donnell line.

The crash was no accident. The sudden string of unusual incidents that led to life-threatening situations for him at school was proof of that. So, he'd left school immediately and disappeared into the shadows of a depraved underworld, taking on a new identity with Finn at his back to ensure his survival. From as early as a toddler at his father's knee, he'd been trained in weapons and martial arts, but the gutter fighting he'd learned in the shadows kept him alive now. During that time, he'd pushed his body to the limit, building his strength and stamina, brawling with the meanest and strongest the streets had to offer. Preparing, planning, waiting for the time when he would resurface to take his vengeance on those who'd destroyed his family.

Five years later, he'd emerged from the shadows a different person than the young man he'd once been. He was stronger and more ruthless than any O'Donnell leader recorded. He inspired loyalty in the people he called his own, but was a viscous, tactical opponent to those who opposed him. He took what he wanted, when he wanted it without remorse. And soon he would take the life of his enemy. The killer who'd taken his family from him. The one who thought his identity was hidden so well.

Cillian lifted the glass of whiskey the bartender placed in front of him. But before it touched his lips, Finn casually took it from his grip. After a covert sniff, then a small sip, Flynn looked at him, waited a few minutes, then nodded in approval and handed him back the glass.

Cillian scowled. "What the fuck am I supposed to do when you die right in front of me?"

"Live to see another day cousin." Finn didn't smile at his cousin's disgruntled behavior. He was used to it. He'd been covering Cillian's ass from the time they were children. It was his legacy. One he took very seriously. Just as his father did for Cillian's. For centuries, his line protected Cillian's. It was an honor to be chosen at birth as the protector of the next generation to lead them. His training started the same as Cillian's. Only his was far more strenuous. He was trained not only to protect himself, but to protect Cillian at all costs as well. A different tactic all together.

"That's not funny asshole." Cillian could feel the tension. That subtle something in the air that caused his senses to come alive. They weren't out of the woods yet. That little fucker Franklinton was too nervous. Billions

8

were at stake over the tiny microchip. Not that Cillian didn't already have billions, but with wealth and power, came enemies.

He leaned casually against the bar, slowly swirling the amber liquid in his glass while he searched the crowded gallery. His senses alert for anything out of place. His neck itched; some sixth sense he'd always had that never failed to heighten his awareness. It was never a good sign. Something of significance was about to happen. "Have the men report in again."

Finn glanced at him in obvious concern before whispering softly into the mic in his ear, then sipped from his own glass. Cillian's instincts were exceptional, and he was never wrong.

Cillian waited calmly for the report. He never buckled under the strain of leadership. He was born to it. But his job wasn't just to lead, it was also to provide stability for his people. To continue his father's legacy.

Unfortunately for him, that meant he'd have to turn his focus to his other responsibilities soon. One in particular that he'd put off long enough.

In following the O'Donnell tradition, he was supposed to be married by the time he was thirty. He'd scoffed at the idea for years. Having only one woman when there were so many to play with, was ridiculous. And given his sensual proclivities, not likely. He'd learned during his time in the underworld that the darker pleasures of the flesh suited his needs.

However, as the years passed, his clan had become edgy. The Irish were superstitious people. They believed in legends, luck and traditions. And his lack of an O'Donnell heir was making them nervous. And a strong leader never left his people feeling insecure.

He'd turned thirty last week. And this past year his people had pushed every eligible woman they could find into his path. Women all too eager to be the queen to his king. And make no mistake, whoever he chose would most definitely be a queen.

He'd been amused at first. Beautiful women; throwing themselves at him. That wasn't new. Even at a young age, because of his appearance, beautiful women were drawn to him. He'd had more than his fair share and had taken advantage of what was offered. But the prospect of being his wife had brought out the most conniving, devious, and in some cases, depraved women he'd ever had the displeasure of meeting. He could almost smell the greed seeping from their pores. Marrying one of them and having to deal with them every day turned his stomach. Soon, though, soon he'd have to pick someone, and the thought pissed him off.

"Jacob reported that Franklinton just pulled out of the parking lot. He's following him to see where the little weasel goes. Zane said no one followed them out. All is quiet outside."

"Something's up. Have them check for a sniper. My neck is itching like a bitch."

"I'm on it."

Cillian swirled the spicy liquid in his glass and watched as an elderly couple made their way to the far-left corner of the room. It was the darkest space on the gallery's main floor. The eerie lighting purposely designed to enhance the setting for the exhibit. Something to do with the impression of Voodoo the artist wanted to portray.

His gaze continued to scan the room, only to repeatedly return to the couple and their direct path into the shadows. He was about to look away again when the elderly woman touched the shoulder of a petite blonde who had her back to them.

When the blonde turned and smiled, Cillian nearly chocked on his whiskey. Years from now, he'd look back on this moment and wonder what sixth sense drew the couple to his attention. Because as she turned, the spotlight on the sculpture fell across her beautiful face, highlighting her smile. And for him; the rest of the room fell away. The brightness of that smile seared directly into his blackened soul. Splitting it open and allowing light in for the first time in more years than he could remember. The sensation was so visceral, he instinctively reached up and rubbed his chest to sooth the burn.

"Damn!" He wasn't sure if the words left his lips or if he'd whispered them in his head. She was absolutely fucking beautiful. Incredibly so. And her smile was open and honest. Innocent. And it lit up her gorgeous face.

The pounding beat of his heart drowned out every other sound. And one magnet drawn to another, a compulsion he couldn't resist, had him instinctively heading in her direction.

"What?" Finn fell into step beside his cousin at his abrupt move, quickly searching for the threat. It only took a second of following Cillian's gaze to see what caught his attention. "Jesus!" Finn's shocked whisper barely registered.

"Excuse me, Miss?"

"Yes." Chloe turned and smiled at the woman who'd tapped her shoulder so softly.

"Do you work here?"

"Yes Ma'am, I'm Chloe. Can I help you find something?"

"Maybe, but I think we've just found it. I'm Phyllis and this is my husband, George." She indicated the elderly gentleman dressed in a slightly rumpled suit standing next to her. "We've been looking for the 'Masquerade of Souls' exhibit. Is this it?" She pointed to the sculpture on display to Chloe's left.

"Yes, it is. Are you familiar with the artist?"

"Oh, yes dear! He's, our grandson. Just look at it, George. Isn't it beautiful?" She clasped her hands together and beamed with pride.

"It looks just grand, Phy, just grand." George smiled sweetly at the delight on his wife's face.

"It is beautiful. And he was very specific on how he wanted it displayed." Chloe couldn't help but smile. They were so sweet. If she had to guess, they had to be in their eighties.

"Oh yes, Greg is very exacting with his art." Phyllis leaned to the side slightly to see the back of the sculpture.

That's when Chloe felt it. That feeling you get when you're being watched. Only this was more intense. It gave her the strangest sensation of being hunted. Self-preservation had her gaze instinctively shifting to the right. And she was caught. Ensnared by the piercing gaze of the most beautiful man she'd ever seen. Deep, sage green eyes stared back at her, gleaming wickedly.

The tiny hairs on the back of her neck stood up in awareness as goose bumps broke out across her skin. Her breath caught in her throat as sizzling heat washed over her.

It took extreme effort to break eye contact and turn back to Phyllis and George. He was openly staring, making her acutely aware of him. Standing only a few feet away, his gaze never left her.

Chloe continued to speak with Phyllis and fought the instinct to look at him again. She subtly adjusted her stance into a defensive position while she tried to figure out why he made her so uneasy. She'd been taught to pay attention to her instincts, and right now those instincts were screaming at her.

Cillian watched as the beautiful angel tried to ignore him. She knew he was there, watching, waiting. And as long as she was aware of him, he was content to wait. It gave him the opportunity to study her.

The black dress fit her gorgeous curves like a glove; not too tight or too short. Its straps crisscrossed over her shoulders and upper back, revealing smooth peaches and cream skin. A little ruffle at the hem hung a few inches above her knees, giving an illusion of innocence. Strappy sandals only added a few inches to her diminutive height. In his experience, beautiful women dressed specifically to flaunt their assets. But not this beauty. And her elegance was captivating.

She had a wealth of long, thick, white blonde hair that his fingers itched to run through and grip tightly. It was held back in a low, sleek ponytail, with the end pulled over one shoulder, resting on her plump breast in a sheet of silk exposing her elegant neck and delicate shoulders.

He caught her subtle shift into a defensive stance. That was interesting. She obviously had some self-defense training and knew when she was a target. And she was definitely a target. He found her self-awareness and ability to stay cool under the pressure of his gaze intriguing.

Chloe watched the couple as they made their way toward the exit. Knowing she couldn't put it off any longer, she took a deep breath, pasted a polite smile on her face to cover her sudden nerves, then turned toward the man closest to her. She kept the other one in sight as she did it. She looked up, then further, craning her neck to meet his gaze. He was well over a foot taller than her and built like a mountain. She fought the urge to take a step back when he extended his hand.

"Hello." Cillian couldn't help but grin at her practiced polite smile. It was a form of defense. He knew it. She hadn't smiled like that at the other couple.

"Hi." Chloe took his offered hand, realizing her mistake too late. His large warm hand engulfed hers causing her skin to tingle in awareness. When she tugged to be released, his hold tightened slightly.

"I'm Cillian O'Donnell." He pulled gently on her hand, steadily drawing her toward him.

Up close, he was even more handsome than she'd initially thought. If it weren't for the small scar over his left eyebrow, she would almost consider him pretty in a masculine way. His strong jaw had just a hint of a five o'clock shadow that was as black as his short, wavy, slightly unkept hair. But it was his eyes that captivated her. Those sage green eyes gleamed with unmistakable interest, and his arrogant smirk indicated he knew exactly how handsome he was. Worse still, he had an intimidating air of power that heightened the intensity of his sensual gaze.

"I'm Chloe." She was so caught up in trying to determine what that smug look in his eyes meant it took her a second to realize he was pulling her closer to him. She subtly planted her feet to try to stop the forward motion.

"Chloe?" Cillian liked the way her name rolled off his tongue. He couldn't help but smile as he waited to hear her last name.

"Yes." She shivered slightly at the sound of her name on his lips. Her gaze shifted to the gorgeous man next to Cillian to include him, minimizing the feeling of intimacy Cillian seemed to create between them. Jeez, where did these two beautiful men come from? "Chloe." She said pointedly.

"Finn." Finn's lips twitching ever so slightly. It was never a good idea to taunt his cousin, and this young woman was inadvertently doing just that. This should be interesting.

12

"It's nice to meet you both. Can I help you find something?"

"I believe, Chloe," He emphasized her name in his Irish brogue, "that I've found exactly what I've been looking for." Using the grip on her hand, he pulled her a little closer.

Chloe tugged on her hand again and pretended to misunderstand him. This wasn't the first time she'd had to deal with a handsome, powerful man. "Oh, yes, the 'Masquerade of Souls' is beautiful. A little dark for my taste, but still beautiful. The jagged lines and sharp curves really bring it to life. Do you follow the artist?"

Cillian's lips twitched. She was quick, he'd give her that. "No. But it is beautiful. You know your art. Are you a sculptor?"

"I wish. I've tried, but I'm not very good at it. Painting is my form of expression." Chloe tugged slightly on her hand again, but he still didn't let it go.

"What do you paint, Chloe?" He rolled her name off his tongue as his smile deepened. She wanted to ignore the heat radiating between them, but her eyes lit up when she mentioned painting. He'd use that little slip to his advantage.

"People, landscapes that sort of thing." The way he said her name sent shivers down her spine. His dialect made it sound softly musical. Damn, he was gorgeous. If Sid were here, she'd definitely call dibs on this guy.

"So, are you displaying your work tonight?"

"No, I'm working. I'm filling in this weekend. I'll start my internship here when I get back from vacation after next week." Crap! She hadn't meant to say that.

"Internship?"

"Yes, it's a requirement for my degree."

"I see." Cillian rubbed his thumb back and forth over the back of her hand and watched her expressive face.

"Do you?" She lifted her brown in question and nearly smirked. She doubted he knew she was working on her Masters. She looked much younger than twenty-four.

"I Do."

I take it from your accent, you're not a local. Where are you from?" He had a distinctive lilt to his deep voice that made her name sound sensual when he said it.

"Ireland." He paused, then pointedly added, "Chloe." He used his accent, purposely playing with her name again, taunting her. He couldn't resist.

Chloe's competitive instinct had her lifting her chin at his subtle taunt. Two could play at this game. "I'd say you're a long way from home." She paused for dramatic effect and then in a thick southern drawl, she added, "Mr. O'Donnell." Holy crap! She sounded like she'd just stepped out of the movie Steel Magnolias. Clairee Belcher had nothing on her!

Finn's eyes nearly popped out of his head. This young woman just made a huge mistake.

Oh, angel. Cillian thought. *Game on.* "Yes, I am, Chloe." He flashed her a sly grin, then raised a condescending eyebrow. This beautiful, enchanting little slip of a woman just deliberately taunted him. Her eyes sparkled with a fire he felt all the way to his cock.

She tilted her head to the side and raised an eyebrow of her own again. As if answering his challenge. Why was she playing his game? Had she lost her mind? She knew better!

She'd learned a long time ago to stay in her own swim lane. Because of her looks, she had to be careful. She was perceptive, confident, and quick on her feet, and she could handle any situation that came her way.

But she'd never been faced with a man quite like Cillian O'Donnell. Oh, she'd held her own with affluent men before. The city was filled with them. All self-centered and puffed up on their own self-importance. But Cillian O'Donnell was in a different class all together. He exuded power. It pulsed in the air around him. And the sizzling attraction vibrating in the air between them was off the charts. Every single nerve in her body was attuned to him. And that had never happened to her before. It was so exhilarating she wanted to throw caution to the wind.

Definitely out of her swim lane. Hell, they weren't even in the same pool! But she couldn't seem to stop herself from sparing with him. Dangerous, yes, but exhilarating. She lifted her chin again attempting to match his arrogance. And with a practiced smile, kept with the script and drawled, "are y'all enjoying your stay here in N'awlins?" Holy hell, she was laying it on thick!

"Yes, it's been productive so far. However, it just got a lot more," he paused for effect, "interesting." He fought the smile that threatened to spread across his face. Damn she was amazing!

"There's a lot to see here in the city." She purposely ignored his last statement. This was getting out of hand. She had no idea why she was being so reckless. This was something Sidney would do, not her. But God, he was sexy!

"Tell me Chloe," he smoothed his thumb back and forth over the pulse at her wrist, "would you like to go to Ireland?"

She just barely stopped herself for saying; Yes please! Instead, she tilted her head as if considering his question. All the while she fought the instinct to say yes. The attraction between them was that intense. She needed an exit strategy, like now! If not, she'd end up throwing herself at him and agreeing to go anywhere he wanted. "Maybe one day. But I'm way too busy right now."

Chloe's gaze shifted away from his mesmerizing stare to roamed the room and found Diane watching her. And there it was, her exit. She smiled brightly at the woman and nodded her head as if there was an unspoken message between them. Then she turned back toward Cillian. "I'm sorry, Mr. O'Donnell, Finn." she nodded at Finn then turned back to Cillian. "But I'm being summoned. I have to get back to work. It was a pleasure meeting you both." She lifted her other hand and captured Cillian's between both of hers, squeezed tightly, then quickly jerked both hands loose. The instant her hands left his, she missed them.

Cillian watched Chloe escape across the room. "Change of plans."

Finn chuckled. "How long."

"A day, two at most."

"I'll make some calls."

Cillian pulled his phone from his pocket, hit a series of buttons, and put it to his ear.

"What's up Boss?"

"Titan, I need everything you can find on a woman named Chloe. She works here at the gallery."

"Got a last name for me?"

"No."

"Not a problem."

"You'll have everything I can find on her in your inbox in a few minutes."

Cillian ended the call and smiled to himself while he continued to watch Chloe from across the room. *Game on angel.*

Cillian and Finn stayed at the gallery a lot later than expected. He couldn't help it. Chloe fascinated him. She was self-assured and confident in her interactions with the patrons during the event. But she knew he was watching her. And he was making her uncomfortable. He liked that.

Finn finally signed loudly at his side. "We have to go. Jacob reported in. Franklinton went to a hotel across the street from ours."

"He can't do much with his piece of the data. Without my program, it's useless." Cillian continued to watch Chloe as she worked.

"He met two men at the hotel bar, then went upstairs. The two men went outside but split up at the corner. Both of them are in our hotel now. One went into the bathroom on the first floor. He came out ten minutes later dressed like the servers in the restaurant. He grabbed a cart and headed up to our floor. My guess is to wait for us. Jacob hasn't found the other guy yet."

"Tell him to stay on the one on our floor. Send Zane after the other one." He looked at Chloe one last time before turning back to Finn. "Let's go."

Cillian followed Finn out of the gallery, where they met Rourke and Patrick Kelly just outside the door. The three surrounded him as they walked toward the SUV. Rourke bleeped the locks, but took a few minutes to search the undercarriage before running the scanner over the entire car to check for any explosive devices. Once he gave the all clear, Cillian got into the back seat. He scanned the parking lot until he found what he was looking for.

"Go park over there by the corner of the building."

"What's the plan?" Finn's question came out of the darkness softly.

"We're going to give Franklinton time to get comfortable."

"We're going to follow her?" Finn had to work hard to suppress the laugh bubbling up in his throat. His cousin had successfully avoided entanglements with women for years, but it looked like that was about to change. And it was about time, too.

"Yes. We are." He didn't bother to look at his men. His orders were always followed. He lifted his laptop out of the pocket in the seatback where he'd left it earlier. It took only seconds to boot up using his fingerprint and a few more to connect to the encrypted hotspot on his phone. "Finn, what hotel did you say Franklinton is in?" It was time to get some answers.

"He's in the Courtyard around the corner from our hotel. We don't know if he's alone."

"We will soon enough." Cillian flexed his fingers and got to work. Within minutes, he'd tapped into the surveillance system of the Courtyard hotel. He found what room Peter Franklinton was in and that he was currently alone. Another few minutes and he'd hacked the hotel security and worked his magic. Franklinton no longer had Wi-Fi. The land-line in his room was disabled and the electronic lock on his door was engaged, then taken off line, sealing him inside.

"He's not going anywhere. Tell Jacob and Zane to move on the other two. Take them to the warehouse on Tchoupitoulas Street. I want to have a chat with them before we visit Peter."

Finn couldn't help but smile. Cillian was a dangerous enemy. He wasn't just a viscous, deadly fighter, he was also a brilliant strategist and his genius IQ made him nearly invincible.

Cillian closed the security feed, then opened his email and worked while he waited for Chloe to leave the gallery. Less than an hour later, Finn shifting in his seat caught his attention. He looked toward the front door of the building and watched as she walked out by herself. He felt his jaw tighten. They had her working late, but no one walked her out to her car? Assholes. He watched her cross the lot and climb into a pearl white Lexus ES.

Finn tapped the headrest in front of him to signal Rourke to drive. "Not to close."

They followed Chloe through the streets of New Orleans and onto St. Charles Avenue. She drove into the historic uptown district where the neighborhoods were classically beautiful. They watched as she turned left on Seventh Street. Then followed at a distance as she navigated the neighborhood until she pulled into the driveway of a large, beautifully appointed home.

"Stop Here." Cillian watched from half a block away as Chloe slowed and pulled through an electronic wrought-iron gate. He clicked a few keys on his laptop and waited for the results. He clicked a few more and was satisfied. When lights came on inside the residence, Cillian closed his laptop. "Ok, head to the warehouse. We have work to do."

Chapter 3: Sexy Irishmen are T.R.O.U.B.L.E!

Chloe resisted the urge to tell Sidney about her encounter with Cillian O'Donnell from the night before. She was on a video call with her and the rest of her friends. They were in the midst of a huge party, and there were people everywhere. The music was loud and her crew were all well on their way to getting smashed. If she told her now, everyone would hear, and how embarrassing would that be?

She'd have to wait until she got there tomorrow, but it was killing her! She was dying to share her experience. Seriously, when the hottest Irishman in the world flirted with you, you told your BFF. And holy crap, he was hot! He scared the bajeezus out of her, but still, he was smokin!

It'd taken her hours to fall asleep last night. Excitement had burned through her veins, causing her senses to come alive for the first time. It left her tingling and anxious, aching with the desire to feel his strong hands again. Only this time on other parts of her body. Sure, she dated hot guys before and even made out hot and heavy with a few. But nothing and no one had ever come close to Cillian O'Donnell and the way he'd made her feel. Thank God, she'd never see him again. If she did, she'd probably throw herself at him, and that would be a huge mistake.

Her instincts were still screaming at her, telling her he was dangerous. But even the danger and his dominant personality left her wanting. The idea of him controlling her in bed, oh yea, that would be hot. She could just imagine his powerful body dominating her while his sexy voice tempted her. And just once, she wanted to be impulsive like Sid. Just once she'd like to be daring.

Sidney was the daring one. Never her. She was more mature than girls her age thanks to her mother. Angela Guidry insisted she receive an education that far exceeded that of a private school in New Orleans. So, she and Sidney had the benefit of spending every summer from the age of thirteen traveling to other countries with their mothers, learning about the world and how to maneuver in it. Getting firsthand knowledge of food, wine and people in other cultures. They'd been to Australia, Spain, Germany, and Switzerland. Then, encouraged by their mothers, they'd taken a gap year after graduation and traveled across Europe. And the entire time, she'd been the responsible one while Sidney took all the risks and if she were being truly honest, having most of the fun. It was her turn now.

But, thinking back over the events of last night, she imagined she just might not be ready for a man like Cillian. She'd been watching when he left the gallery. She'd seen through the glass as those tough-looking men surrounded him when he'd stepped out the door. A shiver had worked its way down her spine at the knowledge that she might have dodged a bullet.

Case in point; she'd tried to Google him this morning and her search came up empty. She couldn't find a single mention of him anywhere on the internet. Not one. Red flag anyone? A man with the kind of power he exuded was important. And that meant there should be something on the web about him. That there was nothing at all, only proved her point.

So, she resisted the urge to tell Sid about him and snuggled in bed while she watched her crew. Sidney carried her phone everywhere she went through the condo so Chloe could be included in the fun, even if from a distance.

"I really wish you would've just driven straight here from the gallery this afternoon. You'd probably only be about an hour away by now." Sidney complained.

"Yea, I know."

"You're being the 'ever responsible' Chloe." Sidney held up two fingers and made the quote sign at the screen.

"Hey, someone has to be the responsible one." And she was. The boring, responsible one. She always had been. Well, last night she'd been completely irresponsible, and she couldn't wait to tell Sid about it. Her first time ever stepping out of her box and taking a risk was with the sexiest man alive. And she'd come out of it completely unscathed. But, maybe just once, she'd like to be, you know, scathed. She nearly laughed out loud at the thought.

"Yea, but does it always have to be you?"

"Why, do you want the role?" After last night, for that sexy as hell Irishman, she'd gladly give it up.

"Me? No way! You know better." Sidney giggled. "Hey, my phone's dying. I need to plug it in. What time are you leaving in the morning?"

"Probably around 4:30."

"That should put you here around 10:00. I'll set my alarm so I can let you in. But call me from the road if you get bored."

"I will. I'll see you in the morning."

"Hey Chloe?"

"Yea?"

"Did you set the house alarm?"

Chloe couldn't help but smile. Everyone thought Sidney was the wild one, but it was all for show. "Yes Mom. Everything is locked up tight." She blew a teasing kiss at the screen.

"Ok, be careful. I'll see you tomorrow."

"Night girl." Chloe disconnected the call, set the alarm on her phone, then turned off the lamp. She was exhausted from lack of sleep the night before. She pulled the chenille blanket her mom gave her several Christmases ago around her. Its softness always helped her sleep. She thought about the long drive tomorrow, but her mind quickly wandered back to Cillian O'Donnell's sage green eyes. She fell asleep thinking about how those beautiful eyes sparkled when he smiled and how she wouldn't mind looking into them every single day.

What felt like only minutes later, Chloe came awake with a start. She didn't know if it was an odd sound or the eerie feeling that she wasn't alone that woke her so abruptly. Before she could reach for her phone, a hand clamped over her mouth and a heavy weight dropped down on top of her.

With a muffled scream, she immediately fought with every bit of strength she had. Terror raced through her mind as she attempted to buck off the heavy body. Seconds later she felt a sharp sting at her neck and to her horror, her arms became too heavy to lift and she couldn't get her legs to move. Within seconds her fear slowly washed away like grains of sand caught in a wave and taken out to sea. She must be dreaming because right before the world went black, she thought she heard Cillian O'Donnell's sexy Irish voice whispering to her.

"Shh angel, just relax."

"You're sure about this?" Finn asked again when Cillian lifted Chloe into his arms.

Cillian didn't answer as he left her room, walked swiftly down the hall, and took the stairs two at a time, leaving Finn to catch up.

"Wait!" Finn hissed in warning. "You can't carry her out the door like that. Put her in the bag."

Cillian growled in response. The idea of putting her delicate little body in a fuckin duffle bag infuriated him.

"She won't wake up." Finn unzipped the oversized black bag he'd left on the floor just inside the front door of the Guidry home.

"She better not." Cillian bent down and gently placed Chloe inside it. He paused, then smiled at the fuzzy purple and gold socks on her little feet.

Shaking his head, he tucked the soft blanket from her bed around her, then zipped the bag halfway closed. He reached to lift it, but Finn's sudden hand on his wrist stopped him.

"I have to carry her."

"You have a bullet hole in your shoulder, or have you forgotten?"

"No. Trust me, asshole, I didn't forget. But she can't weigh more than a hundred pounds soaking wet. Give me a fuckin break. You know you can't be seen carrying a bag when I'm with you. It'll look suspicious. It's my job." Yea, his shoulder hurt like a bitch, but it wasn't the first time he'd been shot.

Cillian held firm to one handle and met Finn's stare, his jaw flexing in frustration. Finn had taken a bullet for him again. Fuck! He hated that shit. His fury at that little fucker, Franklinton, was still simmering. He hadn't expected him to be armed or to start shooting the second the door opened. Watching that piece of shit piss himself before he'd slit his throat still hadn't tamed the beast seething inside him.

"I won't drop her." Finn waited, and it took a few seconds for Cillian to release the handle, but Finn was patient, unmoving. "I understand what this means. Otherwise, we wouldn't be here while the heat is still on. I give you my word. I won't drop her, but we have to go. Now."

Cillian knew he was right. They'd been in the house too long already. Hell, they'd been in the fucking country too long. They should've left after the interrogation last night, but he wasn't leaving without Chloe. He never denied himself anything he wanted, and he wasn't about to start now.

He had to force himself to let go of the handle and watch Finn lift the bag.

Finn whispered into the comm device in his ear, nodded his head to indicate they were clear, then led the way out of the house. He was careful with his delicate cargo. If Chloe Guidry was Cillian's choice, then he needed to ensure her safety at all costs. Their people needed stability. As soon as Cillian brought Chloe onto the island and installed her in the castle, his people would understand her significance and breathe easier. Theirs was an old clan, steeped in tradition. Without an heir, the line would die with Cillian and he couldn't let that happen.

Cillian needed this. He deserved a strong woman. After they'd lost their parents, Cillian lost most of his humanity in the underbelly of the city. He'd had no choice. The dangers they'd faced just to stay alive were unprecedented. He also knew that Cillian had never shown more than a fleeting interest in a woman other than as a means of relief. He used and discarded them quickly. But he'd never reacted to a woman the way he had last night. Finn hoped Chloe Guidry would be the balm that soothed his cousin's hardened soul.

A blacked-out SUV waited at the curb; lights out, door opened. The Kelly twins, Patrick and Rourke, waited in the front seat. The twins were Cillian's guards when Finn wasn't with him. They'd grown up together and were part of Alpha Team One, the only other people Finn truly trusted with Cillian's safety.

Finn quickly made his way to the SUV with Cillian on his heels. He gently placed the duffle bag on the floorboard of the back seat, then stepped back to let Cillian climb inside. Finn shut the door, turned and surveyed their surroundings, then hurried around and got in on the other side.

"Let's go." He tapped the headrest of the driver's seat to signal Rourke to drive. "No lights until we pull out onto St. Charles Avenue."

Rourke already had the SUV in motion when Patrick glanced over his shoulder into the back seat. "Van texted and said the plane is ready for take-off. It'll take us about fifteen minutes to get to the airport." He looked down, hoping to catch a glimpse of the girl who had Cillian acting so out of character.

"Take your time Rourke, don't draw any undue attention." Finn instructed as he and Cillian both glared at Patrick, who just smiled cheekily, then shook his head and turned back around. They made the rest of the trip to the small airport in silence.

Cillian wanted to touch her. He trusted Finn with his life. So, if Finn said the sedative, he'd given Chloe wouldn't hurt her, then it wouldn't. But she was so small. He reached down and slide his hand inside the opening of the bag and stroked her velvety soft cheek with gentle fingers. Fingers of the hand that had slit a man's throat not twelve hours before.

Finn had come through as always. He was good with details and money bought a lot of favors. At the airport, Rourke drove through the gate at the maintenance entrance that had been suspiciously left open and unattended. He continued directly onto the tarmac and parked just a few feet from the jet.

Cillian waited while Patrick and Rourke exited the SUV and carefully surveyed their surroundings before indicating to Finn that all was clear. When Finn came around and opened his door, Cillian reached down and zipped the bag shut, closing Chloe inside. He moved aside, and Finn lifted her out.

It took less than thirty seconds for Finn to carry her up the steps and into the luxurious jet. As soon as he placed the bag on the plush carpet well inside the door and away from prying eyes, Cillian unzipped it. Careful to keep her blanket wrapped around her, he lifted her into his arms and without a backward glance headed toward the back to his private bedroom.

Once closed inside, Cillian sat in the leather chair next to the bed with Chloe in his lap. He fastened the seat belt around him and held her tightly as the plane taxied. It only took a few moments for Van to have them airborne.

Once in the air, Cillian placed Chloe in the middle of his bed. He kicked off his shoes and climbed onto the bed beside her. Pulling the blanket away from her body, he took the time to look her over. She wore a white tank top sprinkled with tiny purple hearts that fit snug over her breasts and barely reached her belly button. The material was pulled tight against her nipples. He tucked his finger into the top and tugged it down to inspect the treasure beneath. His breath caught when her full, perfect breast spilled over the top. The rosy tip puckered quickly from the cool air coming from the vent.

His finger smoothed over the soft swell, then circled the pink tip. His mouth watered in anticipation. His tongue touched the pretty delicate tip, swirled around it as it hardened further. He suckled softly at first, filling his hand with the weight of the firm mound, lifting it higher into his mouth. He scrapped his teeth across her nipple before biting down, sinking his teeth deep into the plump, curved flesh. She moaned softly, but otherwise didn't stir. She smelled and tasted like warm vanilla. The sweetness bursting on his tongue. He had an urgent need to mark her, so he suckled harder. When her breast popped free of his lips, it pleased him to see a dark purple strawberry forming around the marks from his teeth. His cock, already rock hard, nearly split his zipper.

He smoothed his hand down her firm belly to the low-rise shorts she wore. They matched the tank with their little purple hearts. He lifted the band and wasn't surprised to see white lace panties with a tiny satin bow centered just above her mound. He couldn't help but smile at the innocent site. He should've known his little Chloe would wear panties to bed. That wouldn't happen again after tonight, but he had to admit it was cute.

Ignoring his raging hard on, Cillian leaned down and kissed her mound just below the satin bow, then covered her back up carefully. He adjusted the blanket, tucking it around her before he laid down beside her. With his arm bent, resting his head on his hand to better see her, he smoothed the soft wisps of hair away from her beautiful face. He wasn't immune to the fact that in sleep; she looked so much younger than twenty-four.

Thanks to Titan, he knew everything about her that could be found in records, from her athletic awards in high school and her hard-won art scholarship to her worldly travels, her year in Europe and her family and friends. He'd read news articles about her, seen yearbook pictures, and knew she'd dated very little during her year in Manhattan.

He knew she'd been trained in Krav Maga by her father and a fellow Marine. He also knew her brother died in Afghanistan years ago. He and Finn, both found it interesting that there was no body brought back home for burial. And it was odd that a Sergeant Major in the Marines would accept that.

On paper, Chloe Guidry was the perfect young lady. In reality, she was incredible. And she was his. He wasn't naïve, though. Chloe was going to be furious. She'd fight him. He couldn't help but grin. He was going to enjoy that. He was actually looking forward to it. The prospect of conquering this beautiful young woman had his senses firing in anticipation. But eventually she'd come to realize there was no escape, that she belonged to him now. And he always kept what was his.

Chapter 4: Sapphires and White Gold, Oh My!

Cillian sat against the headboard of his bed, surrounded by pillows, Chloe's head resting on his thigh. He couldn't take his eyes off of her. He'd spent most of the long flight back, holding her cradled in his arms and catching up on some much-needed sleep. He'd worked for a few hours, but couldn't concentrate with her lying next to him. It wasn't a good sign. This delicate beauty occupied way too many of his thoughts already. Hopefully, once he'd had her a few times, this obsession, this need would ease up.

He'd called ahead and had his physician meet him at the door to his suite. The tiny silicone GPS microchips he'd designed a few years ago had been sterilized and ready for placement. Dr. Bronson was his staff surgeon. A general surgeon with a surly disposition whom he paid a fortune to remain on his island under his employ.

Bronson had scowled at him when he realized what Cillian expected him to do. But it had only taken the old doctor a few minutes to inject the microchips into Chloe's right ankle, behind her left knee and under the skin behind her left ear, before gathering up his things and stomping out the door. The microchips were invisible to the naked eye, but he could track them from his phone, his watch, and his computer. He could also monitor her vital signs if he needed to.

The minute they were alone, he'd stripped her bare. It was like opening a present on Christmas morning. The excitement and anticipation only heightened as more of her delicate skin was revealed. He'd taken his time. Worshiping every inch of her smooth, soft skin. His hands, his lips and his tongue exploring every peak and valley. He'd been delighted to find her pussy waxed bare. He was curious if she kept it that way or if she'd had it done to prepare for her vacation. Either way, he didn't care. Although he would have preferred to do it himself initially, he'd be the one to keep it waxed from now on.

He brushed his fingers through her hair. It was like pure white silk sliding through his fingers. She was so soft and delicate everywhere. Her aristocratic features; the classic little nose, high cheekbones and her large cornflower blue eyes were an unusual contrast to that lush sinful cupid's bow of a mouth. That full bottom lip of hers was made to be bitten.

She was so small. Compared to his six-five, two hundred and fifty pounds, she was really small. Only about five-three, if he had to guess. But her legs were surprisingly long, firm and toned, like those of a runner. Her belly was flat and her hips were slim, but rounded with soft curves. But her ass. Jesus, her ass was a work of art. Plump and firm and more than a hand full. He'd fantasized about that ass all fucking day.

He released her hair and smoothed his hand over her full breast. It was perfect. For someone so delicate, her breasts were plump and round, just like that peach of an ass. Her nipples were the same rosy pink as her lips. He knew they also matched the lush pink lips of her pussy. He'd taken his time softly exploring that in great detail as well. His cock still pulsed in his jeans. He was about to unsnap them to get some relief when his phone chimed with a text notification.

Finn> *Package arrived*

Cillian> *Meet me at the door*

Cillian eased Chloe's head off his thigh and rested it on a pillow before leaving the bed. He closed the bedroom door behind him and walked through the den, and opened the door of the suite to meet Finn. Rourke was in his usual position, standing guard outside the door. He and Patrick took turns at the role. One never left his post until the other relieved him.

Finn stepped into the room and handed him a long black velvet box. "Omar wants a meet."

"He can wait like everyone else." Omar Abdul, the self-centered, power-hungry piece of shit, was a pain in the ass. He was also a cutthroat terrorist who ruled over a small middle eastern desert oasis and terrorized his own people. He wanted first shot at GhostStorm47. He wouldn't get it, but his continued attempts at negotiation were tiresome. Recently those attempts had turned to veiled threats. The stupid fuck still hadn't learned that throwing his substantial weight around wouldn't get him what he wanted.

"He's making noise about Franklinton." Finn's stony expression didn't change.

"Interesting. How would that piece of shit know about Franklinton?"

"I'm guessing whoever Franklinton was working with had a connection. Or, Omar is the connection."

Cillian would have to find out. It wouldn't matter if Omar had something on them. No one was brave enough to come after him directly. "I'll meet you in the office in a few minutes."

When Finn left, Cillian walked back into the bedroom and approached Chloe. She was still unconscious, and probably would be for a few more hours. He opened the velvet jewelry box and took out the sapphire collar he'd had made for her.

Several years ago, he'd partnered with Landon, a distant cousin of his who made exquisite high-end jewelry for the most discerning customer's. It was a specific line of jewelry that he'd been interested in creating, a private collection if you will, and they'd made a small fortune.

The titanium and white gold infused alloy rendered the collar unbreakable. It was all in the way the metal was fired with the compounds he'd introduced during the firing process. He'd immediately called his cousin after meeting Chloe and instructed him to place the sapphires from Sri Lanka into the piece he'd designed a year ago. And just as he'd thought. The stones matched her eyes perfectly.

Cillian carefully put the collar around Chloe's neck and secured it with the small cylinder like key. It lay against the base of her neck beautifully. He checked the email on his phone, clicked on the link Landon sent, and downloaded the app. Once it finished downloading, he opened it, then held the key up to the screen. Instantly the chip in the key linked the collar to the app, and the GPS imbedded in the tiny clasp of the collar was activated.

Cillian removed his crucifix from around his neck and fed the chain through the tiny ring at the top of the key, then closed it around his neck again. Satisfied that Chloe couldn't escape him, he went into the kitchen to get a bottle of water from the refrigerator. He put the bottle and two ibuprofens on the nightstand next to her. He couldn't resist kissing her soft lips again before he walked out of the suite.

Cillian headed straight for his office, hoping to get the meeting over with quickly so he could return to Chloe. A few steps from the door, he stopped when he saw Roisin (Row-sheen) sauntering toward him from the other end of the hallway. He didn't hide his frown or try to temper his disapproval. Guests weren't allowed in this wing of the castle. It was a blatant disregard for the few firm rules he'd set in place for all visitors. He'd have to speak with Finn about the security at the door to this floor.

Roisin was Finn's second cousin on his mother's side. She was a beautiful young woman, and she knew it. She made sure everyone else knew it too by flaunting her attributes every chance she got. Like now, her skin tight red dress had a plunging neckline that didn't come close to covering the large breasts her parents paid a fortune for. The hem of the ridiculous dress barely covered her ass.

Overindulged by doting parents, she was convinced she could have anything she wanted. And apparently, she'd set her sights on him. Undeterred by his complete disregard, her continued attempts at seduction were wearing on his patience. He considered her a silly woman of little consequence, but he tolerated her, for Finn's sake.

She'd been throwing herself at him since the day she'd turned eighteen. That was nearly eight years ago. To his mind, she should have gotten the message by now.

She was always welcome here because this was Finn's home too, and if he wanted to visit with a relative, that was his prerogative. And she visited a lot. Too often for his peace of mind. Mostly when things got too hot from her constant childish antics back home.

He watched as she approached him on sky high heels, her hips swaying a little too dramatically. "Your welcome here is wearing thin, Roisin." He didn't try to keep the irritation out of his voice.

"What do you mean?" Her breathy response came from pouty lips, slick with shiny red gloss. She lifted her hand to place her palm on his chest, but he caught her wrist before she could make contact and pushed it away.

"Visitors are not allowed in this wing. You're reminded of the rules each time you visit."

"Visitors, of course, but I'm family Cillian. Surely those rules don't apply to me?" She put a hand on her hip, lifted the other to her throat and slid it down her chest to rest at her exposed cleavage. She lifted her face toward him, her best attempt at innocence falling short.

"Roisin, you're a guest in my home for only as long as Finn wishes to see you. I'll be very clear this time so there is no misunderstanding. You are not allowed in this wing of the castle," he turned at the sound of his office door opening and faced Finn before completing his statement. "Under any circumstances."

Finn stopped abruptly when he saw Roisin standing in the hall. "What the fuck are you doing here?"

"There's no need to be so crass, Finn. Really, how gauche for someone of our standing? I was simply looking for you. I thought we'd go for a walk before dinner."

"You're not allowed in this wing of the castle and you know it."

"Oh, good grief. I just wanted to talk to you."

"Go to your room, Roisin."

"What? Seriously cousin? I'm not a little girl to be sent to her room!"

"Go!" Finn's bark caused her the jump slightly. Roisin cast him a furious glare, then turned on her high heels and sauntered back down the hall. Finn lifted his phone from his pocket, pressed a button, then held it to his ear.

"Yes." Jacob answered on the first ring.

"My cousin found her way into the family wing. Make sure it doesn't happen again."

"You go it."

"I want her contained in her room until I get there."

"I'll take care of it."

Finn disconnected the call and looked at Cillian. "I'll handle it."

"See that you do. If she can't follow the rules, she'll no longer be welcome here." Cillian turned and entered his office.

"This unhealthy obsession she has with you is becoming a pain in the ass." Finn followed him in and closed the door behind them.

"You're telling me?" Cillian sat at his desk and using his finger print activated his computer. He clicked a few buttons and the wall across the room slide open, revealing multiple surveillance screens showing several angles of his home. He clicked a few more buttons and the top two screens switched to the image of the hall outside his bedroom door, where Rourke still stood guard and the empty sitting room of his suite. Satisfied there'd been no movement from Chloe, he sat back in his chair and glanced over at Finn.

"Now, what have you heard from Abdul?"

"His man Oden sent a message that they are curious about Franklinton's whereabouts."

"That's all it said?"

"Yes. It's an attempt to get your attention."

"Did you pull the surveillance footage from New Orleans?"

"Yes. We're clear."

"So, he's either fishing, or he partnered with Franklinton to gain leverage in negotiations for the final product."

"My thoughts exactly. Did you scrub the data on the microchip?"

"I did that before we left the parking lot of the gallery Saturday night. Franklinton had a tracer worm imbedded into the encryption. There were four of them, actually."

"Four?"

"Yes. Usually if there's one, there's two. Three's a charm, but the fourth one was imbedded deep into the script of one of the data points. Once I removed it, I scrubbed the rest of the file, moved it into a separate auto scrubber then dropped it into the program I wrote last month that sweeps for any anomalies. It's clean now."

"Shit!" Cillian's genius never ceased to amaze Finn. "Now what?"

"Now I run the algorithms necessary to complete the program and we're in business."

"How soon?"

"A few weeks, maybe more. Then we'll put it out for bid. But tell me if you hear from Abdul again. In the meantime, I'm going to take some time with Chloe."

"You're going to have a fight on your hands with that one." Finn's lips twitched in the small semblance of a smile.

"No doubt." Cillian grinned at his friend. "I'm looking forward to it."

Finn shook his head. "You would."

Chapter 5: Because I Wanted To

The pounding at her temples woke Chloe. It was either that or the severe pressure on her bladder. She wasn't sure which. She forced her heavy eyelids to open, but the bright light in the room sent a searing pain to her already pounding head, so she slammed them shut on a groan.

After a few minutes, she took a deep breath and tried again, much slower. Once she could focus, what she saw made absolutely no sense. The ceiling above her head wasn't hers. This one was at least fifteen feet high with heavily exposed wooden beams. She turned her head to look around and felt a strange weight at her neck, but a sudden wave of nauseousness stole her focus.

She lay still for a few seconds, trying to settle her rolling stomach. She needed the figure out where the hell she was. When she sat up, the blanket covering her dropped to her waist, and she nearly shrieked. She was naked! Completely freakin naked in a strange bed! Oh my God!

She looked around frantically, but thankfully no one else was in the room with her. She reached down and snatched the blanket back up to cover herself and was surprised to see it was her blanket. The one from her bed at home. Oh God! This wasn't a good sign. She wrapped it around herself while she looked around for her clothes. But she didn't see them anywhere.

To the left was an open doorway, and she could just make out the edge of a countertop. That had to be the bathroom. She gripped the blanket tightly then jumped off the bed and raced to it. She slammed the door shut and turned the lock on the knob. Her heart was racing as she leaned back against the door and searched the room for the toilet.

Once she'd taken care of her most pressing need, she was able to concentrate on her surroundings. She didn't recognize a thing. Jesus, where was she? She tentatively approached one of the double sinks to wash her hands and her unease increased. Because sitting on the counter was a bottle of face cleanser. What the hell!? It was the brand she normally used. That had to be a coincidence, right?

She swallowed several times to control her rising panic, but ew! Her mouth felt like it was lined with the same fuzzy material as Juneau's tennis ball. So, she took advantage of the toothbrush, still in its package, and the tube of toothpaste positioned next to the bottle of cleanser. It was difficult to do while trying to keep the blanket secured around her, but she managed to brush her teeth.

When she leaned down to rinse her face, the blanket slipped. She looked down as she reached to catch it and gasped. Then her stomach lurched. She clenched her jaw tightly and swallowed several times. "What the hell!" With trembling fingers, she touched the large hickey on her breast. She traced the reddened spot with her fingertip, noting the teeth marks in the center.

Vulnerability swept over her, and unexpected tears stung her eyes. "This can't be happening." Her whispered words shook with fear. She gathered the blanket tightly around her and closed her eyes, searching her memory for answers. The throbbing ache in her head made concentration difficult. Had she been drugged? Shit! She needed to find a phone. She had to call Sid.

Chloe slowly opened her eyes and looked up into the mirror and almost swallowed her tongue. The heavy weight she'd previously noted at her neck was a beautiful sparkling necklace of what looked like diamonds and sapphires. The sapphire stones were as large as the circumference of her finger. Each brilliant blue stone was edged with tiny diamonds. She lifted its heavy weight with her finger and studied it closely in the mirror. The chain looked like diamond cut white gold linking the stones together. She twirled it around her neck slowly, looking for the clasp to open it.

"It's beautiful, isn't it?"

Startled by the sound of the deep musical Irish voice, Chloe's gaze flew up to see the reflection of the enormous man behind her casually leaning against the doorframe, flipping a key up and down in his hand. She'd been so focused on the necklace; she hadn't heard the door open.

His black dress shirt was untucked and opened down the front with the sleeves rolled up to his forearms. The open shirt revealed a smooth, wide, muscular chest and the taunt ridges of his abs. There was a smattering of black hair in the center of his chest and a thin line of it below his navel that disappeared into faded blue jeans. Jeans that rested low on his hips, displaying a sexy mouthwatering V, then continued down to hug his powerful thighs. His feet were bare, magnifying the sense of intimacy. His short, thick, black hair was unruly, the ends curling slightly around his gorgeous face. She drank in the sight of him, so beautiful, so raw. Yummy. Then reality kicked her stupid, fuzzy brain into focus. What the ever loving hell? "Cillian O'Donnell?"

"Hello, angel."

The soft musical lilt of his voice sent shivers down her spine. He had the same wicked smile he'd worn before. Only now his eyes sparkled with a gleam of satisfaction. And the now familiar sizzle of attraction between them roared to life.

She clutched the blanket in a white knuckled grip as the heat of a blush washed over her. Shit! Had they slept together? Was she in his hotel room? She couldn't remember a thing. She turned slowly and met his sensual gaze head on then boldly lifted a questioning brow. "What? No meeting for coffee or maybe dinner first?"

Cillian's lip twitched at her boldness and shook his head slightly. "Too unimaginative."

She sighed at his arrogance. "Of course, you'd think so. Did we have sex?"

"No," he chuckled.

She looked down at her fist holding the blanked then back up at him. "Then why am I naked?"

He grinned wickedly, but didn't answer. She desperately searched her memory to figure out how she's gotten here. Where ever here is. It took longer than it should've because the throbbing ache in her head was so distracting. And he just watched her, waiting.

Slowly, the memories came back; waking up and knowing someone was in her room, the pinch at her neck, the heaviness of her limbs! Holy shit! "You drugged me!"

"Yes." His blunt admission caught her by surprise.

"Why would you do that!?"

"It was the easiest way to get you onto the plane." He shrugged his shoulders as if it were the obvious answer.

"Plane! What plane? Did you kidnap me!?"

"Yes." He stated simply, those green eyes watching her like a jungle cat waiting to pounce.

She stared at him in stunned disbelief. "Holy shit!" The whispered phrase was barely audible. So much for coming out of this unscathed. Then, her eyes widened with terror at her next thought. "Are you a human trafficker?!"

"No, angel." His deep Irish brogue sounded slightly amused.

"You expect me to believe that?"

He shrugged his shoulders casually. "Yes."

Relief was instantaneous. "Then why!?"

"Because I wanted to."

"What?!" She shrieked and her head nearly exploded. "Because you wanted to?!" God save her from arrogant men! Her head was definitely going to explode! Any second now.

"Yes."

"Where are my clothes?" She demanded to know. She couldn't handle Cillian O'Donnell on her best day, much less standing naked in a bathroom.

"Don't lock the door again, Chloe. Or, I'll be forced to punish you." He tossed the key in the air again.

"What?" She whispered in a stunned breath.

"You didn't take the ibuprofen I left for you on the nightstand." Cillian put the key in his shirt pocket and pulled out two pills, then lifted both hands. One held a bottle of water, the other the two familiar looking green gel capsules.

She looked from his hands back to his face. His expression hadn't changed. Not even when he'd threatened her. "What's happening?"

"Take the pills, then we'll talk."

"I don't think so." Was he serious? He'd already drugged her once. There was no way she was going to let him do it again.

"Chloe, you clearly have a headache. It's an unfortunate side effect of the sedative. This is just ibuprofen." Cillian could see the little crease between her eyes from the ache in her head, and he didn't like it. The idea of her in pain made him edgy. Sensual pain that turned to delicious pleasure was one thing. This was completely different.

"I'm sure you'll understand if I don't believe you."

Her little chin lifted again, causing his eyes to brighten and focus in anticipation at her show of defiance. This is what he wanted, what he'd been waiting for. "Angel, I don't need to drug you again. I have you exactly where I want you."

"Which is where, exactly?"

"Take the pills, Chloe."

She knew she needed something. Her head was killing her! She spotted a small table that held a stack of fluffy towels. She nodded her chin toward it. "Put them on top of the towels and step back."

He slowly shook his head, his intense gaze never leaving hers. "Come here, angel."

Chloe nervously chewed on her bottom lip and stared at him, but she didn't move.

"If you don't, I'll be forced to go to you."

She already felt cornered, and he knew it. But getting too close to him wasn't a good idea. The attraction between them was almost frightening. It felt like a live wire connecting them together with a magnetic force that pulled at her. She needed a clear head to deal with him and distance was key. Especially since she was only wearing a blanket, for God's sake. "Back up, Cillian."

"Come here, Chloe." There was no mistaking the bite in his voice this time.

"I don't think so big guy."

Cillian lost patience and stepped into the room.

She raised her free hand as if to ward him off and instinctively stepped back, bumping into the counter behind her.

He needed to set the ground rules or his beautiful angel would walk all over him. He moved toward her, a huge wall of determined male whose size blocked out everything else. When her hand made contact with his bare chest, he pressed forward in a show of strength that slowly caused her elbow to bend. He placed the water bottle on the counter beside her, then engulfed the hand at his chest, pressing it tighter to him. Her delicate hand burning him like a brand.

The heat of his warm, smooth skin beneath her palm was alarming. Her palm tingled at the contact. She tried to pull it away, but he held it firmly against him. Leaning in close, his head beside hers, he whispered softly into her ear. "You are not in charge here, angel." Then he sucked her earlobe into his mouth, capturing it between strong teeth, and bit down.

She shivered and her deepest core clenched hard and went damp. Then his words penetrated the lust filled haze.

They'd just have to see about that. He wanted to play rough, well two could play that game. Her hands might be pinned between their bodies and useless, but her legs were free. She snapped her knee up toward his groin, but he was ready for it. He shifted his thigh to block the attack and chuckled when she growled.

He lifted his head from her ear and looked at her furious face. He couldn't stop the grin from spreading if he'd wanted to. She reminded him of an enraged little kitten. He leaned in to capture her lips, but Chloe reared back, then lunged forward and head-butted him. He wasn't expecting it, but he should've. His little kitten had claws. Fortunately, his instincts were excellent. He moved at the last second and she caught him in the jaw instead of the mouth.

She was quick. He'd give her that. But his height worked to his advantage. He released her palm and quickly fisted a handful of silky hair at the base of her head and pulled, forcing her head back and her face up to his. The hand holding the pills snaked around her back, pressing her tighter against him.

"Let go!" Chloe seethed as she struggled to get free. He simply squeezed her tighter. She let out an ear-piercing scream of frustration that echoed off the marble tile.

His grin turned into a full-fledged smile. "Chloe, stop struggling. Though I am enjoying it." He pressed his aching cock against her belly to emphasize the impact her struggles had on him.

Shocked, she froze as the hard bulge press against her stomach. His wicked green eyes gleamed down at her. Hers widened in surprise.

He chuckled softly at her reaction.

"Cillian, let go." Her plea sounded desperate, even to her own ears. But if he didn't let her go, she'd probably end up rubbing against him like a cat in heat and she was already in serious trouble here.

Cillian leaned in again, holding her head firmly in place, and pressed soft kisses to the corner of her lush mouth, then her chin, moving slowly to her throat. Her skin was like velvet against his lips. He suckled the tender flesh at her neck, working it tightly against his lips with his tongue.

"Cillian," she whispered helplessly, shivering beneath his soft exploring lips.

He sucked harder, determined to make his point. When he finally released her skin, he was pleased to see another of his dark marks marring her delicate flesh. Satisfied with the results, he lifted his gaze to her heated one. "Every time you act out, you'll be punished." He leaned in and kissed the mark on her skin before meeting her eyes again. "The punishment will fit the crime as I see fit."

If that was his form of punishment, he could punish her anytime.

"Say you understand Chloe."

"Punished." She repeated thoughtfully.

"Say it." He barked. His grip on her hair tightened almost painfully.

"Okay." She flinched, shocked at his sudden change of tone. What the hell?

"Okay won't do, angel. Say you understand that I'll punish you."

Frustrated, she stared at him. This was crazy! This had to be a dream. Any second now, she'd wake up in her own bed at home. But the fierce, commanding look in Cillian's eyes was very real. Clenching her teeth, she forced the words between them furiously. "I understand you'll punish me."

"Good girl." His musical voice purred as he praised her. He nibbled on her chin then slowly released his grip on her hair. He lifted her hand from his chest and placed the pills into her palm, then opened the water bottle, held it out and waited.

Trapped between him and the sink, she had no choice but to put the pills in her mouth. However, she did take a quick look at them to confirm what they were first.

Cillian watched as she took the bottle, lifted it to her lips and drank.
She was definitely dehydrated. And the cool water felt amazing on her
parched throat so she drank nearly half the bottle before lowering it.
"That's better. Now let me show you your new home."

Chloe's jaw dropped at the site that greeted her. She had to force her
mouth closed, but it dropped open again and she was too stunned to speak
as she slowly took in her surroundings. The view was absolutely beautiful.
She was standing on the balcony of what appeared to be a tower at least
four stories high. The light grey stone ledge surrounding it rose to nearly
the height of her chest. Over the ledge, she could see a large stretch of dark
green lawn resembling a golf course and a cobble stoned pathway that led
to a huge stone fountain in the center.

The pathway circled the fountain, then continued off in the distance to
a white sandy beach and crystal-clear water. A very large body of water.
Chloe slowly glanced to her right to see shorter walls that lead to another
tower like the one where she stood, only it wasn't as high. To her left was
the same. Across the lawn, close to the edge of the sand on each side, were
two much taller guard towers. She knew they were guard towers because
there were at least three armed men in each.

Holy shit! A castle. An honest to God castle! Slowly, she turned back
toward Cillian and in a stunned voice asked, "where are we Cillian?"

"Welcome home, Chloe." Cillian stood facing her with his muscled
arms crossed over his massive chest, watching her closely.

Chloe gaped at him. Because really? Was he serious? Then she asked
through clenched teeth, slowly enunciating each word. "Where? Are?
We?"

"Welcome to O'Donnell Island. It's about 80 kilometers off the coast
of Doolin, Ireland." He paused for a second to let that sink in, then his lips
twitched in amusement when he added, "in the middle of the North
Atlantic."

Her jaw dropped open again, and her eyes nearly bulged out of their
sockets. She closed her mouth, only for her jaw to drop again. Then she
screeched. "What?!" This could not be happening! She wanted to slap the
smirk right off of his gorgeous face. "You brought me to Ireland? Why?!"

On any other day, the smile he gave her would have been breathtaking. Not today.

"I told you, because I wanted to."

At his arrogance, her fury ignited. "Because you wanted to?!" She
shrieked! Was he serious! "You can't just kidnap someone and take them
to another country just because you want to!"

"Of course, I can." She was beautiful. A furious little kitten hissing at him. The angrier she got, the more her eyes flashed and her cheeks took on a rosy glow.

"Cillian!" The asshole was toying with her. He appeared so calm, casually leaning there against the wall looking as hot as hell while she was becoming hysterical.

His eyes sparkled with humor as he pitched his voice and mocked her. "Chloe!"

She stomped her foot in frustration and demanded, "take me home!"

"This is your home now, angel." His smooth Irish brogue oozed confidence.

"No, it's not!" That sensuous voice of his slithered down her spine, making her shiver.

He smiled devilishly when he saw it. He liked that delicate shiver. He wondered if she was wet for him.

She stepped toward him and enunciated each work clearly; "I'm. Not. Staying. Here."

Cillian chuckled at her attempt at bravado. "There are only two ways off this island. Air or sea. One of my planes, my helicopter or my yacht. All of which are guarded around the clock so even if you had the skills, any attempt to leave would be unsuccessful."

He stood from the wall and stepped toward her. She instinctively stepped back. He stopped and lifted an arrogant brow. "Where do you plan to run, little rabbit?"

"Cillian you have to take me home." Her parents were going to freak out! Oh shit! Her parents. Sidney! Shit! She gasped audibly. "What time is it?"

Her expression suddenly changed from angry to panicked, causing him to pause.

"It's around 5:00. You were unconscious for longer than expected because I had to give you a second injection on the plane."

"What time is it in New Orleans?"

"With the time difference, it's 11am."

"Oh, my, God!" She whispered, so freaked out she could barely breath. She started pacing the length of the massive balcony. "I should've arrived at the condo by now." She muttered. Sidney would have already started to worry. When she came to the end of the balcony, she turned, paced back in the direction she'd just been, then turned again. If she didn't hear from her soon, she'd panic. "She probably already called in the troops." They'd freak out and, knowing her father, he'd kill someone to get off the cruise ship. She reached the end of the balcony again and turned to retrace her steps. Her mom and dad were going to lose their minds. "So much for coming out of meeting him unscathed. Jesus!" She needed to make some calls.

Cillian watched her as she paced, muttering to herself. For the moment she seemed to forget she was only wearing a blanket. With every turn she made it opened and he got a tantalizing view of her thighs and it was sexy as fuck. He leaned against the doorway, crossed one foot over the other, and enjoyed the show.

On her third trip back, she stopped in front of him. "I need to use your phone."

Cillian simply watched her.

Frustrated at his lack of response, she stomped her bare foot and tried again. "I need to call my parents. And my friend. They need to know I'm ok."

It surprised him that she was more worried about them than about herself. "I don't think you quite understand your circumstances, angel."

"No, it's you who doesn't understand. If I don't call them, they are going to be worried sick. After losing my brother, my parents can't handle this, Cillian. I need to talk to them. Please!"

The anxiety in those blue eyes irritated him. It made his chest tight. He didn't like it. Not one bit. Fuck this. He leaned down, putting his shoulder into her belly, snaked his arm around her thighs, and quickly lifted her up and over his shoulder.

Chloe shrieked!

Chapter 6: Little Hellion

Cillian strode toward the bed with Chloe kicking and screaming over his shoulder. The blanket she'd been wrapped in long forgotten on the floor behind him and her beautiful bare ass under his palm. Two steps from the bed, she bit his lower back.

"Little hellion." Cillian swatted her ass with a sharp slap.

Chloe screamed louder and punched him in the kidneys as hard as she could.

"Behave." Cillian slapped her ass again, a little harder this time.

"Put me down!" The son of a bitch hit her! Twice! And the burn was doing strange things to her. Chloe aimed and punched him again.

"Sure thing, angel." Cillian tossed her onto the bed. But before he could follow her down, Chloe snapped out her leg and hit him with a front kick to the gut. He bent over, winded from the blow, but instead of kicking him again like she knew she should, she punched him instead. She didn't really want to hurt him. So, she'd aimed for his nose, but caught the edge of his sharp jaw.

She screamed as pain exploded in her hand and wrist.

"Damn it! Are you alright?" He paused while leaning over her.

"No!" She followed the right hook with a left jab that hit him in the throat.

Cillian struggled to breathe as he lunged forward, using his weight to push through her attack.

She reacted on instinct, scrambling backward away from his advance. As soon as she had enough room, she did a backflip and hopped off the other side of the bed. Once her feet hit the floor, she raced through the open door. There was a kitchen to the right and a huge set of double doors across the large room. She ran straight toward them as fast as she could.

Cillian planted his foot on the bed and launched himself across it and took off after her. She was fast. Really fast, but so was he. Just as her hand caught at the knob to one of the outer doors, he snaked an arm around her stomach. Before he could jerk her back, she twisted the knob and pulled it open, only to screech at the unexpected site of Rourke's surprised expression as he blocked the exit.

At his growl, Rourke immediately averted his shocked eyes away from Chloe and Cillian kicked the door shut in his face.

"Look what you made me do!" She accused, mortified at being caught naked.

"That wasn't smart, little one." Cillian started back toward the bedroom with a struggling Chloe in his arms. "He saw you naked. Now I may have to kill him."

Kicking her legs wildly, Chloe reached up behind her and grasped handfuls of Cillian's hair and pulled with all her strength. "That was your fault! Now, let me go!"

"Stop." Cillian squeezed her tighter.

Chloe pulled harder. "Let me go!"

Cillian signed when she didn't immediately release her hold. "This is going to sting angel."

Before she could respond, he reached around and slapped her hard between her legs.

At the sudden fiery sting, Chloe gasped. She instinctively let go and folded into a tight ball over his arm.

Cillian carried her back toward the bedroom. She snatched a lamp from a table as they passed through the door. She yanked hard to release the cord and swung it up to slam it into Cillian's head behind hers in retaliation for the slap. He used his free hand to deflect the blow, and the lamp crashed to the floor.

"That wasn't nice you little hellion. I liked that lamp."

"Cillian! This isn't funny!"

"But it is exciting, isn't it beautiful?" Cillian fell onto the bed with Chloe struggling beneath him. He grabbed both of her hands and slowly pushed them above her head and put all his weight on her back, pinning her down. All while raining whisper soft kisses over her neck and shoulder.

Yes, it was exciting, her skin was alive. Every inch tingling with sensations. With each struggling motion, the sensation grew. His bare chest, hot against her naked back, the rough material of his jeans scraping against her bare bottom. His soft kisses at her neck. Never in her life had she felt so alive.

Cillian waited patiently for the fight to leave her as she lost her breath. When she stopped struggling, he tucked his head next to hers and breathed into her ear.

"What now angel?" He chuckled when he heard her muffled scream into the pillow.

He gathered both of her wrists in one hand and reached for the rope he'd attached to the headboard earlier with the other. He quickly slid the slip knotted loop of the soft red rope over her wrists and pulled it snug, securing her hands above her head.

When Chloe felt the rope pull at her wrists, she jerked against it and renewed her struggles.

He lay back down on top of her. His body blanketing hers completely. He tucked the bulge of his aching cock into the notch between her legs and circled his hips. Grinding his cock against her, he whispered in her ear. "This plump little ass is perfect baby." He groaned his need into her shoulder blade, then nipped it with his teeth.

Chloe was completely out of breath and her core was pulsing with heat, aching and needy. The feel of that soft rope at her wrist was exhilarating. She turned her face away from his to try and catch her breath. Because looking at him only made the ache worse. She had to think. Could she do it? Take this wild ride with him? Should she? God, she wanted to. She'd dreamed of this. Only dreams and reality were two completely different things. But, just this once, she wanted to be the daring one. Experience firsthand how exciting life could be. And surely, he'd take her home tomorrow. Why wouldn't he? He'd most likely brought her here to impress her. And she was definitely impressed. This place was gorgeous.

Cillian was assaulting her with sensual kisses and sexy taunts in a musical voice that made her shiver. He was beautiful and charismatic, and with those qualities came a sizzling attraction that burned through her. Making her want to be wild, throw caution to the wind. Just once.

Cillian sat up, careful not to put too much of his weight on her back, and gathered her hair into his hands. "Your hair is amazing, angel. So beautiful and soft. It's like silk."

To her surprise, he began to braid the long locks.

Cillian carefully braided it into a loose French braid to keep it out of her face. He had nothing to tie it with to secure it, so he left it hoping it would stay for a little while at least.

He slid further down her body, pinning her legs before sitting up again. He reached back to press down on her calves and turned around to face the foot of his bed. He flipped her over and quickly sat back down to pin her legs again before she could kick him. He forced her thighs wide, then reached for the ropes at each bedpost, and in seconds had her secured and completely at his mercy.

"Untie me right now, Cillian!" Chloe yanked on the rope at her wrists. She winced when her injured hand protested.

Cillian knelt between her spread thighs and took a moment to admire his treasure. She looked beautiful in his ropes. Just like he'd known she would. He took his phone from his pocket.

"Don't you dare!" She snapped when she realized his intension.

He smiled devilishly and snapped a picture of her, then tossed the phone onto his nightstand. The deep red of the soft rope was gorgeous against her pale skin.

"You better delete that right now!"

"Baby, you're so beautiful." His cock was rock hard from their struggle. It had been the most exhilarating tussle with a woman he'd ever had. She was amazing. So fierce and brave. She'd nearly beaten the shit out of him. And for reasons he couldn't fathom, he was proud of her.

He placed his palm over her bare mound and spread his fingers wide to study the distinct contrast between her pale peaches and cream skin and his sun-tanned hand. The warm, soft skin beneath his palm momentarily distracted him. His eyes lifted to meet the heat in hers as he moved his hand down between her thighs and slid his finger between the delicate lips of her pussy. She was trembling and inhaled sharply. But he needed to be sure she was with him.

"Cillian." She groaned softly and canted her hips involuntarily. Oh God! She was so wet. A blush burned her skin and she wanted to look away. But she refused to let herself. She wanted to experience every heated look, every tortured breath, everything. All of it. She could do this. Take what she wanted. Just this once. And surely, he'd take her home tomorrow.

His eyes fired at the slick wet heat that met his finger tip. It was all the proof he needed. "Oh baby" he whispered and circled her opening slowly, carefully, coating his fingers. She was fucking perfect. "You're amazing."

Holding her gaze, he shrugged out of his shirt and tossed it over his shoulder.

Chloe bit her lip to keep from moaning at the unfamiliar sensations he was causing.

He unsnapped his jeans and lowered his zipper. He groaned when his aching cock sprang free of its confines. He circled the heavy girth and stroked himself as he watched her. "Look baby. This is what you do to me."

Chloe's shock at his brazen act held her transfixed momentarily, but when the rhythm of his hand increased, her senses re-engaged and she gasped.

Cillian chuckled wickedly, then leaned down and abruptly sucked her breast deep into his mouth. As his lips made contact with her skin, Chloe moaned.

"Jeezus!" The shock of his mouth and the tight suction at her breast were so intense her toes curled.

He licked her softly over and over, torturing her tight nipple with his tongue. He took his time, enjoying the taste of her skin. He lightly circled her other nipple with a delicate touch of his finger, still slick with her desire. Soothing her. Teasing her. Arousing her.

She whimpered, her breathing coming in sharp gasps.

"Does that feel good baby?" He whispered against her nipple. His stubble abrading the tender tip.

"Yes," she sighed and pushed up against his mouth.

He soothed her softly. Whispering to her quietly, his lips never leaving her skin. "There you go angel, that's a good girl." He continued to suckle her breast softly. He placed teasing kisses around her tight nipple before kissing a path to her other breast and suckling it just as gently. "You're so soft." He switched hands and lightly teased the deserted, wet nipple, keeping the sensations at a delicious high. "I can't wait to taste your little pussy."

"Cillian." Chloe whimpered. The warm tingling sensations from his kisses caused a flutter deep in her core that conflicted with the fear and anticipation of the unknown.

"So beautiful." He whispered back as he kissed a path down her body, taking the time to lap at her naval before continuing his path down to stop at the top of her mound. He paused and looked directly into her eyes. Using his thumbs, he parted the velvety soft lips of her pussy, still reddened from his slap. "Even here, Chloe. Such a pretty little pussy." Still holding her gaze, he lowered his head and licked her softly. "Jesus, you taste good." He lapped at her clit over and over with slow, gentle flicks of his tongue.

"Oh God. Cillian, I've never, oh, oh my God!" Chloe couldn't breathe. She was dying inside. She didn't know if she was begging him to stop or to keep going.

She pulled against the restraint at her wrists and winced when her abused right hand pulled at the rope. Her back left the bed. She wasn't sure if she was trying to get away from him or move closer.

Cillian didn't take his eyes from hers as he watched the flush of desire wash over her beautiful features. He sucked her clit into his mouth and drew on it while softly lashing the tip repeatedly with his tongue. The more he suckled, the more flushed she became. She squirmed beneath his administrations, trying to pull back, only to push forward again.

He chuckled against her tender flesh and sucked a little stronger, lashed at her clit a little harder. He watched her closely, mesmerized, as he brought her to the edge. When she was close to breaking, he flattened his tongue against her clit, held pressure against the taunt nub, felt it pulse, then scraped his teeth ever so lightly against it. Her back bowed, and she screamed as she exploded against his mouth. He carefully slipped a finger deep into her to feel her pulse around it. She was so tight he had to work it inside of her slowly, but her slick essence eased the way.

Chloe's heart raced. Her skin vibrated, and she couldn't catch her breath. Every instinct she had warned her this was going to be devastating. She couldn't stop her hips from moving, pushing against his wicked mouth. The intensity was frightening as she teetered on a precipice then suddenly found herself tossed over the edge. She heard herself screaming, but could focus on nothing but his hot greedy mouth. It was amazing and terrifying and she couldn't stop it, couldn't slow it down. White hot flashes of pleasure, so intense her brain shut down and her body took over.

Cillian nearly came as he watched Chloe orgasm. She was so beautiful in the throes of passion. And now, lying there, flushed and sated. The site of her tied up for his pleasure, bound in his ropes, her pussy red and swollen from his mouth, was a delicious lick of heat that tightened his balls.

His aching cock pulsed and bobbed against his belly. He was a large man, and she was so small, so tight. She wasn't nearly ready to take him yet. He slid his hand under her ass and lifted her, then wedged a pillow beneath her limp frame. He untied her ankles and pushed her thighs further apart easily. Once he had her in position, he lowered his mouth to her pussy again and drove his tongue deep inside of her.

Chloe groaned at the intrusion. She pulled at her bound hands to get free, to push him away from her over sensitive folds. She tried to squirm away but was held immobile by his large hands at her bottom and her legs held wide by his massive shoulders. His tongue was so deep inside her, the tip touched an extremely sensitive spot that sent heat coursing through her again. She gave a sharp gasp.

"There it is." He chuckled against her wet flesh and lashed the spot again, over and over. Her back bowed, involuntarily pushing her toward his seeking mouth.

This was insanity. She couldn't focus. She wanted it to stop. She never wanted it to stop. She needed more, so much more.

Cillian devoured her luscious heat, paying close attention to every reaction, every sign her body gave him. He quickly found what she liked, what sent her soaring. When he felt her pussy flutter against his tongue, he replaced it with his finger. He moved his mouth to her clit, sucking softly at first as he drove one finger in and out of her. When the flutters quickened, he added a second finger, driving deep.

He suckled fiercely at her clit and was rewarded when she exploded a second time. As she pulsed around his fingers, he nipped her clit with his teeth and dark satisfaction seared his soul when she moaned deep in her throat and more liquid heat bathed his fingers as her pussy clamped down hard around them. His angel liked a little bite of pain with her pleasure. Fuck, she was perfect. Using his fingers and his mouth, he drove her through her second orgasm. When she reached the other side, he lapped softly at her tender folds, slowly bringing her down.

Cillian looked up at his beautiful girl, and that dark satisfaction settled deeper inside him. She was flushed and breathless. Hair the braid no longer held was a mass of white silk spread in a wild disarray across his sheets. Her breathing was quick, causing her plump breasts to sway softly, and the muscles of her belly fluttered in contractions. Her eyes were closed and her bottom lip was swollen and reddened from her teeth. He wanted to bit that lip, suck on its softness. But he knew his girl would probably bite back. She was so fierce. So brave.

He wasn't about to give her time to gather her wits. He needed her. Needed to be deep inside her; that lush little pussy wrapped tightly around him. He got off the bed and quickly removed his jeans, then reached into the drawer of the nightstand and pulled out the toy he'd put there. He settled between her thighs again and nestled the silver bullet between the lips of her pussy, flush against her swollen clit. He switched on the remote and the device came to life, buzzing softly.

Chloe flinched and cried out at the instant stimulation on her overly sensitive clitoris. She instinctively tried to close her legs, but his hips and thighs kept them in place.

"Shh, it's alright baby." He whispered and placed the head of his cock at her slick entrance and slowly pressed forward. The tender folds parting for him. She was unbelievably tight, but so wet. He pushed forward slowly, watching as his cock disappeared inside her. "Fuck baby, you're so beautiful takin my cock." He stretched her wide, and it was as sexy as hell to see her delicate flesh spread tight around his girth. When he looked up to see how she was faring, he was met with wide blue eyes clouded with desire and fear.

Chloe's gaze locked onto his. She could feel the pressure of him pushing inside her. He was so big he stretched her painfully, but the buzzing at her clitoris added another level of sensation that she couldn't rise above. It hurt and it felt amazing at the same time.

Cillian stopped his forward motion when his cock butted up against the barrier of her innocence. Somehow, he wasn't surprised to feel it. Possession, edgy and violent, held him in its grip. He'd never taken a virgin before. Never desired to possess innocence until now. Until Chloe. She was meant to be his. Would always be his.

"Oh, my beautiful girl, you waited for me."

Chloe watched possession heat his eyes. Had she been waiting for him? Is that why she'd never even been tempted by another man before? Was it just him?

He held her gaze for several heartbeats, then smiled. "You belong to me now, angel."

Chloe slowly shook her head but feared he just might be right. She tried to breathe through the delicious sensations tormenting her.

"You already do." His eyes gleamed with possession. His lips pulled back in a devilish smile as he lifted the remote and held it up for her to see.

"No!" She hissed. She wouldn't be able to handle both his intrusion and the vibrations.

He raised an arrogant brow, taunting her, then switched it on to the highest speed, causing the bullet to batter her clit with sharp, quick vibrations that abused the bundle of nerves.

"You bastard!" She yelled as her back bowed from the almost painful yet wonderful sensation. Her already sore throat shredding from it. The wicked dark edge of pleasure was more than she could bare. Her hips flexed violently in his hands, driving his cock deeper inside her.

He chuckled softly. "That's it, baby." He cooed at her. "Just like that." Then he plunged forward, driving into her tight heat to the hilt. When his cock tore through her hymen, she screamed.

Cillian leaned forward, sucked on the tender skin of her neck where it met her shoulder. He sucked it deep into his mouth, then bit down, pinning her in place beneath him. He gripped her ass for leverage and drove into her over and over with deep, powerful thrusts.

Chloe could only accept his thrusts as she tried to adjust to his size. The initial pain quickly turned to heated pleasure as her body rocked with a continuous orgasm that seemed never ending. It threw her into a violently sensuous space where nothing existed but him.

"You're so fucking tight, angel." He lost himself in her. The tightness surrounding him. Her taste, her smell, her body beneath his. "So hot baby."

The buzzing at her clit and the overwhelming fullness of his cock stretching her, thrusting hot and hard against something wicked inside her went on and on.

"Love this little pussy," he groaned. He lifted her legs over his forearms, opening her further for him.

She had no voice left to scream as she exploded! He consumed her. Climbed deep inside her. Opened her up to places she didn't know existed. And the devil that was Cillian O'Donnell left his mark behind.

Her pussy clamped down on his thrusting cock. Milking it as her hips rolled, and she bucked against him, matching his furious pace, meeting it. "Yea baby, that's it, work my cock." He whispered wickedly in her ear. "Feel that baby? That's you, takin what you need from me." Cillian couldn't prolong his own orgasm. His spine tingled, his balls tightened, and his hips flexed as he surged deep. He fisted her hair and lifted her face up to his. "Chloe!" He roared, then bit her lip and exploded as delicious waves of pleasure washed over him.

Chapter 7: Checkmate

Cillian rested most of his weight on his elbows to keep from crushing Chloe. He took several deep breaths, trying to recover from the most intense orgasm he'd ever experienced in his life. His fists still gripped her hair, holding her immobile. He leaned down and kissed her swollen lips. Her expression was oddly blank. "Chloe?" He whispered her name, but she didn't respond. He signed heavily, then slowly pulled his softening cock from the warm, tight grip surrounding it.

He sat back between her legs and looked down at her wet, swollen pussy. He lifted the now silent toy from her folds and saw the little smear of pink, the obvious blood mixed with his semen on her inner thigh and on his sheets. The proof of her virginity sent another quick stab of possessiveness straight through him. He leaned in and kissed the top of her mound reverently. "My beautiful girl." He sighed heavily when she didn't look at him.

He settled a blanket over her and went into the bathroom and turned on the water in the bathtub. Once it was warm enough, he poured in bath salts that would soothe her. After he was sure the temperature was perfect, he left the tub to fill and wet a cloth with hot water and brought it back to Chloe. He climbed onto the bed between her thighs and pressed it against her.

Chloe groaned softly, but she was afraid to open her eyes. She couldn't. She couldn't look at him. Her emotions were all over the place. What just happened between them had been incredible! And she'd actually screamed with pleasure. Screamed!

How could this happen? She'd practically begged him. Actually, she wasn't sure she hadn't. His sexy taunts in that deep Irish brogue had been so hot. She didn't know how to describe what they'd just done. But it had been amazing, and she hadn't wanted it to end. Jesus, she didn't know sex could be like that. Something was seriously wrong with her. Had to be. Because that was the most thrilling experience of her life.

Cillian cleaned her gently, then tossed the cloth onto the floor and moved to untie her. He reached for the rope at her wrist and froze. Her right hand was bruised and swollen. "Fuck! Why the hell didn't you tell me you hurt your hand?" He quickly loosened the slip knot and eased the rope off of her.

When Chloe didn't respond or open her eyes, he signed heavily again and gently lifted her hand to inspect the damage. "Can you move your fingers?" His jaw clenched tightly when she didn't answer. "Chloe, answer the fuckin question."

At his abrupt order, she jerked her injured hand from his. He had no choice but to release it or risk hurting her further. She rolled over and curled her body into a tight little ball, cradling her hand to her chest.

Cillian sat there for a moment, fighting the urge to pull her into his arms. To force her to talk to him so he'd know what she was thinking. But first, he needed a closer look at her hand. So, he got off the bed and went into the kitchen and filled an ice bucket, then took it into the bathroom and put it on a small table next to the tub. He turned the faucet off when the water level was where he wanted it. Then he went to get Chloe.

She was still lying in a tight ball in the center of his bed. She looked so small and delicate in the huge bed. She squeaked when he scooped her up and carried her into the bathroom. He used his foot to push back the antique vanity stool that had been purchased specifically for her and put her down on the marble countertop in front of the huge lighted mirror. He opened a small sterling silver and gold jewelry box that held hair ties. Selecting one, he gathered her long hair into a loose knot on top of her head.

He studied her bowed head for a moment, waiting to see if she would look around at the area his staff had prepared especially for her. When she made no move to do so, he sighed heavily and lifted her again, then placed her gently into the tub. He pulled her hand from where it was still cradled to her chest and placed it in the bucket of ice.

"Keep it on ice for now." He hadn't meant for it to sound like an order, but he couldn't help it. He was used to giving orders, and her continued silence was frustrating.

Chloe rested her forehead on her knees to avoid eye contact with him, but she left her hand in the bucket.

He went back into the bedroom and called Doc. As soon as he answered, Cillian barked into the phone. "Get over here." Then he hung up. He texted Rourke to let him know Doc was on his way, then went back to Chloe.

He climbed into the tub and settled behind her with his legs on either side cradling her. He reached for her, and she flinched.

"Don't." Her whispered plea was barely audible. Her shoulders were hunched in on herself and she was trembling.

Cillian wrapped his arms around her, kissed the top of her head and settled her resisting body flush to his.

Cillian ignored her stiff posture and lifted a sponge from the tray next to the tub and wet it. He squeezed the warm water over her back. Then he added body wash and began to gently wash her back in slow, practiced circles. Once it was covered in suds, he dropped the sponge and used his hands to massage her shoulders, her neck and the muscles of her back. Slowly, the tension in her began to ease.

"Can you wiggle your fingers?"

When she didn't respond, he continued. "I don't think it's broken."

"I don't either." She replied in a low, raspy voice she barely recognized as her own. Her throat was shredded, much like her nerves. She shouldn't be lashing out at him, but she was angry, furious. At him. At herself. And embarrassed. She'd acted so out of character. She'd wanted to be wild and reckless for the first time in her life. But now, facing him was nearly impossible. She didn't know what to do or how to act.

He pulled her resisting body back against his chest. When she tried to cover her breasts with her free arm, he pulled it away and held it down by her side for a few seconds. When he released it, she tried to lift it again, but he blocked the move. "You're in no condition to fight me right now, angel."

"I don't want you to touch me right now." Chloe glanced up from where she now lay with her head cradled against his chest. She could feel his cock pressed against the small of her back. She didn't want to the feel of his warm skin against hers.

"Just lie back and relax."

Cillian didn't like the lost look in her beautiful blue eyes. He added more soap to his palms and began to slowly, methodically, massage her breasts, her belly, and under her arms. Once she was clean, he added more soap and ran his hands down her belly and under the water between her legs. She immediately closed her legs on his hands. He forced them back open with his forearms, then cupped her pussy with his palm. "Are you sore?"

"Yes." She hissed as her temper ignited.

"It'll pass." He circled her pussy slowly with his palm. He brought his other hand back to her breast and massaged it softly.

"Stop Cillian!" She lifted her hand from the ice to push his hands away.

51

Using the hand at her breast, he pushed it back into the bucket. "Leave it in the ice so it doesn't swell."

When she lifted it again; he pinched her nipple. She gasped and flinched at the unexpected sensation. "Ouch! Quit it!"

"I said, put it back." He pinched tighter, holding pressure on the tender tip with his finger and thumb and waited.

"Quit!"

"Put. It. Back."

When she realized, he wasn't going to let go until she did as she was told. She growled, but put her hand back in the ice.

"Good girl." He released her nipple and kissed the top of her head then went back to massaging her breast.

"Jerk!"

Cillian chucked at her little show of temper. This was more like it.

"You didn't use a condom." She'd been trying not to think about that. He hadn't used one and she hadn't thought to ask him to. What was wrong with her?

And right now, she really needed a distraction. His gigantic hands were everywhere. Touching her. Arousing her. Which was a little embarrassing. And now, thanks to his asshole move, her freaking nipple was throbbing!

"You have an implant for birth control that's active for another five months."

Her head jerked back up to see his face. "How do you know that?"

"I know pretty much everything about you angel."

"How?"

"I have excellent hackers. I'm extremely good at it myself, but these days I pay an army to do it for me."

"What about STDs?"

"Well, based on the drops of blood on my sheets and on my cock, I'd say I have nothing to worry about." He chuckled when she blushed a crimson red.

"Jesus!"

"Ah, so sweet and innocent, little one." He touched the tip of her nose with his finger.

Chloe batted his hand away from her face. Her frustration overriding her embarrassment. "What about you?"

"I've never fucked a woman without a condom before you. Regardless, I'm clean. And I get tested regularly. I'll show you the latest results if you like."

She searched his eyes for long moments before sighing heavily. "That won't be necessary. I don't think you'd lie about that."

Cillian reached down to cup her jaw and lifted her face to his. "Chloe, I plan to do a lot of things to your beautiful little body. Most of those things will bring you intense pleasure, some of them may frighten you and I'll likely hurt you at times. I won't be able to stop myself, but I'll make sure you enjoy it. So much, that you'll come to crave it. But, the one thing I will never do is lie to you. Ever. And I'll not tolerate you lying to me."

Chloe could only gape at him. Holy shit, she was in trouble. "You're going to hurt me?"

"You'll enjoy it." He chuckled at her shocked expression. "There's a fine line between pleasure and pain."

"Are you insane? I don't want you to hurt me. I'm not into pain Cillian." She jerked her chin from his hold and turned her head away. Looking into those menacing eyes was unsettling.

Cillian continued to massaged his palm against her pussy gently. "You do and you are."

"No, I am not!"

"Angel, when I bite you or scrape my teeth across your clit, the wet heat that gushes from your hot little pussy is very telling." He moved to massage her inner thighs.

"Jesus!" She covered her face with her free hand.

He grinned at her reaction. "There's nothing wrong with that Chloe. Besides, if you didn't respond to me the way you do, I'd have to teach you to. It's fortunate that we're such a perfect match. We have amazing chemistry, angel."

"We have something, that's for sure." She scoffed.

Cillian pinched her nipple again, but a little gentler this time. "Your pussy was hot and slick for me before I ever touched you with my tongue. I know you're innocent, but don't confuse what just happened between us, angel."

"Stop doing that!" Chloe jerked and slapped his hand away, then growled in frustration when he moved it to her throat.

Cillian chuckled at her outburst. She was such a fiery little thing. "You want me as much as I want you. You can try to deny it if you like. But your pussy was so hot and wet from the very first touch. You're just scared and unsure, but it will pass." He rested his palm on her throat and held her immobile for a few seconds until she settled back against his chest. Then her collar caught his finger, and he lifted it slightly to run his finger under it against her skin.

Chloe had forgotten about the extravagant necklace. She reached up with her free hand and touched it.

"Do you like it?"

"It's beautiful. But I couldn't find the clasp. How do I take it off?"

"You don't."

"What do you mean?"

"The only way to remove the collar is with a key." He called it what it was on purpose, so she would understand.

"Collar?"

"Yes, it's your collar."

Chloe sat up so quickly the top of her head nearly smacked his chin and water sloshed over the rim of the tub onto the floor. The look on her face when she turned toward him was of complete outrage. "It's a collar?" She watched his lips form a devilish grin. "You put a freaking collar on me?!" She screeched and her battered throat protested.

At this rate, she'd have no voice left. She yanked hard, but the stupid thing didn't break, so she yanked harder. "Take it off!"

Cillian didn't try to stop her. She wouldn't be able to break it, and she needed to know it. "It also has a GPS tracker imbedded in it so I'll know where you are every second of the day." He decided not to mention the other microchips he'd had Doc inject into her.

"What?!" She shrieked again. "What am I, a dog?"

"No, little one. What you are, is mine. And in my world, it means you belong to me. You've been collared. Checkmate Chloe."

"Checkmate? Checkmate!" She'd heard that term somewhere before. Sidney had read a book about it once. "Oh my God! Take it off! Take it off right now!"

"No." Cillian's smile was purely wicked. He preferred this furious Chloe so much more than the defeated one she'd been earlier. She was a fighter, and he liked her that way. "It's made of titanium and white gold and the way the alloy is fired, it's basically unbreakable. You can yank on it all you want, but I wouldn't advise it. You'll only bruise your lovely neck."

"Cillian O'Donnell, you can't do this to me!" Chloe was dumbstruck. His arrogance was unbelievable.

"I already have." He said smugly, then stood up and got out of the tub.

Chloe watched him dry off. Like it or not, Cillian was a beautiful man. Not just his fallen angel face, either. His shoulders were wide. His broad back narrowed to a trim, corded waist. His ass was tight and muscular like his long legs. But what caught and held her attention was the massive tattoo covering his back. It was the snarling face of a black wolf. One side of its face dark, completely filled in with black ink except for flecks of his lighter skin and white ink visible for shading in the fur. That side had a gleaming red eye. The other side much lighter. Not as filled in, his skin, the background of the shaded gray image with a flashing green eye. The duality of man. It was as beautiful as it was menacing.

Cillian wrapped a towel around his waist, then picked up another one and reached for her. She tried to slap his hands away, but he simply ignored her. He lifted her out of the tub, paying close attention to her bruised hand, and dried her off.

"I can do it myself." She tried to grab the towel from him, but he didn't let it go.

"You can, but from now on you won't."

Chloe stomped her foot in frustration. "Cillian stop it! And take this stupid collar off of me!"

He dropped the towel on the floor and scooped her up into his arms. "Never."

Cillian carried her into the bedroom and dropped her on the bed. He disappeared into the closet and pulled on a pair of black cotton drawstring pants tied low on his waist. He went to the back of the closet that he'd had prepared for her and opened one drawer after another until he found what he was looking for.

He came back out and handed her a short robe made of silk in a robin's egg blue with a beautiful print of large white tiger lilies. "Put this one. Dinner should be here."

Grateful for something to wear, Chloe put on the robe. Because she was so petite, she was surprised it fit perfectly. And, she had to admit; it was beautiful. "Who does this belong to?" She wasn't jealous. She wasn't! She lied to herself. She just didn't want to wear an old girlfriend's clothes. Well, she didn't want to, but she would if it was the only thing available.

"You."

"Yea, right." She scoffed and slid the soft robe around her shoulders.

Cillian's lips twitched as if he were trying not to smile. "I had my staff fill your closet with a complete wardrobe. You should have everything you'll need."

"When?" She asked skeptically.

"I made the call the moment you walked away from me in the gallery."

"Humph." She tied the belt of the robe tightly around her. It was a little difficult to do with her injured hand. It throbbed terribly, but she didn't want to give him any excuse to get too close to her.

Cillian did smile then. She was so sassy. He reached for her uninjured hand and pulled her out of the bedroom.

Chapter 8: Beauty Fades

Chloe stared at the surly old man as he inspected her hand. His shaggy red hair and the long thick beard covering half of his plump face were both streaked with grey. She had a passing thought that he looked like a deranged Santa Claus.

"How did this happen?" Doc looked up at the beautiful young lady, then over at his boss.

"She hit me." Cillian chuckled.

Chloe blushed beet red. She was going to do more than hit him before this was over. But right now, her hand was throbbing.

"Did you?" Doc mused, fighting a smile.

Chloe smirked at the old man. "Yes. But he deserved it." Then she remembered her current situation and frowned. "You know I'm being held against my will, don't you? And now, I want to go home."

"Chloe." Cillian's voice was a sinful cadence, but his eyes had gone from warm and teasing to hard and cold. "If he attempts to take you from me, I'll kill him. Is that what you want?"

She watched the sudden change in him. Gone was the teasing facade to be replaced with menace. "What?!" She whispered, horrified as the true predator reveal himself.

Cillian crossed his arms over his chest and casually leaned against the chair. "I'll kill him or anyone else who tries to take you from me."

All color leached from her face and fear tightened her nerves. Her eyes slowly shifted from his to the doctors.

"He will." Doc confirmed with a scowl, then lifted her hand higher. "Can you make a fist?"

A loud whirring like a tornado sounded in her head and her throughs started spinning with it. What the hell had she done? All she'd wanted was to be spontaneous. Just once in her life! Throw caution to the wind. And look what happened! She ended up with a psycho! Shit!

Chloe pulled her hand away from his gently probing fingers and slowly back toward the door, careful to keep both men in sight. Her thoughts were spinning out of control as panic set in.

"Don't." Cillian started toward her as her back hit the door. Her good hand slid behind her for the handle.

"I'd like to go home now." She whispered through trembling lips

As Cillian continued to advance, Chloe yanked opened the door and attempted to back out. She screamed when she ran into a hard body and large hands landed on her arms. Panicked, she jerked out of the hold and shifted away, keeping her back to the wall so she could keep everyone in sight.

"Calm down Chloe." Cillian continued to advance as she moved to stay out of his reach. He winced at the terror blazing in her eyes.

"I won't tell anyone. I promise I won't. Just, please. Let me go."

"Baby, you're scaring yourself unnecessarily." Cillian said in a calm, soothing voice.

"I'm not scaring myself! You're scaring me! This whole situation is scaring the hell out of me! You kill people!?"

Cillian stopped his advance because she was running out of wall space. He didn't want her any more frightened that she already was. It was his fault with his careless words. "Rourke, you can go." He ordered without taking his eyes from her. She was trembling violently and the fear in her beautiful eyes cut him deep. He waited until his guard closed the door behind him before saying, "Sweetheart, I'd never harm you."

"Liar! You already said you'd punish me!" She screamed.

Cillian smiled softly and lowered his voice. "Baby, that's different."

"Liar!"

"I told you. I'll never lie to you. Chloe, you're the safest person on this island. No one is going to harm one hair on your beautiful head."

"I don't believe you."

"I know, but you will in time."

"I'm not going to be here. I want to go home."

Cillian moved then. Chloe threw a right hook that was batted away. She executed a quick front kick that was pushed aside. He moved so fast she couldn't track him. One minute he was five feet away, the next she was in his arms. She was good, very good. She'd trained for years. But her defensive moves were useless against his speed and strength. Proving that he'd let her hit him before.

He held her close and whispered softly, "you are home. This is where you belong."

Chloe started to cry. And she hated crying. "Please." She sounded pathetic, even to her own ears.

"Let Doc finish examining your hand baby, then we'll eat something and talk." He kissed her forehead then carried her back to the chair where Doc was waiting with a furious scowl on his old face. Cillian sat with her held securely on his lap, took her swollen hand and held it out. "Finish it."

Doc took a deep breath and cleared his throat then lifted her delicate hand. "Now, let's see. Where were we? Ah yes," he said light heartedly. "Can you make a fist?"

Chloe buried her face in Cillian's chest and cried softly while following Doc's instructions. She winced when it hurt but she did it. He nodded his head, then asked if she would wiggle her fingers for him. It hurt, but she was able to do that too.

" I don't think it's broken but come by the clinic in the morning for an x-ray, just in case."

He wrapped her hand in an ace bandage and told her to ice it until he knew for sure it wasn't fractured. He left prescription pain medication for her, then quickly gathered his bag and stomped out the door, grumbling under his breath about overbearing tyrants.

Finn wheeled in a cart carrying their dinner past the doctor. He frowned when he heard Chloe crying, but one killing look from Cillian and he left. After the door closed, Cillian glanced down at Chloe. "Are you ready to eat?"

He sighed heavily when she didn't answer. "I have a feeling Imogen made something delicious with you in mind."

She lifted her face and regarded him carefully for a moment. "Take me home."

"This is your home now, Chloe. You belong here, with me."

"No, I don't." She assured him. "I promise I won't tell anyone it was you. I promise. Please, just let me go home. I have a family. I have friends and school, my degree!" Her voice rose with her plea until she was yelling. "I have a life!"

Cillian leaned down until they were face to face. "Yes, you do." He gave her a quick, hard kiss, then pulled back, meeting her gaze and continued, "and it's here with me."

He carried her over to the table and put her gently into her chair. "Now eat. You're going to need your strength if you plan to spar with me."

Chloe looked down at the full plate in front of her. Half of a roasted chicken was covered in a rich, delicious smelling gravy resting on a mound of buttery mashed potatoes with crisp green beans on the side. It smelled amazing, but she had no appetite.

Cillian sat across from her and lifted the cover from his plate and smiled at her. "Imogen is an amazing cook." He lifted the opened bottle of white wine from the ice bucket and filled their glasses while she stared down at her plate, ignoring him. "We have our own vineyard on the island. It's been here for over a hundred years."

Chloe eyed the glass miserably before she finally met his gaze. "I really need to call my parents."

"Eat."

"Cillian, they'll be worried sick."

"Eat." Never taking his eyes from hers, he lifted his glass and clinked it against hers before putting it to his lips. When she didn't move to follow his command, he sighed heavily. "Shall we move on to where I teach you about punishments and rewards?"

She cringed, but lifted her fork. She had the passing thought to just stab him with it. But if she killed him, would she be able to fight her way past the guards? Then what? She was on an island in the middle of nowhere.

"Good girl."

Chloe carefully lifted her glass of wine with a trembling hand and took a small sip. The cool crisp wine felt amazing to her abused throat. She scooped some potatoes onto her fork and dipped it into the gravy and ate it. Next, she tried a small bite of chicken. She winced when it hurt her hand to cut it. But before she could try again, Cillian reached over and cut it from the bone for her. It was moist and tender and the skin was crisp. She even managed to eat a green bean or two. The food was excellent, but her stomach didn't care. It was tied in knots. Her throat closed up, so she took another sip of wine, hoping it would help her relax. She lifted her fork again, but couldn't make herself eat another bite.

Cillian watched Chloe push the food around her plate. She should be starving. By his calculations, she hadn't eaten in nearly twenty-four hours. But his careless words had scared her. He hadn't meant to say them, but the thought of someone taking her from him sent him into a murderous rage. His carelessness probably set him back several weeks in his campaign.

He found it hard to concentrate on his own meal with her sitting across from him, looking so delicious. Even frightened, with tears shining in her eyes, she was beautiful.

Her creamy complexion was flushed. Her lips were slightly swollen from her teeth and his kisses. Her hair was a beautiful, disheveled tangle of silk on top of her head, with wisps of it falling around her stunning face and delicate neck. The marks he'd left on her throat just above her collar were dark against her pale skin. The site of them gave him a keen sense of satisfaction.

He shifted slightly in his seat and adjusted his cock into a more comfortable position. At this rate he'd have a perpetual hard on. He'd been hard for her from the first moment he'd seen her smile. And he wondered now what it would take to make her smile like that again.

"Tomorrow, I'll take you on a tour of the island."

"Tomorrow, you can take me home."

"If the weather's good, we'll take the horses out for a ride."

"You can't keep me here."

"What type of paint do you use?"

Chloe sighed heavily, propped the elbow of her good hand on the edge of the table and resting her head in her palm, and answered quietly. "I mostly work with acrylics."

"Do you paint often?"

She took another sip of wine to wet her throat before she answered. "Yes."

"How often?"

"Usually every day. At least I have been lately." She paused, and her voice lowered. "I just completed a piece for my final."

"The Manhattan Art University. Very prestigious. You must be very talented."

"How do you know that?" Because of her sore throat, her shocked question came out very raspy.

Cillian frowned. "What's wrong with your voice?"

Chloe looked at him like he was crazy. Was he serious?

"Chloe?" He hadn't noticed her voice was hoarse before.

"My throat hurts." She glared at him. She hated when he used that tone with her. Even the musical lilt couldn't disguise the autocratic tone. "I assume it's from screaming so much over the last few hours." Her sarcasm didn't sound as sharp as she intended because of the rasp in her voice.

"Why didn't you say something?"

"Yea right."

Despondently, she pushed some of the chicken around in the gravy with her fork. She wasn't hungry. She was scared. And tired. So tired. She felt every ache, every bruise. A silent tear escaped and slid down her cheek.

"Chloe?"

"Please leave me alone." She whispered. She didn't care what he did anymore. What he said or how he said it. She was done. So much for coming out unscathed. She wasn't wild and carefree or adventurous. She was and always would be the responsible one. And, she just wanted to go home.

Cillian watched his beautiful girl for a few minutes. Watched as silent tears slid down her delicate cheeks. He'd pushed her hard today.

Demanded a lot from her. He got up and went to the bar and retrieved a bottle of water from the refrigerator. He replaced her wine glass with it. Then opened the bottle of pills and shook out two tablets, placing them on the table next to the water.

"Take these. Try to eat a few more bites so it doesn't upset your stomach."

Chloe took the pills without even looking at them. She didn't really care anymore what they were. Working awkwardly with her left hand, she forced herself to eat two more bites of the potatoes before lowering her fork.

Cillian lifted the small cover off of the chocolate mousse Imogen had made for her. He spooned up a small amount and held it out. "Try the mousse."

She stared back at him with tired eyes, her lashes spiked and damp from her tears. He moved the spoon closer to her mouth, so she opened for him. He slid it carefully inside and waited while she took his offering. She put her elbow on the table again and rested her head in her hand while she savored the chocolate. It was rich and creamy and as smooth as silk as it slid down her throat. He held up the spoon again. But she shook her head and closed her eyes.

Looking at her despondent face, he knew he wasn't going to get anything more out of her tonight. Instead of pushing her further, Cillian lifted her into his arms and carried her into the bathroom. She didn't struggle at all and that was telling. He placed her on the floor in front of the sink and handed her a toothbrush, then went to take care of his own needs. When she finished, he took her hand and led her back into the bedroom.

Cillian reached for the tie to her robe and she stepped back defensively. He raised an arrogant eyebrow at her and reached out and snagged the knotted belt and pulled her back to him.

Chloe signed, too exhausted to care. She had a fleeting thought that it might be the pain pills dulling her senses.

He untied the robe and slipped it from her shoulders, then picked her up and put her in the center of the bed. After removing his pants, he climbed in beside her. He turned off the lights, then tucked her in tight against him, her back to his front with the covers pulled over them.

He kissed the back of her neck before settling his face in her hair. "I'm not going to tie you up. I don't think it would be good for your hand. But I'll remind you, there's a guard at the door." He curled his body around hers; his leg between her thighs, his arm around her so that his palm cupped her breast. He nestled his hard cock snug between the cheeks of her ass.

She instantly tried to move away from him, but he shushed her and held her firmly in place.

"Don't worry angel, I want you wide awake when I take you again. Just go to sleep now."

She settled quickly. If he had to guess, it was the pain relievers doing their job.

However, several long minutes later she whispered softly into the silence, "why me?"

"Because you're the most beautiful thing I've ever seen." He whispered back.

Right before she dozed off, she mumbled quietly, "beauty fades."

He waited a few minutes after her breathing evened out before he replied just a quietly. "Not your kind of beauty angel."

Chapter 9: The Wicked Ways of Men

Cillian woke up to the smell of Chloe. He opened his eyes and inhaled her scent. Sometime during the night, they'd shifted positions. Her head rested on his chest, his arms around her, holding her close. Her hair was caught in the stubble on his chin. He looked down at her face, relaxed in sleep. She looked so young. He knew she was young. He'd admit it, but she wasn't too young. His own mother had been younger when his father had chosen her.

But Chloe was also strong like his mother, too.

He kissed the top of her head and ran his fingers through her soft hair. The feel of her full breast pressed against his abs was distracting causing his cock to ache for attention. He fought the urge to roll her beneath him and sink into her heat. He could already feel her tight little pussy strangling him. But he wouldn't. He wouldn't take her again until he knew for certain her hand wasn't broken. That wasn't the kind of pain he longed to give her. And laying here torturing himself wasn't helping.

He ran his finger down her cheek and across her full bottom lip. "Chloe?"

"Hmm." She curled into a ball like a little kitten snuggling into him.

Chloe was having the best dream. Cillian O'Donnell was kissing her as they danced slowly across the floor of the empty art gallery. Then he was whispering to her. She moved closer to him to hear his soft words.

He groaned silently as her soft skin rubbed against his. "Angel, wake up."

Chloe's eyes shot open on a gasp and she jerked up to stare dumbfounded down at him.

He couldn't help but grin at her shocked expression. Then his eyes traveled down her naked torso, taking the time to admire her rosy nipples peaked from the slight chill in the room.

"It wasn't a nightmare." She groaned. "It really happened. You really did kidnap me." She reached for the blanket to cover herself, and he let her.

His grin turned to a full-fledged smile. "You are really here, if that's what you're asking."

She stared at his devilish smile for a moment, then looked around warily, taking in the large room. She hadn't paid attention to it yesterday. But she took the time now, if only to put off facing Cillian O'Donnell in the light of day. She wasn't ready for that nor was she ready to admit to her own behavior yesterday.

The room was decorated in shades of cream, light gray and deep blues. The furniture was heavy and looked antique, but didn't detract from the airy feel of the space. The walls were rounded, attesting to the fact that the bedroom was in a tower of a castle. There were large plate-glass windows on two sides, bringing in a lot of natural light. A seating area in the corner included two wingback chairs in cream with dove gray stripes and navy toss pillows. The couch was solid cream with a buttoned tufted back cushion. It was loaded down with more navy and gray pillows and a blanket in multiple hues of gray, blue and white lay across the seat.

Dark hardwood floors gleamed in the sunlight. Several rugs in light shades of cream and beige added warmth.

But the bed was the centerpiece of the room. It was huge! The headboard was a dark wood with intricate designs etched into the wood and framed cut outs that exposed black iron rods which appeared to be part of the design. Four tall posts at the corners held vintage canopy rails across the top of all sides where heavy dove gray curtains were gathered and tied back at each corner. The entire room was like something out of a magazine.

After her perusal of the room, she had no choice but to turned back and face Cillian. As expected, he was watching her, waiting, like he always seemed to do. She tightened her hold on the blanket and winced slightly when her hand protested. She silently took stock of herself. Her hand and wrist still hurt. It was more of a throbbing this morning than the sharp stabbing pain from last night. She swallowed. Her throat was still tender, but not too painful. But more importantly, she was very sore between her legs. She felt her face heat with the burn of a blush.

"I'd give just about anything to know what you're thinking right now." Cillian said as he watched the color rise in her cheeks.

She glared at him. It wasn't fair. How could someone so handsome be a killer? "Alright, my freedom for my thoughts."

He reached over and stroked her cheek with his knuckle. "Not happening."

"Cillian, you know you can't keep me here, right?" In the light of day, she'd hoped he'd see reason.

"Sure, I can." He smiled indulgently.

"No, you can't. It's against the law."

"I make the laws here, Chloe."

She batted his hand away. "You're being ridiculous! Now stop this game you're playing and take me home."

"Not a game. Now come on. We need to get dressed and head down to breakfast." He snaked his arm around her, shoved the blanket out of the way, then moved off the bed, taking her with him.

"Stop it!" She tried to knee him in the nuts, but he was too fast. He swung both of her legs up and captured them with his other arm.

"Be good Chloe," he squeezed her to him, "or I'll spank that perfect little ass."

Shocked outrage held her silent for a split second before she growled at him. "You wouldn't dare!"

"Oh, I would. And I'd enjoy every second of it." He grinned down at her scowling face. "Do you want to play this morning or do you want to go have breakfast?"

When she didn't answer, he stopped, and half turned back toward the bed. "Answer me, or I'll make the choice for you."

She glared at him and hissed, "breakfast!"

"What a shame." Cillian chuckled and carried her into the bathroom. He put her down next to the sink and held out her toothbrush. When she snatched it from him, his green eyes sparkled with laughter. He turned the water on to the shower and, while it heated, brushed his teeth in the sink next to hers.

She ignored him and completely avoided looking at him. They were both naked. He didn't seem to mind his nudity. But she did. She wished she had her pretty robe.

Cillian watched her in the mirror while he brushed his teeth. She was blushing again. He really liked it when she did that. But she'd have to get used to being naked with him. He had no intention of allowing her to hide that beautiful body from him when they were alone.

He waited patiently for her to finish, then reached over and lifted her hand, removed the bandage, and inspected it for swelling. "It's still swollen, but not as bad as it was last night. That's promising."

"It only hurts a little." She tried to focus on her hand instead of the terrifyingly beautiful man in front of her. His cock was hard. Really hard. It was long and thick and reached all the way to his belly button. She couldn't believe it fit inside her. No wonder she was so sore this morning. And at the moment, it was pointed at her stomach, the fat tip touching her belly.

"You should take another pill with breakfast." He leaned down and kissed her palm.

"It doesn't hurt that bad."

"Good." He started toward the shower with her in tow when she pulled against him.

"What are you doing?"

When she continued to resist, he leaned down and lifted her into his arms then stepped into the shower.

"Quit doing that! You can't just pick me up every time you want to take me somewhere I don't want to go."

"Of course, I can." Cillian cupped her face in both hands and lifted it toward his. "I can do anything I want." Before she could reply, he leaned down and kissed her.

She tried to pull away, but his hands held her in position. She couldn't even open her mouth to bite him. And she tried.

After he kissed her, Cillian rubbed his nose against hers for a few moments, savoring the feel of her face against his. Then he removed the band from her hair and watched it fall around her in a cloud of silk.

Chloe tried to step back, but he gripped her hair and held her in place.

"Don't fight me in here, Chloe. You might slip and fall."

"Cillian, please."

"Just be still." He used his voice to soothe her while he washed her hair.

"I can do it."

"I know, but I want to do it and with your bruised hand, it's easier if I do."

She stood stoically with her eyes closed while he lathered the thick mass with his palms. But with the feel of his large hands gently massaging her scalp, she slowly began to relax. When he eased her head back into the spray to rinse the suds away, she opened her eyes and was instantly captured by the blazing heat in his. She got lost in that heat while he repeated the process with the conditioner.

Then he reached for her body wash, and her brain came back on line.

"You are not going to bathe me!" This was too much. His soapy hands running all over her body; massaging and soothing. She'd probably go up in flames!

He couldn't help but smile at her outraged gasp. She'd learn soon enough.

She stepped back, and he advanced, essentially pinning her against the wall. Using his hands, he smoothed suds from her throat down to her breasts, circling them slowly, coating them, then sliding under her arms.

"Oh my God! Stop!" She went to push his hands away and winced when her sore hand bumped into his.

"Chloe, this will go a lot faster for you if you'd stop fighting me."

"Cillian!"

"We can do this the easy way or the hard way, but in the end, I'll get what I want." His serious, intimidating gaze held hers for a moment to make sure she understood. Then he added more soap to his palms and ran his hands down her back and over her hips.

She glared up at him. "I hate you!"

"No, you don't." He chuckled. "You're just afraid." He smoothed his hands down her stomach and slid one between her legs and the other around to her bottom. He took his time cleaning her thoroughly.

"You're right, I am afraid. And with good reason. You kill people, remember?"

"Have you always waxed your pussy?" His hand glided across her soft hairless mound.

She inhaled sharply at the blunt change of subject and turned her face away, but not before he saw the blush that colored her cheeks.

"Chloe?" He slid a finger deep inside of her.

She gasped and lifted up onto her toes. "Ye, Yes."

"Why?" Pleased with her response, he slipped his finger from her and moved to clean her inner thighs.

"Jesus! Personal much?" She frowned at him.

"We're going to get very personal." He slid his hand back up to her pussy with an implied threat. "Answer me."

"Shaving takes up too much time." She said quickly and stood on her tiptoes again to keep away from his finger.

"Good girl. From now on, I'll wax you."

"Oh. No. You. Won't!" She declared between clenched teeth!

He lifted that mocking brow again, then pulled her under the spray and rinsed her off. When she was clean, he guided her down to sit on the bench in front of him. This left her face level with his cock.

Chloe leaned her head back against the shower wall and the asshole laughed! He actually laughed at her!

Cillian had to laugh. If not, he'd end up pushing his swollen cock between those pouty lips of hers. He washed his hair quickly, watching her the entire time. She was definitely getting aroused. She didn't want to be, but she was. Her pouty lip pinched between small white teeth. Her eyes heated as she watched him from under her lashes as he washed himself.

Chloe's eyes nearly popped out of her head when he took his cock in a tight, soapy grip and pumped it with his fist. Shocked, she jerked her gaze up to his.

"Watch me." He whispered harshly. When she didn't look back down, he stepped toward her. She immediately looked down, but held her hand out to hold him off. Satisfied, he stepped back to give her space. "Just watch." His musical voice strained with need. "This is what you do to me, angel. See? You make my cock so hard; it aches. My balls so tight it's almost painful. You cause this baby." He cupped his tight sac with his left hand while pumping his cock with hard sure strokes with his right. He stared at her mouth the entire time. "You, Chloe."

Chloe was dumbfounded. She couldn't believe he was doing this right in front of her. His boldness was intimidating. And sexy as hell. She could actually feel a deep blush wash over her.

"When you touch me, I'll want you to do it with a firm hand. You'll squeeze my cock so tight in your little hand. Your fingers wrapped around me."

Her hand lifted to her chest. Her fingers fluttered there as her breathing became heavier. Oh God this was hot.

"This is yours now, Chloe. It belongs to you." Still looking at her mouth, he groaned and pumped faster. "Can you see the pearls seeping from the tip? That's for you. My desire, my need for you, baby. Do you see it?"

Captivated, she nodded her head slowly. Through the white suds, she could see the thick, clear liquid glistening on the head of his cock.

He ran his thumb over it with each downward slide. "It's warm and slick, baby. So smooth to the touch. Soon. angel, soon, you'll know what it tastes like. What it feels like on your tongue." He groaned, low and deep, when her tongue darted out to moisten her bottom lip. "Just like I've memorized your taste, baby. So sweet, so, so, sweet Chloe." He groaned again. He wasn't going to last. He pumped faster, squeezed his sac tighter. Her mesmerized gaze following his every move. It was so fucking erotic. "I've imagined your pouty lips surrounding my cock. Stretched so tight as you take me deep into your throat. So good, angel."

His spine tingled; his hips flexed, pushing his pulsing cock harder into his hand. He was on his toes. His cock throbbed beneath his palm; his balls tightened further. He pumped faster. "Chloe, baby, so good. It's so good, baby. Chloe!" He threw his head back and groaned out her name as he came with hard, shuddering jerks of his cock.

She watched transfixed as thick spurts of his release blasted into the stream of water to wash slowly down the drain. Chloe gasped and tried to slow her breathing. When Cillian's heated gaze found hers, the lust and longing in those intense green depths caused her to lose her breath again. Holy shit! She was in so much trouble.

Chapter 10: Breakfast in Paradise

Chloe sat in a state of confusion in front of the vanity mirror as she watched Cillian dry her hair. He'd insisted on doing it. She hadn't resisted because she was still a little dazed from watching him in the shower. She didn't know how she felt about what she'd seen. The wicked things he'd said. She knew he was trying to seduce her. She'd been a virgin, but she wasn't naïve. And she never in a million years imagined she'd get to watch a man do that. The way his body took over. The violence of it, the beauty. She was amazed and frightened at the same time. See, completely and frustratingly confused!

"Almost done." Cillian said as he gathered the last section of her hair and pulled the brush through it before switching the blow dryer back on.

When he'd told her to sit at the vanity, he'd opened and searched a few drawers until he found the brush. It surprised her to see so many feminine things in the drawers. When she'd questioned him, he'd reminded her he'd instructed his staff to purchase everything she would need. But she still questioned how they'd known about the brands she regularly used. They were all the same. Even the makeup. He'd done what he always did when he didn't want to answer her questions, he'd simply smiled.

Cillian turned off the dryer when the last of Chloe's hair was completely dried. "We need to discuss a few things before we go downstairs."

Her eyes met his in the mirror. "What things?"

"You'll have a guard with you at all times when you're not inside the castle."

"What, you think I'm going to swim fifty miles in shark-infested waters?" She scoffed.

"No." His serious gaze regarded hers in the mirror. "It's for your safety."

"My safety? I thought you owned this island?"

"I do. And everything and everyone on it. But I trust very few people, especially where you're concerned."

She raised her brow in question at that. But he didn't elaborate.

"Also, while I enjoy sparring with you here in our suite, don't fight me in front of my staff. Don't lash out or misbehave."

When she said nothing, he added, "if you do, I'll be forced to punish you, Chloe. Do you understand?"

She didn't immediately respond as she thought that through. "You said you wouldn't hurt me."

"There are ways to punish you that won't harm you physically." He pulled her hair back sharply, causing her chin to lift. "Tell me you understand?"

"I understand!" She didn't really have a choice. As soon as she answered, he let go of the tight grip on her hair.

"Imogen is head of my household staff. She was also a close friend of my mothers, before her death. She's important to me. You'll meet her this morning."

"She's the one who made dinner last night?"

"Yes."

When she didn't say more, he could almost see the wheels turning in her head. "She can't help you, Chloe. She won't." He divided her hair into three sections and wove it into a French braid. "Everyone on the island works for me. Their very livelihood depends upon me. They are loyal to me. Don't put her or anyone else in an awkward position by asking for their help."

"Perfect!" She grumbled.

Cillian grinned at her disgruntled face then tied off the braid, kissed the top of her head, and left the bathroom. Chloe sat there for a few minutes longer, staring at her reflection. "Just perfect." She whispered dejectedly.

When she finally followed him into the bedroom, she watched while he spread out a pale blue sundress on the bed next to a bra and panty set in sheer baby blue silk. She picked up the bra first. It was soft and delicate, but the cups were completely sheer. Her nipples were going to rub against the fabric of the dress. She rolled her eyes when she noticed the panties were not only sheer but were also a thong.

"You expect me to wear this to breakfast?" Her voice was still a little raspy, so the question sounded harsh even to her own ears. But this was way over the top just for breakfast.

"Yes, the color will look beautiful against your skin."

71

He went back into the closet, so she took advantage of his absence and slipped into the bra and panties. The bra's under wire pushed her breasts up and together, enhancing her cleavage dramatically. The panties rode low on her hips and felt barely there. Just as she'd thought, it felt as if she was wearing nothing at all. She stepped into the short dress just as he walked out of the closet fully dressed in a dove grey button-down collared shirt tucked into dark blue jeans that sat low on his hips and hugged his thighs. His black leather belt matched the boots on his feet. He had a pair of fawn-colored sandals with a kitten heel, dangling from the fingers of his right hand.

He handed her the sandals, then turned her around and zipped up her dress. The dress fell to her mid-thigh and based on everything she'd seen so far; it did not surprise her when it fit perfectly.

They were met at the door by the same man who'd been guarding it last night. One glimpse at him had her averting her eyes. She blushed at the memory. This guy had seen her naked!

Cillian noted it and paused. "Chloe, this is Patrick. You met his twin brother, Rourke, last night. Patrick, this is Chloe."

"Hello Chloe." Patrick's smile was warm and welcoming.

Under different circumstances, she'd have been inclined to smile back. But these weren't different circumstances. Apparently, she was a prisoner and he, a guard at her door. A quiet "hi" was all she could muster as a greeting.

When Patrick held out his hand to shake hers, Cillian scowled at him causing him to laughed.

Patrick wasn't as tall as Cillian, and he was leaner. His muscles not as pronounced but still very much in evidence as they stretched the short sleeves of his polo shirt. But what drew her attention most were the two guns strapped to his chest and the one clipped to his belt.

Cillian pulled her around Patrick and across a wide foyer to the elevator. She didn't miss Patrick instantly falling into step behind them.

Based on the numbers on the panel, Cillian's suite was on the fourth floor. When the doors opened, they followed Patrick out into a brightly lit space and she nearly stumbled.

The marble floors were a glossy white, with gray and beige veins of color throughout the stone. The wool runner on the floor was the only thing keeping their heels for echoing through the corridor. The ceilings were at least twenty feet high, with elegant chandeliers that lit up the entire corridor.

The architecture and decor were luxury at its finest. But it was the artwork that caught and held her attention. A huge marble sculpture of the

Farnese of Hercules was an unexpected and impressive site. And if her memory was correct, an exquisite Imperial Ming Vase that should most definitely be housed behind glass sat casually on a side table. These were just a few fabulous pieces that captured her attention. But the paintings.... Jeezus! She couldn't help but gape at the collection. Stunning canvases behind heavy cases on the walls displaying the works of Van Gogh's Almond Blossoms and Rembrandt's The Storm on the Sea of Galilee and so many others. Forgeries she assumed, but no less awe-inspiring.

Cillian led Chloe slowly through the halls of his home. Her head turned in every direction, taking in the pieces his family had collected over the years. Many of which had been stolen or purchased on the black-market. Transfixed, she'd stumbled a few times and would have tripped if not for his hold on her as he guided her through the rooms.

He felt a sense of pride as he slowed his pace to give her a chance to take in as much as possible. He knew her artist's soul would be captivated.

Chloe looked up at Cillian and caught him watching her, waiting for a reaction. She took several deep breaths, trying to keep from hyperventilating. "Are?" She took a breath, then continued. "Are those originals or just very impressive replicas?"

His green eyes sparkled with approval and no small amount of arrogance. "Originals."

She'd known he was incredibly wealthy, but this, this was unbelievable. As she took in her surroundings; the domineering man beside her, the armed guard in front of her. A shiver of fear slowly creeped down her spine. Her blood turned to ice in her veins and her heartbeat echoed overly loud, thundering in her ears.

Terror; sharp and ugly, battered at her sense of self-preservation. Her mouth went dry as reality sank in. For the first time, clearly comprehending what he'd been saying all along. He absolutely was a law unto himself. And he really could keep her here, locked away from the world, just another treasure for his collection.

Cillian O'Donnell was a very wealthy, powerful man who obviously collected beautiful things. By fair means or foul, he collected them, arrogantly displaying them. She felt sick, the nausea from the previous day coming back with a vengeance. Oh God. She'd lost count of how many times he'd called her beautiful. Now she understood.

Her entire life strangers treated her differently based solely on her looks. Some treated her as if she were special for no other reason than her appearance, while others treated her as if she were not very bright or expected something for nothing. All prejudiced because they only judged the surface, never knowing the person she really was.

But her mother had coached her, in that gentle way of hers, to understand that what she looked like didn't matter. To never let people's opinions of her appearance discredit her or her intellect. To be smart, strong, and confident in everything she did.

But none of that mattered to Cillian O'Donnell. He was just like all those faceless people. He only saw the surface. The packaging. It was never more evident than in this moment, standing here in this beautiful place surrounded by these beautiful stolen treasures. Dressed in a beautiful silk dress that he'd selected for her to wear. He'd dressed her up like a damned doll! For breakfast, for God's sake!

She looked down at the stupid dress then around at his beautiful possessions. "You've got to be kidding me."

Cillian frowned when Chloe scowled. He'd thought his family's collection would delight her. Maybe speak to her artist's soul. "What?"

"Nothing." She grumbled under her breath.

By the time they reached the breakfast room, Chloe was lost in thought. She barely noticed Finn already at the table, eating.

"Good morning." Finn greeted the two as Cillian led Chloe Guidry into the room.

"Morning."

His cousin was scowling. But Chloe didn't acknowledge him at all. Her eyes met his for a brief moment, then looked away. The vivacious woman he'd met at the gallery in New Orleans was nowhere to be seen. He lifted his brow in question at Cillian, who just shrugged his shoulders. He took his time studying Chloe and when his eyes landed on her bandaged hand, he scowled at Cillian.

"What the fuck happened!"

Cillian rubbed his slightly bruised jaw and smiled. "Chloe has a mean right hook."

Finn looked to the petite woman next to his cousin, then back to him and laughed. Delighted. That was more like it. He noticed Chloe didn't look up at either of them. And he was sure that was Cillian's intension. Because when she didn't give any sort of response, Cillian scowled again.

Cillian led her to a chair next to his, then seated himself at the head of the table. The smell of bacon and coffee hung heavy in the air.

"She has an excellent front kick as well. But she doesn't use it to her advantage as she should."

That got her attention. Her gaze jerked to his and she scowled. Yea, she should've kicked him a second time. She just chose not to. At the time, she hadn't really wanted to hurt him.

"Is that right?" Finn's lips twitched in his effort to keep from grinning.

"Yes. She's going to need to continue her training here." Cillian's sly gaze slid from her face to Finn's. "I supposed you'll have to fit her into our afternoon workouts."

"I can do that. If she's willing." Finn reached for his coffee cup. "What do you say, Chloe?"

Chloe stared at Finn for a few moments while she considered him. They were toying with her. And it pissed her off. "Do you train all the victims you kidnap?"

She didn't trust either of them. He was outfitted like Patrick, with two gun holsters across his chest. She bet if he stood up, he'd have one clipped to his belt, too. These men were criminals, killers, kidnappers. And she was sure this one was directly involved in hers.

Finn's sudden grin lit up his stoic face. "I guess we'll find out."

Cillian chuckled beside her. Was he taunting her? "I guess you will."

"Good, that's settled." Cillian spooned a large helping of scrambled eggs and a few slices of bacon onto her plate. Her stomach turned. She reached out to push the plate away, but at that moment, an older woman stepping into the room from a side door caught her attention.

She was tall and thin and wore a simple black dress and low-heeled black pumps. Her long black hair peppered with grey, was pulled back in a tight bun at the back of her head. Her pretty face was slightly rounded with age and her smile was as welcoming as her kind, pale green eyes. Eyes that quickly zeroed in on Chloe, and her smile got even bigger.

"Good morning." Her chipper melodic voice conveyed her Irish heritage. She carried a pitcher of orange juice over and placed it next to Chloe's plate.

"Chloe, this is Imogen." Cillian watched her closely, waiting to see if she would follow his instructions.

She glanced from him to Imogen. "Hello." Her voice was raspy and strained, causing Cillian to frown again.

"Hello, Chloe. It's very nice to meet you." Imogen smiled kindly at her. She reminded Chloe of a matronly grandmother, but she was learning that looks could be very deceiving around here.

"Can I get you some coffee or juice, perhaps?"

"Coffee please." She purposely kept her gaze pointed over the woman's shoulder. If she looked into those kind eyes, knowing that the woman wouldn't help her, she'd probably start bawling like a baby.

Imogen walked over to the side buffet and returned with a cup of steaming black coffee and a small tray of cream and sugar. She placed both in front of Chloe and seemed to be waiting anxiously for her to try the coffee.

Grateful for the distraction, Chloe added cream and two spoons of sugar into her coffee and stirred it slowly.

"You may find our Irish coffee a bit stronger than you're used to. If you'd prefer something else, please let me know."

Chloe took a small sip of the hot, rich, coffee and relished the warmth on her abused throat. Since Imogen seemed to be waiting for a response, Chloe nodded slightly. "This is very good, thank you." She was used to strong coffee. New Orleans was famous for it.

Imogen smiled, obviously pleased. She nodded back, then noticed her bandaged hand. She looked over at Cillian, then back at Chloe and her smiled turned to a look of concern.

"Imogen, is there more coffee for me?"

"Of course, Finnigan." She turned quickly and refilled his empty cup, but glanced back at Chloe anxiously before she left the room.

As soon as Imogen left, Cillian looked over at Finn. "Anymore from Abdul?"

"Nothing new."

Cillian filled his plate with the American breakfast foods he was sure Imogen had made especially for Chloe. "Just as I expected. He'll lie low for a few weeks, hoping we'll stew over his latest inquiry."

"No doubt. But he thinks he has something or wants us the think he does, so we'll hear from him again soon." Finn sipped his coffee and regarded the two at the end of the table.

Cillian pulled his phone from his pocket and started reviewing his emails while he ate. "Did Van leave yet?" He wanted all visitors off the island before he took Chloe on a tour.

"Not yet. A slight mechanical issue."

Cillian didn't take his eyes from his phone as he clicked through the messages. "Mechanical issue?"

"Just a part that needs to be replaced. We have it in stock so it shouldn't take long."

Ignoring their conversation, Chloe spied a rack of thick toast. She took a piece and spread butter on it before taking a small bite. The warm bread settled her stomach almost immediately. She saw a little bowl of orange jelly, so she scooped up a small amount and spread it on her toast.

She concentrated on the toast and jelly while the men continued their conversation. She tried a few bites of the eggs and ate half a piece of bacon, but preferred the toast with the jelly. She ate a second piece, licking the sticky sweetness from her fingers when she finished. The sudden silence in the room caught her attention and she glance up to see both men staring.

Well, technically, Finn was watching Cillian. Cillian was staring at her with heat in his eyes. Eyes that had deepened to a dark electric green.

"What?" Did she have jelly on her face or something?

"You like marmalade, angel?"

"Yes, it's good." She lifted her coffee and concentrated on it to avoid his gaze.

"Excellent. Imogen will be please. Finish up so we can start your tour."

Chloe finished her coffee, then looked around the table and the side buffet for some water but didn't see any. She thought about asking Cillian, but decided to try her luck at getting it herself. It would give her a chance to get away from him for a few minutes. When she stood, both men's attention came quickly to her.

"Where are you going, little one?" Cillian asked.

"Which way is the kitchen?"

"What do you need?" Cillian cocked his head to the side and watched her closely.

Did he think she was going to run? Probably. And she should. That would serve him right. "I thought I'd grab a bottle of water before we left." She lifted her chin and waited.

He raised that condescending eyebrow. "The kitchen is through that door." He nodded to the door Imogen had used." Take a left and the kitchen is the first door on your right."

Finn stood up before she could make her way across the room. "I'm going to check in with Van to make sure he has what he needs." When Cillian nodded at him, he left through the door they'd used earlier.

Cillian's attention came back to her when the door swung shut behind Finn. "Go ahead angel. I have a few more emails to return, so I'll wait for you here."

Chloe wondered if Finn was circling around somehow to follow her, but changed her mind when Patrick stepped into the room from the door Finn had used. He walked past her and held the other door open for her.

She frowned up at him, then looked back at Cillian, who had a knowing grin on his face. "You said I only needed a bodyguard when I was outside the castle."

Cillian cocked his head and stared at her thoughtfully. A moment later, he nodded slightly. "As you wish angel."

She lifted her chin at the arrogant ass, sniffed disdainfully, and turned on her heel and marched past a grinning Patrick, leaving them both behind.

Chapter 11: What a total BITCH!

Chloe followed the directions Cillian had given her and stepped into a well-appointed, professionally equipped kitchen. The warm blue, gray, and brown slate tiles on the floor gave the room a homey feeling. Two professional gas cook tops held large steaming pots. Two long stone countertops and a huge center island were filled with colorful bowls of fruits and vegetables. Another countertop along the far wall was covered in flour, where two women were kneading dough. The sounds of water running, pots clanging and dishes rattling were comfortable, familiar sounds.

People were bustling around everywhere, stirring pots, chopping vegetables and washing dishes. The low chatter and laughter that buzzed through the room stopped almost immediately with the sound of the door closing behind her. Everyone turned toward her and stared.

Chloe was used to it and returned their stares with interest of her own. There were so many faces, both young and old, all going about their lives as if it were just another day, while hers was in complete turmoil. They watched her as if waiting for something to happen.

She plastered her practiced, polite, smile on her face as her gaze traveled quickly around the room until it landed on the refrigerator. At least it looked like a refrigerator. It was about five times the size of the one back home. She absently wondered how heavy the door was going to be on something that size.

She crossed the room under the avid stares of her audience and was only a few steps away from her intended destination when Imogen came through a side door and stopped short, delighted surprise showing on her face. "Hello Chloe. Did you need something?"

"Oh hello, yes, I wanted a bottle of water."

"Of course, dear. Would you like sparkling or flat?" Imogen glanced around at her staff, only just realizing their silent focus. She clapped her hands three times in quick succession and immediately everyone turned back to their work.

"Um, just plain water is fine."

"Plain water? *Really?"*

Chloe and Imogen both turned at the sound of the snide feminine voice coming from the door Imogen had just entered through.

A beautiful woman sneered at Chloe as she stomped into the room on sky high platform heels the same shade of hot pink as the very tight leather miniskirt she wore. Her white, silk, tailored, blouse was extremely tight and cut so low; Chloe wasn't sure how her large breasts didn't simply pop right out. She was tall and curvy, with long black hair that hung in soft waves around her face and shoulders. Her flashing green eyes were diamond hard and her full, red lips were pinched into an unflattering snarl.

Imogen attempted to block her path into the kitchen. "Roisin, I'll bring your coffee out to you shortly. Why don't you"

"Well, if it isn't the latest castle whore?" The beauty interrupted. Her venomous glare still focused on Chloe.

"Roisin!" Imogen's horrified gasp echoed through the suddenly silent room.

Chloe looked behind her to see who the woman was referring to, only to find no one there. She turned back to face the woman as she advanced and realized she was talking to her. "I think there must be some misunderstanding."

"Do you really think anyone cares what the fuck you think, whore?"

Chloe gasped. A hushed silence settled over the room. Stunned, she glanced around at the shocked faces staring back at her. Castle whore!? The latest castle whore!? Is that what everyone thought?

"Chloe," Imogen advanced, but Chloe lifted a hand trembling in fury to stop her.

She looked down to take a breath, trying to calm down, and her gaze landed on the beautiful dress. The stupid dress Cillian insisted she wear. The site of it on top of everything else was just too much! Her head started buzzing as her temper ignited. Whore! Really? A whore! They thought she was a whore! How fucking dare they! Chloe took a deep breath as anger turn to molten rage. Bright hot rage! Whore! After all she'd been through? Now she was being called a whore?

Chloe lifted her chin and faced the bitch. "Let's see if I have this right," she hissed, and held up a finger on her bruised hand and started counting. "I was asleep in my own bed when a stranger broke into my house!" She lifted a second finger, her frayed voice rising. "I was drugged!" She lifted a third finger and yelled, "kidnapped and brought to an entirely different country!!" She lifted a fourth finger. "I'm being held prisoner against my will!" The last finger of her injured hand went up as she screamed, because seriously, she'd had enough! "And you people are all acting like its business as usual! So no, I don't think you care what I think!" She was shrieking now. "But I'm gonna tell you, anyway! I think you are all a bunch of criminals," she waved her hand to encompass everyone in the room, "and you should all be in jail!" Then she pointed her finger at Roisin. "And you! You are a fucking BITCH!" She shrieked the word as loud as her tattered voice allowed.

Imogen went completely pale as she gaped at Chloe.

"Bitch!? You little slut, you need to learn your place!" Roisin lunged at Chloe. Her long arm raised, her hand swinging towards Chloe's face.

Chloe instinctively blocked the blow with her forearm and punched Roisin in the nose with a quick left jab. The satisfying crunch of bone was loud in the otherwise silent room. Blood exploded from Roisin's nose as she shrieked and stumbled back, holding her face. Both doors flew open simultaneously. Finn entered behind Roisin and Cillian from behind Chloe.

"Cillian!" Imogen tried to intervene, but Roisin's screams drowned out her next words.

"That horrible woman attacked me, Cillian!" Tears and blood covered her face. "She broke my nose!" Roisin screamed, then turned and fell into Finn's arms. A pitiful, sobbing, bloody mess.

Cillian cast furious eyes around the room, taking in the scene, then landing on Chloe, who now faced him, her chin held high in defiance, daring him. The monster inside him reared its ugly head and focused steely eyes on its prey. He'd warned her. Oh, he'd fucking warned her. The little hellion. Now she would pay.

"Cillian!" Finn barked from across the room. He didn't like the look on his cousin's face or the set of his shoulders. He tried to push Roisin into a chair in order to get to Chloe, but she clung to him like a leech.

Ignoring Finn, Cillian placed his hand on the back of Chloe's neck and marched her out of the room. As soon as the door closed behind them, she began to fight. Pulling against his hold, punching out in an effort to get free. In his fury, he moved his hand from the back of her neck to her throat, squeezing slightly, just enough to get her attention. He grabbed both her arms and pinned them tightly behind her back and forced her resisting body toward the stairs.

Cillian pushed Chloe through the door of his office and kicked it shut behind him. "You will obey me." He hissed. "I warned you angel. Don't say I didn't." Cillian whispered harshly into her ear.

Chloe's fear had escalated with each step they'd taken. Cillian hadn't relaxed his hold at all. She'd jumped at the sound of the door slamming behind them. Her arms ached from being held so tightly at her back, and his harsh words added to her fear. Was he going to hurt her now? Punish her?!

Cillian lifted his phone, stabbed at the buttons with his thumb, then put the screen in front of her face. A video began to play and Chloe froze, her fear turning instantly to debilitating terror. She couldn't breathe. On the screen, she could plainly see her parents. Their beautiful faces. Hear their achingly familiar voices as they spoke to each other. The video showed them having breakfast on the deck of the cruise ship. They were holding hands like they always did and watching the horizon.

"I see I have your attention now." He seethed against her neck.

She couldn't take her eyes off the screen, soaking up every second while the video continued to play.

"It would be a shame for them to meet with an unfortunate accident. Now wouldn't it, angel?"

Cillian released her and stepped around her, still holding the phone in front of her face.

She looked up at him in horror. "How did you get that?"

"I have a man on the ship keeping an eye on them."

"No!" She felt sick. Her mouth instantly salivating with the first signs that she was going to be ill.

"He boarded the ship at their first stop late Sunday afternoon. Shall I show you the video of their home and the men waiting for them to return?"

She swallowed several times, trying to keep from vomiting. This couldn't be happening. Her worst nightmare realized. Her mom and dad. Oh God!

"Their safety and continued good health are completely up to you, angel." Cillian leaned against the back of the couch and watched as Chloe stared at him in horror. Her anguished tears falling unchecked down her pale cheeks pleased the monster inside him. "Do we understand each other now?"

At her mute nod, he continued. "The rules are simple. One, you can spar with me all you want in the privacy of our suite, but you will not undermine me in front of my people. Two, you will not lash out at them. Three, you will not leave this island without me, under any circumstances. Ever."

Chloe looked over his shoulder as he spoke, unable to meet his piercing gaze. The site of him sickened her. She could almost feel shards of ice slowly coming together around her heart. Building a shield, block by block. She'd always thought of hatred as a hot emotion, full of heat and violence. But she'd been wrong. Hatred wasn't hot. It was cold. Very, very cold.

Cillian watched her delicate face close down. "Chloe?" She lifted her chin in response, but didn't look at him. "Four, you will not attempt to harm yourself in any way. If you do, your parents will pay the price."

Chloe stared at the wall over his shoulder as she came to terms with her new reality. She was a prisoner, subjected to the whims of a monster. She wasn't sure she could take much more. She could feel herself shutting down. The ice closing her inside, hiding her away. Blocking everything out. And she didn't fight it. The safety of her parents depended on it, so she let the ice close her into the security of its frozen grip. Locking her away.

Her lifeless eyes met his now, but there was no spark. No heat. There was simply nothing.

"Now, to your punishment." He'd thought his wicked tone would spark her temper, but there was nothing. He reached out and took her wrist and led her around the couch where he sat and maneuvered her between his legs. "Ly across my lap."

She didn't protest like he expected. To his frustration, she didn't fight him at all. No sassy comments, no attempt to hit him. She simply lay across his lap, face down, her arms over her head like a silent offering. And his monster howled in fury.

He lifted the hem of her silk dress, exposing her gorgeous ass. His hand smoothed over the warm globes. Chloe didn't flinch. He slipped his finger beneath the silk of her thong, the monster inside him wanting to tear it away. He breathed through the need and followed the silk down between her cheeks and slowly circled the opening of her pussy. She didn't respond. When she didn't move against his finger as he circled her opening, he slid his finger further down and began stroking her clit softly, around and around in a tight circle.

Finally, after several minutes of intimate torture, against her will, her body responded. When she tried to edge away from his stroking finger, he used his other hand to hold her down. Soon, under his practiced hand, her body took over. When her pelvis flexed against his hand, adding friction against her clit, he slipped it from between her thighs and swatted her ass with a sharp slap. He expected her to squeal and was disappointed when she didn't.

His cock was swollen, hard and painful against her stomach as her slight weight pressed against it. She was so soft and wet. His need was nearly unbearable. But this was a lesson for her. She had to learn. He slid his finger back to her clit and repeated the process again and again, circling it over and over then slapping her beautiful ass with sharp stinging strikes. Soon, she was grinding against his hand until she was soaking wet with need and her ass was a beautiful bright red. Satisfaction coursed through him as he slipped his finger deep inside her warm wet heat, pumping with measured thrusts, bringing her to the very edge of orgasm and finally, finally the monster within him settled.

Chloe was furious with herself. She'd tried to ignore the hands on her body, coaxing it to life. But there had been no reprieve from those determined fingers that strummed her body like a master musician with a treasured instrument. He knew exactly how to touch her, stroke her. Shatter her resistance. And she hated him for it. Right when he brought her to the very edge, seconds from tipping over, he stopped. Abruptly pulling his fingers from her pulsing heat. Her body cried out with need, hungry for release, only to be denied, and her hatred grew. He'd done it on purpose. A punishment. To prove a point. To prove that he was in control.

Cillian sat back against the couch, enjoying the feel of her pressed against his raging cock, leisurely stroking her beautifully reddened ass. It was gorgeous. He took his time, waiting patiently for her to get her breathing under control; for his cock to stand down. He wouldn't take her now. He wanted her simmering, needing him.

Chloe closed her eyes and focused on home. Anything to take her mind off of the heat. She imagined running with Juneau. Having breakfast with her parents around the kitchen table. Lying by the pool with Sidney on a hot, humid, Louisiana day. Familiar. Home. All those things she'd taken for granted. Slowly her breathing settled, but the heat didn't dissipate. It burned on a slow simmer. She knew that was his intention. So, she focused on the pool she and Sidney spent so many summers lounging in. The icy water splashing over her as she dove into the deep end. The rush of cold against her heated skin. Closing over her head, submerging her in its icy silence. Losing herself in the freezing depths. Cold. So cold. And the heat inside her raging body finally eased.

Cillian pulled Chloe's dress down to cover those pretty reddened cheeks. He lifted her into a sitting position on his lap and slid his arms around her. He held her close, his chin resting on top of her head. He expected to sooth tears, was looking forward to the closeness of aftercare, but his angel wasn't crying anymore. She simply sat there with her eyes closed, not making a sound. "Do you understand the rules now, angel?"

He sighed heavily when she didn't respond. "Answer my question, Chloe."

"Yes." Her voice was bitter. The frosty sound of disdain.

He nudged her to indicate she stand then he turned her to face him. Strained patience evident in his voice when she didn't meet his gaze. "Chloe?"

At the sound of her name, she moved her gaze from over his shoulder to meet his searching one.

Of all the looks she'd given him so far. The resistance she'd shown. Her fiery spirit. Her sassy mouth. Even her fear, her sadness, her pleas. Nothing had prepared him for this. This silent void, this lack of emotion. There was no anger, no accusation, no recrimination, nothing. There was nothing at all. And he didn't like it.

She just needed time, he assured himself. He knew she was young and unfamiliar with his world, but with time, she'd adjust. That was all. Time to adjust to her new life, to him and his expectations. Cillian rose to his feet. Taking her by the wrist, he led her out of his office, down the stairs and through the main hall. They passed members of his staff as they made their way through the castle, but no one spoke as he pulled the silent beauty out the front door.

Patrick waited next to the Side-By-Side 4-wheel drive ATV parked by the front steps. Cillian seated Chloe beside him in the back while Patrick got behind the wheel.

Chloe noticed the cold bottles of water in the cup holders. Imogen must've put them there. She reached for one and, twisting the top off, took a long drink, washing the bile from her throat.

Cillian reached for her hand and held it tightly as the vehicle moved forward.

Chloe kept her face averted from Cillian's and watched the scenery go by as they traveled over the terrain. She lost sight of the ocean as they followed a path through the trees. It opened up a few feet later into a wide-open field. Men with hardened eyes carrying guns were everywhere. Some were training in large groups spread out across the grass. Some were sparring, some were exercising and others were lined up across several lanes shooting riffles at targets that flipped up sporadically in front of them. Far off in the distance, over a grassy hill, was a golf course. Much farther in the distance, on the other side, was a thick line of trees.

They traveled past the field, and Cillian was telling her about the security on the island. Apparently, there were guard towers everywhere that were manned around the clock, as well as drones that filmed every inch of it. He added that all the windows in the family wing of the castle were bullet proof.

They pulled up in front of a white building that she soon learned was the clinic. Doc was stitching a cut on a man's arm when they walked in. When the guy looked at her, his menacing eyes scanned her from head to toe, sending shivers down her spine. His perusal made her extremely uncomfortable.

Doc stabbed him with the needle to get his attention. "Arnie, keep this clean and come back to see me in a few days."

When Arnie didn't move to leave, Cillian got impatient. "I believe you're done." He nearly barked.

Once Arnie left, Doc x-rayed her hand and determined it wasn't fractured, just bruised. He tried for small talk, but she wasn't interested. Instead, she kept her eyes averted and waited for Cillian to lead her out the door.

After leaving the clinic, Cillian continued to provide information as they toured. There were two hundred and eighty-three people living on the island. Many housed in the barracks. The rest in the castle or in homes he provided in a small community about five miles away. The island itself was twenty-seven miles wide and thirty-one miles deep. A mountain range spanned over four of those miles. It stopped at a cliff with a sheer drop off facing the ocean. The rock wall protected them from storms coming in from the ocean on that side.

As they continued their tour, he pointed out the golf course that his grandfather had built. The tennis court he'd recently had resurfaced. They stopped, and he picked an apple for her in the orchard his great grandmother had planted. It was located just through the tree line behind the golf course. On the other side of the castle, a short distance from an enormous vegetable garden, were several buildings and a stable with a large corral. They pulled up to the stable doors, and Patrick turned off the motor.

Cillian took her hand and led her through the huge double doors of the stable. "I think you'll like this part of the tour, angel." Chloe had been silent for so long. She hadn't asked any questions. He wasn't even sure she was listening as she took in the sites. Given the concerned glances Patrick kept giving them, her stony silence had caught his attention as well.

As he led her down the center of the stable, he paid close attention to her reaction. And as he'd hoped, the horses piqued her interest. The prized thoroughbreds and Connemara ponies in his stable were beautiful, well-trained animals of superior lineage.

"Hey Boss, come to see how the common folk are getting along?" Peter, his stable manager, greeted him at the end of the aisle.

"Peter." Cillian released Chloe's hand to shake his. "Chloe, this is my stable manager, Peter. Peter, this is Chloe."

"Very nice to meet you, Miss Chloe."

Chloe peered over Peter's shoulder. "Hello."

"I'm showing Chloe around today, but I need to talk to you about a new acquisition. Do you have a few minutes?"

"Of course!"

Chloe stepped away from Cillian and walked over to the closest stall. A beautiful brown mare with a patch of white between her eyes stuck her head out to greet her. She reached out and ran her fingers over its face.

"Chloe, Peter, and I are going to talk in his office. Why don't you stay here and get to know the horses."

When she didn't reply, he added "Patrick will be close by if you need him."

She knew he meant Patrick was watching in case she tried anything. She didn't turn from the horse she was petting, but she nodded her head.

After Cillian followed Peter into a side room. Chloe walked further down the rows of horses, petting those that stuck their heads out in greeting. When she reached the back door, she stepped out into the sunshine. At the sound of hoofbeats, she shielded her eyes from the glare, searching out where it was coming from. An old man wearing a tan cowboy hat, denim shirt, faded jeans and beat up cowboy boots was in a back corral with a beautiful solid black horse. He was holding onto the horse's bridle and was peering into its eyes, whispering softly while the horse twitched restlessly.

Chloe skirted around several steamy piles left by the horses as she made her way over to the corral. She figured Patrick wasn't very far behind her, but she didn't care. She put her hands on the top rail and rested against the fence to watch the horse. As soon as she rested her chin on her hands, the horse's head swung toward her and it whinnied loudly.

The old man turned his head and saw her then frowned at Patrick Kelly a short distance away. Puzzled, his gaze moved back to her. His bushy grey eyebrows and the wide brim of his hat nearly hid pale blue eyes that widened in surprise when he got a good look her. "Now you've done gone and interrupted our lesson." He barked in his usual cantankerous voice.

Chloe spared him a quick glance, her vacant stare barely registering his weathered face sporting a thick gray mustache that looked as if it should have its own zip code. Instead, her attention turned back to the horse. He was beautiful. His sleek muscles flexing as he paced the width of the fence on the far side of the corral.

"You're dressed a little too spiffy to be out here, lass." He groused.

Chloe ignored him and in a sad voice that lacked enthusiasm, she nickered to the horse like she'd done a thousand times to her own horse on her grandfather's ranch across Lake Pontchartrain.

The horse stopped pacing and stared at her. The old man watched avidly. She nickered again, and the horse reared up on its hind legs, then stomped its feet at her. Chloe smiled sadly at the beast.

"He don't like strangers." The old man tilted his head, watching her closely. "He hates his bit, so he's an ornery sort."

Chloe touched the collar at her neck absently. She knew the feeling. She nickered to the horse again.

To the old man's stunned disbelief, the meanest horse he'd ever met slowly, cautiously walked over to the most beautiful girl he'd ever seen. A beautiful girl with the saddest eyes. He watched them closely and inched toward them in case he needed to intervene. It wouldn't do for the horse to hurt her.

The horse walked up to Chloe and nudged her hand where it rested on the rail. She lifted it slowly and touched his face. "Hey fella." She whispered. "You're magnificent, aren't you?"

From a distance, she heard the old man grumble.

"Well, I'll be damned," before adding, "he may bite you, lass." Watching the two, woman and horse, 'kindred souls' came to mind.

The horse whinnied at her, and she smiled. The horse nudged her again. And only then did she remember she still held the apple Cillian had given her when they'd visited the orchard. "Ah, so it's not me you want, is it handsome?" Chloe didn't take her eyes from the beautiful animal but asked in a soft voice. "Can he have the apple?"

"I suppose." It wasn't a good idea, but how could he deny her? "But you best toss it over the fence to him. He might take a finger or two."

Chloe held out the apple in her palm, keeping it as flat as possible. The horse snagged the apple without mishap. She watched him eat it and come back to her for another. He nudged her arm again, and she touched his enormous head with her small hand. "That's all I have, big guy."

The horse's head came up quickly, and she knew immediately that she was no longer alone. He backed away, and she instinctively flinched and shrank in on herself. She didn't need to turn around to know Cillian was behind her.

Cillian's heart was in his throat. He wanted to yell out for her to get away from the troubled horse, but didn't want to startle it. As soon as he got close enough, he snaked an arm around Chloe and pulled her away from the fence and against his chest. "Jenkins, you old fool! What did you think you were doing?"

"Dad, Storm is too dangerous to be that close to Chloe." It shocked Peter that his father had allowed her near the horse. He'd been working with the animal exclusively because it went crazy if anyone else tried.

The old man eyed Chloe quizzically. It was obvious she was very uncomfortable with Cillian O'Donnell's arm around her.

Chloe looked between the stable manager and the old man. She could see the resemblance between father and son now that they were standing close together. "I'm sorry." She whispered. "It was my fault. He told me to stay away." She turned to look over her shoulder at Cillian, then carefully stepped out of his hold. "I'll wait for you in the ATV." Before anyone could say a word, she turned and headed back toward the stables.

Chapter 12: Life's a Beach

They'd gone straight back to the small dining room for lunch after the tour.

Finn was already seated at the table when they'd arrived. She answered his greeting with a simple hello. His hardened expression as he looked her over was intimidating. Finn was as gorgeous as his cousin, but he had a menacing air about him that scared the crap out of her.

Imogen came in as soon as they were seated. She went straight to Chloe's side and placed a pitcher of ice water next to her plate. "How was the tour, Chloe?" Her voice was filled with anxiety, and she was wringing her hands worriedly in front of her.

Chloe really wished everyone would just leave her alone. She felt it was the least they could do if they weren't going to help her get off this island. "It was fine."

"You've been gone a while; you must be hungry." The anxiety in her voice was still very evident.

Chloe wasn't sure what she had to feel anxious about. "A little." She wasn't at all, but her comment seemed to please Imogen because she smiled.

"Imogen, Chloe needs some hot tea with honey. She has a sore throat. And she'll need ice for her bruised hand." Cillian reached over and clasped her left hand on the table and squeezed it lightly.

Her eyes darted to their joined hands, then up to see his face. But he was looking at Imogen.

Imogen glared at him. So, he raised his brow in inquiry. She ignored that and turned back to Chloe. "Oh dear, I hope you aren't catching a cold."

How did she tell the woman her throat ached because she'd screamed her head off the day before? "I'm fine."

"I'll be right back." She hustled out of the room, leaving a strained silence behind her.

As soon as she was gone, Chloe attempted to pull her hand from Cillian's. He held firm for a moment until she met his gaze. Once he had her attention, he smiled and squeezed it lightly as if to convey a message, then released it. She stared at him with cold blue eyes. Why didn't he just pat her on the head for a job well done? The jerk! God, she he wanted to punch him!

Instead, she tucked her hand into her lap so he couldn't do it again. He loaded her plate with fried fish and potatoes before doing the same to his. She ignored the plate of food, but her salad bowl held a mixture of summer vegetables in a light vinaigrette that was delicious and her stomach didn't protest, so she ate most of it.

"Did Van make it back yet?"

"He did. And none too soon. Says you owe him." Finn kept his usual stoic expression in place as he shoved a piece of fish into his mouth.

"Humph. That bad huh?" Cillian didn't lift his eyes to Finn, but he chuckled and shook his head and kept right on eating.

"We'll need to talk later."

"After Chloe and I finish her tour."

The dining room was thick with tension and stilted conversation. Chloe didn't know what they were talking about, and she didn't care. She didn't have much of an appetite so after eating most of the small vegetable salad, she picked at the 'fish and chips' on her plate, mostly just pushing it around. The fish was excellent, but it wasn't anything like the spicy, thin fried fish she was used to.

When Finn finished eating, he stood to leave, but on his way out, he stopped at the door and looked back at her. The tiny hairs on the back of her neck stood up as she waited to hear what he'd say. She exhaled the breath she'd been holding when he just turned and left without a word.

"You didn't eat much Chloe. Didn't you like the fish?" Cillian waited for her to look up at him. The frown he'd been wearing through the entire meal turned to a scowl when she didn't lift her head.

"It was fine. Thank you." She forced the words out, then sipped her tea.

"You should eat more." They'd had a long morning. He would have thought she'd be starving. She hadn't eaten much the night before or at breakfast that morning.

She didn't reply. Her stomach was in so many knots she'd be physically ill if she tried to eat anymore. It wasn't her fault that he'd loaded her plate with so much food.

"All right. If you're finished, I'll show you around the castle." He tossed his napkin down on the table and held out his hand to her.

She looked around the room and, realizing they were alone, stood up, but didn't take his hand. "Lead the way."

Cillian reached out and took her hand anyway and pulled her out the door.

He led her through the monstrous castle, explaining its history. There were so many rooms, she'd never find her way around. They started in the massive hall, just inside the grand foyer. The ceiling in there was two stories high, so it was very impressive when you first entered through the front door. Two grand staircases on either side of the room led up to the second floor. There was an open entryway under the stair cases straight ahead that led into the heart of the castle.

They went that direction first. They walked through a labyrinth of rooms, including a huge formal dining room that was next to the small dining room they'd been using. He also showed her a library, a media room, a billiard's room and an indoor pool with a glass wall that separated it from a gym. Other than the pool and gym, the expensive artwork she'd noted earlier was displayed everywhere.

There was a separate hallway next to the kitchen that led to where most of the housekeeping and gardening staff lived. He guided her into a huge sunroom that spanned nearly the entire width of the castle. The entire back wall was glass, with electronic gliding doors that opened onto a covered patio with a large seating area overlooking the outdoor pool. If all the doors were opened to include the outdoor living space, the room could accommodate hundreds of people. Plus, there was a magnificent view of the golf course and the mountain range off in the distance.

He brought her back into the main hall and led her up the staircase on the left. A set of double doors across the landing of both stair cases opened into an enormous room that he explained was a ballroom. It took up nearly the entire second floor, with floor to ceiling windows overlooking the back grounds.

They walked back out to the landing, and Cillian pointed out a side door to the right that led to a guest wing. They didn't go in that direction, but he said that wing had ten bedroom suites. There was also access to a third-floor turret, which had seating where guests could take in the views and watch the sunset.

They took the entrance next to the left staircase that opened into another smaller foyer and extended down a long hallway, but had a door to the left. He said the hallway led to the second and third guest wings, which were replicas of the first.

"This is the entrance to the family wing." He lifted his hand and pressed his thumb to a screen beside the doorknob. A green light on the

91

screen flashed. He smiled at her, then took her through the door and up a flight of stairs to the third floor.

Cillian led her past his office door, farther down the wide hallway, and showed her a private media room, library, game room, a second gym and a parlor that included a feminine antique desk in the corner. There were also ten suites, or apartments really, on this floor for the family. She wasn't sure what family occupied the rooms, but didn't ask about that either.

He said no one was allowed in the family wing of the castle except a select few. He added that only long-term trusted members of the cleaning staff were allowed in to care for the family. After touring the wing, he led her back to the stairway and up to the fourth floor. The door opened up next to the elevator, across from the double doors of his suite. Patrick was standing guard by the door.

Cillian brought her into their suite. "Come on, I have one more thing to show you." As he led her through the den, he pointed toward a door next to the kitchen. "There's three more bedrooms and a weight room in there." He pointed toward a door on the other side of the fireplace from theirs. "That's the nursery. The kitchen is stocked, but we'll eat breakfast and lunch downstairs."

She followed him into the large walk-in closet in his room. Masculine clothes hung from rods at the top and bottom on both sides. There was a set of drawers built into the middle of one side, with a small island in the center holding smaller drawers. The back wall had a large open doorway in the center with build-in shelves on each side that held rows and rows of shoes.

Cillian took her hand and pulled her through the opening, then around in front of him. Chloe found herself in a room nearly the size of her bedroom at home. She looked in all directions. It was a closet. A very massive, very feminine closet. She looked over her shoulder at Cillian questioningly.

"Go ahead. Look around."

The soft, plush carpet on the floor was as white as snow. The walls were a soft muted rose pink. She slowly walked around a huge center island. It was white and held multiple drawers on both ends with built-in shelves filled with colorful sweaters folded and stacked neatly along each side.

When she looked down at the top of the island, she gasped and brought her hand to her mouth automatically. The entire top was glass displaying blush pink velvet jewelry drawers. Little crystal drawer pulls sparkled under the edges of the glass top all the way around the island.

Each velvet drawer was filled with delicate pieces of gold and silver jewelry, some with diamonds or jeweled stones of blood red rubies, sparkling sapphires, green emeralds, pearls and so many others. Too many to take in so quickly.

She reached up and fingered the diamond studs in her ears. A gift from her parents on her sixteenth birthday. She never took them out. She absently looked away from the case and took in the rest of the room. Two walls held rods filled with women's clothing, top and bottom. There were short dresses, long dresses, formal dresses, slacks, jeans, shirts, sweaters, jackets and coats. Half of the third wall held shelves and shelves of shoes and boots of every style and color she could imagine. The last wall had a white antique make-up table with a mirror and a matching chair with a pale pink, velvet, cushion. The entire wall was a mirror from floor to ceiling. Built in little boxes on one side went all the way to the ceiling filled with purses of handbags.

Chloe turned slowly back to Cillian to find him watching her. "What is all this?"

"This is your closet."

She stared at him, trying to imagine how he expected her to react.

When Chloe said nothing, he continued, "I told you I had my staff purchase everything you would need. Do you like it?" He reached out and took her hand.

"It's a lot to take in." She hadn't asked for this, so what did he expect her to say?

"If there is anything else you need or want, just let me know."

She wondered how he could be so charming one minute and so horrible the next. She felt like she was walking on eggshells. "Do I get to wear what I want?" She bit her lip as she waited for his response. A nervous habit she'd only recently acquired.

He stared at that plump lip tucked between her teeth. "Most of the time." He added pressure on her hand, pulling her closer.

"What do you mean?"

"When we're here in our suite, you won't wear anything at all."

"What?" Her heart pounded in her throat. She didn't want to even think about walking around naked in front of him all the time. She pulled on her hand and tried to step back, but he wouldn't let her go.

"I prefer to see your beautiful body bare for my pleasure." He lifted his other hand and gently placed it at her throat, using his thumb to stroke her neck softly. His eyes followed the path of his thumb.

She frowned and ignored his last statement, but she could feel the heat of a blush staining her cheeks. She was determined to get through this conversation. "Can I wear what I want otherwise?"

"Mostly. However, sometimes I'll want you to wear something that I prefer. Like the dress you're wearing now."

"Why?" She asked indignantly.

"I knew the color would look beautiful on you and wanted to see you in it. I was right." He used his thumb to hold her chin up and leaned down and kissed her. Before she could jerk away, he lifted his mouth from hers and regarded her stoically. "I prefer you wear dresses, but I know that's not always appropriate for the occasion."

She studied him a moment, then turned to look around the room again without commenting. She didn't know what to say, so she stepped back and when she pulled at her hand again, Cillian let it go.

"Take your time looking through your new things. I have some work to finish, so I'll be in my office." He turned and headed out the door.

"Cillian?"

"Yes?" He turned, hand on the doorframe, and glanced back over his shoulder at her.

"Can I go outside?" She lifted her chin stubbornly. Her eyes didn't reflect her inner turmoil. They reflected nothing.

"Outside where?" He watched her skeptically.

"The beach. Maybe a walk. Anywhere?"

He held her gaze for a long moment, searching for some hint of what she was thinking. When she showed him nothing, he sighed, "yes. But only if you take Patrick or Rourke with you. Whichever one is on duty."

"Ok."

"Do not attempt to leave without one of them with you, Chloe."

"Your rules were very clear, Cillian."

He stared at her broodingly for a long moment. "After dinner tonight, I'll program your prints into the keypads necessary to access this wing."

"Alright."

"Enjoy yourself, Chloe." He watched, waiting for her reply."

She simply stared at him. Enjoy herself? Really? What an asshole.

When she didn't so much as bat an eyelash, he gave a heavy sigh of frustration, then turned and left.

Chloe flipped through the hangers, taking a quick inventory of the clothes. Most of them weren't what she would usually wear around the house. She searched the drawers in the center island, and that's where she found what she was looking for. One side was completely filled with bras, sports bras and panties, but she hit the jackpot on the other side with shorts, leggings and more casual tops. She didn't see a single t-shirt, but the tops would do. She also found running shoes and flip-flops. The flip-flops were another surprise. Whoever filled her closet did a good job.

She changed into shorts and a tank and slipped on flip-flops, then stopped in the kitchen to grab a bottle of water. When she opened the outer door, Patrick was waiting.

"Hi Chloe, ready for your walk?"

His smile was friendly and open, but the site of the guns strapped to his chest and waist terrified her. Would he use them on her?

"Yes." She tried to sound polite, but it came out stilted.

If he noticed, he didn't say. They took the elevator down to the first floor and when they walked outside; she surveyed her surroundings then headed for the beach. As soon as she reached the sand, she stopped.

She shielded her eyes and looked up at Patrick. "Can you hang out here and wait, or do you have to stay by my side?"

"You're not going to swim for it, are you?" He teased.

She scowled at the asshole. "I don't believe I'm ready to be chum for the sharks, so no." She didn't think he was funny. And the joke was definitely in poor taste.

"Ok, then I'll wait here. Just stay in sight." He said cautiously.

Chloe stomped away from him and kicked off her flip-flops and stepped onto the sand. She expected it to be hot, but it wasn't. Back home this time of year the sand on the beaches could burn the bottoms of your feet. She walked to the water's edge and stared out at the horizon longingly as the waves crashed at her feet.

She took her time exploring the beach. Getting a feel for the area and enjoying being by herself for the first time since her abduction. She found a long stick that had washed up on the shore and was making designs in the sand when a thought came to her. She glanced off in the distance to see Patrick leaning against a rock, his gaze moving from the beach, to the water then to the lawn behind them as if constantly looking for a threat. She glanced up toward the guard towers in the distance and wondered if the guards were paying attention. She decided it was worth the risk, so she turned back to the wet sand and using the stick wrote CHLOE GUIDRY in large block letters about three feet high. Underneath it, she wrote the word HELP! When she finished, she added a Fluer de lis. She drew an exact replica of the one used by the New Orleans Saints football team. When the tide came up in the evening, the water would erase it, but if she could write it every morning, hopefully some satellite somewhere would pick up the image. She didn't know if it would help someone find her, but it was all she had at the moment.

She continued down the beach, using the stick to draw designs sporadically, so she didn't draw Patrick's attention to her message. On her way back, she stopped at a row of large boulders jutting out into the water. The tallest was about eight feet high, with smaller ones all around it. She climbed the rocks until she made her way to the highest one. The top was about four feet wide, with a flat surface. She sat on the stone warmed by the sun and watched the waves crash on the rocks below her.

She wondered what Sidney was doing. Her disappearance no doubt ruined her vacation. She would've freaked out and gone home when Chloe didn't show up. Her parents had probably already been notified and were more than likely home by now. Silent tears fell as she wondered how her mom was handling it. She'd be distraught. Her dad would be worried, but mostly he would be angry, very angry. He'd be strong for her mom, though. She'd need that.

Chloe laid down on the warm stone facing the water with her head resting on her folded hands and watched the waves roll in. If she wasn't rescued, she'd be stuck here forever. Or until Cillian tired of her. What would he do then? He couldn't let her go. Would he kill her? "Way to go Chloe, just scare the crap out of yourself, why doncha?"

She thought about all she'd miss out on. Spending the summer with Sidney before she went back to Manhattan for her final year. This was supposed to be the best summer yet. Then there was school. All that work and she wouldn't get to finish. She'd never get to find that first job and use her degree. Never find her own place and learn to live on her own. She'd gone from living with her parents to living in a dorm, then to the house with her other roommates in Manhattan to this. It wasn't fair. She'd miss out on everything.

Chloe let the tears fall. Here, alone with her thoughts and the waves crashing, there was no one to see. No one to care.

She spent hours on that rock. And in that time, she came to think of it as hers. Her place of solace away from the beautiful monster who'd stolen her life.

Chapter 13: Silken Ties that Bind

Chloe startled awake when Patrick pulled on her foot. She was slightly disoriented and squinted from the sun as she looked up at him.

"Wake up Chloe, lass. The boss is looking for you."

Chloe jolted up and quickly took in her surroundings. She was disgusted to see that she was still on the rock, still on the island. The last she remembered; she was lying here feeling sorry for herself. Her father would be so disappointed.

"I didn't mean to dose off. How long have you been waiting?" She was afraid he'd be pissed, so she avoided eye contact.

"You've been on this rock for about four hours, Chloe. But don't worry. I don't mind being outside. But you're a little sunburned. You need a hat, lass."

"Still, it was rude of me to stay so long and to fall asleep while you had to wait."

"It's really not a problem, Chloe. You shouldn't concern yourself with me. Just do what you like, I'll adjust."

She scowled at him. "What I'd like is to go home."

He smiled sheepishly. "Well, I can't adjust to that. The boss called. He wants to know why you're still out here."

"Well, let's not keep the 'boss' waiting." She didn't even try to hide the sarcasm in her voice.

"That's never a good idea." He chuckled at her grumbled reply. "Come on, lass."

On the walk back to the castle, she thought about her last conversation with Cillian in the closet. He'd said she could go anywhere as long as she took one of her guards with her. She decided to test that theory. "Who's on duty early tomorrow morning?"

He looked down at her questioningly. "I come back on in the morning, why?"

"I usually run about 5 miles every morning around 5:30. I'd like to get back to my routine tomorrow. Will that be a problem?"

"No. I don't always relieve Rourke by then, but I'll make a point to."

"I don't mean to change your schedule."

"Chloe, your routine is now our routine." He looked down at her intently. "This is kind of new to all of us. But it wouldn't be fair to ask Rourke to stand outside your door all night then take off on a 5 mile run at the end of his shift. It's not a problem. Besides, I could use the run."

"If you're sure?"

"I am. I'll be ready whenever you are. No worries, Chloe." He bumped her shoulder as if they were old friends and smiled at her.

For some reason, she found the move endearing and for the first time in what seemed like forever. She smiled.

Cillian was leaning against the bar, sipping whiskey when she walked into their suite. His patience had worn thin. He'd been waiting for her to come back from the beach, but she'd been down there for hours. He needed to see her. There had been no life in her beautiful eyes when he'd left her earlier, and it was eating at his conscience. Being preoccupied with a woman was a new experience for him. And he didn't fucking like it.

His steely green eyes captured hers with a flash of impatience. "Where have you been angel?" His musical voice growled.

Chloe's chin lifted at his show of impatience. "You have a GPS on me, Cillian, so you already know the answer to that question." She replied sarcastically. She'd decided while sitting on that rock, lamenting her future, that if she had to stay here, she was going to be herself. He'd said he wouldn't harm her so she would not be cowed by him. If he kept his word she'd follow his rules, but only to keep her parents safe.

Her father would expect her to hold her own against him. He'd also want her to find some kind of control in this chaos. She could lose herself in her grief on her rock, because there was no one to see it. But now that she'd let her emotions free for a little while without an audience, she felt much better.

He raised an eyebrow arrogantly and grinned at her. "I do. You were at the beach for a long time." He felt his pulse quicken. His cock thickening. This is what he craved. This sass. This spark.

She unconsciously put her hand on her hip. She hated that arrogant smirk almost as much as she hated him. "So?" She absently wondered how much he'd had to drink. His face was flushed.

"What were you doing out there for so long?" His lips twitched. His little hellion was finding her feet again. Good. He mentally rubbed his hands together in anticipation.

"Mourning the loss of my future. You know, the one you stole from me?" When his eyes sparked, she had a passing thought that she probably shouldn't be goading him.

He straightened from the bar and stepped toward her. "I didn't steal your future angel. I just gave you a different one." This little slip of a woman stood up to him like no woman ever dared. Defying him. It fired his blood.

Chloe didn't agree, but she didn't tell him so. And when he stepped toward her again, she took a step back, but as she did, he advanced again. She turned her head subtly to peek over her shoulder, judging the distance to the door.

"Try it." He whispered, taunting her. "You won't make it." He needed her to run. Ached for the challenge.

His whispered dare caused her pulse to race. He was stalking her across the room.

She knew better than to turn her back on a threat. But he was advancing too fast, so she turned and raced toward the door.

Cillian lunged. He planted his foot on the coffee table between them and launched himself at her. He senses alive. Exhilaration pulsing through him at the challenge she presented.

Chloe was nearly to the door when both his arms encircled her and lifted her off her feet. "Let go asshole!" She kicked back at his shins and used her fist, beating on his arms. Clawing with her nails. Trying to reach behind her to strike him in his head.

She fought like a wildcat, and he loved every second of it. He chuckled when she landed a blow to his temple. "Oh, hellion, you'll pay for that." He bit her shoulder, hard in retaliation. She'd wear his teeth marks for days. That thought cause his already stiff cock to throb.

He threw her on the bed he'd prepared while waiting for her to come back. Anticipating her return. He was ready. When she landed, he immediately flipped her over and straddled her, tucking her arms under his knees, pinning her in place. She tried to buck him off a few times, and he couldn't help but laugh at her tenacity. He outweighed her by more than a hundred pounds, and he used his weight ruthlessly.

When she finally settled, he lifted slightly to relieve some of the pressure his weight caused so she could breathe easier. She was red faced and panting from exertion.

"Get off of me!"

"Oh baby, I'm going to be on you, around you and inside of you." He leaned down to kiss her, and she tried to bite him. "Keep it up and I'll gag you. Is that what you want?"

"No! I want you to get off of me."

Cillian leaned over and picked up the soft silk pink ties he'd placed on the bed and held them up for her to see. "We'll use silk tonight. We would have used it last night had I known your hand was injured."

"Don't tie me up Cillian!"

"Oh, my beautiful girl, I'm going to do more than tie you up." He used the silk to bind her left wrist, then lifted his knee to release it and brought it over to her right, binding them together.

"Stop!" She pulled unsuccessfully against his hold.

He pushed her bound hands above her head and connected the tie to a hook on the back side of the headboard.

"What now, hellion?" He asked in a playful voice he knew would piss her off further.

She yanked several times, but the soft ties held. "Un. Tie. ME!" She enunciated each word through gritted teeth. The idea of him binding her in silk caused her to shiver and her core to pulse. The reaction startled her, making her uneasy.

"Let's see how flexible you are." He reached back and forced her left foot up and flat on the bed so her calf was flush with the back of her thigh. She'd lost her flip-flops somewhere between the door and the bed. Using another tie, he bound her ankle to her thigh in that position. She pushed frantically against the tie, but couldn't straighten her leg. He repeated the process with her right leg.

"Untie me right now!" She was stuck. Completely stuck! And the wicked gleam in his eyes only confirmed it.

He lifted the knife from the open drawer of his nightstand and showed it to her. And her eyes got as big as saucers.

"What are you doing?" At the sight of the dagger, her mouth went dry. "Oh, God! Please don't hurt me!"

Cillian leaned down and kissed her. He thrust his tongue deep relishing the taste of her, not caring that she didn't kiss him back. At least she didn't bite him. When he leaned away from her, he brought the knife up for her to see. "I would never hurt you. Now be very still little one."

Her breath was coming out in sharp gasps, terrified. Tears burned her eyes as she tried to prepare herself to feel the blade slice into her skin.

Cillian tucked the tip of the blade into the neck of her shirt and sliced it open down the middle, exposing the delicate sheer, blue, bra he'd selected for her that morning.

She breathed a sigh of relief, but it was short lived because he leaned down and sucked her nipple deep into his mouth. Her back arched into the moist heat as her senses came alive.

"Mm angel, you're delicious." The sheer silk material of the bra abraded the tip of her nipple as he worked it ruthlessly with his tongue.

When he had her squirming and pushing against his mouth, seeking more, he did the same to the other one. Taking his time with each, going back and forth between both nipples. Slowly and relentlessly working her into an agitated state, as sensations wreaked havoc on the bundle of nerves at each tight little tip.

"Cillian, please!" The release of adrenalin that washed over her when she thought he was going to cut her had her breathless. Her head was spinning. She was drowning as heat pulsed through her veins. Her skin was alive with tiny goosebumps. The fiery ache in her nipples sent fissures of pleasure to her core. His hot tongue, soft warm lips, sharp teeth, relentlessly attacking, over and over. Large, strong hands cupping, kneading. It went on and on forever. Building. A burning, sizzling heat settling deep into her bloodstream, coursing through her veins.

He brought her to the very edge, then lifted from her. She moaned at the loss of the heat.

She was a glorious site, writhing beneath him. "Be still." His command was met with another moan. He smiled to himself and placed his knife at the band of her shorts. With two careful, precise slices, he cut them away from her body. He tossed the knife back into the drawer and leaned into her again.

He spread her bound legs wide to accommodate his shoulders, taking the time to inhale the intoxicating scent of her need. The shear silk covering her pussy was drenched. He used the silk ruthlessly with his tongue, rubbing it against her clit, sucking and licking again and again until her thighs were shaking, her hips flexing, back bowed. She was close, so close.

He palmed her ass, lifting her tight against his mouth and devoured her. He pulled her cheeks apart, putting pressure on the tiny rosette between them. Using his finger, he moistened it with her slick juices, then rubbed repeatedly on the little opening softly at first, then gradually adding pressure, circling and rubbing, pressing relentlessly until it finally opened for him. He sucked her clit deep into his mouth, lashed at it with the tip of his tongue over and over at the same time he pushed his finger to the first knuckle into her back entrance.

At the sudden dark, twisted pleasure enveloping her, she screamed and came in a glorious blast of sensation, bucking wildly against his mouth. Pulling frantically at the silk binds at her wrists.

Pumping his finger in and out and sucking ruthlessly at her clit, Cillian drove her through a seemingly endless orgasm. When her peak receded, he slowly brought her down the other side. Nuzzling her pussy softly, burying his face there. His finger in her ass stopped pumping, but remained in place, stretching her.

He waited for her to relax and catch her breath, then his fiery green eyes, alive with lust and need, captured her gaze. Chloe groaned. The pressure in her ass increased as he suddenly pushed his finger all the way into her. "Jesus!"

He leaned down and licked her clit through the damp silk again, over and over, his eyes glued to hers.

"It's too much!" She panted and tried to close her legs, but his shoulders held them open. Her oversensitive clit couldn't take anymore. "Please, Cillian."

"Again, angel." He commanded against the wet silk.

Within seconds, her breathing escalated. She couldn't stop it. The dark, sensual pressure in her rear. His wicked tongue, overwhelming. Twisting her into a dark maelstrom of desperate aching need.

He reveled in her pleas and, using his finger in her ass and his tongue at her clit, ruthlessly brought her to the edge again. But just before she tumbled over, he stopped.

"No! Please!" She was right there. The edge so close. She was on fire. He couldn't stop!

He chuckled wickedly and pulled away from her.

"Cillian!" The ache was so sharp, almost painful. Oh, God, she needed more, so much more. And he was taunting her, the devil. And he was; the fucking Devil!

He used the knife again and cut her shirt, bra and panties away, then reached up and lifted the silk strap from the hook at the headboard and lifted her. He turned her trembling body to face the side of the bed where he'd positioned a full-length antique mirror earlier. He placed her on her knees in front of him on pillows lined up before it to lift her to the right height he needed. He looped her bound wrist up and over his head.

He met her blue eyes, glazed with need, in the mirror. "Look at us, angel. Look at how we fit." He positioned the head of his aching cock between her splayed thighs at her slick entrance and slowly pushed inside her from behind. Planting himself to the hilt in her tight heat. Stretching her. "Watch us. Watch your pretty little pussy take me."

"Oh, my God!" Her heated channel clamped down on his invading cock. Her need overriding common sense. His head beside hers, his beautiful face next to hers, his mouth whispering wicked things into her ear. His eyes locked onto hers in the mirror. The image of them together was staggering.

One of his large hands was at her breast, cupping it, a long finger stroking the very tip of her tight nipple. His other doing the same at her clit. The contrast of her peaches and cream skin against his weathered from the sun was startling. He thrust deep inside her, over and over. The image of his cock sliding in and out of her, slick from her release, was mesmerizing.

"You were made for me, baby. Look how perfectly we fit. How beautiful." His harsh whispers increased with the fast rhythm he set, bringing her back to the edge almost instantly.

In this position, he hit that overly sensitive spot inside her over and over with each powerful thrust. Her arms tightened around his neck, her back bowed of its own accord. She couldn't stop the overpowering sensations rolling through her. They took her deep into a dark world where only the two of them existed.

She was so beautiful. A golden goddess in his arms. He wanted her to soar higher, to need him as much as he needed her. She had to. He pinched her nipple and her clit, thrusting deep. Holding the tender tips in the tight grips of his fingers, adding a darker element, a fierce bite to the pleasure.

She moaned deep in her throat. When her pussy flexed on his cock, he released her nipple and her clit and moved his hands to her hips for leverage, and powered into her with violent thrusts. Over and over, going deeper and deeper. Her plump breasts bounced with each thrust. The image of them together, of him taking her, was so hot it scorched his senses and sparked a violent need to make her see. To prove to her she was his.

"This is us, Chloe. Do you see?" He panted into her ear.

She couldn't stop the explosion. She screamed as she came. Her body violently pulsing around his. Her hips pumping, meeting his brutal thrust, desperately seeking a deeper penetration. Deeper, harder, faster. Nothing mattered but this, him.

"Yes, baby that's it." He crooned wickedly. "Fuck me, Chloe! Fuck me!" Cillian forced her hips down onto him in an unbreakable hold. Pushing himself as far into her tight heat as his pulsing cock could go. When he exploded into her, he bellowed, "Chloe!" Her name sharp and loud in her ear.

Chloe woke up when Cillian untied her wrists. She was lying in the middle of the bed with her chenille blanket tucked around her. She could hear bath water running in the other room. Once he had her untied, he lifted her, cradling her to his chest, and carried her into the bathroom. He stepped into the tub filled with warm bubbles and settled her in front of him, placing her hand into the bucket of ice he'd prepared.

She was limp in his arms. Her weight settling softly against his. He took his time lathering her entire body with the thick body wash, noting the slight sunburn on the side of her neck and her arm. When he was finished, he pushed her up and massaged her neck, shoulders and the tight muscles of her lean back. "You're quiet." He noted.

"Hmm". She was staring down at the water, lost in thought.

"And you're sunburned." He ran his hand over the pink of the burn.

"It's fine. I burn easily, but it'll turn to a tan by tomorrow."

"Does it hurt?"

"No". She answered him absently.

"How's your hand?" He lifted it up and inspected it.

"It doesn't hurt that much anymore." She pulled it from his grasp.

"Keep it in the ice for now."

"It's fine, Cillian." She leaned back against him. Her thoughts all over the place. She didn't understand how, but he was changing her. Molding her into someone she didn't recognize. It was frightening. Nothing in her life had prepared her for this, for him.

He filled his palms with her breasts, rubbing the bubbles into her tender skin. That was the fourth 'fine' he'd gotten from her today.

"Cillian?"

"Yes." He kissed the spot where her neck and shoulder met. Nibbled. Suckled. Marked her.

She shivered at the feel of his lips on her skin in that tender spot. "Is it always like that?"

"What do you mean?" He nibbled on her earlobe. Her delicate skin against his lips was so soft and sweet it was addictive.

"That intense. Is sex always that intense?" She tried not to blush, but it was hopeless.

"It's never been like that with anyone else." He used the sponge to rinse the suds from her breasts.

She didn't know if she believed him or not. He'd said he wouldn't lie to her, but there was no way for her to know for sure. What she did know was that this affect he had on her was dangerous. She needed to shield herself. To fight it.

"Come on, little one. Let's go eat something before you fall asleep."

Cillian dried her off before doing the same for himself. He dropped the towel on the floor and lifted her into his arms.

He placed her on the bed and disappeared into the closet. He came back out a minute later wearing nothing but a pair of black athletic shorts and carrying her blue robe. She slipped into it, but when she moved to tie it, he placed his hand on hers to stop her.

"Leave it open."

"Cillian."

"I'm making a concession for you by letting you wear it at all. I want to see you. Leave it open or give it back to me." He held out his hand and waited.

She blew out an aggravated breath and left the robe open, but marched past him into the other room. She'd rather be partially covered than completely nude. And anyway, with her luck, if he didn't get his way, he'd take out that big knife again and cut the beautiful robe to pieces.

He smiled and followed at a much slower pace. He'd won that round rather easily, but a little of her sass was back.

The table was set with covered plates that smelled delicious. She removed the cover from her plate, and her stomach growled. She hadn't eaten much lately, and it was catching up to her.

She took a bite of the delicate salmon and nearly groaned. "This is delicious."

Cillian reached out and positioned her robe open to frame her breasts, then filled her wineglass with a light Riesling. "Imogen is an excellent cook. Try the wine."

Chloe scowled at him, but she sipped the wine. "It's light." She tasted it again. "I like it."

He smiled when she went back to eating the fish with gusto.

The wine was excellent, but the salmon was amazing. She ate the entire thing, as well as the spinach with lemon and garlic butter sauce.

"Does Imogen cook all the food herself? I saw a lot of people in the kitchen this morning."

"For security purposes, Imogen cooks everything I eat and now, everything you eat. I employ a lot of people on my kitchen staff because they cook for my men."

"Security purposes?"

"Yes." He sipped his wine and waited for her to look up at him. "What better way to strike fear into the hearts of your enemies than to take out your greatest adversary in his own home under the watchful eye of his security."

"Poison. You think someone would try to poison you?"

"One can never be too careful. When we're off the island, Finn will taste your food before you eat it."

"What? But if it's poisoned, he could die!"

"It's his job to protect us from any threat."

"You have enemies?"

"Yes."

"What do you do? Wait," she held up her hand to stop him, "never mind, I don't want to know." She figured if she knew too much, once he tired of her, he'd have to kill her.

"No, you don't. But rest assured, I'm more powerful and ruthless than they are. And," he paused for an intense moment, "you will follow the security protocols I set for you no matter what."

She swallowed audibly. "No one even knows I'm here. And besides, why would they care about me. I'm nobody."

"You belong to me." His steely gaze swept down from her face, over her collar, to her bare breasts, then back up with his eyes reflecting stark possessiveness. "That's enough."

When she didn't respond he added, "my parents and grandparents were murdered several years ago."

"I'm sorry. That must've been awful."

"It was."

"What happened to them?"

"My father's plane was tampered with. It exploded."

"Oh, my God. That's terrible. Did they ever find out who did it?"

"No, but I know. I've spent years uncovering his identity."

"Are you going to turn him in to the authorities? Do you have proof?"

"I have proof, but no, I won't be turning him in."

"Why not?"

"Because I'll get my revenge my way."

"Your way?"

"Yes, my way." He stared at her for a moment as if gaging her response before continuing. She needed to know exactly who he was. "I'm destroying everything he holds dear. Everything he loves. Once that's complete, then I'll kill him. Slowly."

Chloe's heart skipped a beat at the reminder of who he was. "Kill him?"

Glittering eyes stared into hers for a moment. "Yes Chloe, I'm going to kill him."

Chloe took a measured breath to calm her racing pulse. Cillian O'Donnell scared her to death.

Chapter 14: Dude, It's just a hat!

Chloe awoke in the dark to fire flooding her veins and Cillian's mouth between her legs. Need, sharp and mean, burned low in her core. Her back arched; her pelvis thrusted toward his mouth. And she reached for his head.

Cillian caught both of her hands and, clutching them tightly, surged up over her, bringing them above her head. In a seamlessly fluid motion, he thrust deep inside her pulsing heat. When her slick, velvety channel surrounded him, he groaned. "You feel so good, baby. So tight." Using both their hands, he gripped fists full of her hair and pulled. The motion lifting her face to his in the dark. He captured her lips before she could catch her breath. His kiss was rough and forceful, taking her mouth like he took her body.

She tasted herself on his lips, salty and subtly sweet. His kiss consumed her, leaving her helpless to his sensual assault. His thrusts were measured at first, slow and deep. She followed his lead as her hips moved with his, both finding a rhythm together. His leisurely pace, meant to entice, increased as she rocked beneath him. Her pulse quickened; her heart raced. Her hips grinding, working to take him deeper, chasing the burn.

"There's my girl." He groaned in her ear. "Yes angel, just like that. Fuck me baby." His whispered words calling to something dark and sensuous inside her. Her fiery channel clamped down, her legs encircled his waist, clutching him, holding him close. Need building so high, she was flying. Soaring. It was too much, too fast. Chloe opened her mouth and, without thought or reason, bit down hard on his shoulder as she came.

The erotic pain of her bite, her teeth on him, her pussy squeezing him, milking him. Perfection. He groaned as his release poured into her, his pelvis grinding against her clit, triggering another explosion in her.

Once her body's grip on his relaxed, he rocked his hips softly, sliding inside her slowly, raining kissed on her face and neck as he brought her back down. Eventually easing her back into sleep.

What felt like hours later, Chloe barely stirred as she felt Cillian pull slowly from her. His warmth lifting away, only to be replaced with soft chenille as he tucked her blanket securely around her.

"Sleep baby. I'll be back in a few hours to take you to breakfast." He whispered against her cheek in the early dawn, then kissed her lips softly and eased from the bed. He'd be late for his workout with Finn if he didn't leave now.

Chloe woke again to the sound of the outer door closing. She glanced sleepily toward the clock, wanting nothing more than to snuggle down into the soft chenille and doze back off. The digital numbers read 5:15. She sighed wearily. She didn't want to face the mirror this morning. She was too disgusted with herself. But if she was going to find her way, she had to get up now. She couldn't lay here and feel sorry for herself. So, rolling out of bed, she made her way to the bathroom by the light of the early dawn coming through the windows.

Chloe stopped short when she was met by Rourke instead of Patrick at the door. Her face flamed red at the memory of her first encounter with him, but she persevered. "Good morning. Where's Patrick? We're supposed to go running this morning."

He smiled and tilted his head, regarding her thoughtfully. "Good morning, Chloe. It's nice to finally meet you. How did you know I wasn't Patrick?"

"Don't be silly." She looked at him quizzically when he silently waited for her answer. "Patrick's hair is more brown than black. Yours is more black than brown. And his eyes are a lighter blue than yours." She paused, but when he still didn't respond, she asked, "should I go on?"

"You know, no one really notices those things. How is it you do?"

She shrugged. "I'm an artist. I see details more than most, I guess." Especially now that she wasn't a panicked mess. "Is Patrick coming?"

"Yes. He radioed; he forgot something. But he should be here any minute."

The elevator door opened as if on cue and Patrick stepped out wearing running clothes with his gun holsters strapped across his chest. He was carrying a ball cap in his hand that had a small tube of sunscreen tucked into it. He held it out to her.

"Here, you'll need this."

She frowned at him. "What for?"

"You got sunburned yesterday. Imogen threatened to withhold my dinner if it happened again. I didn't think I'd ever hear the end of it."

Rourke chuckled. "I heard she was scolding you in the kitchen last night. Is that why?"

Patrick scowled at his twin. "Yes! She was relentless." His gaze moved to Chloe's, "so do me a favor, put on the sunscreen and wear the cap to shield your face. I'd like to eat today."

Chloe's gaze moved between the two guards, confusion marring her brow. Why would Imogen care if she got a little sunburned?

Rourke grinned, "have pity on him Chloe. He's a growing boy."

Chloe looked at both of their expectant faces, then down at the hat Patrick still held out. "Oh, good grief." She took the hat and put it on, pulling her ponytail through the back opening. She quickly applied the sunscreen to her face, neck, arms and shoulders around the edges of her tank top. When she was finished, she tossed the tube to Rourke with a quick flip of her wrist. "Here, happy now?"

"Yes!" They both said in unison, flashing pleased smiles.

She rolled her eyes, then looked up at Patrick. "Can we go now?"

Patrick smiled and stepped back, sweeping his arm out dramatically toward the elevator. "After you."

Chloe signed and shook her head at the two goofballs. For as intimidating as they appeared, their antics were pretty silly.

Patrick led Chloe on a route he'd mapped out for her that would bring her back to the castle at the five-mile mark, but allow her to see some of the island. They exited the castle onto the back patio, where they stretched and warmed up. Then they set a fast, steady pace as they ran across the golf course and through the apple orchard. The shade of the trees kept them cool as they followed a trail to several caves buried deep in the woods. Chloe made a mental note to ask about them later.

They followed the trail through the woods, where it circled around the back perimeter of the training area. They came out behind the clinic and ran past the field where men were training.

Chloe felt exhilarated as her muscles stretched and heated with exertion. She increased her pace as her breathing leveled out and her endorphins kicked in. The familiar burn, a comfortable reminder of who she was. The wind in her face. Her arms and legs pumping out a rhythm. It was fluid and peaceful. And for the first time in days, her mind settled.

She felt light on her feet and eager to push herself as they raced toward the stables. When they passed the corral, she wished she'd picked an apple. Jenkins was already out working with Storm. He stopped and watched her and Patrick as they ran by. She smiled to herself when she heard Storm whinny loudly at her. *Next time handsome*, she thought and made a mental note to make sure she had an apple tomorrow.

"What the fuck!" His moment of inattention cost him. Seconds later, Cillian was on his ass from the blow of Finn's fist connecting with his jaw. He rubbed at it absently, but his eyes never left the sight of his woman running past. Long legs bared in little black running shorts. The white tank top hugging her plump breasts as they swayed with her body's movements. Skin gleaming with sweat. Long white gold ponytail trailing out of a green cap that wasn't his. His beautiful girl was graceful as she ran. And fast. Really fast. But the sight of that cap on her head infuriated him. Even more so, the man who paced beside her.

He scowled up at Finn. "Do you want to tell me why my woman is running across the island with another man?" He'd left her tucked in, warm and sated, asleep in his bed. He was going to fucking murder someone. No, not just someone. Patrick fuckin Kelly.

Finn watched as Chloe and Patrick disappeared behind the castle. He turned back to Cillian and commented thoughtfully, "she's fast." He looked around at the rest of his men. They'd all stopped training and were staring after the woman. He pursed his lips and let out a sharp, loud whistle, bringing their attention to him. "Back to work!" His order was met with an instant response.

Cillian looked around at his men and scowled. Their attention to Chloe only pissed him off more. He surged to his feet and got in his cousin's face. "You didn't answer my question."

Finn eyed him carefully. It never boded well when Cillian lost his temper. And if experience taught him anything, his cousin was very close to doing just that. "She didn't tell you?"

She hadn't said a fucking word about it last night, but he wasn't about to tell Finn that. "Why don't you fill me in?" Cillian was seething. His angel was spending time with someone else.

"Cousin, he's one of her guards." Finn reminded carefully. "His job is to protect her. You assigned the brothers to her detail."

"So what? That doesn't explain what I just saw." His head was going to fucking explode! She'd looked so carefree and beautiful. And with that fucker Patrick running beside her; they looked so natural together it infuriated him.

"Chloe told him yesterday that she wanted to go for a run this morning. Apparently, running is a part of her normal routine. And Chloe wants to get back to some semblance of normalcy. This is a good thing. And, where she goes, he goes. You know that."

He did. He just didn't like it. She should've told him she wanted to run in the mornings. "Why didn't he tell me? For that matter, why didn't you?" He planted his broad hand on Finn's chest and shoved.

Out of respect, Finn stepped back. Physically, they were evenly matched. But Cillian was a lot meaner and very dangerous when he lost his temper. "Cousin," his calm voice tried to soothe him, "you want her to settle into her new life. You've got to give her a little freedom."

Cillian knew he was right. He knew it. He just didn't care. The monster inside him demanded her. Needed her. Wanted to keep her all to himself. Hidden away. She was his. He tried to breathe through the need for violence. His shoulders were tense, his fists clenched. It had only been a few hours ago that he'd been buried in her luscious heat. If he closed his eyes, he could still feel her tight little pussy closing around him.

"Cillian!" Finn needed to extinguish the fire in his cousin's eyes. He couldn't let him make an irreparable mistake where Chloe was concerned. He was already on unstable ground when it came to the tiny little American. He also couldn't let him make an ass of himself in front of his men. "Finish the workout."

Cillian's fury was a living thing. His eyes burned with it. "Alright cousin," he sneered and launched himself at Finn. He landed a flying front kick to Finn's shoulder. Finn fell backward, but rolled quickly and swiped Cillian's legs, and their grappling session was back on track. Only now the intensity was amplified.

Imogen met Chloe and Patrick on the back patio with a pitcher of ice water. "Good morning, Chloe. How was your run?"

Chloe was winded, hot and sweaty, but she felt exhilarated. She had no idea it showed so plainly on her face. "It was great." She took the offered glass of water and chugged half of it. "Whew, thanks."

"She runs like a girl." Patrick laughed and dodged out of the way when Chloe tried to kick him.

"Are you ready for your breakfast?" Imogen smiled at the two of them. She was so glad to see the petite little lady smiling for the first time.

"I'm starving, but I want to shower first. I'll be back down in a few." She turned toward Patrick. "After you." And repeated his move from earlier by holding out her arm in a dramatic sweeping motion toward the door.

Freshly showered and dressed in grey leggings and a lavender silk top, Chloe was brushing out her wet hair when Cillian stormed into the bathroom. He was drenched in sweat and had a cut over his left eye that was oozing blood.

He stalked directly to her and abruptly lifted her out of her chair. He planted her on the vanity counter, roughly pushed her thighs apart and wedged his hips between them. He put his hands on the counter at her sides, caging her in.

Chloe leaned back away from him to take in the dark look of suppressed fury in his eyes.

"Did you enjoy your run, angel?" His voice was low and menacing.

"Yes." Ignoring the dangerous tone in his voice and the intensity of his narrowed gaze, she looked at the cut over his eye. "You're bleeding." She'd decided that she would not let him intimidate her anymore. And she wouldn't. So, she focused on the cut in order to ignore the nervous flock of butterflies in her belly.

He leaned further into her, his hand going up to slide through her hair. He fisted the wet strands, holding her face up to his. "You didn't tell me you planned to go for a run this morning." He was practically growling.

"You said I could go anywhere as long as I had Patrick or Rourke with me. Did I do something wrong?" Chloe lifted her chin slightly, tugging against his hold. Her eyes meeting his stubbornly while her heart pounded in her throat.

He considered her, taking in her reaction, then leaned closer, nearly nose to nose. "No, baby." His gaze moved slowly, possessively, from her eyes to her lips, then back to her eyes again. She was so fucking brave. He made an effort to temper his tone slightly. "I'm going to take a shower, then we'll go down to breakfast." He kissed her nose and turned toward the shower, stripping as he went.

Stunned, Chloe watched him walk away. The glittering flash of hostility in his eyes and that silky velvet voice belied his words and actions, so she waited to see if he would turn back around. He didn't.

Chloe dried her hair while Cillian showered. She was braiding it when he came to stand behind her. She glanced up and met his eyes in the mirror. The cut above his eye was still oozing. "You're still bleeding Cillian. What happened?"

"I was training this morning and got distracted."

"Where's the first aid kit?"

Cillian cocked his head and watched her in the mirror for a minute. "It's under the sink."

Chloe stood, but when he didn't back up, she scooted past him. She retrieved the first aid kit, then hopped up onto the counter in front of him. She pulled out an alcohol wipe and butterfly bandage and held them up. He slowly bent toward her, watching her with a bemused expression. She carefully wiped the blood from the cut and applied the bandage it over his eye, working gently to close the wound.

"There. All done." She held her breath. He was angry. She could see it in his eyes.

"Thank you, Chloe."

When she didn't respond, he did. "Hungry?"

"Starved."

"Let's go to breakfast, angel." Cillian grabbed her hand and helped her down from the counter, then pulled her out of the room.

It surprised Chloe that Finn wasn't already at the table when they arrived. She took her seat and immediately reached for the toast and marmalade. Cillian loaded her plate with eggs benedict and potatoes. "I can't eat all that."

"You should. Especially after a long run. You need the calories."

His voice was still that growly tone, so she stopped buttering her toast to look over at him. "Are you angry that I went running this morning?" He stared back at her without answering. "Cillian?" She waited anxiously, but when he didn't reply, she continued; "I took Patrick with me, like you said. I didn't break any of your rules."

"No, I'm not angry that you went for a run. Tomorrow, I'll join you."

"Oh, um, ok." She didn't want to run with him. This morning had been so peaceful because he hadn't been there.

Imogen slipped into the room and discreetly placed an ice pack next to her on the table. Chloe looked up just as she slipped back out the door. She iced her hand while she munched on her toast. Her hand didn't really hurt that much anymore. The bruising was already turning yellow.

Finn walked slowly into the room, capturing hers and Cillian's attention. Chloe gasped when she saw him. He had a black eye and his lip was cut.

She frowned as she watched him make his way to his seat. It looked like he was limping slightly, but she couldn't tell for sure. "What happened to you?" She immediately snapped her mouth closed. She hadn't meant to ask; it just came out. But seriously, it looked like he'd had the crap beaten out of him.

"This morning's workout was intense." He eased into his seat and glared at Cillian.

Chloe glanced between the two men. Cillian wasn't even paying attention to his cousin. He was looking at her.

He reached over and captured her hand. "After breakfast, we're going to program your fingerprints into the security system to give you the access you'll need. We should've done it yesterday, but you were at the beach longer than I expected."

"Alright. I'd like to go back to the beach for a while after we're done." She wanted to go out and write her message in the sand again.

His penetrating stare pierced right through her for a few seconds. "There's something I want to show you first. Then you can go."

"Alright."

"Finn, have you decided how you're going to fit Chloe's workouts into our training schedule?" He glanced at his cousin, who was sipping his coffee carefully.

"Yes. Since you run in the mornings, you'll train after lunch every day." Finn glanced at Chloe as he lowered the cup.

"You expect me to train every day? Why?"

Both men looked up at her question. But it was Cillian who answered.

"Because I want you to be prepared for anything."

She frowned at both of them. "Like what?"

"Everyone here is trained in some capacity in case the unexpected happens. You'll need to sharpen your existing skills and add some additional ones."

"You'll be burning a lot more calories, so make sure you eat full meals every day." Finn added.

At that, Cillian pushed her plate a little closer as a reminder for her to finish her breakfast. Chloe looked down and was surprised to see that she'd eaten most of it, anyway. Her run that morning had obviously increased her appetite.

"You should also eat a banana before you run each morning." Finn added.

"When I'm at home, I always do." She snapped. She already knew that, but this wasn't her house.

Both men grinned at her. She didn't find the situation funny, so she ignored them and finished her breakfast.

Cillian took Chloe to his office and spent several minutes moving her fingers over a metal pad on his desk. With each pass it loaded parts of her fingerprint into the system. When the light on the top flashed green, he'd move on to the next one. She didn't understand why she couldn't do it herself, but he'd insisted on holding her wrists the entire time. Hovering over her, crowding around her so close that every breath she took smelled of him. The subtle sandalwood scent made her insides quiver. When she tried to step back, hoping to put some distance between them, he moved in closer. Essentially pinning her between him and his desk.

"Your fingerprint will allow you into the family wing, our floor and a few other areas on the island that I'll show you, eventually."

"Other areas?" She looked up at him in surprise.

"Yes." He didn't elaborate. It wasn't the time to show her those areas yet. She wasn't ready.

When the last fingerprint was uploaded, he took her to the door by the stairwell and had her test it. Once he was sure it was working properly, he leaned against the wall and pulled her toward him.

Chloe resisted the tug, but he was persistent and a lot stronger than her.

"How far did you run this morning?" He spread his long legs apart and, with his hands at her hips, pulled her closer into him.

She met his gaze, wondering why he was asking about her run again. "Five miles."

"How long have you been doing that?" Holding her in place, he leaned down and kissed her forehead.

"What. Running?"

"Yes."

"Since I was fourteen." Chloe tried not to panic. This was the side of Cillian that scared her the most. This tender, sexy man was such a contradiction to the intense domineering force he usually displayed.

"Did you run by yourself?" He kissed her cheek.

"No. Dad would've never allowed that."

"He ran with you?" He kissed the top corner of her mouth.

"Yes, him and Juneau until I was in seventeen. Once he was sure Juneau was trained well enough, he let us go by ourselves."

"Juneau?" He slid his hand up her back and captured the end of her braid, twirling it around his finger.

"Yes." She looked at him quizzically. She thought he knew everything about her. When he stayed quiet, she continued. "Juneau's my dog."

"Ah, I knew you had a dog." He kissed her nose. "I just didn't know her name. What breed of dog is she?"

"Well, she is a he. And he's a white German Shepard." She smiled. "He's, my baby."

"Your baby, huh?" He kissed the corner of the other side of her mouth.

"Yes." She hesitated. "Um, Cillian?"

"Hmm?" He nuzzled her neck.

"What are you doing?" She put her hand on his chest, trying to put a little distance between them.

"Relax Chloe, we're just talking." He grinned at her attempt to move back. He continued to twirl the end of her braid and fingered her collar with his other hand. "How was Juneau trained?"

"One of my dad's friends was a dog handler in the Marines. Juneau is trained in obedience and as a guard dog. That was the only way dad would let us go by ourselves."

"So, you like dogs?"

"I like all animals, but I love Juneau."

"Do you want to go horseback riding today?"

"Sure. I was planning to bring Storm an apple, anyway."

"Storm is dangerous Chloe."

"I don't plan on riding him Cillian. I'm just going to give him an apple."

"Why?"

"Because he seems so sad. And he likes apples." She'd felt an instant connection with Storm, for that very reason.

"Alright. We'll go after lunch. Come on, I have something to show you." He hadn't wanted to remind her of her situation. He wanted to distract her from it.

Cillian took Chloe's hand and walked a few steps past his office door and opened a door across from it that led out onto the roof. There was a large outdoor fireplace and a massive seating area.

"Wow, this is nice. Do you come out here often?"

"Sometimes. But this isn't what I wanted to show you."

They crossed to the turret on the other side of the roof.

"This turret does not open into the guest wing on this side. The only access is through here," he said and opened the door. He stepped inside the brightly lit room and turned to watch her reaction.

Chloe paused just inside the door. The room's walls were round like those in Cillian's suite, but there were more windows. Floor to ceiling windows nearly all the way around the room allowed natural light to flood the space. In the center was an easel that held a blank canvas. Off to one side, by a window, was another. A long table against a wall held containers filled with paintbrushes of all different sizes. Labeled bins holding tubes and bottles of several types and colors of paint were stacked on a shelf next to the table.

"Oh my God!" She whispered slowly, then crossed the room and started pulling open the bins, checking out the supplies. In addition to paint, there were charcoals, clays for sculpting, sketch pads, cups and palettes. She found a razor knife, scissors, a staple gun, canvas stretching tools, and bars. Under the table, stacked in racks, were canvases and boards and more sketch pads in different sizes. It felt like Christmas morning!

Chloe tentatively turned back toward Cillian. He'd closed the door behind them so she could see hooks on it with small smocks and a few aprons dangling from them.

Cillian waited for her to look up at him. Finally, after taking it all in, she met his gaze. And there it was. It was tentative at first, but Chloe smiled. Big and bright and so beautiful, it lit up her face. He'd waited days to see it again. Days.

"Did I get everything you'll need?" He'd enjoyed watching her exclaim over everything as she'd opened and investigated the supplies.

"I don't think there's anything missing. This is unbelievable." She quietly exclaimed. "Is this for me?"

"Of course."

"Why would you do this?" Most of the time he was menacing, domineering and even frightening, but like now, there were moments when he could be so gentle and sweet. She was more afraid of the gentle sweet Cillian than anything because he could so easily cause her to relax her guard. And that would be a huge mistake.

"I told you angel. I want you to have everything you'll need. You're an artist. You need supplies and a quiet place to work." When she just stared at him, he continued. "There's a lavatory behind that door." He pointed to a corner she hadn't noticed. Next to a closed door was a black leather chaise lounge with red toss pillows, a small coffee table and a silver mini refrigerator. "I believe Imogen filled the refrigerator for you."

She stared in awe at the room he'd created for her. Her artist's soul was singing with excitement, but her stomach was tight with anxiety. "I don't know what to say." She'd missed painting so much that her fingers ached to grab a brush and start a project right away. She always painted when her thoughts were troubled, and she'd never been more troubled than she was now. But could she accept this? If so, what message would it send to him?

"You don't have to say anything." He moved to open the door. "I'll leave you to explore. I have some work to finish up before lunch. I'll be in my office if you need me."

"Cillian?"

With one hand on the doorknob, he peered over his shoulder. "Yes?"

"Thank you for this." She waved her hand to encompass the room.

He watched her face for a moment then nodded, "you're welcome angel."

Chloe left the art studio and went straight to their suite. She changed into shorts and flip-flops and applied sunscreen, then went to get the baseball cap Patrick had given her earlier. She'd left it on the island in her closet, but now it was gone. In its place was a dark blue one with the letter O on the front. She rolled her eyes at what the O implied. Obviously, Cillian wanted her to wear this one. She searched through the closet for Patrick's, but couldn't find it anywhere.

She went back into the bedroom, lifted the house phone and asked the person who answered to have Patrick call her. Less than a minute later, the phone rang. She grinned to herself.

"Patrick?"

"Hello Chloe. What's up?"

"I want to go to the beach for a while."

"I'll meet you downstairs at the front door."

"Thanks."

"Chloe?"

"Yes?"

"Don't step outside until I get there."

She signed heavily "I won't."

She made her way down to the front foyer and leaned against the wall to wait for Patrick. The castle was bustling with people. There were armed guards walking through the rooms, as well as the housekeeping staff bustling around doing their chores. The staff smiled tentatively at her as they passed, but didn't speak to her. The guards didn't acknowledge her at all, which was a little creepy, so she was relieved when Patrick showed up.

With a boyish grin on his face, Patrick reached up and tapped the bill of her hat."

"I'm sorry. When I went to get yours from my closet, I couldn't find it anywhere. This one was sitting in its place instead. Did the maid get it back to you?"

"Oh, I got it back. Don't worry, lass." He wasn't about to tell her it had been torn to shreds. Or that Cillian had knocked the shit out of him when he'd returned it himself that morning.

"There's a lot of people in this place." She noted as they walked toward the beach.

"It takes an army of staff to maintain the castle."

"There are guards everywhere."

"Yes, that's usually the case. But don't worry, they won't hurt you."

"Yea right. As long as I don't try to off their boss." She scoffed. "Just let me hold a gun on him to negotiate my way out of here and watch what they do then."

Patrick laughed and nudged her shoulder. "That would be an amusing sight to see."

"It wasn't meant to be funny." She scowled.

"Oh, but it was lass. They'd probably shit themselves. They all know that Cillian would kill them if they harmed one hair on your head. Even if you had a gun pointed at him."

"Humph! I doubt that."

"Don't doubt it, lass. But do me a favor, make sure I'm around if you decide to do it. I'll want to record it."

"Stop laughing! It's not that funny."

They'd reached the sand, and Patrick stopped at the edge just like the day before. He looked over at her and his voice got very serious. "All joking aside Chloe, Cillian would never allow you to put yourself in harm's way like that. He'd disarm you before you could blink, then you'd have to face the consequences."

"You think so?"

"I know so. Cillian had the learn the hard way to be faster and meaner than everyone else. And he is. So please don't be foolish."

Chloe turned and kicked off her flip-flops, then stomped down the beach. She let the waves crash over her feet for a while as she surveyed the horizon. She peeked over her shoulder a few times and when she was sure Patrick wasn't paying attention to her so much as her surroundings; she walked further down the beach and found the stick from the day before. Just as she'd thought, her message had washed away with the tide. She wrote the message again, making sure the write other designs across the sand in case Patrick was watching. When she finished, she climbed up on her rock and pulled her knees up to her chest and watched the waves.

She'd been here three days now. It felt like three weeks. It was hard to believe that only a week ago she'd completed the first year of her Master's program. She'd been so excited to be one step closer to starting the next chapter of her life. Now she didn't know if she'd ever get that chance.

She had no idea how to get herself out of this. Cillian ruled this place. His word was law. The only way to get off this island was through him, unless she planned to swim. It'd serve him right if she could do it. But she wasn't stupid. Fifty miles was a long way to swim through shark-infested waters. And anyway, if she died trying, he'd kill her parents. He'd as much as said he would.

God, she missed home. Her mom and dad had to be frantic. Every time she thought about them, her heart hurt. She could barely hold back her tears. The fear they must be feeling. Not knowing if she was dead or alive. And the worst part was that it was all her fault. If she'd just gone to the beach like she'd planned, things would have been different. She would've never even met Cillian O'Donnell.

How could she ever face them again after what she'd put them through? The pain in her chest increased. Her tears flowed freely as she rocked back and forth. She knew she had to be strong. If nothing else, to prove she could survive. But here, with the waves crashing around her, she could let the tears fall and no one could see. No one would know she was so weak.

Cillian sat at his desk, staring at the largest screen on the wall, watching his girl. She was crying again. Except today, she was folded in on herself, rocking back and forth. He didn't like it. His Chloe was a fighter, full of fire and sass.

He had hoped she'd paint today. Had hoped the art studio would keep her occupied and off that fucking rock. He'd given her a closet full of beautiful clothes, shoes, and jewelry. Stunning pieces he'd selected just for her. But his angel hadn't gotten excited over those things. No, not his girl. And there she sat, out in the elements on a rock, barefoot in shorts and a tank top. His hat tucked low over her bare face. She looked so young like that.

He didn't turn his eyes from the screen or Chloe when Finn walked into his office. Finn stopped short when he saw what he was watching.

"She's out there again?" Finn scowled at the screen.

"Yes."

"Didn't she like the studio?"

"She did." Cillian watched Chloe for a few more seconds, then lifted the remote and lowered the image of her into another smaller screen, off to the side for now.

"I suppose I'll have to go out there and wipe away another message in the sand later."

"It appears so." He couldn't help but smile. His girl was smart. She just didn't know how advanced his security was. "Any word from George?"

"Yes. Roisin's nose is broken. But instead of simply fixing it, she had the surgeon give her a new one."

"I'll just bet she did." Finn's second cousin was way too vain and self-centered not to take advantage of the opportunity.

"Yea well, George is insisting you pay for it." Finn crossed his arms over his chest, his expression stoic. He hated his great uncle almost as much as he hated his great grandfather. Both men were devious criminals who'd tried several times to move up in their world, only to be beaten back like rabid dogs. George was mean, but he was stupid. However, his great grandfather Silas was a different story. And they had plans for him. Very specific plans.

"Pay it."

"Alright. Now we need to discuss the Russians and the Swede's."

Chloe stepped into the art studio and closed the door behind her. She couldn't sit around feeling sorry for herself. She wasn't made that way. She needed to paint. She wasn't sure how Cillian knew that, or even if he did. Either way, it didn't matter. She needed it. Her hand itched to hold the brush, smell the fumes, and let the familiarity of it all close in around her.

She selected the brushes she wanted and the colors she needed and began mixing them to create the perfect hue she desired while the primer dried on the canvas. She'd found a small fan under the table and placed it in front of the wet canvass over by the window so it would dry quickly. Afterward, she went through all the supplies, carefully arranging them the way she wanted.

Placing the now dried canvas on the easel, she made her first brush stroke in what seemed like ages. It felt so natural, so familiar, that she lost herself in the lines, the shades and smudges as she brought the image in her head to life on the canvas.

Jet black fur, the gray hues and white flecks creating shadows. Faded blues with just the right amount of white and gray to fade the denim. Browns with enough red to age the leather. The canvas course and rough under her fingertips as they smoothed and rubbed. The brush delicate and sure.

Cillian watched her from the doorway. She didn't know he was there. So focused and content as she slowly brought the painting of Storm and old man Jenkins to life. She was amazingly talented. He felt a pain in his chest as he watched her talent revealed. He'd known she'd be good. But to see it in reality was truly astonishing.

When she stepped back to view her work, he cleared his throat. She didn't turn around as she continued to study the canvas.

"How long have you been standing there?"

"Not long. You're very talented." He walked further into the room to stand beside her as he, too, studied the beginnings of a beautiful painting.

"Hmm." She whipped her hands on a rag and looked up at him. "Is it time for lunch already?"

"Yes. Are you hungry?" Just then, her stomach growled loudly. He chuckled. "That's what I thought. Come on, little one, let's get you something to eat." He held out his hand for hers.

Chloe looked down at the paint covering her hands, then back up at him. "I need to clean up and washout the brushes. It'll take a few minutes."

"I'll wait over there." Cillian nodded his head toward the leather chaise. "Take your time."

Chloe looked over toward the chaise, then back at him before looking down at her paint smudged hands again. "Alright."

Cillian watched her from the leather sofa as she bustled around the room. Chloe was in her element, with paint covering her hands and smudged on her delicate face.

Imogen seemed to bounce with excitement when they entered the dining room. She smiled brightly at Chloe and pointed to the table. "I made hamburgers and 'French fries.' I hope you like it, Chloe."

"I'm sure I will. It smells delicious. Thank you, Imogen." Chloe took her seat and reached for a burger before Cillian could do it. But he beat her to the fries. He loaded her plate with them. She frowned at the amount. "You know I can't eat all that."

"You should try. We're going horseback riding after lunch. You need the calories."

"You and Finn keep saying that. You do know I'm not a teenaged boy, right?" She asked sarcastically before realizing what she'd said.

Imogen giggled and hurried out of the room.

Cillian's expression turned decidedly wicked, and he leaned over and tugged on her collar. "Trust me angel. I definitely know you're not a boy."

Before she could avoid it, he kissed her. His lips were rough at first, forcing hers open, his tongue thrusting deep, claiming her then slowly gentled to soft nibbling kisses. When he lifted his lips from hers, he was gratified to see the dazed look in her eyes and her lips swollen and red from his. He released her collar and sat back, obviously pleased with himself.

Chloe glared at him and hissed. "Stop doing that!" She thrust her chair back.

Cillian reacted quickly, catching her wrist and holding her in the chair when she tried to stand. "Stay there and eat." His eyes gleamed with anticipation.

"Let go." She tugged on her wrist, but he didn't release it. He used his foot to catch the leg of her chair and pulled it back to the table.

"Eat, Chloe."

The silky tone of his voice should have warned her. Instead, her stubborn chin lifted, and she yanked hard, but unsuccessfully, on her wrist.

"Unless you'd rather go up to our room? We can continue this discussion while you're tied to our bed. Those sweet thighs spread wide for me."

"Looks like I'm late for lunch." Finn said carefully and moved from the doorway to take his seat.

"Not at all. Chloe was just deciding if she wants to eat." He chuckled under his breath when she blushed. She instantly stopped pulling at her wrist and relaxed in his hold. He let go, but patted her hand gently and whispered, "good girl" before lifting a French fry from his plate and popping it into his smiling mouth.

She was so angry; she wanted to scream. He was such a condescending asshole. 'Good girl'? What the hell! She thought about kicking him under the table, but wasn't sure what he'd do in retaliation. The jerk!

Peeking over at Finn, she was only slightly mollified that he wasn't paying them any attention. So instead of kicking him, she ignored him and took a bite of her burger. It was fabulous. Cooked to a perfect medium with the cheese melted just right. Crisp lettuce and sweet tomato. Delicious.

Imogen came back in with a wide grin on her face and put a bottle of ketchup next to her plate. "I ordered this for you Chloe". She said softly, then hurried out of the room.

Chloe stared at the familiar bottle for a second before she picked it up. Her throat tightened. It was the only brand her mom ever bought because it was her dad's favorite. She swallowed a few times and took several breaths to fight back the tears that threatened to fall. She knew by the excitement Imogen had been displaying about today's lunch that she'd planned it just for her. If she started crying over a dang bottle of ketchup, then she'd probably hurt the older woman's feelings. And she'd look like an idiot.

"Chloe?" Cillian didn't like the look on her face. She'd been full of fire just a few minutes ago. Her face had been flushed, her eyes sparkling with fury. His girl was beautiful, but when she was angry, she was stunning. Now she just looked devastated.

"Yes?" She didn't take her eyes off the bottle as she squeezed some onto her plate.

"We'll take the horses up the coast so you can see more of the island."

"Ok." She just needed to concentrate on eating. The food was delicious. And she promised herself she'd get through this.

"You do know how to ride, don't you?"

"Of course. My grandfather has a ranch on the Northshore. I have my own horse." She looked up as she popped a French fry into her mouth.

"Excellent. We'll leave as soon as you're

took Chloe to his office and spent several minutes moving her fingers over a metal pad on his desk. With each pass it loaded parts of her fingerprint into the system. When the light on the top flashed green, he'd move on to the next one. She didn't understand why she couldn't do it herself, but he'd insisted on holding her wrists the entire time. Hovering over her, crowding around her so close that every breath she took smelled of him. The subtle sandalwood scent made her insides quiver. When she tried to step back, hoping to put some distance between them, he moved in closer. Essentially pinning her between him and his desk.

"Your fingerprint will allow you into the family wing, our floor and a few other areas on the island that I'll show you, eventually."

"Other areas?" She looked up at him in surprise.

"Yes." He didn't elaborate. It wasn't the time to show her those areas yet. She wasn't ready.

When the last fingerprint was uploaded, he took her to the door by the stairwell and had her test it. Once he was sure it was working properly, he leaned against the wall and pulled her toward him.

Chloe resisted the tug, but he was persistent and a lot stronger than her.

"How far did you run this morning?" He spread his long legs apart and, with his hands at her hips, pulled her closer into him.

She met his gaze, wondering why he was asking about her run again. "Four miles."

"How long have you been doing that?" Holding her in place, he leaned down and kissed her forehead.

"What. Running?"

"Yes."

"Since freshman year in high school." Chloe tried not to panic. This was the side of Cillian that scared her the most. This tender, sexy man was such a contradiction to the intense domineering force he usually displayed.

"Did you run by yourself?" He kissed her cheek.

"No way. Dad would've never allowed that."

"He ran with you?" He kissed the top corner of her mouth.

"Yes, him and Juneau until I was in eleventh grade. Once he was sure Juneau was trained well enough, he let us go by ourselves."

"Juneau?" He slid his hand up her back and captured the end of her braid, twirling it around his finger.

"Yes." She looked at him quizzically. She thought he knew everything about her. When he stayed quiet, she continued. "Juneau's my dog."

"Ah, I knew you had a dog." He kissed her nose. "I just didn't know her name. What breed of dog is she?"

"Well, she is a he. And he's a white German Shepard." She smiled. "He's, my baby."

"Your baby, huh?" He kissed the corner of the other side of her mouth.

"Yes." She hesitated. "Um, Cillian?"

"Hmm?" He nuzzled her neck.

"What are you doing?" She put her hand on his chest, trying to put a little distance between them.

"Relax Chloe, we're just talking." He grinned at her attempt to move back. He continued to twirl the end of her braid and fingered her collar with his other hand. "How was Juneau trained?"

"One of my dad's friends was a dog handler in the Marines. Juneau is trained in obedience and as a guard dog. That was the only way dad would let us go by ourselves."

"So, you like dogs?"

"I like all animals, but I love Juneau."

"Do you want to go horseback riding today?"

"Sure. I was planning to bring Storm an apple, anyway."

"Storm is dangerous Chloe."

"I don't plan on riding him Cillian. I'm just going to give him an apple."

"Why?"

"Because he seems so sad. And he likes apples." She'd felt an instant connection with Storm, for that very reason.

"Alright. We'll go after lunch. Come on, I have something to show you." He hadn't wanted to remind her of her situation. He'd intended to distract her from it.

Cillian took Chloe's hand and walked a few steps past his office door and opened a door across from it that led out onto the roof. There was a large outdoor fireplace and a massive seating area.

"Wow, this is nice. Do you come out here often?"

"Sometimes. But this isn't what I wanted to show you."

They crossed to the turret on the other side of the roof.

"This turret does not open into the guest wing on this side. The only access is through here," he said and opened the door. He stepped inside the brightly lit room and turned to watch her reaction.

Chloe paused just inside the door. The room's walls were rounding like those in Cillian's suite, but there were more windows. Floor to ceiling windows nearly all the way around the room allowed natural light to flood the space. In the center was an easel that held a blank canvas. Off to one side, by a window, was another. A long table against a wall held containers filled with paintbrushes of all different sizes. Labeled bins holding tubes and bottles of several types and colors of paint were stacked on a shelf next to the table.

"Oh my God!" She whispered slowly, then crossed the room and started pulling open the bins, checking out the supplies. In addition to paint, there were charcoals, clays for sculpting, sketch pads, cups and palettes. She found a razor knife, scissors, a staple gun, canvas stretching tools, and bars. Under the table, stacked in racks, were canvases and boards and more sketch pads in different sizes. It felt like Christmas morning!

Chloe tentatively turned back toward Cillian. He'd closed the door behind them so she could see hooks on it with small smocks and a few aprons dangling from them.

Cillian waited for her to look up at him. Finally, after taking it all in, she met his gaze. And there it was. It was tentative at first, but Chloe smiled. Big and bright and so beautiful, it lit up her face. He'd waited days to see it again. Days.

"Did I get everything you'll need?" He'd enjoyed watching her exclaim over everything as she'd opened and investigated the supplies.

"I don't think there's anything missing. This is unbelievable." She quietly exclaimed. "Is this for me?"

"Of course."

"Why would you do this?" Most of the time he was menacing, domineering and even frightening, but like now, there were moments when he could be so gentle and sweet. She was more afraid of the gentle sweet Cillian than anything because he could so easily cause her to relax her guard. And that would be a huge mistake.

"I told you angel. I want you to have everything you'll need. You're an artist. You need supplies and a quiet place to work." When she just stared at him, he continued. "There's a lavatory behind that door." He pointed to a corner she hadn't noticed. Next to a closed door was a black leather chaise lounge with red toss pillows, a small coffee table and a silver mini refrigerator. "I believe Imogen filled the refrigerator with bottles of water and fruit."

She stared in awe at the room he'd created for her. Her artist's soul was singing with excitement, but her stomach was tight with anxiety. "I don't know what to say." She'd missed painting so much that her fingers ached to grab a brush and start a project right away. She always painted when her thoughts were troubled, and she'd never been more troubled than she was now. But could she accept this? If so, what message would it send to him?

"You don't have to say anything." He moved to open the door. "I'll leave you to explore. I have some work to finish up before lunch. I'll be in my office if you need me."

"Cillian?"

With one hand on the doorknob, he peered over his shoulder. "yes?"

"Thank you for this." She waved her hand to encompass the room.

He watched her face for a moment then nodded, "you're welcome angel."

Chloe left the art studio and went straight to their suite. She changed into shorts and flip-flops and applied sunscreen, then went to get the baseball cap Patrick had given her earlier. She'd left it on the island in her closet, but now it was gone. In its place was a dark blue one with the letter O on the front. She rolled her eyes at what the O implied. Obviously, Cillian wanted her to wear this one. She searched through the closet for Patrick's, but couldn't find it anywhere.

She went back into the bedroom, lifted the house phone and asked the person who answered to have Patrick call her. Less than a minute later, the phone rang. She grinned to herself.

"Patrick?"

"Hello Chloe. What's up?"

"I want to go to the beach for a while."

"I'll meet you downstairs at the front door."

"Thanks."

"Chloe?"

"Yes?"

"Don't step outside until I get there."

She signed heavily "I won't."

She made her way down to the front foyer and leaned against the wall to wait for Patrick. The castle was bustling with people. There were armed guards walking through the rooms, as well as the housekeeping staff bustling around doing their chores. The staff smiled tentatively at her as they passed, but didn't speak to her. The guards didn't acknowledge her at all, which was a little creepy, so she was relieved when Patrick showed up.

With a boyish grin on his face, Patrick reached up and tapped the bill of her hat."

"I'm sorry. When I went to get yours from my closet, I couldn't find it anywhere. This one was sitting in its place instead. Did the maid get it back to you?"

"Oh, I got it back. Don't worry, lass." He wasn't about to tell her it had been torn to shreds. Or that Cillian had knocked the shit out of him when he'd returned it himself that morning.

"There's a lot of people in this place." She noted as they walked toward the beach.

"It takes an army of staff to maintain the castle."

"There are guards everywhere."

"Yes, that's usually the case. But don't worry, they won't hurt you."

"Yea right. As long as I don't try to off their boss." She scoffed. "Just let me hold a gun on him to negotiate my way out of here and watch what they do then."

Patrick laughed and nudged her shoulder. "That would be an amusing sight to see."

"It wasn't meant to be funny." She scowled at the laughing loon.

"Oh, but it was lass. They'd probably shit themselves. They all know that Cillian would kill them if they harmed one hair on your head. Even if you had a gun pointed at him."

"Humph! I doubt that."

"Don't doubt it, lass. But do me a favor, make sure I'm around if you decide to do it. I'll want to record it."

"Stop laughing! It's not that funny."

They'd reached the sand, and Patrick stopped at the edge just like the day before. He looked over at her and his voice got very serious. "All joking aside Chloe, Cillian would never allow you to put yourself in harm's way like that. He'd disarm you before you could blink, then you'd have to face the consequences."

"You think so?"

"I know so. Cillian had the learn the hard way to be faster and meaner than everyone else. And he is. So please don't be foolish."

Chloe turned and kicked off her flip-flops, then stomped down the beach. She let the waves crash over her feet for a while as she surveyed the horizon. She peeked over her shoulder a few times and when she was sure Patrick wasn't paying attention to her so much as her surroundings; she walked further down the beach and found the stick from the day before. Just as she'd thought, her message had washed away with the tide. She wrote the message again, making sure the write other designs across the sand in case Patrick was watching. When she finished, she climbed up on her rock and pulled her knees up to her chest and watched the waves.

She'd been here three days now. It felt like three weeks. It was hard to believe that only a week ago she'd completed her junior year in college. She'd been so excited to be one step closer to starting the next chapter of her life. Now she didn't know if she'd ever get that chance.

She had no idea how to get herself out of this. Cillian ruled this place. His word was law. The only way to get off this island was through him, unless she planned to swim. It'd serve him right if she could do it. But she wasn't stupid. Fifty miles was a long way to swim through shark-infested waters. And anyway, if she died trying, he'd kill her parents. He'd as much as said he would.

God, she missed home. Her mom and dad had to be frantic. Every time she thought about them, her heart hurt. She could barely hold back her tears. The fear they must be feeling. Not knowing if she was dead or alive. And the worst part was that it was all her fault. If she'd just gone to the beach like she'd planned, things would have been different. She would've never even met Cillian O'Donnell.

How could she ever face them again after what she'd put them through? The pain in her chest increased. Her tears flowed freely as she rocked back and forth. She knew she had to be strong. If nothing else, to prove she could survive. But here, with the waves crashing around her, she could let the tears fall and no one could see. No one would know she was so weak.

Cillian sat at his desk, staring at the largest screen on the wall, watching his girl. She was crying again. Only today, she was folded in on herself, rocking back and forth. He didn't like it. His Chloe was a fighter, full of fire and sass.

He had hoped she'd paint today. Had hoped the art studio would keep her occupied and off that fucking rock. He'd given her a closet full of beautiful clothes, shoes, and jewelry. Stunning pieces he'd selected just for her. But his angel hadn't gotten excited over those things. No, not his girl. And there she sat, out in the elements on a rock, barefoot in shorts and a tank top. His hat tucked low over her bare face. She looked so young like that.

He didn't turn his eyes from the screen or Chloe when Finn walked into his office. Finn stopped short when he saw what he was watching.

"She's out there again?" Finn scowled at the screen.

"Yes."

"Didn't she like the studio?"

"She did." Cillian watched Chloe for a few more seconds, then lifted the remote and lowered the image of her into another smaller screen, off to the side for now.

"I supposed I'll have to go out there and wipe away another message in the sand later."

"It appears so." He couldn't help but smile. His girl was smart. She just didn't know how advanced his security was. "Any word from George?"

"Yes. Roisin's nose is broken. But instead of simply fixing it, she had the surgeon give her a new one."

"I'll just bet she did." Finn's second cousin was way too vain and self-centered not to take advantage of the opportunity.

"Yea well, George is insisting you pay for it." Finn crossed his arms over his chest, his expression stoic. He hated his great uncle almost as much as he hated his great grandfather. Both men were devious criminals who'd tried several times to move up in their world, only to be beaten back like rabid dogs. George was mean, but he was stupid. However, his great grandfather Silas was a different story. And they had plans for him. Very specific plans.

"Pay it."

"Alright. Now we need to discuss the Russians and the Swede's."

Chloe stepped into the art studio and closed the door behind her. She couldn't sit around feeling sorry for herself. She wasn't made that way. She needed to paint. She wasn't sure how Cillian knew that, or even if he did. Either way, it didn't matter. She needed it. Her hand itched to hold the brush, smell the fumes, and let the familiarity of it all close in around her.

She selected the brushes she wanted and the colors she needed and began mixing them to create the perfect hue she desired while the primer dried on the canvas. She'd found a small fan under the table and placed it in front of the wet canvass over by the window so it would dry quickly. Afterward, she went through all the supplies, carefully arranging them the way she wanted.

Placing the now dried canvas on the easel, she made her first brush stroke in what seemed like ages. It felt so natural, so familiar, that she lost herself in the lines, the shades and smudges as she brought the image in her head to life on the canvas.

Jet black fur, the gray hues and white flecks creating shadows. Faded blues with just the right amount of white and gray to fade the denim. Browns with enough red to age the leather. The canvas course and rough under her fingertips as they smoothed and rubbed. The brush delicate and sure.

Cillian watched her from the doorway. She didn't know he was there. So focused and content as she slowly brought the painting of Storm and old man Jenkins to life. She was amazingly talented. He felt a pain in his chest as he watched her talent revealed. He'd known she'd be good. But to see it in reality was truly astonishing.

When she stepped back to view her work, he cleared his throat. She didn't turn around as she continued to study the canvas.

"How long have you been standing there?"

"Not long. You're very talented." He walked further into the room to stand beside her as he, too, studied the beginnings of a beautiful painting.

"Hmm." She whipped her hands on a rag and looked up at him. "Is it time for lunch already?"

"Yes. Are you hungry?" Just then, her stomach growled loudly. He chuckled. "That's what I thought. Come on, little one, let's get you something to eat." He held out his hand for hers.

Chloe looked down at the paint covering her hands, then back up at him. "I need to clean up and washout the brushes. It'll take a few minutes."

"I'll wait over there." Cillian nodded his head toward the leather chaise. "Take your time."

Chloe looked over toward the chaise, then back at him before looking down at her paint smudged hands again. "Alright."

Cillian watched her from the leather sofa as she bustled around the room. Chloe was in her element, with paint covering her hands and smudged on her delicate face.

Imogen seemed to bounce with excitement when they entered the dining room. She smiled brightly at Chloe and pointed to the table. "I made hamburgers and I believe you call them 'French fries.' I hope you like it, Chloe."

"I'm sure I will. It smells delicious. Thank you, Imogen." Chloe took her seat and reached for a burger before Cillian could do it. But he beat her to the fries. He loaded her plate with them. She frowned at the amount. "You know I can't eat all that."

"You should try. We're going horseback riding after lunch. You need the calories."

"You and Finn keep saying that. You do know I'm not a teenaged boy, right?" She asked sarcastically before realizing what she'd said.

Imogen giggled and hurried out of the room.

Cillian's expression turned decidedly wicked, and he leaned over and tugged on her collar. "Trust me angel. I definitely know you're not a boy."

Before she could avoid it, he kissed her. His lips were rough at first, forcing hers open, his tongue thrusting deep, claiming her then slowly gentled to soft nibbling kisses. When he lifted his lips from hers, he was gratified to see the dazed look in her eyes and her lips swollen and red from his. He released her collar and sat back, obviously pleased with himself.

Chloe glared at him and hissed. "Stop doing that!" She thrust her chair back.

Cillian reacted quickly, catching her wrist and holding her in the chair when she tried to stand. "Sit down and eat." His eyes gleamed with anticipation.

"Let go." She tugged on her wrist, but he didn't release it. He used his foot to catch the leg of her chair and pulled it back to the table.

"Eat, Chloe."

The silky tone of his voice should have warned her. Instead, her stubborn chin lifted, and she yanked hard, but unsuccessfully, on her wrist.

"Unless you'd rather go up to our room? We can continue this discussion while you're tied to our bed. Those sweet thighs spread wide for me."

"Looks like I'm late for lunch." Finn said carefully and moved from the doorway to take his seat.

"Not at all. Chloe was just deciding if she wants to eat." He chuckled under his breath when she blushed. She instantly stopped pulling at her wrist and relaxed in his hold. He let go, but patted her hand gently and whispered, "good girl" before lifting a French fry from his plate and popping it into his smiling mouth.

She was so angry; her head was going to explode. He was such a condescending asshole. 'Good girl'? What the hell! She thought about kicking him under the table, but wasn't sure what he'd do in retaliation. The jerk!

Peeking over at Finn, she was only slightly mollified that he wasn't paying them any attention. So instead of kicking him, she ignored him and took a bite of her burger. It was fabulous. Cooked to a perfect medium with the cheese melted just right. Crisp lettuce and sweet tomato. Delicious.

Imogen came back in with a wide grin on her face and put a bottle of ketchup next to her plate. "I ordered this for you Chloe". She said softly, then hurried out of the room.

Chloe stared at the familiar bottle for a second before she picked it up. Her throat tightened. It was the only brand her mom ever bought because it was her dad's favorite. She swallowed a few times and took several breaths to fight back the tears that threatened to fall. She knew by the excitement Imogen had been displaying about today's lunch that she'd planned it just for her. If she started crying over a dang bottle of ketchup, then she'd probably hurt the older woman's feelings. And she'd look like an idiot.

"Chloe?" Cillian didn't like the look on her face. She'd been full of fire just a few minutes ago. Her face had been flushed, her eyes sparkling with fury. His girl was beautiful, but when she was angry, she was stunning. Now she just looked devastated.

"Yes?" She didn't take her eyes off the bottle as she squeezed some onto her plate.

"We'll take the horses up the coast so you can see more of the island."

"Ok." She needed to concentrate on eating. The food was delicious. And she promised herself she'd get through this.

"You do know how to ride, don't you?"

"Of course. My grandfather has a ranch on the Northshore. I have my own horse." She looked up as she popped a French fry into her mouth.

"Excellent. We'll leave as soon as you're finished."

Chapter 16: Kindred Spirits

Chloe stared at the clothes laid out on the bed for a moment, then looked over at Cillian. "Why can't I just throw on some jeans?"

"Because I want you to wear this." Cillian stood with his arms crossed over his chest as he studied Chloe.

"But why?" She fingered the soft buff colored riding pants. The expensive thick woven cotton and spandex would allow for easy movement on the horse. She could understand that, but the white long-sleeved silk blouse was very elegant.

"You'll be seeing the people who live here for the first time."

"It's a bit much, don't you think?" She raised her eyebrow at him. She knew what he was doing. He was dressing her up to show her off. Her frustration was growing by the second.

He frowned. "Not for you. You should be properly attired when riding."

"But,"

"Chloe." He cut her off. "Change so we can go." She was going to use the beautiful clothes he'd bought for her, whether she liked it or not.

She huffed out a breath of irritation and snatched up the riding pants and the shirt and stomped toward the bathroom.

He stopped her with a hand on her arm. "Where are you going?" He grinned at her show of irritation.

"Obviously, I'm going to change." She snapped. She hadn't meant for it to come out so sarcastically, but he was getting on her nerves. She tried to twist out of his hold, and his grin got wider.

"Change here."

"No way!" She edged toward the bathroom.

His smile deepened as he matched her, step for step.

"Back off, Cillian." She held her hands out to stop him. He was stalking her again. She hated when he did that.

"Do you like the top you're wearing?"

She looked down, confused by his question. "Yes." It was the closest thing in the closet to a t-shirt.

"Take it off before I rip it off." When her eyes got a round as saucers, he chuckled.

"Cillian!"

"Chloe!" He pitched his voice high and mocked her teasingly. His fallen angel face so beautiful as he toyed with her.

"Quit being an ass!" Her stubborn chin went up. She hated that look. It never boded well for her.

His expression turned serious, anticipation sparkling in his eyes. "I want to see you."

His silky voice sent shivers down her spine. "No. I'm going to change so we can leave."

He reached for her shirt and before she could react; he gripped the neckline in both hands and jerked hard, ripping it completely in two. He dropped both pieces of torn fabric to the floor and reached for the band of her shorts.

"Alright! Stop!" She jumped back away from him and glared furiously as she pulled down her shorts.

"That's more like it." He sat down on the side of the bed and watched her while she changed into the clothes, he'd selected for her. He couldn't help but grin as she mumbled under her breath.

He went into her closet and returned with a soft pair of tall leather riding boots. The dark brown, supple leather was soft. They fit perfectly. After zipping them, she stood and waited for him to finish putting on his own boots.

Cillian walked up to her and unbuttoned the top two buttons on her shirt. He ran his finger over the now visible jeweled collar at her throat, then down to her exposed cleavage. She looked down at his hands as he did it, then off to the side, carefully looking over his shoulder, waiting for him to finish. Then she let him take her hand and lead her out of their suite.

She was surprised when Patrick didn't fall into step behind them, but she didn't comment. However, she understood why when they reached the foyer and Finn was sitting in a chair by the door, looking at his phone. He was wearing jeans and a pair of riding boots. When he saw them, he immediately came to his feet. He handed Chloe an apple. When she looked up at him, he simply said, "for Storm." He didn't smile, but he rarely did. Neither did she.

When they arrived at the stable, Chloe rushed out to the back corral, but didn't see Storm. She looked around and noticed Finn had followed her out and was standing by the back door to the stable, watching for any threat. Old man Jenkins was heading in her direction so she leaned against the fence and waited for him to make his way to her.

"Still looking a bit too fancy, but at least you're dressed right." He grumbled at her.

Chloe glared at the cantankerous old man. She got the feeling he enjoyed growling at everyone. She kicked out her leg to show off the boots and in her best southern drawl asked, "can't be too careful where I step now, can I?"

"Humph. Better than whatcha had on before, I suppose. Watcha doin out here again?"

"Where's Storm?" She couldn't help but notice the gleam in his eye. He really did like to portray a grumpy old man.

He looked her over as if assessing her, then noticed the apple in her hand and shook his head. "You're goin ta spoil the beast if ya keep that up." He nodded toward the apple.

"Maybe he needs to be spoiled a little."

He assessed her for another minute before coming to an internal decision, then nodded his head in a direction over his shoulder. "Well, come on then. You're supposed ta be ridin today, not messin' around with a demon like our Storm."

He turned and headed toward a separate stable she hadn't paid much attention to. Chloe fell into step beside him. She peeked back over her shoulder, and sure enough, Finn and Cillian weren't far behind her.

There were several stalls in this stable as well, just not as many as the first one. Only one stall at the end was occupied. As they approached, Storm stuck his head out over the door to greet her. He whinnied loudly.

Chloe nickered back, causing Storm to whinny again. "Why is he secluded back here?"

"Because he's a mean sonovabitch. Why do ya think?"

"Why is he so mean? Was he abused?" She looked at him sharply. She didn't think they abused horsed here, she had seen no signs of neglect, but she'd only been here once before.

"Settle down there, lassie. We don't abuse animals around here."

He'd looked so insulted; she couldn't help but believe him.

"No, just people." She mumbled under her breath. She turned back to Storm when he bumped her shoulder with his head. "Hey there handsome." She reached to touch his head tentatively, and he let her.

Frank Jenkins watched the horse react to the woman. The usually unruly animal gentled under her touch again. Kindred spirits, those two. Both so sad. He turned and glared at Cillian O'Donnell. He remembered Cillian's mother. She'd had the same look in her eyes when she'd first come to this island. He hadn't liked it then, and he didn't like it now.

Chloe giggled softly when Storm nudged her again. "I know, big fella. You want your treat, don't you, handsome?" Chloe stuck her hand out flat again with the apple resting in her palm. The horse nipped it off her hand, same as before. She watched him eat it and smiled when he came back for more. "That's it today, big guy." She petted his face and cooed to him for a few minutes.

"Chloe, we're ready to go." Cillian had been holding his breath the entire time. He wanted to pull her away, but the horse didn't seem to react to her the way it did to everyone else. At the sound of his voice, however, the horse raised its head and backed away.

"I'll be back tomorrow." She whispered to the beautiful animal. She turned to see the three men staring at her intently. "Are we going?"

"Yes." Cillian tried not the let his aggravation show. He couldn't believe it; he was jealous of a fucking horse. He took her hand and led her outside to where a stable hand waited with their mounts.

He'd selected a gentle mare for her to ride. He wanted to see her skills for himself before he felt comfortable putting her on one of the more powerful thoroughbreds in his stable.

Chloe petted the neck and face of the pretty, light brown little mare. She was dossal and allowed the attention. "What's her name?" Her question wasn't posed to anyone in particular.

"Butterscotch." Cillian watched her pet the horse as she whispered to it softly.

"Hello Butterscotch. It's very nice to meet you." Chloe introduced herself and patted the horse's nose. Then, without waiting for help, she took the reins from the stable hand and, using the stirrup, mounted the horse with ease. She pulled the reins slightly to the left and was pleased to see the horse responded immediately and turn left. Chloe turned her around in a circle to face Cillian and Finn again to find them watching her. "Are ya'll ready to go?"

They traveled through the dense forest, Cillian beside her with Finn in the lead. The temperature dropped significantly under the shade of the trees. The weather here was much different than the muggy heat of a New Orleans summer. In the sunlight, the temperatures were in the lower eighties, but here in the shade it felt more like the mid to high sixties.

"This trail will lead us out to the coast on the west side of the island." Cillian's melodic voice echoed in the stillness.

Chloe tried not to pay attention to Cillian when he talked. His voice could mesmerize her. The cadence; a deep, musical Irish brogue that made her shiver. It frustrated the crap out of her. So, she didn't respond to his continued attempts at conversation. She needed a break. Instead, she focused on the familiarity of the movement of the horse. The familiar smells of horse and pine.

Her mind wandered back to her grandfather's ranch and the weeks she and Sidney had spent there every summer from the time she was six years old. It had been so much fun learning to ride her horse, swimming in the pond at the back of his property, and riding dirt bikes through the trails. Several times in the earlier years, Brock would show up unexpectedly and ride with them.

Those times were the best. He didn't seem to mind entertaining two young girls, letting them run wild and making them giggle at the crazy stories he'd invent.

She was quiet. Too quiet. Cillian talked about the trails and the terrain. They'd stopped to watch a fox scurry across the path several yards ahead of them. She'd smiled at the fox, but didn't comment. He couldn't say she was sulking. That wasn't her way. No, she was thinking, contemplating, completely wrapped up in her own head.

About an hour later, they exited the forest onto a white, sandy beach similar to the one in front of the castle. They traveled a few miles down the coast before turning back into the trees. The warm breeze off the water was a welcome contrast to the coolness of the shaded forest. A mile or two back inland, the forest opened up again. Wide-open fields of gold stretched out in the distance.

"What kind of crop is this?"

"It's barley." He'd been pointing out points of interest and telling her a little about the island. But other than nodding every once in a while, Chloe hadn't spoken a word in over an hour. She was obviously comfortable with silence. He was surprised, especially given her age. Most of the women he'd met over the years chattered incessantly. Normally her silence would've been a welcome change. But if she didn't talk to him, he had no way of knowing what she was thinking. And he could almost see the wheels in her head turning.

"What do you make with it?" She continued to lead her horse along the trail through the fields, but watched the tractors as they moved along the rows of crops.

"Whiskey."

She nodded, but didn't take her eyes off of the fields.

"We have a distillery here on the island. We'll pass it on our route so you'll get to see it. We also have a vineyard and winery. It's further inland, so the occasional high winds off the coast cause less damage to the grapes."

"So, you're in the whiskey and wine business?" She hadn't realized the island was so largely utilized.

"Among other things." He waited to see if she would ask about the 'other' things. But she didn't.

They rode past the distillery and took a dirt road that cut through another wooded area. A few miles further and they came to a village of small cottages. There were about twenty of them and a small store. When they stopped in front of the store, she dismounted before Cillian could help her down.

He scowled when she followed Finn's lead and tied off the reins to a post. She was quick and obviously a very accomplished rider. He held out his hand to her and dared her with his eyes to deny him.

Chloe peeked over her shoulder and saw several people outside of their homes, watching them.

Cillian raised his eyebrow in that arrogant way she hated. Daring her.

She sighed in resignation. If she didn't take his hand, she'd be breaking one of his rules. So, she kept her eyes focused over his shoulder, and put her hand in his. He wrapped his large warm palm around her smaller, colder one and pulled her into his side. She gritted her teeth, but didn't fight him.

"You're cold." Her hand was like ice. She hadn't complained about the lower temperatures as they'd traveled through the woods. Not once.

"Not really." She wasn't freezing or anything.

They followed Finn into the small store. The place smelled heavenly. Like warm apple pie and spices. A frail elderly woman at the counter greeted them with a huge smile. Her shoulders were hunched with age and her once red hair was streaked with gray, curling wildly around her thin face. She wore bright red lipstick and her green eyes were alive with mischief.

"Hello Finnigan, Cillian. What a wonderful surprise. And who is this beauty you've brought to meet me?" Her smile widened and her eyes lit up when then landed on Chloe and Cillian's joined hands.

"Anita, this is my woman, Chloe. Chloe, this is Anita. She runs the store." Cillian wrapped his arm around Chloe and pulled her in front of him as he introduced her.

She instinctively stiffened in his hold.

Cillian felt her go rigid, so he squeezed her back tight against his front and kissed the top of her head. When he did, she subtly moved her foot on top of his and pressed down hard with the heel of her boot.

He chuckled in her ear and squeezed her tighter in retaliation.

Anita beamed at Cillian's introduction. "Hello Chloe. Call me Nettie. Everybody does." She bustled around to the front of the counter and took

Chloe's hand. "My heavens, Frank said you were lovely, but his description didn't do you justice, lass."

"Frank?" Chloe wondered who Frank was. She clasped Anita's hand for fear she might trip in her enthusiasm.

"Frank Jenkins. My grouchy, pain in the ass little brother. Oh, my, but your hands are freezing! I have just the thing. Molly!" Nettie yelled over her shoulder. A second later a pretty young brunette came from the back of the store, wiping her hands on the apron around her waist.

"Gram, you don't need to yell." The brunette chided, and came to stand beside Nettie.

"Chloe, this is my granddaughter, Molly. She makes the best apple hand pies you'll ever eat. Sells um all over Ireland."

Molly smiled sweetly. "I would shake your hand Chloe, but they're covered in sugar. It's very nice to meet you."

"Hello, it's nice to meet you, too. Apple hand pies? Is that what smells so delicious?"

"Yes. I just pulled a batch out of the oven. Come on back. I'll fix you a hot chocolate too. That should warm you up." She smiled openly at Chloe, then motioned over her shoulder.

"That sounds wonderful." Chloe pointedly stepped out of Cillian's hold, leaving him and Finn with Nettie, and followed Molly to the back of the store. Dozens of small pies were lined up on a counter to cool. "Nettie says you sell these all over Ireland?" Chloe asked as Molly handed her a warm pie wrapped in baker's paper.

"Yes. Try it, but be careful, they're hot."

Chloe broke off a corner piece, blew on the steamy confection, then popped it into her mouth. The sweet, tart filling burst on her tongue. And the crust was so delicate and buttery. She rolled her eyes in appreciation. "Oh my gosh, these are so good!"

Molly beamed with pride. "Thank you. It took a few years to perfect the recipe. I've been working on it for a while. In the beginning I just baked for the people here on the island and they had to be my taste testers while I worked to perfect it. Now my business has expanded and is doing really well."

"I'll bet. These are delicious."

Molly smiled. "I'm glad you like them. Have a seat, I'll fix you some hot chocolate to go with it."

"Molly, Finn and I'll have some of that hot chocolate too if you don't mind." Cillian came to stand behind the Chloe's chair, placing his hands on the bar in front of her, caging her in.

It was nearly dark when they made their way back to the castle. Chloe had learned a lot from their visit to the store. Like the fact that Old Man Jenkins was indeed Frank Jenkins, Nettie's younger brother. He'd been the head stable manager until he partially retired several years back. He and Nettie had lived on the island all their lives.

Nettie proudly told her that her family had lived on the island and worked for the O'Donnell's for generations. Her husband had been one of Cillian's grandfather's personal guards. He'd died of colon cancer over ten years ago.

Molly was her only grandchild and together they ran the store for the people who lived on the island. Molly's husband worked for Cillian at the distillery and they had a three-year-old daughter named Annie. Molly was six years older than she was and other than her years away at college, she'd lived on the island her entire life.

While they'd chatted, Molly had carefully packed up several pies and insisted she take them with her back to the castle for later.

She liked the two women. She didn't want to, but like Imogen, they seemed to be really nice people.

The rest of the ride across the island had taken another two hours. She'd gotten to see the vineyard and toured the winery. Cillian's wine and his whiskey businesses were thriving industries. He'd also explained about the horses, telling her about the breeding programs and stud services of their champion lines. She imagined he did really well for himself. However, considering the number of soldiers on the island, she didn't think that all of his enterprises were entirely legal.

About a half an hour ago, Cillian and Finn had both suddenly gotten quiet. Cillian had been preoccupied with his phone and the muscle in his jaw was twitching as if he were furious. As soon as they'd walked into the foyer, he'd kissed her forehead. Then he and Finn had excused themselves and disappeared into his office.

She'd gone up to their suite and taken a shower to wash away the dust and sand from the ride. Now she was sitting at the vanity dressed in her robe, drying her hair. Cillian came up behind her. The closed off expression on his face was an unfamiliar look. She switched off the drying and met his eyes in the mirror and waited.

"I have to leave for a few days, angel." Cillian ran his fingers through her soft hair. He wasn't ready to leave her so soon, but one of his crews had been ambushed. There were casualties, but they'd still completed the shipment. He needed to assess the damage and unfortunately, it had to be in person.

"Alright. Am I going with you or staying here on the island?" She asked calmly. She tried not to look or sound too excited about the possibility of being away from him.

"You're going to stay here." He wondered if she'd wanted to go with him so she might have a chance to escape or if she wanted to stay so she would have time away from him.

"Ok. Do I have to stay in the castle?"

"No. You can go pretty much anywhere you want on the island, but not without Rourke or Patrick. Is that Understood?"

"Yes."

"Don't forget the rules, angel." Cillian stared at her for a few seconds more before moving to take his shower.

He dressed and packed his bag in record time. Finn was probably waiting for him downstairs by now, but he didn't care. He found Chloe sitting on the couch in the front room. He dropped his bag by the door, walked over, and picked her up. He sat on the couch and positioned her on his lap, her legs straddling him. He fisted her hair in one hand, tilted her head back and, using his other hand, held her jaw open for his kiss so she couldn't bite him in retaliation. He drank his fill of her sweetness.

When he finally lifted his head, her lips were swollen. He touched her full bottom lip with the tip of his finger, then ran it down her chin and throat to her collar. He lifted it slightly and moved his finger slowly under the jewels. He stared into those cornflower blue eyes for a few minutes longer, then whispered, "Be good, Chloe." before releasing the collar. He lifted her off his lap and settled her on the couch again, then headed toward the door.

"Cillian?" She needed to know for her own peace of mind.

His hand on the doorknob, he glanced back over his shoulder at her. "Yes?"

"Are you ever going to let me go?" She chewed on her bottom lip while she waited for his answer.

"No." He watched her for a moment longer. Watched her face fall in dejection. Watched the tears slide down her cheeks, let the image of her in this moment burn into his brain. Then he turned and left without another word.

Chloe laid on the sofa and cried for what felt like hours. After she'd cried herself dry, she'd gotten angry. Then she'd searched their suite for a weapon she could use on Cillian when he came back. There were knives in the kitchen, but she wanted a gun. He could probably take the knife from her before she did any damage, but a gun she could use from a distance. She didn't find anything other than the suspiciously locked wardrobe against the wall in the bedroom. It was huge, with double doors, both locked up tight. She wondered what was in there, but she had no idea how to pick the lock. She had the passing thought to try it, but what did you use to pick a lock with?

While she was considering what would work best, Rourke knocked on the outer door, startling her, causing her to jump with a squeak. She blushed beet red, as if she'd been caught with her hand in the cookie jar, so she glared at the closed door. "What?"

"Food's here."

She opened the door so he could roll the cart inside.

"Cillian wanted me to tell you that if you need anything while he's gone to just ask Imogen. You can also ask me or Patrick." Her eyes were swollen and red and it was obvious she'd been crying.

"Do you know when he'll be back?" She was disgusted that he could tell she'd been crying.

"No. Could be a day or two, could be a week." Rourke looked around the suite, then back at the cart before looking at her. "What are you doing in here, lass?"

"Nothing."

He grinned, "You have a terrible poker face."

"Humph." She crossed her arms over her chest and cocked her leg out.

That made him chuckle. "Do you need anything else right now?"

Chloe looked around the room. She wanted to rip him a new one, but it wasn't his fault his boss was an ass. "Um, I didn't see a TV."

"There's one in the bedroom."

She frowned. "Where?"

"Come on, I'll show you." He walked into the other room and went to the coffee table in the sitting area. He opened a drawer under the table and pulled out a large keyboard and showed it to her.

When she didn't take it, he held it up for her to see and hit a large button in the center. She gasped in surprise when a panel slid away to reveal a TV and stereo system. "No way!"

Rourke smirked. "Pretty clever, huh?"

"I'll say. How do you turn it on?"

Rourke spent a few minutes showing her how to use the weird keyboard remote to turn on the TV, change channels and to switch it to stereo. "Do you need anything else?"

"I don't think so. Thanks." She was fascinated with the remote, and so engrossed in finding something to watch that she didn't notice when Rourke discreetly left.

Cillian was already logged in to Netflix, so she started scrolling through the library when an idea came to her. She clicked back to the main menu and logged out of his account. Then she tried to log into her own account so it would send the notification to her parents that it usually sent. She couldn't remember if the notification included a location, but at least they'd know someone was using her account. When she hit enter, the screen turned black, then a message appeared in bold yellow letters that read; "Nice try Chloe," with a 'smilie face' beneath it. "Sonovabitch!" Before she could try again, the screen changed back, and the system logged back into Cillian's account.

Disgusted at the level of Cillian's security, she scrolled through the library. She found Friends and clicked on season one to start the first episode. At least that was familiar. Friends' reruns were always playing on one channel or another at home. She went back to the dinner tray and removed the cover. She smiled when she saw the steak and baked potato. She also found cheesecake with a chocolate sauce for dessert. Her stomach growled in anticipation. She ignored the opened bottle of wine in the ice bucket and brought her plate and a glass of water back into the bedroom and ate in front of the TV.

When she returned her empty plate to the cart, she poured a glass of wine and brought it back to the couch and cuddled into her blanket to watch another episode. On her second glass, the show on the television faded into the background as her thoughts turned to her current situation.

She couldn't live like this. Feeling vulnerable and unsure all the time. She needed to figure out how to get through this until she could escape. She took a mental assessment. Aside from that horrible woman, Roisin, the people here had been nice to her. The weird thing was, they all seemed very pleased that she was here. She still hadn't figured that one out. Even her guards, Patrick and Rourke, those big, mean looking, scary as hell men seemed to go out of their way to be nice to her.

Now that she had time to think about it, even Cillian hadn't hurt her. Not really. He hadn't beaten her. Even when she'd hit him, he hadn't retaliated with violence. It could have been so much worse than a few swats on her ass. If anything, he'd been gentle, teasing, and charismatic, just determined to get what he wanted.

Chloe wrapped the blanket tighter around herself and took a third glass of wine out onto the balcony. She huddled in a chair and quietly listened as the waves crashed onto the shore off in the distance.

While she watched the stars, she thought about all the things Cillian had done to her and felt a blush burn across her skin. Jesus, it was intense. He could make her need his touch. In the heat of the moment, even crave it. That need, that craving, and then there was that little bite of pain, the edginess of it setting her senses on fire. It was as if he could see inside her to that secret place of longing. Yea, she'd secretly dreamed of a dominant lover, of how sexy it would be. Which was probably why no other man had ever piqued her interest before.

But not like this. She'd been struggling with the shame of feeling so much pleasure when her parents' safety was a risk. She should not enjoy his touch the way she did. And certainly not at the expense of her family.

Chloe looked up at the stars and made that promise to herself. Never again. She would never again feel ashamed of what she couldn't control. She'd do what was necessary to ensure the safety of her parents, but she wouldn't be ashamed anymore. And, she'd still fight him. She made that promise as well. She'd never go to him willingly. Not as long as he threatened her parents.

She cuddled into the chair on the balcony and sipped her wine. Now that she'd made that decision, she felt lighter. Her conscience felt clear. She'd follow his stupid rules, and she'd learn to find peace in this place. At least until she figured out how to both escape and keep her parents safe at the same time. And she would escape. The first chance she got.

At 30,000 feet over the Atlantic, Cillian watched Chloe through the live feed on his phone until she went out onto the balcony. He cursed himself for not installing cameras out there. He was restless. There was work to be done. His men needed leadership. They relied on him, so he had to stay sharp. With a frustrated sigh, he closed the app on his phone and turned his chair back to his desk and faced Finn again. And they continued to strategize.

Chloe's internal clock woke her at 5:15 the next morning. She rolled out of bed and dressed for her run, then went into the den. There was a bowl of fruit on the bar in the kitchen, filled with apples and bananas. She smiled, remembering Finn's instructions for her to eat a banana before she ran in the mornings. This must be his way of ensuring she did what she was told.

She grabbed a banana and peeled it as she opened the door. Patrick was leaning against the doorframe, dressed for their run. As always, gun holsters on display.

"Where's the hat?"

"Shoot, hold on." She finished off the banana as she went to get the baseball cap. She pulled her ponytail through the back hole and she adjusted in low over her eyes. "Ready?" She tilted her head way back to see Patrick under the bill.

"Let's do this."

They took the same route as the day before. The burn of her muscles and the breeze on her heated skin making her feel alive. On the last stretch, she put on a burst of speed and raced Patrick across the manicured lawn. She was laughing by the time they reached the back patio.

"I almost had you, old man." She laughed as she tried to catch her breath.

"Who're you callin an old man?"

"If the shoe fits?" She caught her breath and turned just as Imogen hurried through the door, carrying a tray with a pitcher of ice water and two glasses.

"Watch it runt."

"You two got back faster than you did yesterday. I'd meant to have this waiting for you." She put the tray on a table and filled the glasses.

"That's because Chloe thinks she can outrun me." Patrick bumped Chloe's shoulder on their way to the table.

She bumped him back and reached for the glass.

"Chloe, are you ready for your breakfast, or do you want to shower first?"

"I'll shower first. I won't be long." She refilled her glass and took it with her up to her room.

She showered and dressed in khaki shorts and an ice blue silk top and slipped on a pair of light brown leather sandals. She'd pulled her hair into another ponytail because it was still slightly damp, but she was too hungry to care.

When she stepped into the dining room, the aroma of syrup and bacon had her mouthwatering in anticipation. She absolutely loved pancakes. She put two on her plate, looked around at the empty room, then added a third. She dipped bacon in the warm syrup and relished in the salty, sweet combination. At her second bit of the fluffy pancakes, Imogen came in with fresh coffee.

Chloe looked around again while Imogen filled her cup. It was strange to be in the dining room without Cillian and Finn. Until Imogen had come in, the silence had been weird. "Um Imogen?"

"Yes?" Imogen placed the small tray with the cream and sugar Chloe liked next to her coffee cup.

"Would it be strange, um, I mean, do you think I could eat in the kitchen? Would it be too disruptive for the staff?" She tried not to look too hopeful. But sitting here by herself wasn't fun.

"Of course not." Imogen looked around the empty room, then back at Chloe. "Grab your plate, I'll get your coffee."

She did as she was told and followed Imogen into the bustling kitchen. When she came through the door, all chatter and movement stopped as the staff stared at her. She paused at their intense regard, but she refused to feel self-conscious. Instead, she lifted her chin and smiled at them. "Good morning."

No one spoke, but several nodded, and all of them smiled.

"Back to work with you now." Imogen instructed as she led the way to a small kitchen table off to the side. The staff immediately went back to their chores at her command.

When Chloe looked up, she was surprised to see Patrick and Rourke at the table. Both shoveling pancakes into their mouths. They looked up at her with matching surprised expressions. She rolled her eyes at them, causing them both the grin.

Rourke scooted over to make room for her.

"I thought you'd be sleeping by now." She took her seat and Imogen put her coffee next to her, then left them to eat.

"I'll be finding my bed soon enough. It's much easier to sleep on a full stomach." Rourke patted his hard belly.

"Do you always take the night shift?"

"No, we swap up every other week."

"Is this a new assignment because of me?" She'd wondered that from the beginning.

"No. We always guard Cillian, and now you." Rourke shrugged his shoulders and went back to eating.

"Why?" She knew why they were guarding her. She was a prisoner, but why Cillian.

"Because we're assigned to you now. Your safety is our responsibility when Cillian and Finn aren't around." Patrick answered.

"No, I mean why have you always guarded Cillian?" He seemed strong enough to take care of himself, as far as she was concerned.

"He's a powerful man, lass." Patrick answered. When she lifted a delicate brow, he grinned and continued. "And he's one of the last living descendent of a very powerful line of rulers here in Ireland. There are some who want to extinguish his line completely and it's our job to keep that from happening."

"What do mean, like royalty or something?" She looked between the brothers as Rourke choked on his coffee and she was sure Patrick kicked him under the table.

"Something like that." Rourke choked out.

Patrick put down his fork and faced her. "You see, hundreds of years ago, Ireland was led by only a few powerful families. Those families, the wealthiest and the strongest, ruled over specific territories and governed as they saw fit. That select few were held in high regard by their people because they kept them safe and provided for them."

"As decedents died off or were killed, the other families absorbed those territories," Rourke added. "Or sometimes a new leader would step into power if he was strong enough and had the resources at his disposal to take it. But that never happened without massive bloodshed as they waged war on those who were too vulnerable or lacked allies to help them keep it."

Chloe thought this sounded like an old fable. She took another bite of her pancakes and chewed while she thought it over. "But what does that have to do with Cillian?"

"The O'Donnell's have always held this territory. Through the centuries, they have proven to be the strongest, the most vicious, as well as the most cunning of all the ruling families. Now, they're the wealthiest as well."

"That sounds like something out of a movie."

"It's not." Both brothers said at the same time.

"I was pretty good in history and I've never heard of this before."

"That's because the Irish are steeped in tradition and have always kept to the philosophy of 'don't ask, don't tell.'" Rourke said and popped his last piece of bacon into his mouth.

"So, this island is the O'Donnell territory, and Cillian governs it?" Holy crap! She exhaled slowly, trying to ease the butterflies in her stomach.

Patrick dreaded telling her this part, but she needed to know. He couldn't have her trying to escape. "Not just the island. The O'Donnell territory extends hundreds of miles into the mainland as well. But the island is the O'Donnell strong hold because of its terrain. The sheer rock wall of the mountain facing the back has protected it from attack for centuries. It's the main reason his ancestors claimed this island so long ago. It's nearly impenetrable."

Chloe stared at the brothers. This was awful. Even if she were to escape the island, she'd have to travel for hundreds of miles to get out of his territory? "What about local government or the police?"

The brothers shared a measured look before Patrick answered carefully. "Chloe, the local Garda are all on Cillian's payroll as is the commissioner."

She felt the pancakes settle into her stomach like a led weight. A feeling of hopelessness assailed her. How the hell was she supposed to get out of this!

Chloe went straight to the beach after breakfast. She was careful to follow the same routine as the day before, and when she settled on her rock, she took a shuddering breath. Now that she knew who Cillian really was, she didn't think her message in the sand was going to help, but she needed to do it, anyway. She had to feel like she was helping herself. She couldn't just sit here and do nothing. She watched the waves and thought about all that the brothers had told her.

This was bad. This was really bad. If he was that powerful, no wonder he thought he could have her just because he wanted her. He really was used to getting what he wanted. Jesum Petes! Wasn't that just her luck? Well, she wasn't going down without a fight. Chloe picked up a pebble from the loose gravel on her perch and, with a flick of her wrist, hummed it into the waves.

"Woow! That went really far. I bet I can throw one farther."

Chloe looked to her right at the sound of a boy's voice and was surprised to see one working his way up to her perch. "Who are you?"

"I'm Ian. Are you Chloe?"

"How do you know my name?"

"Everybody's knows who you are. You really are as pretty as they say. I just wanted to see. Gram says I'm not supposed to bother you though. Am I bothering you?"

Chloe couldn't help but smile. Ian perched on the rock below hers and stared up at her with big green eyes. Short red curls blew around his head like a mop in the brisk breeze. A small smattering of freckles dotted his tanned face, evidence he spent a lot of time in the sun. The hopeful expression on his adorable face was hard to resist. "No, you're not bothering me."

Chloe looked over Ian's shoulder to see where Patrick was, in case this kid might be in danger. She was relieved to see that, although he was watching, he hadn't attempted to approach them.

"Gram says you're from America."

"I am."

"You talk funny."

"I could say the same about you."

"I guess. What are you doing out on this rock?"

"I like to sit here and watch the waves. It's a good place to think."

"What are you thinking about?"

"Nothing in particular. Who's your gram?"

"Imogen. I live here with her now."

"You do?"

"Yes. I used to live in Doolin with my mum and my da but they died, so I had to come live here."

"I'm so sorry to hear that. When did that happen?"

"When I was five."

"How old are you now?"

"I'm twelve and a half. I'll be thirteen in November."

Chloe scooted over and patted the surface beside her. Ian climbed up the rest of the way and sat down. He was a little gangly, but agile, with a boy's athletic build. At twelve, he was already bigger than she was. "I'm sorry you lost your parents." She couldn't imagine losing hers. She'd lost Brock at ten and it had devastated her.

"Me too. But I get to live here now."

"Do you enjoy living here?"

"Sure, but there's no baseball or football or anything. So, it's boring sometimes."

"I played softball in school."

"Were you any good?"

"Yes."

"Maybe we could throw sometime."

"I supposed we could, but I don't have a glove here."

"That's ok. I can ask Gram. She can get you one."

If she had her way, she wouldn't be here long enough for that. But since it was a possibility, she didn't think it would hurt.

"Well, if you can come up with a glove, I'll throw with you. Where do you go to school?" She hadn't seen a school anywhere, but wondered if Cillian had brought in tutors for the kids on the island.

"I take on-line classes. I have literature in an hour."

He didn't sound too pleased about it. "Literature is fun."

"No, it's not. You have to write papers all the time."

"Don't you like to write?"

"No. It's boring. Plus, I never know what to write about."

"Does your teacher let you pick the topic?"

"Yes."

"Then write about what you like to do. My best friend loves to write. She going to school to be a writer. She says that you just have to pick something you like and then start writing about it without stopping for ten minutes. She says that's the best way to get started."

Ian picked up a pebble and flicked his wrist and it went sailing out into the water, much further than hers did. He cut his eyes to her and grinned triumphantly. "Told you I could through it farther."

"I didn't know we were in a competition." She picked up another pebble and threw it. Hers fell a little short of his mark.

She sat with Ian and they threw rocks into the waves until he had to leave for class. After he left, she climbed off the rock and headed for her studio.

Chloe found a rhythm over the next week. Running in the mornings and visiting the beach and sitting on her rock after having breakfast in the kitchen with the twins. Sometimes Ian showed up to sit with her. He'd bring a sack of small rocks for them to throw when he came. They kept a continuous score and so far, he was winning. Somehow, he'd also found a glove for her. So, some days they spent time on the lawn playing catch.

And she painted. She painted a lot. Imogen brought her lunch in a picnic basket every day and every afternoon, Chloe brought the basket back to her before changing her clothes and heading out to ride.

She went to see Storm and verbally sparred with Frank before each ride because she always brought an apple with her. Frank's habit of glowering at her was amusing, so she gave as good as she got. When his lips twitched as if fighting a smile, she'd consider it a point for her and make a tick in the air with her finger. Then he'd scowl, which caused her to giggle.

She visited Nettie and Molly at the store every day. Molly was always ready with hot chocolate and a pie and they'd sit for an hour and chat. She learned a lot about the people on the island through them and met several as they came and went to do their shopping. On the third day, she got to meet Molly's little girl, Annie. And she had fun playing dolls on the floor behind the counter with the precocious toddler.

But her evenings were spent in her room, where she ate in front of the TV. With Cillian gone, it was easier to get into a routine that she could live with. And every night, she spent time on the balcony thinking about her family. Wondering what Sidney was doing, how she was spending her summer. If she was so worried about her that she wasn't enjoying her time before going back to

laid on the sofa and cried for what felt like hours. After she'd cried herself dry, she'd gotten angry. Then she'd searched their suite for a weapon she could use on Cillian when he came back. There were knives in the kitchen, but she wanted a gun. He could probably take the knife from her before she did any damage, but a gun she could use from a distance. She didn't find anything other than the suspiciously locked wardrobe against the wall in the bedroom. It was huge, with double doors, both locked up tight. She wondered what was in there, but she had no idea how to pick the lock. She had the passing thought to try it, but what did you use to pick a lock with?

While she was considering what would work best, Rourke knocked on the outer door, startling her, causing her to jump with a squeak. She blushed beet red, as if she'd been caught with her hand in the cookie jar, so she glared at the closed door. "What?"

"Food's here."

She opened the door so he could roll the cart inside.

"Cillian wanted me to tell you that if you need anything while he's gone to just ask Imogen. You can also ask me or Patrick." Her eyes were swollen and red, so it was obvious she'd been crying.

"Do you know when he'll be back?" She was disgusted that he could tell she'd been crying. That just pissed her off more.

"No. Could be a day or two, could be a week." Rourke looked around the suite, then back at the cart before looking at her. "What are you doing in here, lass?"

"Nothing."

He grinned, "You have a terrible poker face."

"Humph." She crossed her arms over her chest and cocked her leg out.

That made him chuckle. "Do you need anything else right now?"

Chloe looked around the room. She wanted to rip him a new one, but it wasn't his fault his boss was an ass. "Um, I didn't see a TV."

"There's one in the bedroom."

She frowned. "Where?"

"Come on, I'll show you." He walked into the other room and went to the coffee table in the sitting area. He opened a drawer under the coffee table and pulled out a large keyboard and showed it to her.

When she didn't take it, he held it up for her to see and hit a large button in the center. She was shocked when a panel slid away to reveal a TV and stereo system. "No way!"

Rourke smirked. "Pretty clever, huh?"

"I'll say. How do you turn it on?"

Rourke spent a few minutes showing her how to use the weird keyboard remote to turn on the TV, change channels and to switch it to stereo. "Do you need anything else?"

"I don't think so. Thanks." She was fascinated with the remote, and so engrossed in finding something to watch that she didn't notice when Rourke discreetly left.

Cillian was already logged in to Netflix, so she started scrolling through the library when an idea came to her. She clicked back to the main menu and logged out of his account. Then she tried to log into her own account so it would send the notification to her parents that it normally did. She couldn't remember if it sent a location with the notification, but at least they'd know someone was using her account. When she hit enter, the screen turned black, then a message appeared in bold yellow letters that read; "Nice try Chloe," with a 'smilie face' beneath it. "Sonovabitch!" Before she could try again, the screen changed back, and the system logged back into Cillian's account.

Disgusted at the level of Cillian's security, she scrolled through the library. She found Friends and clicked on season one to start the episode.

At least that was familiar. Friends' reruns were always playing on one channel or another at home. She went back to the dinner tray and removed the cover. She smiled when she saw the steak and baked potato. She also found cheesecake with a chocolate sauce for dessert. Her stomach growled at the delicious smells. She ignored the opened bottle of wine in the ice bucket and brought her plate and glass of water back into the bedroom and ate in front of the TV.

When she returned her empty plate to the cart, she poured a glass of wine and brought it back to the couch and cuddled into her blanket to watch another episode. On her second glass, the show on the television faded into the background as her thoughts turned to her current situation.

She couldn't live like this. Feeling vulnerable and unsure all the time. She needed to figure out how to get through this until she could escape. She took a mental assessment. Aside from that horrible woman, Roisin, the people here had been nice to her. The weird thing was, they all seemed very pleased that she was here. She still hadn't figured that one out. Even her guards, Patrick and Rourke, those big, mean looking, scary as hell men seemed to go out of their way to be nice to her.

Now that she had time to think about it, even Cillian hadn't hurt her. Not really. Well, he'd had sex with her against her will. No means no. But he hadn't been violent about it. He hadn't beaten her. Even when she'd hit him, he hadn't retaliated with violence. It could have been so much worse than a few swats on her ass. It stung, but wasn't anything she couldn't handle. No, if anything, he'd been gentle, teasing and charismatic, just determined to get what he wanted.

Chloe wrapped the blanket tighter around herself and took a third glass of wine out onto the balcony. She listened to the waves crash onto the shore off in the distance.

As she watched the stars, she thought back to the things Cillian had done to her and felt a blush burn her skin. Jesus, it was so intense. He could make her to need him. In the heat of the moment, even crave him. That need, that craving, and then there was that little bite of pain, the edginess of it setting her senses on fire. It freaked her out. She'd felt ashamed of the way she reacted to it. To him. But no more.

Chloe looked up at the stars and made that promise to herself. Never again. She would never again feel ashamed of what she couldn't control. Oh, she'd still fight him. She made that promise as well. She'd never go to him willingly. Ever. Her dad raised a fighter, so she'd fight.

She cuddled into a chair on the balcony and sipped her wine. Now that she'd made that decision, she felt lighter. Her conscience felt clear. She'd follow his stupid rules, and she'd learn to find peace in this place. At least until she figured out how to both escape and keep her parents safe at the same time. And she would escape. The first chance she got.

At 30,000 feet over the Atlantic, Cillian watched Chloe through the live feed on his phone until she went out onto the balcony. He cursed himself for not installing cameras out there. He was restless. There was work to be done. His men needed leadership. They relied on him, so he had to stay sharp. With a frustrated sigh, he closed the app on his phone and turned his chair back to his desk and faced Finn again. And they continued to strategize.

Chloe's internal clock woke her at 5:15 the next morning. She rolled out of bed and dressed for her run, then went into the den. There was a bowl of fruit on the bar in the kitchen, filled with apples and bananas. She smiled, remembering Finn's instructions for her to eat a banana before she ran in the mornings. This must be his way of ensuring she did what she was told.

She grabbed a banana and peeled it as she opened the door. Patrick was leaning against the doorframe, dressed for their run. As always, gun holsters on display.

"Where's the hat?"

"Shoot, hold on." She finished off the banana as she went to get the baseball cap. She pulled her ponytail through the back hole and she adjusted in low over her eyes. "Ready?" She tilted her head way back to see Patrick under the bill.

"Let's do this."

They took the same route as the day before. The burn of her muscles and the breeze on her heated skin making her feel alive. On the last stretch, she put on a burst of speed and raced Patrick across the manicured lawn. She was laughing by the time they reached the back patio.

"I almost had you, old man." She laughed as she tried to catch her breath.

"Who're you callin an old man?"

"If the shoe fits?" She caught her breath and turned just as Imogen hurried through the door, carrying a tray with a pitcher of ice water and two glasses.

"Watch it runt."

"You two got back faster than you did yesterday. I'd meant to have this waiting for you." She put the tray on a table and filled the glasses.

"That's because Chloe thinks she can outrun me." Patrick bumped Chloe's shoulder on their way to the table.

She bumped him back and reached for the glass.

158

"Chloe, are you ready for your breakfast, or do you want to shower first?"

"I'll shower first. I won't be long." She refilled her glass and took it with her up to her room.

She showered and dressed in khaki shorts and an ice blue silk top and slipped on a pair of light brown leather sandals. She'd pulled her hair into another ponytail because it was still slightly damp, but she was too hungry to care.

When she stepped into the dining room, the aroma of syrup and bacon had her mouthwatering in anticipation. She absolutely loved pancakes. She put two on her plate, looked around at the empty room, then added a third. She dipped bacon in the warm syrup and relished in the salty, sweet combination. At her second bit of the fluffy pancakes, Imogen came in with fresh coffee.

Chloe looked around again while Imogen filled her cup. It was strange to be in the dining room without Cillian and Finn. Until Imogen had come in, the silence had been weird. "Um Imogen?"

"Yes, dear?" Imogen placed the small tray with the cream and sugar Chloe liked next to her coffee cup.

"Would it be strange, um, I mean, do you think I could eat in the kitchen? Would it be too disruptive for the staff?" She tried not to look too hopeful. But sitting here by herself wasn't fun.

"Of course not." Imogen looked around the empty room, then back at Chloe. "Grab your plate, I'll get your coffee."

She did as she was told and followed Imogen into the bustling kitchen. When she came through the door, all chatter and movement stopped as the staff stared at her. She paused at their intense regard and nearly stumbled, but she refused to feel self-conscious. Instead, she lifted her chin and smiled at them. "Good morning."

No one spoke, but several nodded, and all of them smiled.

"Back to work with you now." Imogen instructed as she led the way to a small kitchen table off to the side. The staff immediately went back to their chores at her command.

When Chloe looked up, she was surprised to see Patrick and Rourke at the table. Both shoveling pancakes into their mouths. They looked up at her with matching surprised expressions. She rolled her eyes at them, causing them both the grin.

Rourke scooted over to make room for her.

"I thought you'd be sleeping by now." She took her seat and Imogen put her coffee next to her, then left them to eat.

"I'll be finding my bed soon enough. It's much easier to sleep on a full stomach." Rourke patted his hard belly.

"Do you always take the night shift?"

"No, we swap up every other week."

"Is this a new assignment because of me?" She'd wondered that from the beginning.

"No. We always guard Cillian, and now you." Rourke shrugged his shoulders and went back to eating.

"Why?" She knew why they were guarding her. She was a prisoner, but why Cillian.

"Because we're assigned to you now. Your safety is our responsibility when Cillian and Finn aren't around." Patrick answered.

"No, I mean why have you always guarded Cillian?" He seemed strong enough to take care of himself, as far as she was concerned.

"He's a powerful man, lass." Patrick answered. When she lifted a delicate brow, he grinned and continued. "And he's the last living descendent of a very powerful line of rulers here in Ireland. There are some who want to extinguish his line completely and it's our job to keep that from happening."

"What do mean, like royalty or something?" She looked between the brothers as Rourke choked on his coffee and she was sure Patrick kicked him under the table.

"Something like that." Rourke choked out.

Patrick put down his fork and faced her. "You see, hundreds of years ago, Ireland was led by only a few powerful families. Those families, the wealthiest and the strongest, ruled over specific territories and governed as they saw fit. That select few were held in high regard by their people because they kept them safe and provided for them."

"As decedents died off or were killed, the other families absorbed those territories," Rourke added. "Or sometimes a new leader would step into power if he was strong enough and had the resources at his disposal to take it. But that never happened without massive bloodshed as they waged war on those who were too vulnerable or lacked allies to help them keep it."

Chloe thought this sounded like an old fable. She took another bite of her pancake and chewed while she thought it over. "But what does that have to do with Cillian?"

"The O'Donnell's have always held this territory. Through the centuries, they have proven to be the strongest, the most vicious, as well as the most cunning of all the ruling families. Now, they're the wealthiest as well."

"That sounds like something out of a movie."

"It's not." Both brothers said at the same time.

"I was pretty good in history and I've never heard of this before."

"That's because the Irish are steeped in tradition and have always kept to the philosophy of 'don't ask, don't tell.'" Rourke said and popped his last piece of bacon into his mouth.

"So, this island is the O'Donnell territory, and Cillian governs it?" Holy crap! She exhaled slowly, trying to ease the butterflies in her stomach.

Patrick dreaded telling her this part, but she needed to know. He couldn't have her trying to escape. "Not just the island. The O'Donnell territory extends hundreds of miles into the mainland as well. But the island is the O'Donnell strong hold because of its terrain. The sheer rock wall of the mountain facing the back has protected it from attack for centuries. It's the main reason his ancestors claimed this island so long ago. It's nearly impenetrable."

Chloe stared at the brothers. This was awful. Even if she were to escape the island, she'd have to travel for hundreds of miles to get out of his territory? "What about local government or the police?"

The brothers shared a measured look before Patrick answered carefully. "Chloe, the local Garda are all on Cillian's payroll as is the commissioner."

She felt the pancakes settle into her stomach like a led weight. A feeling of hopelessness assailed her. How the hell was she supposed to get out of this!

Chloe went straight to the beach after breakfast. She was careful to follow the same routine as the day before, and when she settled on her rock, she took a shuddering breath. Now that she knew who Cillian really was, she didn't think her message in the sand was going to help, but she needed to do it, anyway. She had to feel like she was helping herself. She couldn't just sit here and do nothing. She watched the waves and thought about all that the brothers had told her.

This was bad. This was really bad. If he was that powerful, no wonder he thought he could have her just because he wanted her. He really was used to getting what he wanted. Jesum Petes! Wasn't that just her luck? Well, she wasn't going down without a fight. Chloe picked up a pebble from the loose gravel on her perch and, with a flick of her wrist, hummed it into the waves.

"Woow! That went really far. I bet I can throw one farther."

Chloe looked to her right at the sound of a boy's voice and was surprised to see one working his way up to her perch. "Who are you?"

"I'm Ian. Are you Chloe?"

"How do you know my name?"

"Everybody's knows who you are. You really are as pretty as they say. I just wanted to see. Gram says I'm not supposed to bother you though. Am I bothering you?"

Chloe couldn't help but smile. Ian perched on the rock below hers and stared up at her with big green eyes. Short red curls blew around his head like a mop in the brisk breeze. A small smattering of freckles dotted his tanned face, evidence he spent a lot of time in the sun. The hopeful expression on his adorable face was hard to resist. "No, you're not bothering me."

Chloe looked over Ian's shoulder to see where Patrick was, in case this kid might be in danger. She was relieved to see that, although he was watching, he hadn't attempted to approach them.

"Gram says you're from America."

"I am."

"You talk funny."

"I could say the same about you."

"I guess. What are you doing out on this rock?"

"I like to sit here and watch the waves. It's a good place to think."

"What are you thinking about?"

"Nothing in particular. Who's your gram?"

"Imogen. I live here with her now."

"You do?"

"Yes. I used to live in Doolin with my mum and dad but they died, so I had to come live here."

"I'm so sorry to hear that. When did that happen?"

"When I was five."

"How old are you now?"

"I'm eleven and a half. I'll be twelve in November."

Chloe scooted over and patted to surface beside her. Ian climbed up the rest of the way and sat down. He was a little gangly, but agile, with a boy's athletic build. At eleven, he was already bigger than she was. "I'm sorry you lost your parents." She couldn't imagine losing hers. She'd lost Brock at ten and it had devastated her.

"Me too. But I get to live here now."

"Do you enjoy living here?"

"Sure, but there's no baseball or football or anything. So, it's boring sometimes."

"I played softball in school."

"Were you any good?"

"Yes."

"Maybe we could throw sometime."

"I supposed we could, but I don't have a glove here."

"That's ok. I can ask Gram. She can get you one."

If she had her way, she wouldn't be here long enough for that. But since it was a possibility, she didn't think it would hurt.

"Well, if you can come up with a glove, I'll throw with you. Where do you go to school?" She hadn't seen a school anywhere, but wondered if Cillian had brought in tutors for the kids on the island.

"I take on-line classes. I have literature in an hour."

He didn't sound too pleased about it. "Literature is fun."

"No, it's not. You have to write papers all the time."

"Don't you like to write?"

"No. It's boring. Plus, I never know what to write about."

"Does your teacher let you pick the topic?"

"Yes."

"Then write about what you like to do. My best friend loves to write. She going to school to be a writer. She says that you just have to pick something you like and then start writing about it without stopping for ten minutes. She says that's the best way to get started."

Ian picked up a pebble and flicked his wrist and it went sailing out into the water, much further than hers did. He cut his eyes to her and grinned triumphantly. "Told you I could through it farther."

"I didn't know we were in a competition." She picked up another pebble and threw it. Hers fell a little short of his mark.

She sat with Ian and they both threw rocks into the waves until he had to leave for class. After he left, she climbed off the rock and headed for her studio.

Chloe found a rhythm over the next week. Running in the mornings and visiting the beach and sitting on her rock after having breakfast in the kitchen with the twins. Sometimes Ian showed up to sit with her. He'd bring a sack of small rocks for them to throw when he came. They kept a continuous score and so far, he was winning. Somehow, he'd also found a glove for her. So, some days they spent time on the lawn playing pitch and catch.

And she painted. She painted a lot. Imogen brought her lunch in a picnic basket every day and every afternoon, Chloe brought the basket back to her before changing her clothes and heading out to ride.

She went to see Storm and verbally sparred with Frank before each ride because she always brought an apple with her. Frank's habit of glowering at her was amusing, so she gave as good as she got. When his lips would twitch as if he were fighting a smile and she'd consider it a point for her and make a tick in the air with her finger. That always made him scowl, which caused her to giggle.

She visited Nettie and Molly at the store every day. Molly was always ready with hot chocolate and a pie and they'd sit for an hour and chat. She learned a lot about the people on the island through them and met several as they came and went to do their shopping. On the third day, she got to meet Molly's little girl, Annie. She's had fun playing dolls on the floor behind the counter with the precocious toddler.

Her evenings were spent in her room, where she ate in front of the TV. With Cillian gone, it was easier to get into a routine that she could live with. But every night, she spent time on the balcony thinking about her family. Wondering what Sidney was doing, how she was spending her summer. If she was so worried about her that she wasn't enjoying her time before going back to school.

Chapter 18: This is Us

Cillian sat straddling a metal chair while Andrei Chernoff's naked body swung, bloody and bruised, from a chain in front of him. Andrei was the last living member of the Russian mercenaries who'd ambushed his crew.

Cillian twirled his K-Bar 1211 with its seven-inch blade in his right hand while he eyed the Russian. Shallow, precise one-inch cuts oozing blood covered the entire front of his body, from the top of his head to the bottom of his feet. Not a space had been overlooked. Every fingernail and toenail had been ripped away. Thanks to Finn, five toes, three on one foot and two on the other, were missing, leaving his hands and feet a bloody mess. The acrid smell of blood and urine was a pungent stench in the windowless warehouse. It burned his nose and ignited his fury.

His men from Alpha Team One were exhausted. He was exhausted. They'd been running on fumes for the past few days as they'd closed in on this last asshole. Team One, led by Finn, was a ten-member crew of elite fighters who went wherever he did. His own personal guard. They were the men who'd been with him the longest. Those he trusted most. They were two men short, but that had been his call. He'd ordered Rourke and Patrick to stay back and guard Chloe. Until he figured out who was behind the attack, he wouldn't trust anyone else with her safety.

The surviving three of the eight-man squad of Russian mercenaries had split up immediately upon realizing the attack on his shipment wasn't going to reap the spoils they'd been promised. You'd think they would've done their homework. Based on the information he'd forced from the other two stupid fucks; they'd been completely misinformed. Evidently, whoever hired them said his Team Three was simply an unorganized group of gun runners who were new to the business. Their assignment was supposed to be simple; kill the entire team and keep the weapons' supply for themselves as a bonus. What he needed to know now was who'd hired them.

Their Russian sniper had taken out two of his men before Team Three turned the tables on them. When the tide turned, the remaining three had scattered across the globe. It had taken him fifteen days to run them down. He didn't believe in leaving loose ends, so he needed a name. He knew the first two didn't have it because they would've given up their own mother to make the pain stop. He was very good at inflicting pain. He knew more about the subject than he cared to admit.

Cillian nodded to Finn and watched him cut off another toe. The mercenary's screams echoed off the metal walls of the building before he passed out again. Cillian stood and picked up the bucket of ice water Zane kept refilling and threw its contents into the Russian's face. When that didn't revive him, he lifted the wooden mop handle with a rag wrapped tightly around the end of it, out of the bucket of ammonia, and held it up to the unconscious man's nose. He bucked against his chains as he came awake.

"All you have to do is answer the question and this will stop." Cillian soothed in his musical Irish brogue. "It's very simple."

"I told you; I don't know!" Andrei screamed, tears of pain and rage mixing with the blood on his battered face.

Cillian viciously kicked him in the crotch with a swift front kick, making sure the heel of his boot connected with the man's flaccid, bleeding cock. The blow sent Andrei swinging violently as he let out a blood-curdling scream.

He waited patiently for the screaming to turn to moans before continuing. "Come now Andrei, all I need is a name." His soothing voice such a contrast to the viscous blow.

"Fuck you!" Andrei spat.

"If you insist." Cillian nodded at Finn. Holding him back was difficult. Everyone thought Cillian was the more vicious of the two. He wasn't.

Finn smiled as he picked up the modified, long-handled cattle prod from the table next to Cillian's chair. He held the end out to Terrance, who coated it with lubricant. He'd created it himself and it was one of his favorites.

Terrance was a six-foot, eight-inch black man with a shaved head and a deep jagged scar that ran from the top of his left cheek, down his neck to disappear under the collar of his shirt. He was from England and they'd run across him during their third year of living underground.

Terrance had been an elite soldier for the Queen's army until slavers abducted his sister. He'd lost their trail in Ireland and was fighting in an underground club when Cillian faced him in the rink. It had been a bloody fight that nearly killed them both.

Cillian had been so impressed with his skill and endurance that when the fight was over, he'd offered Terrance a job. That's when they found out about the sister. Cillian used his connections to locate her, then helped him get her out. The girl was a mess by the time they'd found her. Terrance had taken her tiny broken body back home to his family, only to return a few months later after she'd taken her own life. Now he was a mean, emotionless machine. He was vicious, but he was loyal to Cillian to a fault.

Terrance stepped behind Andrei, grabbed his ass cheeks, and forced them apart. Then Finn shoved the prod high up into his rectum and pulled the trigger. The electrical current pulsed continuously as the man convulsed and let out a scream that could probably be heard a mile away.

Cillian watched dispassionately for a minute as the man thrashed violently before nodding at Finn to stop. When Andrei's limp body stopped convulsing, Cillian stepped closer. "We can do this for hours, mate. But you've kept me away from my woman for fifteen fuckin days. That's a long time. So, unless you want Finn here to fuck your ass for a good long ride with that prod, you'll tell me what I want to know. But I'll warn you, in case you get off on that shit, your cock is going to be locked up tight in this trap while he does it."

Cillian lifted the steel spring loaded trap with serrated teeth from the table and held it up for Andrei to see.

Andrei's eyes nearly bulged out of his battered face. "Email! They contacted us through email," he shrieked. Then his pathetic voice pleaded; "we texted after the initial email came through. That's it, I swear!"

Cillian smiled. His gaze moving to Jacob "get his phone." He turned back to Andrei. "Password?" When he didn't immediately start speaking, Cillian opened the steel trap and moved it toward Andrei's cock. "I suppose we're not finished here." The man immediately started babbling numbers.

Jacob, another member of Team One, nodded and held up the phone. "Got it. We're in."

Cillian took the phone and, scrolling quickly, found the email he was looking for. The sender was a series of numbers and letters that didn't tell him shit at first glance. But he'd send the information to Titan. Titan would get what they needed. At least now they had a starting point. He turned back to Andrei and without another word, slit his throat.

Two nights later, Cillian stood naked in the darkened room watching Chloe sleep. His cock swollen and thick. The tip leaking with need. He ached for her. It had been sixteen nights since he'd been inside her tight heat. He'd stared at her pictures on his phone. Watched the live feed of her when he could. He'd jacked off to the first picture he'd taken of her tied to his bed so many times he'd lost count. But he wasn't appeased. He needed her. He craved her. She consumed his thoughts. Distracted him.

She was so fucking beautiful, so innocent. The urge to tarnish that innocence pulsed through his veins. She'd unwittingly engaged in a verbal battle of wits with the devil and lost. The payment? Her freedom. He looked down at his hands. Hands that always seemed to be covered in blood. Hands that shouldn't touch something so pure. The thought made the beast inside him, the one seething with need for her, roar in fury.

His inner beast had been pacing, restless. Furious at being separated from her. Furious at the sour taste of fear on his tongue. Fear that whoever was attacking his shipments would get to her. Would somehow get past his guard and harm her. He needed to touch her. Needed to sooth his soul and remind himself that she was safe.

On the bed next to her now, was a pile of items he would use tonight. The need to make her submit, riding him hard. Using measured movements so as not to wake her, he slowly cut away the T-shirt and panties she wore. He'd buy her more. Hell, he'd buy her whatever she wanted.

Her beautiful skin gleamed in the moonlight. He gently rolled her to her side and took the black silk tether and carefully tied her wrists behind her back. As soon as he tightened the knot, she woke with a start.

"What the hell!" Chloe tried to roll away, tugging relentlessly on her arms to free herself. The hard hand at her waist held her in place. She used her legs to try to scoot round to get leverage to kick him. All she could see was a shadow, but she knew him.

"Oh, no you don't." He laughed wickedly and flipped her back over onto her stomach and, using his weight, pinned her down.

"Get off me!" She screamed into the pillow.

"I missed you baby." He whispered at her ear. He suckled at her neck in the sensitive spot where her neck and shoulder met. Taking his time, enjoying the taste of her skin, marking her while she thrashed beneath him. He worked his way back up to her ear and sucked the lobe into his mouth and bit down.

"Stop it!" Chloe attempted to buck him off, but it was no use. He was too heavy.

Cillian reached down and slipped a black silk tether tied in a loop over her ankle. He pulled it up to the top of her thigh, then jerked her ankle back. He twisted the silk into a figure eight, then slipped the second loop over her foot and smoothed it further up her ankle, pinning her leg in a bent position. She screamed and thrashed wildly, so it took him a little longer to repeat the process with her other leg.

When she was secured, he flipped her onto her back on top of several pillows to ensure her arms wouldn't hurt from her weight. Reaching over, he turned on the bedside lamp to get a good look at his work and settled between her open thighs.

"Hello, angel." He grinned at the blazing fury displayed in her beautiful blue eyes. He was thrilled at the lack of fear.

"Untie me, asshole!" She huffed out a harsh breath to get the hair out of her face. His smile was cunning, with a hint of cruelty that caused a quiver low in her belly. She never could decide if he had the face of an angel or the devil.

"Such naughty words from such beautiful lips." He teased. "I like it." He reached out and smoothed the hair from her face. He was tempted to braid it, but he wanted to see it spread out on his pillows.

"I swear to God, if you don't untie me, I'm going to kill you! I swear it!"

He lifted her collar with his finger and tugged slightly to sooth the jealous beast inside him. A reminder that she belonged to him. With her arms secured behind her in this position, it forced her breast to thrust forward. He moved his finger down to her nipple. He circled around the tip continuously until it puckered, then he did the same to the other one.

"Little hellion. I missed you." He leaned in and captured her nipple with his lips, and suckled sharply. When he had the peak hard and tight and wet from his mouth, he lifted away and reached toward his pile of treasures. He held up a white gold chain with sparkling sapphires for her to see. The chain matched her collar perfectly.

"What's that?" Chloe eyed the chain with the weird clips at the ends.

"I had this made for you baby." Very carefully he attached the clamp of one end to her nipple and tightened it just a little too tightly.

"What are you doing?! Ouch!"

He chuckled softly, then bent down and sucked her other nipple deep into his mouth. He lashed the tip with his tongue while she squirmed restlessly beneath him. He lifted away and pushed her breast closer to the other one, then carefully attached the second clamp. The chain between the clamps was just short enough to hold her breast up and out so that when he released her breast, the chain pulled against the weight. He knew the dual pulling and pinching sensations would be intense.

"Oh my God!" Chloe gasped. It was too much. The pressure sent shooting arrows of sharp pleasure and ripples of stinging pain, to her core.

"You're going to love this angel." He licked the tips of both clamped nipples softly over and over, adding a different, softer sensation to the mix, causing her to shiver uncontrollably beneath his tongue. He reached between her thighs and pleasure seared his soul at the wet heat that met his fingertips. His sweet girl liked her clamps. She may not want to, but she did.

He held up his glistening fingers for her to see, and grinned wickedly. Chloe scowled at him. The arrogant asshole.

He chuckled again and licked his fingers clean, then leaned in and scattered warm soft kisses around each nipple, her plump breasts, her neck and face. He was careful as he nipped the corners of her mouth to ensure she couldn't bite him in retaliation, then nibbled on the lower edge of her plump bottom lip. He followed the same path back to her nipples and continued softly lapping at the clamped tips, like a kitten lapping at cream.

She couldn't breathe. Her fingers flexed behind her back. Her toes curled into the sheets. The difference in the pulling, the tight pinching and the soft, warm, delicate touch of his tongue was intoxicating. She couldn't keep up, couldn't compartmentalize the sensations. Pleasure and pain, the softness of his lips, the warmth of his breath, the hard clamp of metal. She arched her back and pushed her breast closer to the heat of his mouth.

He kissed his way down her torso to her mound. "Pretty baby, you look so beautiful with your skin flushed. You're wet for me angel." He whispered against her skin. "Your little pussy is so warm and wet." He pushed her thighs wide with his shoulders and, without warning, drove his tongue deep inside her.

"Oh, God!" Chloe threw her head back and inhaled sharply. Her legs pulled against the ties that held them.

Cillian devoured her sweetness. "Chloe, baby, you taste so fucking good." He drank her in. Using his tongue, thrusting deep, his lips sucking hard, his teeth nipping at her folds, he threw her into an orgasm within seconds. When her pussy clamped down on his tongue, the jealous monster experienced gratification, but wasn't yet appeased. He squeezed his cock in a tight grip to keep from plunging into her.

He reached for the next toy, and the wicked creature again lifted its evil head. He coated the slender toy with lubricant and squirted a small amount onto his finger. He lapped softly at her now overly sensitive clit to distract her. "You're so soft baby, so sweet." He slid his finger slowly back to the puckered rosette of her ass. She gasped in shock when he circled the opening gently, over and over, until the dual sensations of his finger and his tongue brought her close to the edge a second time.

Before he let her fall, he eased the tip of the toy to her back entrance, then flipped on the remote and brough it to life, vibrating softly. She jerked, as if attempting to escape him. He held her down with a muscular arm across her abdomen. "Relax Chloe. Take it for me. It's going to be so good, baby."

She squealed as he gently pushed the vibrating plug deep until the ring of her sphincter closed around the tapered end, locking it in place.

"Cillian! Oh God! Oh my, oh! Please!" Her head thrashed back and forth; her shocked blue eyes glued to his evil green gaze.

"Yes." He soothed in the wickedly low voice that sent shivers down her spine. "Get ready angel. I'm going to make you fly." He held up the remote and hit a button and the vibrations increased. When she gasped and lifted off the bed in reaction, he smiled again. "See, baby. It's going to be so good." He crooned to her softly.

She was beautiful. Absolutely fucking beautiful and he couldn't resist temptation. So, he reached for his phone and took several pictures, wanting to capture this image forever. He tossed the phone back onto the nightstand and crouched between her thighs. He lapped softly at her clit and teased the opening of her pussy with tiny whisper soft flicks of his tongue as the vibrating plug in her ass and the pinch and pull at her nipples battered her, bombarded her with sensual decadence.

She was dying. The sensations were overwhelming. It was too much! Oh God, he was doing it again. Awaking the darkness inside her. Making her crave the darkness in him. Bringing it to life to meet his, to match it. He set off cravings she didn't know existed. The need, the ache, the want. Yes, she wanted it. Oh God! She wanted it.

"Cillian! Please!" Here she was again, begging. Begging him for more? The vibration so deep. The pulling at her nipples. It was too much!

"Please what, baby?" He chuckled wickedly and circled the opening of her warm wet pussy again with a delicate touch of his tongue then sliding it over her clit ever so slightly.

The need was dark and violent. She ached with it. Every time she moved, the chain clipped to her nipples pulled, pinched. A delicious burn.

"Please what, baby? Do you need me, angel?" He whispered against her tender folds and she thrust her hips, trying to get closer.

"Oh, my God!" When she flexed her hips again, her heavy breasts swayed with the motion. The chain, oh shit, the chain swayed with them, pulled so tight! She needed her hands free. Needed to hold her breasts. They rocked back and forth with each movement. It was torture. Delicious torture.

"Say it angel." He clicked the remote again, sending the vibrations into overdrive, and suckled softly on her clit again, never hard enough to send her over the edge. Her muscles tensed further, her back bowed. She thrust her pelvis and pushed against his lips. He couldn't help but chuckle against her tender, wet heat. "Oh yea, you need me don't you, hellion. Say it baby and I'll make it all better." He coaxed, pinching the head of his swollen cock tighter to keep from losing it.

The need built into a raging inferno. The fire so hot, so intense. Shit! Shit! He was the devil! The freaking Devil! "Yes! Please Cillian, I need you!" She screamed. Begging him to ease the burn.

And there they were, finally. The words his beast craved. He didn't make her wait. He palmed her ass and lifted her to him and slowly, relentlessly, pushed his aching cock deep into her. She immediately convulsed around him. Her pussy clutching at him. The plug in her ass making her already small channel tighter. She was squeezing him so hard. The slick heat, a sumptuous haven for his aching cock. When he was finally sheathed, once she'd taken every inch of him, he paused and waited for her pleading eyes to meet his. "This Chloe, this is us. You and me. We belong together."

She shook her head frantically. Trepidation warring with need on her beautiful face. "No." Her pleading voice belying her flexing hips as she tried to get closer.

He pulled halfway out of her heat and waited. It nearly killed him, but he waited.

She bowed her back and pushed her pelvis toward him in an effort to seat him again.

When he held her still and simply waited, she screamed in frustration. Her little pussy pulsing around his shaft.

His smile was evil. "Say it baby. Say you belong with me."

"No! Please Cillian!"

Her pleading voice was almost his undoing. "Say it. Say it and I'll give you everything you need. You know it's going to be so good, angel." He flexed his hips, sliding deep then pulling halfway out again and waited.

"I hate you!" Frustrated tears streaked from those beautiful blue eyes.

"No, you don't. Now say it!" He barked, his eyes blazing. He pulled a little further out of her quacking depths. Fuck, she needed to submit! He needed this. She felt so good. Molten lava convulsing around him. He needed to thrust back into her so hard and deep. The need so sharp. But she had to give him this. She had to.

The vibrations deep inside her and the tight pull and pinch. His thick cock filling her, stretching her. The heat and need all combined was her undoing. "Yes!" She screamed desperately at the devil taunting her. "I belong with you!"

Cillian thrust forward to the hilt and she exploded around him. Quacking, pulsing, tightening, her pussy, milking his cock. Clamping down to keep him locked inside. He pounded into her, riding her hard through two glorious orgasms before throwing his head back, seating himself to the hilt again, and finding his own. His hot seed bathing her womb, flooding her with him.

Finally, when the vicious bite of need was sated, he slowly eased in and out of her as they both came down. Her pulsing wet heat and the soft slide of his still partially hard cock were soothing. He shuffled through the sheets and pillows until he found the remote and turned the vibrations off, then dropped onto his elbows on top of her. He was careful not to put his weight on the clamps still attached to her nipples.

He fisted his hands in her hair to hold her face still and kissed her. He forced her mouth open and thrust his tongue deep, exploring her depths, pushing against her tongue, demanding a response. When her tongue moved against his, he lightened the pressure as he taught her to kiss him the way he wanted her to. When her tongue chased his, he savored her surrender for long moments, then eased back and ended the kiss with soft nibbles on her swollen lips.

He watched her carefully as she watched him. Both of them still breathing harshly from exertion.

"What are you doing to me?" She whispered as she stared into his beautiful face. The harsh angles now relaxed in satisfaction.

"Making you mine." He whispered back and kissed her lips with a soft quick peck.

Chapter 19: Tiaras and Tea Parties

Chloe pushed Buttercup a little faster as they hurried to reach the store before it rained. She was sore and achy between her legs, so the movement was uncomfortable, but she pushed the horse, anyway. She could smell the rain coming and the fresh scent would've been welcome if not for the tense alertness of the men surrounding her.

The number of men traveling with them on the short ride surprised her. She'd thought Patrick would welcome a break from their daily rides, but he was mounted and following behind her with a man named Jacob.

Now that Cillian was back, she was meeting a lot of really fierce-looking men. When Cillian had introduced them earlier, Jacob had smiled at her, but his solemn intensity made her uneasy. She'd looked from him to Cillian and then finally to Finn, whose lip twitched slightly as if fighting a grin. That little twitch was enough to put her at ease.

But now she was late. With Cillian back, her routine was off. The delays had started early this morning. When she'd attempted to get out of bed, he'd pulled her back into him and rolled her beneath him. With her hands clasped in his above her head, he'd thrust deep into her, taking her hard and fast, almost desperately. Afterward, with his warmth wrapped around her, she'd nearly fallen back to sleep. She'd had to force herself to get up. She knew Patrick would be waiting.

When she'd come out of her closet dressed for her run, Cillian was waiting and apparently planned to go with her. Patrick fell in behind them outside their door and Finn and a huge black man named Terrance greeted them on the back patio.

Terrance was more menacing looking than Jacob, with his bald head and jagged scar, but he'd greeted her with a kind, if not tentative, smile. She'd searched the faces of the men, wondering why today was so different from any other day. She hadn't tried to escape or anything, so she couldn't help but think it was overkill. And she made a point to tell them so.

They didn't relent, and their unusually stoic expressions and quiet resolve made her anxious. In the end, they ran as a group with the men surrounding her. It totally sucked. She felt stifled. Having their tense presence around her diminished the joy she usually felt at the freedom of racing over the grass with the wind in her hair, her muscles firing, her adrenalin surging.

Breakfast was another bone of contention. She'd had to go back to eating in the dining room again. She missed the hustle and bustle of the kitchen and the easy flow of banter with Patrick and Rourke. Conversation in the dining room had been stilted and quiet until Finn mentioned her training. He'd mapped out a plan for her that involved practicing the moves she already knew before introducing new ones. He'd explained his need to see what she knew and test her strength.

With breakfast finally over, she'd gone straight to the beach with Patrick and, surprisingly, Terrance in tow. Afraid they might see her if she rushed, she painstakingly took her time following her normal route, ensuring her message was written in the sand. She'd been slightly disappointed when Ian hadn't shown up on the rock this morning, so she hadn't stayed at the beach long.

Lunch had been a whole separate issue. Imogen had been bringing her lunch every day, so she'd been eating in her studio for over two weeks. It was a routine she liked. If she was honest with herself, she enjoyed the few quiet moments with Imogen while she discovered what delicacies the woman had prepared for her. And she knew Imogen enjoyed looking at her paintings.

But not today. Today Cillian had shown up at exactly eleven forty-five to bring her down to the dining room. When she'd told him she would eat later, he'd simply waited her out. She hadn't been able to concentrate with him watching her. The intense heat of his gaze burning into her back was completely distracting. So, she'd washed her brushes then stomped over to the leather chaise where he'd been sprawled out like a lazy panther and, with hands her on her hips, she'd glared at him. And what had he done? The arrogant ass. He'd grinned that wicked grin of his and reached out, snagged her hand and jerked her onto his lap. He'd kissed her protests away, then lifted her and carried her out the door.

After lunch, they'd gone straight to the training field. The workout had been challenging. And Cillian and Finn were both relentless. There was a sense of urgency and determination in the way they tested her skills. She'd grappled with them, each taking turns, then coming at her at the same time repeatedly for over two hours as they'd worked through her kicks and jabs.

Cillian had taunted her the entire time, challenging her, daring her to punch harder, kick faster. Finn was stoic as usual, but he'd been patient while showing her how to use her size against an opponent with a takedown move. She understood the mechanics, but hadn't been able to execute it. He'd pushed her hard. And by the time they were finished, she'd been exhausted.

His gruff voice was stern when he informed her that she needed to practice every day until she got it right. She didn't know if it was possible, but she'd try because she liked the idea of throwing him on his ass.

She'd been excited when they'd moved to the shooting range. Cillian had gently put protective ear plugs into her ears himself, then eyed her carefully before handing her a nine-millimeter Baretta. Right before she'd taken it from his hand, though, he'd pulled it back slightly. When she'd met his gaze again, the ass blew her a kiss as if daring her to shoot him. Then he'd handed it over.

The gun was heavy and a little awkward, but she could load it and shoot at the target. She just needed two hands to keep it steady. She hadn't hit the bullseye, but at least she'd hit the dang target. Cillian had teased her about not being able to shoot him if she tried, which only made her more determined.

They made her unload and reload the gun and switch the safety on and off, over and over, until her fingers were numb. When she'd finished, Cillian had turned to Finn and told him to purchase her a Nano. Finn had nodded, but said she still needed to know how to handle every weapon they had. She didn't know why she needed to know how to do that, but she enjoyed shooting, so she didn't comment. However, she asked Cillian what the heck a Nano was. He'd explained it was a smaller, more compact weapon that would be easier for her to handle. Then he'd grinned and tapped her on the nose and joked that she'd be better able to shoot him with a lighter gun.

Chloe hadn't known she'd be training most of the afternoon, and now she was late. She noticed the heavy rain clouds moving in, but they were so close.

Finn held up his hand to signal everyone to stop, then looked up at the sky. "The storms moving in faster than we expected."

Cillian followed his lead and watched the clouds. "We better turn back before we get a wet ass."

"No, it's just a little further." She spoke before she thought better of it.

Cillian eyed Chloe carefully, trying to read her pensive stare. "Baby, it's going to rain."

"Please, Cillian, we're almost there." She needed a little normalcy today. She was tense. There were more men than usual surrounding her for some reason. And he kept touching her and kissing her and teasing her. Last night had been intense, and she still hadn't processed it. She wasn't ready. What she needed was her little slice of normal.

Cillian watched her, searching her expression before nodding. "Alright angel." For whatever reason, this trip was important to her. He knew she and Patrick rode the horses to the store every couple of days, but they could just as easily return tomorrow.

Chloe breathed a sigh of relief when they broke through the trees and the little store came into view. She quickly tied Buttercup to the now familiar post and was about to charge up the steps when Cillian captured her hand and pulled her into his chest.

She looked up at him, and he could easily read her frustration. He leaned in and kissed her softly. She tensed beneath him like she always did. But he took his time tasting her, exploring her mouth with gentle licks until she relaxed against him and tentatively met his tongue with the delicate swipe of her own. Once he was satisfied that her attention was focused back on him, he ended the kiss and let her go.

It took Chloe a second to catch her breath, then she scowled at him. She couldn't retaliate because his men were surrounding them and he knew it. He was taking advantage of the rules. The smug bastard. She turned on her heel and nearly dragged him in her haste to get inside.

When she stepped through the door, the warm, homey scents and sounds soothed her frayed nerves.

"There she is." Nettie's gravelly voice greeted her.

"Hi Nettie." As soon as she spoke, the sound of little feet rapidly hitting the wooden floor captured everyone's attention.

At the unexpected sound and the flash of movement, Cillian and Finn quickly pushed in front of Chloe, as if facing a threat.

She rolled her eyes at the unnecessary show of protection and forced her way between the two men. But Cillian grabbed her arm to move her back behind him. Quickly shaking off his hold, she smiled with delighted pleasure and crouched down. With her arms open wide, she caught the tiny body flying into her.

"Chlowee! You'we hewe!" Annie shrieked as she raced across the floor and threw herself into Chloe's outstretched arms. She was dressed in her favorite pink and purple princess dress, with a plastic, silver crown perched precariously on her head.

"Hi princess! I'm sorry I'm late." The force of Annie's body hitting hers nearly knocked her over. If it weren't for Cillian's legs behind her, she would have fallen on her butt. Chloe hugged the little girl to her chest and squeezed her tight. When she let her go, Annie grabbed her hand and tugged with all her little might.

"Come on Chlowee! I've been waiting and waiting and waiting! Mommy said we can have peppowmint tea with chocowate cookies for ouwa tea pawty!" She squealed with delight as she started dragging Chloe toward the back of the store.

Chloe smiled at Molly and mouthed her apologies for being late over Annie's head.

Molly smiled back and winked at her. "No worries honey. You're not that late. She's just excited."

"I can tell." Ignoring the men, she allowed herself to be tugged around behind the counter by the little girl, then down onto a quilt laid out on the floor. A little white china tea set painted with pink and red rose buds was already set up for service for two in the center of a miniature wooden table.

Once Chloe was seated, Annie clapped her hands. "Isn't it pwetty Chlowee?" She asked proudly.

"It's beautiful, sweetheart." Chloe settled onto one of the two pink pillows positioned at the little table.

"This is fow you." Annie lifted another plastic crown from the table and Chloe ducked so she could put it on her head. Annie clapped again after Chloe helped her secure in into her hair. "Now we'ae both pwincesses!"

"I love my crown! Thank you, Annie." She couldn't help but smile at the angelic little girl. This is exactly what she needed today. A pleasant distraction from the domineering presence Cillian posed. She hadn't been prepared for him to return, and now that he was here, his constant attention was unnerving.

"You welcome. Mommy, can we stawat now?" Annie looked at her mother hopefully.

"Yes, baby."

Cillian looked at Finn, then they both turned to stare after Chloe with equally surprised expressions. Then they frowned at Patrick when he chuckled behind them.

Nettie cackled at their dumbfounded expressions. "Go on, take a look." She nodded her head toward the back of the store. Then she wagged her finger at them. "But don't you disturb those two. An invitation to a tea party is a serious thing." When they both glared at her, she grinned through bright red lips. She'd known these two men their entire lives. She'd slipped them candy, then shooed them out of this very store more times than she cared to count. And she was way too old to be intimidated by their posturing, both standing there with arms crossed over massive chests, equal scowls on their faces. Ha! That would be the day!

Cillian headed toward the back of the store with Finn on his heels. They both peered over the counter to see what Chloe was doing. To say he was pleased was an understatement. He glanced back at Finn and the look on his cousin's face told him he was, too.

He'd never met a woman like her before. Of course, he'd had beautiful women, a lot of them. But they paled in comparison to Chloe. And to see someone who looked like her without an ounce of artifice should have been surprising. But with Chloe, it wasn't. He remembered the way she'd smiled so openly at the elderly couple in the gallery the first time he'd seen her. As if she were delighted to spend time with them. She'd been patient and kind, and even when she'd become aware of his presence, she hadn't brushed them off. None of the women he knew would have been so attentive to them.

Watching her now, he couldn't imagine a single woman he'd ever fucked sitting on the floor playing with a child unless she sought to gain something from it.

He pulled out his phone and surreptitiously snapped a picture of her with the silly crown on her head and a teacup in her hand before he moved quietly to the end of the counter and sat on a stool to watch. The longer he watched, the more frustrated he became. She'd obviously had plans today, but hadn't said a word to him about them.

The sound of rain hitting the roof caught his attention. He glanced at Finn, who was texting on his phone. "We'll need a vehicle."

"I know. I just texted Peter. He's on his way with a few stable hands to collect the horses. He'll leave the SUV for us."

After Molly finished serving tea and cookies for the tea party, she moved to the counter and poured coffee for the men. After she filled Cillian's cup, she met his gaze carefully. "Thank you for letting her come here today. Annie has been looking forward to it." She whispered under her breath. He didn't look happy, and she was terrified he'd be angry that Annie was taking up Chloe's time. Cillian O'Donnell took care of his people, but he was not a gentle man.

Cillian smiled to put Molly at ease. "I'm sorry she was late. I didn't realize she had a prior commitment."

They both turned when Ian came in from the storage room, carrying a stack of boxes. They watched as he carefully maneuvered around Annie and Chloe, as if he already knew they were there.

"Hi Chloe." Ian grinned at the crown on her head. Annie had tried to get him to wear the dang thing earlier. No way was he doing that.

"Hey Ian. What are you doing here?" Chloe frowned at the stack of boxes he was carrying.

"I help Molly with packaging when she has large orders." He placed the boxes carefully on the back counter next to pies that were cooling on a rack.

"I missed you this morning." She could feel Cillian's eyes on her, but ignored the urge to look in his direction. She'd had her fill of him already today.

"I'm sorry about that. I had to reschedule my test to this morning so I could be here to help Molly."

"Well, how did you do?" They'd been studying together out by the beach for the last few days.

"I aced it, thanks to you."

"Congratulations!" She held up her fist, and he bumped his against hers. "But I didn't do anything."

"Yea ya did. Reviewing my notes with me helped a lot."

"All I did was call out questions to you. You're the one who knew the answers, so that A is all yours."

Cillian scowled at the two of them. He wondered when they had become so close. He'd obviously missed out on a lot while he'd been gone.

"You look good in a plastic crown." Ian smirked at the lopsided crown on her head.

"I know, right?" Chloe giggled and reached up to touch it.

The sound of her laughter caused a tightening in Cillian's chest. He absently rubbed the sensation away.

"Ian wouldn't wear the cwown. He's a mean boy." Annie pouted.

"Aw Annie, don't be mad. I gave you a piggyback ride instead, remember?" Ian walked over and patted Annie's shoulder.

"Oh Yes! It was fun, Chlowee. We wode awound and awound."

Cillian watched his woman as she charmed those around her. She was captivating, sitting on the floor in an old store, playing with a small child. She was surrounded by people with whom it could be said; helped to keep her hidden away on his island. He couldn't take his eyes off of her. Seeing her so relaxed helped to sooth his anger, his frustration. She hadn't told him she had plans today. Even when he'd tried to turn them back toward the stables because of the weather, she'd insisted on continuing to the store, but hadn't told him why. Hadn't bothered to tell him the importance of her being here. And it obviously was important to her. He also didn't know she was helping Ian with his studies because she hadn't told him that either.

Sure, his people reported when and where she went in his absence, but not exactly what she was doing. They'd been together most of the day, at breakfast, lunch, and even during her training. But never once during all that time had she bothered to share anything about her time here on the island. Not a word. She was simply going through the motions with her interactions with him. In her own quiet way, she was excluding him from her inner circle.

She'd told him she would never belong to him, and he supposed this was her way of ensuring it. She was deliberately closing herself off, refusing to let him in. And it pissed him off.

The thunder clapping outside matched his turbulent mood. His palm itched to spank her tight little ass for daring to try such a thing. But at the same time, he wanted to smile at the challenge she'd inadvertently thrown out. He did love a good challenge.

Chapter 20: Mean Girls

It had been five weeks since Cillian had been back on the Island, and the challenge of conquering Chloe was taking all of his focus. She was still as fiery as ever when they were alone. She continued to fight him every night and when she was able to score a blow; he wore the bruise proudly. If truth be told, he relished every second, because her surrender was so much sweeter for it.

She spent several days a week at the store with her friends while he and her security detail were relegated to the sidelines. She'd even charmed old man Jenkins and that crazy ass horse he was so tempted to sell. She and Ian were getting closer every day. More than once he'd left his office and gone in search of her, only to find her in the kitchen baking cookies with him and Imogen.

She still spent every morning on the beach, writing her message in the sand. But she didn't linger, and she no longer stared out at the waves with tears streaming down her cheeks. He would take that as a win.

Her training was coming along. Chloe was naturally athletic, and she obviously enjoyed the challenge of learning new ways to fight him. She followed directions well out on the training field. Finn was concerned that her sweet nature would keep her from using her skills if she needed to. He'd assured his cousin that Chloe didn't hesitate to use them on him regularly. Part of the reason he enjoyed their evening scuffles was that it gave him a chance to ensure her reactions were what they needed to be. And he could honestly say from experience that her skills were improving.

He grinned at that thought and touched the bruise under his eye. Just last night he'd experienced it first-hand. When he'd led her out of the bathroom, still warm and damp from their shower and she saw what he'd planned, she'd immediately gone on the attack. By the time he'd subdued her and had her tied to the bed, she'd been as pissed as a scalded cat. His cock hardened at the memory.

She'd cursed like a sailor while he'd meticulously waxed under her arms, her legs, then finally her pretty little pussy. She was smooth and soft again without a single hair left. He'd soothed her afterward, rubbing warm oil into her tender skin, but she hadn't calmed down. He'd had no choice but the pull the puffy lips of her pussy open and lick her clit with soft flicks of his tongue until she came. He'd been so hard afterward that he'd crouched between her legs and jacked his cock while she watched under hooded lids until he coated her belly with his come. It had been so fucking hot.

She'd sulked all evening after he'd cleaned her up and untied her. She hadn't eaten much at dinner, and she still hadn't spoken a word to him. She was very good at giving him the silent treatment. Early this morning, when she'd tried to get out of bed for her run, he'd pulled her beneath him and fucked her slow and deep. He'd never felt the need or desire to be gentle with a lover until Chloe. He constantly craved the feel of her tight little pussy clamping down on his cock. The satisfaction of her beautiful body tightening around his, needing his. But the intense orgasm hadn't soothed her anger in the least. So, he was giving her until after lunch to get over her sulk.

He tapped a few keys on his keyboard and activated the camera in her studio. She was painting. He spent way too much time watching her paint. Her delicate face was always so relaxed. All of her defenses seemed to melt away when she had a brush in her hand. Beautiful canvases lined the walls of her studio. Gorgeous pieces that included little Annie wearing her crown, another with Ian sitting in the grass. The first one she'd finished of Frank Jenkins and Storm was leaning against the back wall. There was a portrait of her parents and her dog. Several landscapes of the island. He watched her for a few minutes longer, then turned his focus back to his work.

Another shipment had been attacked. There were no casualties this time because his crews were expecting it. Finn left several days ago with team Two to check on the men, gather any additional details and to ensure they completed the delivery. He agreed with Finn that he should stay back with Team One. His neck itched, and that was never a good sign. Something was brewing, some unseen anomaly that he couldn't put his finger on.

Titan was close to finding the source. The email address was a ghost account that pinged several servers across the globe, but Titan was narrowing the search. He thought he recognized the work of the analyst who created it and was following up on it. Soon they would have the answers they needed.

Cillian had a feeling he knew who was hiring the mercenaries, but he had to be sure. He was always certain before he made a move to take someone out. His reputation demanded that he be absolutely positive of a target before moving on it.

Against Finn's wishes, he'd lifted the lock down on the Island. Most of his people had family on the mainland, and it wasn't fair to keep them apart. Within days of doing it, Roisin had shown up.

He'd known her since she'd been a small child, and she really couldn't help the way she behaved. Her parents had spoiled her from the time she was born. A family of power hunger vipers who thought they were smarter than they were. But they adored Roisin. She was their pride and joy no matter how much trouble she seemed to find herself in. But other than her penchant for putting his staff in what she felt was their place, she hadn't caused any trouble here. She was mostly just a nuisance.

When he'd told her that Finn wasn't in residence and that he wouldn't be back for several days, she'd appeared to be surprised. Her coy smile was a little unsettling, but he was used to it. He'd been ignoring her adolescent attempts at flirting with him for years. She'd pouted prettily when she told him she and Finn had arranged for her to visit this week. Then she'd sighed dramatically and played at being annoyed, saying she'd just have to wait for him to get back.

He really didn't care what she did as long as she stayed out of his way. But if everything went as planned, Finn would be back tomorrow and he could deal with her himself.

Chloe ignored Cillian when he stepped into her studio. She was too angry to deal with him today. After last night, she didn't even want to look at him. Not only had that shit hurt, but it had been a painful reminder of her spa appointments with her mom, Ms. Sara and Sidney back when they were in high school. Sure, waxing really only hurt a little now that she'd been getting it done for so many years, but that wasn't the point.

Once a month they'd go to the spa downtown and their moms would let them sip wine while they got facials before they were waxed. Afterward, they'd have lunch and go shopping. It was one of those days that she and Sidney always looked forward to. But last night was a stark reminder of her current situation and the lonesome feeling that those days were over.

Cillian waited patiently for her to acknowledge him for nearly five minutes. When it became obvious that she had no intention of doing so, he lost patience. He stepped up behind her and wrapped his arms around her waist, and pulled her into him. When she tried to jerk away, he bit the back of her neck in punishment.

"How long are you going to sulk?"

Chloe elbowed him in the ribs as hard as she could. She only had a moment of satisfaction at his gasp before he jerked her around to face him. Her paint brush went flying across the room to land on the floor with a splat. Brown paint splattering everywhere. When she saw the extent of the mess, she scowled at him.

"I asked you a question Chloe." The sparkle of anticipation in his eyes belied his stern voice.

And it pissed her off even more. He thought it was funny! The asshole. She snapped up her knee, aiming for his crotch. She nearly hit her mark before he sifted.

"Oh, little hellion. Is that how you want to play it?" He jerked her paint covered smock open, buttons ripping apart and flying everywhere.

She snapped out her fist, attempting to punch him in the throat. He captured her flying fist and her other hand before she could use it, so she head-butted him. He leaned back so the blow landed on his chest, causing her to scream in frustration.

Cillian laughed. He couldn't help it. She always looked like a furious little kitten when she was angry. He shoved the smock off of her arms and when it fell to the floor; he bent down and put his shoulder into her belly and lifted her into the air. He carried her kicking and screaming over to the leather sofa in the corner. He sat and flipped her down over onto his lap. "You asked for this, angel."

"Don't you dare asshole!" She squirmed and kicked her feet frantically.

"Asshole?" He clucked his tongue jokingly. "So naughty." He put pressure on her back with his palm essentially pinned her in place. His other hand snagged the waistband of her shorts and panties and yanked them down to her knees, pinning her legs.

"Don't do it!" She tried unsuccessfully to raise her torso.

He landed a sharp slap to her ass and fire raced through her. "Ouch!" She was going to freakin kill him!

He landed three more blows before rubbing his palm over the heated skin. "Look how pretty. I love this shade of pink baby." He slid his fingers between her thighs and stoked her clit, using his thumb to circle the opening of her pussy. He stroked and circled, playing her body like an instrument until his fingers were coated with the proof of her desire and she was moving against them.

He pulled his fingers away and licked them clean. "You taste so fucking sweet."

Chloe groaned when he pulled his fingers from her. "No." Oh God, it felt so good. She knew if he kissed her now, she'd taste herself on his lips.

He lay four more sharp strikes, watching her heated skin turn a beautiful shade of red. He rubbed the heat into her skin before sliding his fingers to her clit again. He worked his magic until her pussy was flooded, slick, and wet. He circled her clit over and over, his thumb pumping in and out of her until she moaned, pushing against his hand.

"Oh God. Stop." The groan came from deep in her throat.

"Take your punishment baby." His Irish brogue was husky with need. "You know you've earned it." He thrust two fingers deep inside her while he jerked her shirt over her head with his other hand. He unclasped her bra while his fingers pumped deep. She was thrusting against his hand when he pulled his fingers from her.

"No!" Oh God, she was so close. She could feel the hard bulge of his cock beneath her belly. So, she rubbed herself against it. Trying to entice him to give her what she needed.

Cillian was in glorious hell. His sassy little hellion was always so responsive to his touch. She was like a living flame. He slapped her gorgeous ass two more times and watched the fiery red stain spread across her delicate skin before sliding his fingers deep into her pulsing heat. She arched her back and thrust into his hand.

Chloe was furious, frustrated, and so in need. Desperate need.

Cillian pushed her shorts and panties from her legs and lifted her to straddle him. She was grinding against him, seeking the connection that would send her over. He opened his fly and when his cock sprang free; he palmed it. Aligning it with the opening of her pussy, he pushed her down onto it. "Take what you need, baby." He thrust up as he forced her down, seating himself to the hilt. Chloe instantly exploded around him. He clutched her to his chest and pumped into her furiously, guiding her as she rode him. Teaching her to use him, to take what she needed. And she did. She rode him through her release and clung to him through his.

They held on to each other for long moments, their harsh breathing the only sound in the otherwise quiet room. He held her close, rubbing her back soothingly while they both came down. When he could move again, he laid her down and went to the sink to clean up. Then he cleaned her gently as she watched him through heavy-lidded eyes that still sparked with fury.

He smiled and kissed her swollen lips. "Still mad?" He closed his fly and gathered her clothes for her.

"I promise, the first chance I get, I'm out of here." She'd probably regret that statement, but she couldn't stop herself from making it.

His teasing smile turned menacing, and green eyes blazed into hers. "I'd find you and bring you back."

"You won't find me." Her stubborn chin lifted, and she snatched her clothes from his hand.

He grabbed her chin and forced her face closer to his. Those terrifying green eyes drilled into hers. "I'll always find you, Chloe. Always. And I'll kill anyone; anyone who tries to keep you from me."

She yanked her chin from his grasp and scowled.

Cillian clasped Chloe's hand tightly as he led her into the dining room for lunch. They were both on an emotional razor's edge. The violent release and the tense conversation afterward had both of their tempers simmering.

Chloe nearly stumbled when she saw Roisin sitting at the table. Well shit!

"Cillian, really?" Roisin's snide voice grated on Chloe's nerves. "Is this how you allow your mistress to dress?" She raised her lip in disgust at Chloe's leggings and simple top.

"Chloe is not my mistress." He didn't have time to deal with her mouth today.

"Now Cillian, don't get testy. I didn't mean anything by it." She smiled sweetly at him, then looked at Chloe and clucked her tongue.

"Roisin." His voice warned her to stop.

"There's nothing to be done about her morals, but the least I can do is show her how to dress appropriately." Roisin used the soothing voice she always used with her grandfather. He fell for it every time and no doubt Cillian would too. Men were so easily led. "I mean really, Cillian." She sighed heavily. "If you intend to keep her for a while, her appearance will be a direct reflection on you. On all of us, really. I'd be more than happy to show her what's expected." She wanted to scratch the little whore's eyes out. It was obvious the two of them had held up her lunch because they were fucking.

"Roisin, that's enough out of you." Cillian warned.

"Cillian darlin'" Chloe responded in an overly exaggerated southern drawl, calling on her inner Designing Women's Julia Sugarbaker. Her mother used to love that show. "It's alright. In the south, we don't ask if you have crazy people in your family, we just ask which side they're on. You see, everybody has them. And we put ours right out on the front porch for everyone to enjoy." She grinned sweetly at Cillian, completely ignoring the loud gasp from the she-devil across the table.

Cillian fought the grin that wanted to spread across his face. It wouldn't do to encourage her.

"But I'll tell you one thing." Chloe continued, "we at least make sure they're properly clothed. My goodness, what would the neighbors think if we let them out in public dressed like that! Why the poor dear must've put on some weight recently. Her clothes are two sizes to small. We'd be the talk of the town. I'll be sure to let Finn know to buy her a new wardrobe. Maybe two or three sizes larger so they fit her properly."

She turned to Roisin and continued as if speaking to a small child, "would you like that dear?" She batted her eyelashes at Roisin for affect. She wasn't the first mean girl Chloe had ever encountered, and probably wouldn't be the last.

Cillian couldn't stop the snort that left his lips.

Roisin turned an alarming shade of red and glared at Chloe, then looked innocently at Cillian. "Cillian, we're practically family, you and I. I've known for years, so I know how you like your women, but this one's a bit mouthy, don't you think?"

"Enough. Roisin, finish your lunch." He glared at the stupid woman. Her little games were getting tiresome. Chloe was already furious. There was no telling what she'd do if this kept up for much longer. As it was, she had a white knuckled grip on her fork. He wondered if she was considering stabbing Roisin with it or him.

He reached over and snagged her free hand. "You and I are going to play a few games of pool after lunch."

"What? Why aren't we training?" She still didn't want to speak to him, but she couldn't ignore him in front of the stupid woman. It would break the rules. Plus, she really wanted the training session today. She needed to get rid of the anger coursing through her veins. And it would give her a good reason to hit him a few times.

"Because I want to play pool." He squeezed her hand, then released it. "Do you know how to play?"

"Yes. I've played with my dad for years."

"Are you any good?"

"I do alright."

"Good. I'm looking forward to the challenge." His phone chimed with an email, so he spent the rest of lunch catching up on those he'd missed while he'd been in Chloe's studio.

She and Roisin finished lunch in hostile silence.

Cillian was leading Chloe through the halls toward the billiards room when his phone rang. He glanced at the caller, then over at her. "I have to take this. You go on ahead. I'll join you in a minute."

When she rounded the corner, Roisin stepped out of the library.

"Hi Chloe." She greeted sweetly. "I wanted to apologize for my behavior earlier. Do you have a minute?"

Chloe stopped in her tracks and eyed her speculatively.

"Please." Roisin wrung her hands together worriedly. "I behaved so badly and Finn isn't going to be happy with me."

Chloe sighed dramatically and nodded. "Alright."

Roisin gave her a relieved smile and motioned for Chloe to proceed her into the library.

She walked a few steps into the room and turned when she heard the door slam shut. Roisin was right behind her, a lot closer than she'd expected, with a hateful glare on her face. She was also holding a steak knife from the lunch table in her hand.

The hair on the back of Chloe's neck stood on end. "What the hell are you doing?" She stepped back, but Roisin stepped with her, matching her step for step.

"The only way to get rid of you is the make Cillian think you're more trouble than you're worth."

Before Chloe could respond, Roisin's glare turned to a purely evil snarl. She lifted the knife high, Chloe reached for it to defend the attack. But to her surprise, Roisin stabbed herself in the arm with it. Chloe was stunned speechless when Roisin shoved the bloody knife into her hand, then jumped back, clutching her arm. She shrieked at the top of her lungs as blood dripped down her arm.

The library door flew open and Cillian rushed inside. He froze when he took in the scene in front of him.

Chloe's stunned gaze moved from his face to Roisin, who was screaming, then down to the bloody knife in her hand.

"She attached me again, Cillian! Your whore tried to kill me! All I wanted to do was apologize to her!" Roisin screamed. "I was just trying to apologize!" Huge tears streamed down her agonized face.

"Cillian!" Chloe dropped the knife, and it clattered to the floor. She tried to speak over the screams, but was interrupted when Rourke and Jacob flew through the door behind him with their guns drawn.

He couldn't believe it. He couldn't fucking believe it! He'd known she was pissed, but he'd never thought she would retaliate like this. She had no way of knowing Roisin would be here, which meant she'd planned to use the knife on him. Why she'd lashed out at Roisin instead, he didn't know and he didn't care. His fury was a living, breathing animal who'd slipped its leash. The demon inside him reared its furious head. Demanding retribution.

Rourke took one look at the scene and the expression on Cillian's face and moved to step between him and Chloe.

"Don't!" Cillian roared. "Put pressure on that wound! Jacob, call Doc. Get him over here." His large palm wrapped around the back of Chloe's neck and forced her from the room. He had his phone in the other hand while he propelled her down the hall to the stairs, then up toward his office. He'd warned her.

He was barking instructions into his phone the entire time he herded her up each step.

Chloe's shock turned to terror when her brain finally caught up with what was happening. She struggled in Cillian's hold, shoving and pulling, trying desperately to slow him down. She had to tell him what happened, but he wasn't giving her a chance. "Cillian, stop! Please! You don't understand! Listen to me! Please!" She yanked at the arm holding her, but the blood coating her fingers kept slipping so she couldn't get a grip.

He kicked his office door closed and marched her over to his desk, never once relaxing his grip on her neck. He dropped his phone on the desk and stabbed at the buttons on his keyboard. His grip tightened almost painfully because she was struggling and pulling against his hold. The panels on the wall across the room moved, and the monitors came to life.

His furious voice was deathly calm at her ear. "I want you to remember that you did this angel." He turned her to face the screens. Chloe froze instantly when she saw her parents on the screen in front of her. She watched in horror as three men in hoods entered the kitchen of her home. Terror squeezed her heart so tight she couldn't breathe. When her mother screamed and tried to run, one man caught her by the arm and forced her into a chair at the table where he tied her hands to the back of the chair.

"Oh, God! No! Please don't do this!" She screamed and jerked violently in Cillian's hold.

His grip tightened to almost bruising force to keep her face pointed at the screen. To make her watch, to force her to see the results of her actions. His demons were riding him hard. Furious that she would dare to test him in such a way. The roaring in his ears drowned out her sobs.

The sound of her father's voice suddenly echoed through the speakers into the room. He was cursing and fighting with all his strength. He was in excellent shape for a man in his fifties, but he was no match for the two highly trained men. And they were skilled as they steadily worked him over while her mother was forced to watch. The third man held her head in his palms, forcing her gaze to watch as they beat her husband.

This was her worst nightmare come to life. She heard her father's voice rising above her mother's screams, "Chloe Bell, listen to me! This is nothing, do you hear me? Nothing! You survive! No matter what happens here, you survive! We'll find you; I promise! This is nothing, honey! No matter what, you survive Chloe Bell!"

Her dad was shouting a message to her. He was being beaten, her mom terrorized, but through it all, he was shouting a message to her as if he knew she was watching. He must've found whatever cameras Cillian had placed in their home, and he'd left them there. It would've felt like such a violation. But he'd left them there, somehow knowing they were linked to her disappearance.

Her heart shattered into a thousand tiny pieces. Never, never would they fit back together. Tears streamed down her face as she listened to the sound of his voice. As she watched the attack, knowing this too was her fault. Everything they'd been through rested solidly on her shoulders.

"I warned you." Cillian seethed. His ominous voice cold and hard.

Bile surged into her throat. She gagged, then bent over as far as she could, pulling against his hold, and vomited on the floor at her feet. When her stomach emptied of its contents, she threw her head back in what little space he allowed, and she screamed in anguish.

Chloe collapsed at his feet. He expected her tears. He expected her to beg and plead with him to spare her parents. She didn't. Instead, she'd vomited on his floor, and now she was nearly sitting in it. She was screaming so loud he was sure it could be heard for miles. He released her and picked up the phone again and gave to order for his men to stop. He watched on the screen as Gregory and Jude eased David Guidry into a chair and Nathan gently cut the rope from Angela's wrists. Then, like the ghosts they were, they disappeared from the room.

He turned the monitors off, then pulled a tissue from the box on his desk and crouched in front of Chloe. She was still screaming.

"Chloe, stop!" He barked. "It's over." His demon had settled, his temper abated for the time being, but only because she looked so distraught. She was covered in blood and vomit. He reached out with the tissue to wipe her mouth, but she shrank away as if he'd hit her. "Chloe, it's over."

She had no voice left, but she was still screaming inside her head. The monster reached for her, and she launched herself away from him. She scurried backward in terror until she hit the wall. She was never more aware of exactly how dangerous Cillian was until that instant in the library.

The deadly look in those furious eyes focused intently on her. His unwillingness to listen to her. She'd followed his fucking rules, all of them. She hadn't given him reason to doubt her, but he'd punished her parents, anyway.

"Chloe, calm down. It's over." He tried to move toward her, but slipped in the mess on the floor.

She used the wall as leverage to stand, then reached for the doorknob and yanked the door open. She raced down the hallway, just barely remembering to use her fingerprint to unlock the door. She took the stairs two and three at a time.

"Chloe, God damn it! Stop!" Cillian slipped several times in his attempt to go after her. He couldn't get his feet under him because of the wet floor. If she didn't slow down, she was going to break her fucking neck.

She tripped halfway down and tumbled head over heels until she fell on the landing on her back in front of a distraught Imogen's feet.

"Chloe! Are you alright?!" Imogen reached for her and was shocked when Chloe shuttled across the floor to get away. Stark terror written all over her beautiful face.

"Chloe?" Imogen tried again.

Chloe found her feet, the screaming in her head louder now. She raced through the castle and out the front door. She didn't stop when she heard Imogen call her name. The sound coming as if from a great distance. She didn't stop when Rourke yelled for her to either. Maybe he'd shoot her with one of those guns he always wore. If he did, she hoped the shot was fatal. Anything to stop the excruciating pain tearing her soul apart.

She could hear pounding feet behind her, so she ran as if her life depended on it. Because it probably did. She crossed the grass and hit the sand at a dead run. She raced down the beach and launched herself up the pile of rocks, cutting her hands and knees on the jagged edges. She collapsed in a heap on the familiar surface at the top and curled into herself. The screaming in her head was so loud her ears had to be bleeding.

Rourke Kelly stopped several yards from the pile of rocks Chloe was perched on. He didn't know if he should approach her or not. She could jump into the ocean and he wouldn't be able to stop her. He was sure he could get to her before she drowned, but he'd prefer it if she didn't jump.

He glanced over his shoulder at the sound of someone approaching and was relieved when Cillian ran past him. A furious Terrance followed close behind him. Terrance hadn't liked the idea of Cillian taking Chloe, but after Finn had assured him it was not the same as what had happened to his sister, he'd settled down. But now the fury clear in his stormy eyes might just be a problem for all of them.

Cillian approached Chloe slowly. He didn't climb the rocks in case she jumped. "Chloe, come down." His frustration increased when she didn't respond. She was curled into a ball, rocking back and forth, staring out at the horizon.

He looked over his shoulder at his men, then turned back to her. "Chloe, come down. Now!"

His temper ignited when she ignored him, but he wasn't about to start another altercation within earshot of his men. Plus, from her position on the rock, she could jump. But she'd earned the punishment. Now she'd have to get over it. He had calls to make and a situation to assess. He turned back to Rourke. "Watch her."

Chapter 21: Black

Chloe sat on the rock by the ocean for several hours. She was bruised and battered and covered in vomit and Roisin's blood. It was disgusting. Her throat was raw. It felt like she'd swallowed glass and her head was pounding. Her father's voice echoed off the walls in her head. Her mother's screams would haunt her for the rest of her life. He'd caused that. Cillian.

She closed her eyes and focused on the darkness, the stillness, the black space. A sea of black. She wanted to hide in the darkness, in the black. But, while temporarily comforting, she knew it wouldn't protect her. But when she concentrated on it, she didn't feel so helpless. As if all she had to do was focus on the darkness, and maybe she'd be safe. That wasn't likely to happen, though.

She'd tried so hard to keep herself closed off so he couldn't hurt her, but he'd found a way. She was at his mercy. Subject to the whim of a monster. She had to find a way off this island, or at least figure out how to protect herself. To keep what was left of herself protected. To hide any vulnerabilities.

Resolved, she stood and, ignoring her stiff muscles, climbed off the rock. She knew she must look terrible, but Rourke and Terrance didn't comment. Their solemn expressions said it all. She was too exhausted to speak, nor was there anything left to say. She was a prisoner here, and she'd just been given a harsh reminder. She wouldn't forget again.

Chloe slowly looked around her studio. The only place she'd been able to find an ounce of solace here. Then she looked at the sofa where they'd had sex only hours before, and she felt bile rise in her throat again. Her stomach turning violently. Before she could stop it, she vomited what little was left of the contents in her stomach. She wiped her mouth with the back of her hand. Then, with measured steps, she found and opened a can of paint. She dipped her brush and stared into the void. She took her time, her brush strokes meticulously covering every inch of the canvas resting on the easel. The slight sound of the brush against the canvas in the silence was comforting. The soothing acrid scent of the paint so familiar as she worked tirelessly to close off the only pieces of herself that were left open to him.

Slowly, steadily, she rebuilt her defenses, coating the beautiful colors with a shield. A protective barrier to hide the images away for safekeeping. When it was finally covered in a solid wall of black, dark enough to match her soul, she moved on to the next one. It took over two hours to painstakingly cover them all. When she was finished, she dropped her brush on top of the last one and walked out of the room for the last time.

She went to the suite she now shared with a monster and curled up in a chair on the balcony to listen to her father's words as they replayed in a loop over and over in her head. It had been strange, but comforting when he'd called her Chloe Bell. Only Brock had ever called her that. Now it was a stark reminder of all she'd lost.

Cillian checked the app and saw that Chloe was in her studio. Good. At least she was off that fucking rock. He'd give her space, but only so much. Satisfied, he went back to reviewing the accounts for his various enterprises. But something about the earlier scene with her parents tugged at the back of his mind. Some piece of information he was overlooking. Something that shouldn't be there. The attack had been recorded. He was in the habit of recording everything, and he'd already watched it once. Frustrated that it was taking his focus away from his work, he watched the video again, trying to figure out what he was missing.

He paused the screen on David Guidry's face. There was something familiar, something important about his face. Was it because he recognized small traces of Chloe around her father's eyes? He stared at the image for long moments, trying to figure out what was bothering him about David. When nothing came to him, he decided it had to be the traces of Chloe he recognized. He switched the screen to his coding program and immersed himself in writing the final code for his latest weapon.

He created and sold his weapons to various countries all over the world, including the US. He had an unspoken understanding with them all. He agreed not to sell his weapons to certain terrorist groups and in return; They gave him certain concessions. So, even if they knew he had Chloe, they wouldn't dare come after him.

Hours later, his head pounding and his neck sore from bending over his keyboard, he finally left his office for the day. He used the app on his phone again to locate Chloe. She was in their suite where she should be at this hour.

When he stepped off the elevator, he was surprised to see the twins standing guard at his door. Usually, it was one or the other, but never both. Their regular, jovial countenance missing in their somber faces. When he lifted his brow in question, neither of them responded. He didn't know why they were there, and he didn't care. He was ready to see Chloe.

It took him several long minutes of searching their suite to find her. She was sitting out on the balcony curled up in a ball, her arms hugging her knees, staring at the ocean. When he called out to her, she didn't react. He stepped in front of her, and she stared right through him.

"Chloe?" She was wearing the same tank top and shorts from earlier in the day, still covered in blood and vomit. Only now her knees and her fingers were scrapped and bloody and she had black paint all over herself. "Jesus! Why didn't you shower?" He lifted her chin. Her skin was like ice. "You're freezing. Why the fuck are you sitting out here in the cold?" He looked into her eyes and felt his chest tighten. Her usually sparkling blue eyes were dull and vacant.

He lifted her into his arms, tense and ready for her attack. Anticipating it. Relishing the battle to come. But she didn't attack him. She didn't acknowledge him at all. This is not at all what he expected. His little hellion should be furious. She should've at least taken a swing at him.

He carried her into the bathroom and placed her on the counter to get a better look at her. He started the water in the bathtub, then went back to assess the damage. Besides Roisin's blood and the vomit, she had bruises on her legs, and her hands and knees were scraped and covered in more dried blood. He lifted her shirt over her head, and when he looked in the mirror at her reflection, he scowled. Her back was covered in bruises as well. "Did you fall?"

He sighed heavily when she didn't answer. This was getting them nowhere. Once the tub was filled, he turned off the water, but turned on the shower. He finished undressing her, then himself. He pinned her hair up before he picked her up and carried her into the shower. He washed her gently, being careful of her scrapes. "You know, this silent treatment is getting tiresome." Once she was clean, he carried her out of the shower and stepped into the tub. When he sank down into the warm water with her, he was surprised she didn't flinch as the water hit the scrapes on her hands and knees.

He settled back with her resting against his chest. The warm water should help with the soreness from her bruises. He cupped her breasts, massaging them gently. He tugged at her nipples, rolling them between his thumbs and fingers. "Are you ready to talk?"

She had no intension of ever talking to him again. He could do whatever he wanted. She was done.

"You earned your punishment." He was getting angry. His demons were riding him hard. He hated when she ignored him. She wasn't in control here, he was. He pinched her nipples in retaliation. To his surprise, she barely flinched. His demon roared. He jerked her up and turned her around to straddle his lap. Water splashed over the sides of the tub at the violent movements. He held her face close to his while he glared at her. "So, this is how you want to play it!"

Her knees burned from the scrapes hitting the bottom of the tub, but who cared. She just stared back at him showing no sign of fear or intimidation. There was simply nothing there.

Cillian pulled her face closer to his and bit her lip. When there was still no response from her, he rested his forehead against hers, attempting to calm down. "You know angel," he said thoughtfully, "it's not a good idea to piss me off any further."

Late into the night, Cillian reached for Chloe, but she wasn't there. He sat up and looked toward the bathroom, but there was no light under the door. He flipped on the lamp beside his bed and scanned the room. He found her lying curled up in a ball, naked on the floor by the balcony door with her back to him. Crouching next to her, he realized she was asleep. He gently lifted her and carried her back to bed.

They'd had a rough night. She hadn't eaten a single bite of her dinner, nor had she spoken a single word. No amount of bullying or coaxing had worked. When he'd put her to bed, he tried to fuck her, just to get a response. He was eager for a fight. Any response at all. But that hadn't worked either. She just laid there like some sacrificial lamb, which pissed him off further. She hated being tied up, but when he tied her hands, she hadn't fought him. She'd stared at the ceiling and let him touch her as he'd wanted. He'd been so disgusted with himself; he'd ended up untying her and holding her until she'd fallen asleep.

Now her skin was freezing from being on the floor. He covered her with the blanket and curled his body around hers, hugging her close. It took him over an hour to fall back to sleep. Only to wake up again several hours later, alone for the second time. He found her back on the floor by the door. Once he had her back in bed this time, he didn't sleep. He held her and watched as hours later, dawn lit the sky.

The time for her run came and went, but she didn't get up. He ran his fingers through her hair to wake her. When she opened her eyes, there was no sparkle in the now hauntingly beautiful blue. He scooped her up out of bed and carried her into the bathroom. On autopilot, she went about her morning routine in silence. Once she was dressed, he took her hand and together they walked out the door.

They were met by both Rourke and Patrick again. The twins smiled at Chloe. But it was Patrick who spoke.

"Good morning, Chloe." He eyed her anxiously when she didn't respond. "You missed your run."

She just stood there, looking straight ahead. She couldn't let them in anymore. It would make her too vulnerable. Instead, she concentrated on the screams in her head. Her mother's screams.

When Cillian led her into the elevator, she didn't see Patrick scowl at him.

In the dining room, Imogen fussed over Chloe. She made her coffee just the way she liked it. She placed the syrup bottle she preferred next to her place. She hovered close, wringing her hands when Chloe barely sipped the coffee. Cillian filled her plate with the pancakes and bacon he knew she loved, but she just pushed them around on her plate, hardly eating any of it.

His phone chimed with an email that momentarily distracted him. He was typing a response when Chloe stood up and left the dining room without a word.

"Cillian." The worry in Imogen's voice was clear as she stared at the door Chloe had just walked through.

The muscle in his jaw ticked in frustration. "She'll be fine." He'd make sure of it.

Finn was exhausted. He'd gathered the details of the attack and sent them to Titan, then stayed with the men to finish the delivery. Other than a quick nap on the plane, he hadn't slept much in the last 72 hours. He was heading toward the castle when he glimpsed Roisin walking toward the barracks. He sighed and shook his head. His second cousin was a pain in the ass. He was glad she hadn't spotted him. She wouldn't have wanted him to know she was sneaking off to the barracks. But from the distance, he could see a bandage on her arm. He wondered why she was here and what she'd been up to.

He walked around the front of the castle and seeing Patrick and Rourke standing out by the beach, he headed in their direction. He stepped up beside the twins, but neither of them turned to greet him. He shielded his eyes with his hand and followed their gazes out toward the rocks. He frowned when he saw Chloe curled up in a protective ball.

She looked so sad and alone. Nothing like the girl she'd been when he'd left a few days ago. His instincts pricked with warning. "What happened?" When neither of the twins answered, he turned and face them. "I said, what happened?"

They both scowled at him. But surprisingly, it was Rourke who answered. "Ask the boss. We weren't there."

Finn watched the two brothers for a few heartbeats, then looked back at Chloe before he turned and headed toward the castle.

He found Cillian at his desk, watching Chloe on the monitors.

Cillian looked up at his cousin when he walked through the door. "Any problems?"

"Nothing I couldn't handle." He sat in the seat across from Cillian's desk and kicked out his feet.

"Good." Cillian turned his gaze back to Chloe.

"Why is Chloe back on that fuckin rock?" He eyed his cousin carefully. When Cillian simply stared stoically at the screen, he continued. "I saw Roisin heading to the barracks again. What's she doing here?"

"You tell me. She said you were expecting her."

"You know that's bullshit."

"Yea, but that's what she said."

"She must've pissed someone off again and needed a place to hide out. What happened to her arm? I saw the bandage." He chuckled softly. "Don't tell me she did something stupid like attack Chloe again?"

Cillian's his gaze shot from the monitors to his cousin's face. "What did you say?"

Finn gave him a puzzled look and tensed. "Did she attack Chloe again?"

"What do you mean, attack Chloe?"

Finn tilted his head to the side and stared at Cillian in confusion. "Roisin attacked Chloe in the kitchen the first morning she was here. You already know that. I'm just asking if she did it again."

Cillian scowled at him. What the fuck? Roisin was a spoiled, pampered woman. She'd be too concerned about breaking a nail to attack anyone. But his Chloe was a fighter. "Finn, Chloe is the one who attacked Roisin in the kitchen."

Finn frowned and sat forward in his chair. "Why the fuck would Chloe attack Roisin? Didn't Chloe tell you what happened?"

Cillian tried to think back to that morning. Had he even asked her what happened? "Chloe didn't tell me anything."

At the puzzled look on his cousin's face, Finn added, "Imogen and the entire kitchen staff saw it. Didn't you look at the security feed?"

Cillian turned to his computer and jabbed at several buttons on his keyboard, then searched through the log of videos listed by room and date until he found the day he was looking for. He fast forwarded through the breakfast rush until he saw Chloe enter the kitchen. He hit the play button and watched the scene unfold. He heard Chloe's furious rant as she'd announced to the entire kitchen staff what had happened to her. Saw the fear and anguish on her beautiful face. Then he heard the terrible things Roisin said to his woman. His chest tightened, his spine stiffened, and fury surged through his veins as he watched her lunge at Chloe, her hand raised to strike her.

He paused the video and looked over at Finn, his fury a living, breathing thing boiling beneath the surface. "She didn't tell me." He thought back to that morning and tried to remember. Had he given her a chance to?

"So, what happened to Roisin?"

Cillian clicked through the log until he found yesterday's footage from the library. When he clicked play, Finn turned in his chair to face the screens behind him. Together they watched as Roisin stabbed herself then thrust the bloody knife into Chloe's hand. They observed the shock on Chloe's face, then watched as it turned to terror when she saw the anger on his when he'd stormed into the room.

"Fuck!" He roared in fury and with a violent swipe of his arm, cleared his desk. Glass shattered, plastic splintered, and metal clattered to the floor. In all the years of leadership, he'd never made a move without knowing all the facts. Never, until Chloe. Until it mattered the most.

Finn jerked around at the sudden noise. He assessed the livid expression on Cillian's face; the tense flexing of his muscles. "What did you do?"

"What the fuck do you think I did?!" He roared. "I had the crew in New Orleans work her father over a little."

"You didn't?" Finn scowled at him.

"Of course, I did! And that old man of hers? That motherfucker yelled messages to her the whole time. Like he knew she was watching. Fuck!"

"Jesus! Did they hurt him?"

"No! Of course not! But he's a mean son of a bitch. He fractured Nathan's jaw and cracked Jude's rib. They were taking it easy on him, but he didn't hold back! The fucker had to know the men weren't really trying to hurt him."

Even though the situation was dire, Finn couldn't help but chuckle. Chloe had come by her fighting spirit honestly.

Before Finn could comment further, there was a timid knock on the door. They both turned as Imogen opened it without invitation. Her eyes bulged when she saw the mess on the floor, but her worried expression locked onto Cillian.

"Not now, Imogen!" Cillian snapped.

"Cillian," Imogen's voice shook, so she cleared her throat. She was wringing her hands in front of her. She took a breath then continued as tears threatened to fall. "I went to tidy Chloe's studio. I always do it while she's at the beach so I don't disturb her."

Cillian froze at the whispered words, the anguish in her voice.

Finn stepped forward and took Imogen's hand. "It's alright. Tell us."

"Her beautiful paintings, all of her work." She looked from Finn to Cillian.

Finn followed her gaze to Cillian. But he was already rushing toward the door before Imogen finished talking. Finn fell into step behind him, with Imogen taking up the rear as they quickly made their way to the studio.

Cillian stood in the center of Chloe's studio staring in stunned disbelief. He turned in a slow circle, taking in the room. He couldn't believe it! Her beautiful paintings. Ruined! All of them. Completely ruined. The canvases depicting those beautiful scenes, the ones he'd admired just days before, were all completely covered in solid black paint. They weren't carefully displayed against the walls anymore, beautifully depicting her time here on the island. Instead, they were strewn across the floor, all black, evidence of her anguish, her pain. Nothing else had been destroyed, just her creations. "Fuck!"

"Jesus! What the fuck did you do?" For the first time in his life, Finn questioned his cousin's judgement. He was appalled at the implications of what this could mean. He'd helped take Chloe because he'd been so sure she was the one. The one to give his cousin back his humanity. She was strong and clever and so self-assured. And Cillian had never, not once, ever wanted a woman for his own. He'd never considered simply taking a woman until Chloe Guidry. That's when he'd realized who and what Chloe was.

Initially, the thought had been staggering and so out of character for Cillian. So, he'd convinced himself that she was the one. His cousin's mate. He'd justified taking her, knowing that she would be the queen to his king. Throughout history, the reigning O'Donnell's were notorious for taking their mates. Legend was that the O'Donnell men knew instantly when they met their woman. It was instinct. As late as Cillian's own mother, it was just the way it was always done. And the O'Donnell's mated for life. Never had there been a divorce.

How could they have gotten it so wrong? And worse still, how were they going to fix it? How did they give her back? Finn looked around at the ruined paintings, then back to Cillian's tormented face. He faced his cousin squarely, ready for an attack. His anger more than clear in his threat. "You fix this, or let her go."

Cillian turned deadly cold eyes on the one man he trusted more than anyone in the world. "Never."

Cillian filled Chloe's plate with roasted duck, sauteed spinach and sweet potato souffle. She was going to eat, whether she wanted to or not. But she never even picked up her fork. She simply stared down at her lap. Finn was still scowling at him, but he didn't give a fuck. He watched Chloe closely out of the corner of his eye while he waited.

He didn't have to wait long. Roisin sauntered into the room like she owned it. The smug smile on her face caused his boiling blood to simmer as it always did right before a kill. Earlier, after ordering Terrance, Patrick, and Rourke not to let anyone near Chloe under any circumstances, he'd gone to the training field. There he and Finn worked through most of the adrenalin coursing through his veins. They'd nearly beaten the shit out of each other, but it had helped to clear his head and it had kept him from doing something he might later regret.

"Really, Cillian!" Roisin gasped dramatically. "You expect me to sit at the same table as your whore after she tried to kill me?" Roisin pressed her hand to her chest in shocked indignation.

"Sit down, Roisin." Finn hissed.

"Well, hello to you too, cousin." Her snide voice was cutting. She flipped her hair over her shoulder, arrogantly. "Maybe you missed it, but his shiny new toy tried to kill me yesterday."

"Sit down!" Cillian barked.

Roisin paled slightly, but undeterred, she made a show of arrogantly taking her seat. She flashed a smug, extremely satisfied smile in Chloe's direction when the girl didn't acknowledge her.

Cillian deliberately took a slow drink of iced tea while he watched the bitch closely. "You know Roisin, I never cared that you used the soldiers in my barracks for your own personal stud service."

Roisin gasped and dropped her fork. "I beg your pardon?"

"As long as there was no in-fighting among my men, I didn't care who you fucked."

"What the hell are you talking about?" Mortified, she glanced quickly at Finn who watched her coldly then at Chloe before finally coming back to Cillian's steely gaze.

"I actually found it amusing that they were all ok with taking turns at you. Passing you around, maybe drawing straws to see who was next, probably comparing notes afterward."

"How dare you!"

Cillian look over at Finn and they shared a menacing grin. "Did it bother you, Finn? Did you care that your cousin here was slipping my soldiers up to her room at night for a quick fuck, or that she was slithering out to the barracks in the wee hours of the morning when she thought no one was watching?"

"Second cousin, once removed." Finn reminded. "But no, I didn't give a shit. We both know she's been doing it for years and she's a grown woman. If she wants to play the whore for the men, why should I care?"

"You can't say that about me, Finn! My father will kill you!" Roisin screamed. Her face was red with fury.

"I found it strange though that she actually thought you'd want her after she'd been passed around so much between your men." Finn added fuel to the fire.

"You fucker!" Roisin screamed again and stood so fast her chair crashed to the floor behind her. She picked up her glass and threw it at his head.

Finn moved his head to dodge the glass, but stayed seated. The door behind Roisin burst open and Terrance, Rourke, and Patrick stepped into the room. Terrance moved to stand behind Chloe's chair. He crossed his arms over his massive chest and stoically stood guard over her. Rourke and Patrick each grabbed one of Roisin's arms and held her in place.

She yanked hard, struggling to break free. "What the hell do you think you're doing?! Do you have any idea who I am? Let go of me, this instant!"

Cillian slid his knife from its sheath. The sound causing her to freeze in place.

Chloe's head lifted at the sound, her eyes tracking Cillian in time to see him step in front of Roisin and hold the knife against her throat. When he put pressure on the blade, blood trickled down her throat to her overly exposed chest.

"No!" Chloe screamed. She couldn't stop herself! He was going to kill her, and his men weren't trying to stop him. Who were these people?

Cillian turned those diamond hard green eyes on her at the interruption and she inhaled audibly. The fury, the suppressed violence, was more than obvious, and it was another terrifying reminder of who held her prisoner.

"Quiet, baby." He hushed her. His cruel gaze roaming impudently over her beautiful face before he turned his attention back to the bitch.

"Don't!" Chloe pleaded. Oh, God! He was going to do it!

Cillian grabbed a handful of Roisin's hair and yanked her head back as he leaned in. "Did you honestly think I wouldn't see what you did to my woman?" His voice was deadly quiet as he put pressure on the blade, and more blood trickled down her neck.

Roisin went as white as a ghost and recoiled, trying to put space between her throat and the knife.

"Every fucking inch of this castle and the grounds are under twenty-four hour video surveillance. I see and hear everything. From the men you've fucked to your preference for threesomes in the woods. Fucking my men down in the dirt and twigs when you think no one can see. I see it all. I see everything, bitch!"

"Cillian," her voice trembled. "I,"

"Shut the fuck up!" The monster in him was seething for vengeance. He glanced back over his shoulder at Chloe. Her beautiful blue eyes held terror. That terror fueled his need for vengeance.

"Please!" Chloe couldn't stand Roisin, but she didn't want her dead. Holy shit!

Resolved, Cillian turned back to the bitch and hissed between clenched teeth. "If Chloe wasn't here, I'd slit your fucking throat." He looked back at Chloe again and glared. The demon inside him livid at being denied. "For you, I won't kill her. Do you hear me?!" He roared, "for you!" His loud bark echoing off the walls of the dining room.

Chloe jumped at the sound and covered her head with her arms.

"No! You look at me, Chloe!"

Chloe couldn't stop the tears from sliding down her cheeks, but she lifted her head slowly and met his tormented gaze.

"It's my right to kill this bitch. She deserves it for what she did to you and you fuckin know it! But for you, I'll let her live. Only for you, Chloe. Do you understand what that means?"

She was so terrified; she was crying uncontrollably. She had no idea what he meant.

"Do you?!" He increased the pressure on the knife at Roisin's neck.

"N..No," she stuttered through trembling lips.

"You will soon enough." Cillian looked over at Patrick and Rourke. "Get this whore off my fuckin island." He looked back down at the bitch. "Finn will pack your shit and send it back to you after he's searched it."

"But you can't,"

"Take her!" He wiped the blood off of his blade on her blouse, then sheathed it and watched as the twins dragged her from the room. They could hear her curses and threats fading in the distance. When the room was silent again, he turned back toward Chloe.

Cillian slammed his palms down on the table directly across from her. His penetrating glare seared her from the inside out. "Finish your lunch. We have things to do this afternoon."

Chapter 22: Running Away Little Rabbit?

Cillian gripped Chloe's hand tightly as they walked through the apple orchard. Her back was rigid, her hand stiff in his. He'd instructed their security detail to give them some space. She hadn't eaten a single bite of her lunch, and she still wasn't speaking. Not just to him, but to any of them. That stopped now.

Using his hold on her hand, he pulled her around and placed her back against the trunk of a large apple tree. He braced himself against the tree at her shoulders, caging her in. Her mutinous gaze was focused over his shoulder.

"Look at me." His voice echoed with barely controlled rage. When she didn't shift her eyes to his, he slid a finger beneath her collar and lifted it high, bringing her up onto her toes, her face close to his, capturing her attention.

"You are going to forgive me. I don't fuckin care if you want to or not, you are." He decreed.

Chloe scowled at him. "Or what? You'll slice my throat too?"

"No, never." Her response soothed the beast pacing beneath the surface. Her bravery knew no bounds. Now they were getting somewhere. And if this weren't so important, he'd give in to the urge to grin at her little scowl. Instead, he leaned down, pressed his forehead to hers and whispered softly, "I'm so sorry."

Chloe closed her eyes to avoid his beautiful eyes.

"No baby, look at me. I'm sorry."

She was terrified; trembling so hard her teeth were chattering. She didn't want to hear this.

"Your father is fine, Chloe. He's a strong old man. He wasn't seriously injured." He chuckled to break the tensions between them and added, "But my men didn't fare so well against him. He nearly beat the shit out of them."

She knew her father was strong. She didn't need him to tell her that. But that changed nothing.

"I should've checked the surveillance first. That's on me and I'm sorry."

She opened her eyes and met his sincere gaze. But she wasn't going to be taken in by his handsome face again. She was done making deals with the devil.

He released her collar and clasped her hip in one hand and her chin in the other and turned her face up to his. "Chloe?"

She jerked her face from his hold. "Leave me alone!"

"Baby."

"Don't! You lied! I followed your stupid rules and you hurt my parents, anyway!" She was hyperventilating as fear and anger chocked her. "And you were going to kill her. I saw it in your eyes. You said you'd never lie to me and you did! You're a monster! And I promise you, I'll never forget that again! So just leave me alone. You holding me prisoner here and you've turned me into your whore. What more do you want?!"

Cillian grabbed her chin and forced her face closer to his. "You are not my whore!" His voice; a whiplash of reprimand. "Those words better never cross your lips again! Do you hear me? Ever!"

She refused to shed another tear. Never again. She jerked out of his hold and ran toward the castle as fast as her feet would take her.

Cillian nearly bolted after her. But he had plans to make. So, he nodded his head at Patrick to indicate he should follow her. Then he watched as she disappeared into the distance.

A week later Cillian found Chloe curled up in a chair in the library reading a book about Italian artists. They'd been circling each other for days. Her silently ignoring him, him teasing her at every turn, hoping to crack the ice she surrounded herself with. Every night he'd hold her as she drifted off to sleep, only to wake up hours later to find her on the floor by the door again.

He snagged the book from her hands, and she scowled at him. He tried unsuccessfully not to grin. She couldn't close herself off completely. The warrior in her wouldn't allow it. "Come on, we have things to do."

"I don't want to train today." Her emotionless voice matched the void in her eyes.

"I didn't say we were training." He pulled her to her feet by her wrist and practically dragged her to their suite. He left her by the bed and went into her closet and came back with a pair of jeans and boots. "Put these on." He tossed the jeans to her and dropped the boots at her feet, then went back into the closet.

She frowned at the jeans. The fabric would rub against the cuts on her knees so she went into the bathroom and put band aids over them, then slipped into the snug denim.

He came back out and handed her a jacket. "Let's go."

They walked out of the castle together, and she was surprised to see a set of trail bikes waiting for them. Finn and Jacob were sitting casually on bikes of their own.

"Do you know how to ride?" Cillian pulled her over to the smaller of the two bikes.

"Yes." She didn't look at him or her guards. Instead, she focused on the bike. The Yamaha 250 trail bike was smaller than the 450's the men were sitting on, but it was still very cool.

Cillian lifted the helmet from the seat and put it on her head. They stared at each other while he buckled the strap under her chin. His eyes searching her disinterested ones. Once he had the buckle fastened, he leaned in and kissed her mouth quickly before she could pull away. "Let's ride, baby."

She jerked away from the asshole and ignoring his chuckle, mounted the bike. Hoping to drown out anything he might say, she started it and revved the engine.

They spent the afternoon riding the bikes around the entire island. She got to see where the main airstrip was located. That's how they got supplies to the island and shipped out their own products. She also got to see the dock where his yacht was berthed. She'd carefully looked around for any sign of another boat. One not so heavily guarded. But there wasn't one. Everywhere she looked, there were men with guns.

At one point, they parked the bikes at the bottom of the mountain and climbed for a while. Cillian explained it would take several hours to reach the top, but that the view from the cliff was amazing. He said he planned to bring her back later to spend a day showing her the mountains.

They rode through trails from one end of the island to the other. It was nearly dark when they pulled back up to the castle. She was dusty and exhausted, but exhilarated. Her adrenalin was still pumping. It had been an amazing way to spend the afternoon. She'd had to focus on controlling the bike through all the twists and turns, so she hadn't had time to think too much.

Cillian removed his helmet, then unbuckled hers. "Your covered in dust, baby." He touched the tip of his finger to her dusty nose.

She looked up at him and instinctively giggled before she could suppress her reaction. "So are you." Without his helmet, his face looked like he was wearing a dirt mask. She imagined she looked the same way.

His eyes sparkled at her reaction, and a pleased smile spread across his face. "Let's get cleaned up. You must be starving."

"I am." And to her surprise, she really was.

He tossed her helmet to Jacob then together; they went up to their suite.

Cillian stepped into the shower just as Chloe was rinsing her hair. He leaned under the other shower head and quickly washed up. When they'd entered their room earlier, she'd immediately tensed up and closed herself off again. As if she were stepping back into a place she didn't want to be. And he wasn't ready to lose the carefree woman from moments before.

After rinsing the soap from his face and hair, he flashed her a devilish grin and reached up to wipe her face. "You missed a spot."

Just as he expected, she reacted by rubbing at her face. "Where?"

"Here, let me." He soaped up his hands again and dabbed his fingers on her face. "What about me? Did I get it all off?"

She searched his face for a moment. "Yes, you're clean." It wasn't fair that he was so handsome. His hard body so beautiful. That sexy smile triggering flutters in her belly.

He moved into her, edging her up against the wall. His soapy hands smoothing over her skin.

"Stop." She lifting her hands to his chest to push him away.

He crowed closer, taking her hands in one of his and pushing them above her head. He was determined to move them past this hurdle. He crouched and slid his aching cock between her thighs. Gliding his hard length back and forth through her delicate folds.

"Don't, Cillian!" She hissed.

He ignored her and leaned in and suckled at her neck. He kept up a steady rhythm, gliding through her delicate folds over and over, until she softened against him. "I need you baby," he whispered at her ear, then suckled the sensitive skin of her neck again. His free hand slid through the suds on her slick skin to cup her breasts, wet fingers circling her nipples, pinching gently.

She shivered and arched her back at the delicious sensation, pushing her breasts into his hand. She couldn't fight her body's response. It recognized his, responded to his, craved his, even when she didn't want it to. She hated it, and she hated him. God, did she hate him. But the aching need he awakened deep inside her was unbearable. He made her crave him, crave his touch. And that realization was devastating.

When she rocked against the hard edge of his cock, he released her hands to slide his down to her thighs and he lifted her, pinning her between him and the shower wall. He wrapped her legs around his waist, captured her lips. He kissed her as he slid deep into her tight sheath. She was slick and hot, tightening around him. Squeezing him.

She was enveloped in a cocoon of strength. His hands at her bottom, his arms flexing as he carefully guided her up and down onto his driving cock. His mouth at her neck, suckling the sensitive area, nibbling, then biting down to hold her in place. She took him deeper than ever before in this position. It was new and different, and she felt so full. She squeezed her legs around his waist and canted her hips to accept his thrusts. The head of his cock sliding across that sensitive spot deep inside her. His pelvis rubbed against her clit. She was losing herself in pleasure. Lost in a place where there was no thought, no anger or remorse, only delicious pleasure. A driving need taking over. Pushing her toward the rush she craved.

Chloe came alive around him. Her response to his touch driving him forward. Encouraging him to thrust deeper, harder. The need to make them one, to stay connected so deep was instinctive. She was a living flame burning into his soul. When she cried out and pulsed around him, he gloried in the scorching heat that clamped down so tightly as she fought to keep him deep. A rush of liquid fire bathed his cock. He exploded with her, coating her womb with his own fire. Needing to brand her as she had branded him.

Cillian carried an exhausted Chloe from the bathroom, straight to the kitchen. His stomach growled at the delicious aroma coming from the table. He sat in his seat with her cradled in his lap.

"I can sit in my own chair." She protested sleepily.

"Shh, let's eat so you can rest." Her restless sleep for so many nights was catching up with her. He fed her small bites of the seafood cannelloni with red pepper Alfredo sauce and several bites of the green salad before she dozed off in his arms. He finished his own meal with her bare, soft warmth cuddled into him.

After he finished eating, he continued to sit for a few minutes longer, just caressing her soft skin. He wasn't foolish enough to think their battle was over. He'd claimed her body. She'd never be able to dispute that, but he didn't have all of her yet. She'd been keeping him at an emotional distance purposely. Now it would be even worse. But he had no intention of allowing it. She had to forgive him so they could move forward. And she would forgive him. He wouldn't give her a choice.

That night Chloe left their bed again, unable to bear lying next to him; her skin touching his. It was terrifying to have a monster wrapped around you when you were sleeping.

Cillian found Chloe in the same place as so many nights before, naked on the floor facing the ocean. Her blanket from home was only six feet away, draped over the back of the sofa. He thought it odd that she hadn't used it to cover herself. She was instinctively moving away from him in her sleep.

As with every night for the last week, he carried her back to bed and tucked her in. He pulled a silk tie from his wardrobe and tied her wrist to his. Once she was secured, he curled around her and went back to sleep. He woke a few hours later to the pull on his wrist. In the dark, he dragged her back beneath him, hushed her protests, then held her until she settled back down. Within moments, she was asleep again.

Just before dawn, Cillian woke Chloe with his mouth. His tongue thrusting deep into her luscious heat. He ensured she came awake hot and needy, with fire racing through her veins. When she moaned and arched her back, he lifted over her and drove his cock deep into her heat. Wrapped tightly in his arms, he took her over the edge before she was fully awake. Then he held her close, kissing her softly until she dozed off again.

When the sun began to rise and Chloe didn't move to get up for her run, Cillian bullied her out of bed and forced her to get dressed. He had no intension of allowing her to continue closing herself off from him or the people she'd come to care for on the island. So, he dragged her out to the back patio where they were met by his men. They ran their usual route with her in the center, silently keeping pace with the group.

She was also quiet at breakfast while he and Finn discussed his latest project. He watched her closely while she ignored the eggs and only nibbled on a piece of toast.

Chloe needed air. She felt like she was under a microscope. Cillian and Finn were both stealing glances at her, and it was unnerving. She finished her toast and stood to leave.

"Where are you going?" Cillian asked as he and Finn both turned when she stood.

"I'm going for a walk out on the beach."

"Running away, little rabbit?" He taunted.

She narrowed her eyes at him. Was he kidding? She would not dignify that with a response.

"Don't be long, we're going to play golf today."

"Why?"

"You do know how to play golf, don't you?" He knew the best way to keep Chloe engaged was to challenge her. To poke at her natural competitive spirit.

"Yes."

"Good, then I won't have to take it easy on you. Hurry back." He winked at her, then purposely turned back to Finn to continue their conversation.

She frowned at his back, then turned and stomped out of the room. She could swear she heard male laughter behind her.

She was sitting on her rock, watching the waves crash, when Ian silently climbed up and sat beside her. Neither spoke for long moments. Finally, he whispered in a tortured voice, "does he beat you up Chloe?"

Her gaze flew to his face at the sound of the anguish in his voice. But he wasn't looking at her face. Instead, he was looking down at the scrapes on her knees and the bruises on her shins. From the worry in his eyes, it was obvious that he cared about her. Just as much as she'd grown to care about him in the short time she'd been there.

She couldn't tell him what Cillian had done to her father or to Roisin. This was his home. She didn't want to make him feel unsafe. This was her problem, not his. She reached out and stroked his unruly curls back from his face. "No, he doesn't beat me."

"But, the bruises,"

"We had an argument, and I got upset. I ran and then tripped and fell down the stairs."

He eyed her suspiciously, as if he didn't believe her. "You promise?"

"Yeah buddy. I promise. He doesn't beat me. He wouldn't do that." As soon as the words left her lips, she realized she didn't know anymore. Initially, she hadn't thought he would, but now she wasn't so sure. Cillian was violent and deadly. She'd seen that for herself in the past few days, and it was terrifying.

But thinking back over the time that she'd been here and all the times she'd fought him, he'd never retaliated with violence toward her. And more than once he'd kept her from hitting the floor when she tripped during their scuffles. Instead, he teased her in that sexy way of his and then overpowered her. But he'd never struck her in anger. That didn't mean he wouldn't, only that he hadn't yet.

Only when he'd thought she'd stabbed someone had he gotten furious with her. Even then, he hadn't physically hurt her, not really. Her father, yes, and she would never forgive him for that. But not her. He'd never laid a hand on her in violence other than to hold her in place to watch the screen. And even then, he hadn't bruised her neck. She'd checked.

She smiled at Ian to put his mind at ease. He was too young to understand hers and Cillian's insane relationship. Hell, she didn't even understand it. But she really didn't want to talk about it with a kid, so she changed the subject. "How are you doing in math?"

The next month passed with Chloe spending more and more time in the library. There were tons of books on art history. It seemed that every other day, a new one appeared in the collection. She enjoyed learning about famous artists and the time periods of their work. It was fascinating, but she missed painting.

She refused to go back to the studio. She wouldn't open herself up in that way ever again. Instead, she painted in her head. There, she created intricate designs and colorful images, one brush stroke at a time. It was no substitute for holding a brush and smelling the fumes, but it was all she would allow herself.

To make matters worse, every day Cillian came up with a new way for them to spend time together. It was almost as if they were dating. It was disconcerting being around him so much, and it made it harder to keep an emotional distance. He was charming and flirted relentlessly. He worked in his office while she read in the library, but when lunch and their training sessions were finished for the day, he always had plans for them.

He teased her about her skills when they'd played golf, trying to coax a smile from her. He took her hiking up the mountain to show her the view from the cliff. During the climb, he told her about his childhood and asked questions about hers. She gave him very little and focused on the climb. Once they'd reached the top, he'd wrapped his arms around her, squeezing her tightly when she tried to pull away. Then he's rested his chin on top of her head while they silently took in the view.

He took her out on his boat several times and taught her to scuba dive. There was a whole unknown world under the ocean, and it fascinated her. She'd gotten to see some of the most beautiful marine life. It had been amazing, and she'd loved every minute of it. He took her snorkeling on the reef on the west side of the island. The coral was delicate and beautiful. He took her deep-sea fishing for Tuna and she'd shown him up by catching more fish than he did. That was something she knew how to do really well.

Cillian challenged her and piqued her interest constantly. He goaded her and teased her as he fueled her adventurous spirit and her desire to learn new things. It was as if he could see inside her head and knew her triggers. No matter how hard she tried to keep him at arm's length, he was steadily working his way into her heart. If he hadn't had her father beaten, she imagined she'd probably be one of those stupid women who fell head over heels for her abductor. But he had, so she wouldn't.

At the end of each day, he'd take her to their suite, and every night she fought him with all her strength. She refused to go to him willingly. He'd taken too much from her already. But her emotional stability was teetering on a razor's edge, her nerves stretched thin. She wanted to hate him, needed to hate him, but he was slowly wearing her down.

Cillian was having trouble controlling the furious beast raging inside him. He wanted Chloe. All of her. But his angel had a way of politely keeping him at an emotional distance that he couldn't dispute. And it pissed him off. She was carefully following the rules, not causing any rift. She barely spoke to anyone now and when she did, it was only to respond when spoken to directly, except for Ian and little Annie.

Every day, she pasted a polite smile on her face that didn't reach her eyes. He hated that fucking smile. She hid behind it, using it to keep him from getting too close. It was time to change that.

Even though it was out of character for him, he'd tried to be nice. He really did. He'd given her enough time to accept him and her new life, but his little hellion continued to be stubborn. So be it. He was a selfish bastard by nature, and it was time to take what he fucking wanted.

.

Chapter 23: Now You Want to Talk?

The sound of the door closing had Chloe looking back at Cillian. Her apprehension increased a little more. He'd been unusually quiet on the ride back to the castle, too quiet. Every time she looked at him, he'd been staring at her. They'd spent the afternoon at the store with Molly and Annie. She hadn't seen them in weeks because Cillian kept planning activities, but today she'd asked to go to the store and he'd taken her.

On the drive back, he'd refused to release her hand, his thumb stroking her palm softly in a mesmerizing rhythm. Now he was leaning against the closed door with his arms crossed over his chest, his legs spread wide, watching her intently.

"Did you have fun with Annie today, angel?" He was done with the emotional distance. It was never more evident than when he watched her interact with her new friends. She gave them pieces of herself that she refused to give him, and he was at the end of his patience. It stopped today.

"Yes. She's a sweet little girl."

"Do you think it's wise to goad me?"

"I'm not goading you." Is that what his problem was? She instinctively put her hands on her hips and cocked her leg out slightly. He was trying to intimidate her and she wasn't having it.

His eyes narrowed at her defiant stance. He dropped his arms and placed them behind him on the door to keep from turning her over his knee. His palm actually itched to spank her. Her little sassy attitude was hard to resist. "Do you intend to hold me at arm's length forever?"

"Do you intend to hold me hostage forever?" Her chin went up automatically.

He watched her for a few minutes while he made up his mind. She wasn't going to give in without a fight. And if she wanted a fight, he'd give her one. "Go take a shower, dinner will be here soon."

"Alright." She escaped into her closet for her robe before he could say anything else.

Cillian made a quick call to the kitchen, then unlocked the huge antique chest and carefully laid out a few items on the bed. He smiled to himself while he did it. She thought this was over, but it wasn't. Not by a long shot. When he had everything set up, he closed the bedroom door leading into the den, then followed her into the bathroom.

Chloe was rinsing the conditioner from her hair when Cillian stepped into the shower. She watched him carefully through half-closed eyes while her head was under the spray.

He washed quickly. Their eyes locked as they circled each other in a silent battle of wills. The trepidation in hers soothed him.

When Chloe finished drying off, she slipped into her robe and went to the vanity to deal with her wet hair.

He stepped up behind her and took the brush from her hand.

"I can do it." She tried to take the brush back.

"Let me." Menacing eyes simmering with heat met hers in the mirror, so she lowered her hand. He quietly brushed most of the water from her hair, then braided the slightly damp locks. As soon as he tied off the braid, he took her hand and led her out of the bathroom.

Chloe should've known she was in trouble when he led her toward the bed and not the kitchen. "I thought we were eating?"

"In due time, angel." Cillian suddenly shoved her face down on the bed in a move so abrupt she couldn't have avoided it if she tried. He had her pinned beneath him in the next breath.

"What the hell are you doing? Get off me!" He'd shoved her far enough onto the bed that her feet were dangling in the air over the side so she had no leverage. That didn't stop her from wriggling and squirming to dislodge him.

"Now, hellion, it's time you understood a few things." He whispered in her ear.

She stopped squirming as unease settled over her. "Cillian, please get off of me." She tried to keep her voice as calm as possible. "If you want to talk, we can. Let's talk over dinner."

"Now you want to talk?" His frustrated voice whispered in her ear. "Oh no, angel. You've had weeks to talk to me. Weeks. I've given you ample time, but you chose not to." He pushed the robe off of her, then jerked both of her hands behind her back and clasped them together in one of his. He wrapped a small piece of black rope around her wrists and tied it in a knot to hold her hands in place so he could work.

Cillian sat on Chloe's thighs and used a simple Shibari rope technique to wrap a soft sapphire blue rope meticulously around each arm from bicep to wrist, making sure not to pinch her delicate skin, kissing and licking as he went. He weaved a gorgeous sapphire, diamond pattern that when the light caught the weave it sparkled against her skin. The pattern included an inline double coin knot that connected her wrists together. He loved seeing her in his ropes.

"Cillian, don't do this!" Her unease grew as she shivered at the feel of the rope combined with his warm hands and his soft lips sliding gently over her skin. He tied her often, but usually just her hands. This was different. It was sensual, tantalizing. He was seducing her and she couldn't like this, she wouldn't. But the rope was soft and delicate against her skin, like the sleeves of a silk blouse.

"I apologized. Didn't I baby?"

"Cillian?"

"No, I apologized. I never do that. But for you, I did," he whispered against her spine. Once she was secured correctly, he removed the black rope, then moved down her legs, using his weight to keep her in place. He tied her ankles with it to keep her still so he could complete the intricate diamond weave down each of her legs from just above her knees to her ankles. He tied the ends together with the same knot, only this time leaving about twelve inches of slack between her ankles.

Chloe closed her eyes and breathed through the sensations. "I know you did, but you still hurt my parents." The rope wrapped around the bottom half of each leg felt like soft, strappy little sandals against her skin. It wasn't tight, it didn't cut off her circulation. Instead, it was soft, and delicate, and warm.

"They weren't hurt." Cillian took his time, wanting her to feel every touch of his hands against her skin. Every soft, lingering kiss. The slide of the rope as it caressed her. He paid close attention to his work to again ensure the soft rope didn't pinch her skin. When he tied off the knot between her ankles, he left a six-inch length of rope as a tether. He removed the shorter black piece and sat back to admire his work. She was so beautiful.

Cillian checked each twist and weave a second time. He wanted her to love his ropes, to crave the feel of them against her gorgeous skin. Once he was assured it wouldn't pinch her, he lifted the tether to her wrists, causing her feet to lift with it. He slipped it through the knot between her wrists and pulled it tight until her ankles and wrists were connected, then tied it off. In this position, with the pattern he'd chosen, she looked like a beautiful butterfly.

She was breathless. "Please, um, un...untie me." Her skin was alive, overly sensitive.

He'd already folded down the blankets before he'd gone into the shower, so he positioned her in the center of the bed surrounded by white satin sheets.

Chloe turned her thoughts inward to try and understand why the ropes felt so sensual. How they could make her feel so secure. And the satin sheets against her bare skin were luxurious.

When she was in the position he wanted, Cillian went to the nightstand to get his phone and took several pictures of her. When he was satisfied with the pictures, he dropped his phone and picked up a blue silk scarf.

"Oh no, no Cillian!" She was definitely panicking now.

"Eventually you're going to realize that word doesn't work with us angel." He slipped the silk over her eyes and tied it behind her head.

"It should!" She hissed.

"Relax baby. I'm not going to hurt you." He started at her cheek, raining soft kisses down the side of her neck, over her shoulder to the center of her back. He continued down her spine, around the knots, and through the weave of the rope. His hands slid from the sides of her breasts, down her torso to her hips. He caressed and kissed every inch of her.

"You expect me to believe you?" She huffed out her breath at the feel of his soft, warm lips and those large gentle hands.

"Yes." He whispered against her skin. "You should know me by now. You're just mad because I have control. But that's ok little hellion. I bet if I untie you, you'd come up swinging. Wouldn't you baby?"

"Yes."

"Yea, you would." He laughed softly against her hip. She was such a sassy little thing. "You're withholding something from me, aren't you, angel?"

"No."

"Yes, you are." He whispered and continued to slide his hands gently over her skin.

Her tense muscles slowly relaxed under his knowing hands. "No, I'm not."

"Such a little liar." Came his quite response as he caressed her and teased her with gentle kisses for long moments before he released the tie holding her ankles to her wrists and lowered her legs. He smiled knowingly when she let them fall languidly where he put them. He lifted her torso and shoved several pillows beneath her belly so her head was on the bed, but her ass was raised up high for him.

"What are you doing?" she groaned in a whispered voice.

"Relax, baby." He framed her ass with his hands and kissed each cheek, nipping her with his teeth. He nudged her thighs wide and felt a deep sense of satisfaction at the site of her glistening little pussy. He slid his fingers through the wet heat his ropes and his caresses had caused. "Baby," he crooned, "you like my ropes, don't you?" His angel was perfect. He leaned in and sucked her already swollen clit into his mouth.

Chloe groaned at the wicked sensation.

Cillian suckled her softly, adding the pressure of his finger, pushing gently in and out of her until she was right on the edge. When she was thrusting against his mouth, trying to get a deeper penetration, he pulled back.

Her breath escaped in a loud rush as she moaned softly.

He reached for the toys he'd prepared for her. He put lubricant on the plug, then hit the button on the remote. When it started vibrating, he pressed the tip to her ass.

Chloe flinched slightly when she felt the now familiar wet tip touch her there.

"Easy baby." He lashed at her clit with quick strokes of his tongue.

"Oh, God!" The decadent sensations were overwhelming. The delicious heat intoxicating.

He worked the wet tip of the plug at her ass, circling it with the slick vibrating point until she opened for him. Then he slowly pushed the plug all the way inside of her. Once it was seated in place, he flipped the remote again, increasing the speed of the vibrations a little higher. He palmed the cheeks of her ass, pulling them wide apart, stretching her little opening further, adding another level of sensation against the vibrating plug. "Your tight little ass is fuckin perfect baby."

"Ci... Cillian. I can't take this." She pleaded as the pulsing, stretching sensations nearly drove her insane.

She was writhing against the pillows, pushing her pelvis toward him. He palmed her pussy and used his fingers lightly at her clit. "Shhh, baby. Just relax. You can take it." He soothed her with his soft Irish brogue.

When she was fully focused on the vibrations and his stroking fingers, he reached for another toy. He used the lube to moisten the electronic Ben Wa balls, then slowly pushed the three smooth little glass orbs attached to a soft silicone string deep inside her, one at a time. The balls were small, like oversized marbles, so they would move inside her freely, but not painfully.

"Cillian!"

He chuckled and hit the button on the remote for the balls, and watched with satisfaction as she jerked against her bindings when they came to life buzzing against the walls of her tight channel. She shrieked when he turned up the vibrating plug, increasing the speed even higher.

The vibrations of the plug and the balls at different speeds would drive her insane.

"Oh My God!" Chloe shrieked at the unfamiliar sensation. "What is that!?"

"Those are Ben Wa balls. They'll vibrate and move inside you as you move and as the plug vibrates. You're going to love it."

"Oh" She groaned, the plug caused those vibrating balls to move softly, buzzing ever so slightly against that sensitive spot inside of her. It felt so wicked.

Cillian lifted Chloe with one arm and arranged the pillows against the headboard before putting her on her knees with her ass resting on her heels, her thighs spread wide. Her back against the pillows.

She gasped loudly as the balls shifted inside her at the movement.

He crouched on the bed between her knees and, holding onto her hips, leaned in and sucked her breast deep into his mouth. The sensations wracking her body already had her nipples diamond hard. He loved how those hard pink tips felt against his tongue.

Chloe's head fell back, and she gasped again. She was losing herself, sinking deep, then she heard the clink of the familiar chain. "No. It's too much!"

"Shh. baby, it's going to be so good." Cillian soothed her while he attached the clamp on her nipple and tightened it down.

"Oh shittttt!" She breathed through the expletive, panting through the sensation. She couldn't stop shaking her head. Her back bowed, pushing her breast out toward him.

To assure himself, he reached between her legs and felt the pulse of warm wetness as it gushed from her, coating his fingers. Yea, she was with him. He smiled to himself and licked the luscious essence from his fingers. His cock tightening at the sweet taste that was only Chloe.

He lifted her other breast high and lashed the nipple with his tongue until she was shivering violently. He attached the second clamp, then purposely released her breast quickly, so the motion caused it to sway. The chain pulled and her other breast swayed with it.

She gasped loudly and tried to squeeze her knees closed as the sharp tug and pull at her nipples sent fiery sparks of need to her core.

Cillian stopped her with his hands on her thighs, holding her open. "Cillian!"

"Breath through it, angel." He placed his mouth at her neck, where it met her shoulder, and suckled.

"I need," she moaned and rocked her hips uncontrollably. Her head fell back, exposing her neck to him, needing the connection of his warm soft lips. The delicious heat adding to the electric stimulation. He kissed and suckled her neck and face, nibbling at her lips until her head was swimming.

"You need to come, don't you baby?" He whispered against the tender skin of her neck.

"Yes," She whimpered. Her senses were alive with anticipation. She was so close to that blissful place only he could take her.

Cillian reached between her tights and cupped her pussy again, circling her clit with his thumb. When she ground against his palm, trying to increase the friction, he removed his hand.

"Cillian!" She was right there, just a second longer. One more stroke.

"Shh." He soothed. He lifted his mouth away from her skin and turned down the vibrations on the plug and the balls to their lowest settings. Resting his hands on her outer thighs, he waited long minutes for her breathing to settle.

Chloe didn't understand why he'd stopped. She'd been so close to the edge that she ached with unsatisfied need. It took several minutes for her pulse to slow back down. It felt like she was under a sensual attack from every angle. She rocked back and forth in frustration.

Cillian stroked his cock as he watched her come down. His need to punish her, warring with his need to fuck her. She was so beautifully responsive to his touch. His cock ached like a gaping wound. The head throbbing as moisture beaded, then oozed down to his balls. The desire to push inside the tight heat her body promised; nearly his undoing. It would be ecstasy. Heaven and hell combined in a collaboration of sensual oblivion.

But his little hellion needed to learn a lesson. He hit the switch on the remotes and brought the devices to life again. Her back bowed at the sudden vibrations. He tongued her clamped nipples with delicate flicks of his tongue repeatedly. His hand moved between her legs again, his thumb casually circling her swollen clit. She went up so much faster this time. Teetering on the edge.

"Oh, God!" Shivers racked her entire body. Sweet heat flooded her, firing her blood. It was beautiful torture. Her hips flexed, pushing against his hand. It was so good.

"You're so sexy, baby." He whispered at her neck.

She was drowning. Every movement adding to the sensual heat. She needed to come. She needed to come so badly. "Cillian." She moaned his name in a desperate whimper.

"What baby? What do you need?" He suckled at her neck, her shoulder.

"I need to... Oh God!"

"Do you need my cock?" He moved back to her nipple and flicked softly, then closed his lips over it and suckled gently.

"Yes!" Her voice broke on a gasp. She was ready to fly.

His thumb slowed its circling motion when her clit flexed against it. She was right at the edge again. Her sweet hips grinding, trying for a deeper connection. Satisfaction flooded through him and he moved his mouth and hands away from her.

"No! No!" She growled in frustration. She was desperate. The need so sharp her entire focus was centered on him and the ache so deep inside her.

He petted her thighs, keeping them open when she tried so hard to close them. "Breathe through it. You can do it." He soothed her. His head next to hers, keeping the connection he knew she'd need.

She was in hell! She was drowning in a sea of violent longing. Closed off in darkness with only his touch, his ropes binding her skin and the pinches and pulls, the vibrations; she was drowning.

Cillian ruthlessly brought Chloe close to the edge again and again, never letting her tip over. He forced her through a relentless onslaught of emotions. She screamed at him; she cursed him; she begged him and through it all, he mercilessly brought her up, then slowly brought her back down, always withholding that last little touch that would send her flying.

Finally, nearly an hour later, she broke. He was beginning to think she never would. His strangle hold on his own restraint deteriorating.

Her mind was flooded with the need for his touch. It overshadowed everything else. Tears drenched the silk covering her eyes. She ached. Her skin so sensitive, it burned for the warmth of his. "Why?" She gasped. "Why are you doing this to me?" Her voice was wrecked, so exhausted it wavered with her tears.

He kissed her swollen lips. Swollen from the sharp edges of her teeth. His tongue soothed them softly. "You know why." He kissed her chin, her neck, nuzzling her.

"Why? Please! What do you want?!" She pleaded through her tears. Showing a weakness, she knew she'd hate herself for later.

He licked her nipple. When she gasped, he continued, "You. I want you baby. You're refusing to forgive me, so you're closing yourself off from me, from everyone. I won't allow it any longer."

"Cillian." Her defeated whisper was barely audible.

"No more, Chloe." His voice was harsh, his demon riding him hard. "We can do this all night, baby. All fucking night."

"But my dad,"

"Is just fine." He interrupted her. "My men were holding back and he knew it. It was just for show. He did more damage to them than they did to him. I swear it. And, your mother didn't suffer a single bruise, not even a chipped nail. I apologized for acting before knowing all the facts. And I don't ever fucking apologize." He hissed viciously. "It's time for you to forgive me." Beyond frustrated, he clicked both remotes, bringing them back to life.

"Ah, God!" she gasped desperately.

"They're perfectly fine. Now, give me what I want and I'll give you what you need. Everything you need." Cillian wrapped his arms around her, holding her close. Her clamped nipples were hard points against his warm chest.

"I can't!" She lay her forehead on his shoulder as she sobbed.

"You can baby." He leaned down and bit her shoulder, then sucked the tender skin into his mouth. He slipped his hand between her thighs and palmed her pussy, circling the tender, over sensitive flesh. "I promise, they weren't harmed." His thumb pressed against her clit. "Forgive me baby." When she flexed into his hand, he removed it again.

"Ok! Oh God Cillian, please!" She begged. She was shivering, goosebumps rising all over her flesh. She'd give him anything to ease the burning need, the desperate ache.

Cillian untied the blindfold and peered into her beautiful blue eyes. Eyes filled with desperation and soaked with tears. "Promise me, Chloe."

She blinked heavy lids. Tears sliding unchecked down her cheeks. His menacing stare; laser focused on her, smoldering with heat and triumph. "I promise." Her defeated voice rang with truth.

"Good girl." He crooned. Still holding her gaze, he turned the vibrations off, reached between her legs and released the knot holder her ankles together. Then he slowly pulled the little balls from her channel.

Chloe moaned deep in her throat when they slid out. The sensation was so intense she fell forward against his chest again.

He lifted her onto his lap and guided his cock to her. Chest to chest, her legs over his thighs, he slowly drove her down onto his aching cock. Replacing the little balls with the added width and length of him.

She hissed out a breath as he slid in deep. When he was seated completely inside her, he clicked the button to activate the plug again and sent the vibrations to the highest setting. "Take what you need, angel."

Chloe screamed. She screamed and screamed as she came, pulsing around the thick length as his cock flexed deep inside her. The pressure, the unfamiliar sensation, terrifying and darkly sensual. It was heaven. It was hell. And she knew now that he truly was the devil come to temp her. She couldn't control her hips as she slammed down onto his driving cock, over and over, riding him while her orgasm burned through her. One flowed into another. It lasted forever, tearing through her, laying waste to everything she was. It was horrible and beautiful and she never wanted it to end.

Cillian thrust deep inside her pulsing heat again and again, the incredibly tight fit strangling his sensitive cock. Using her hips to force her down as he drove so high inside her, she would feel him for days. She was wild in his arms as she sought to extinguish the raging fire, he'd stoked so deep. His beautiful angel was glorious as she took him. When her orgasm finally subsided, she lay limp and exhausted in his arms. He palmed her head to his shoulder, gripped her hip and pounded into her, chasing his own release, following her into oblivion.

Hours later, Chloe barely stirred in his arms as Cillian lifted her and carried her back to bed. Her shivering had finally subsided. Earlier, after he'd untied her, he'd cleaned her up, applied soothing cream to her tender nipples, then carried her into the other room where he held her on his lap and fed her small bites from his own plate. She hadn't objected, and she silently ate what he fed her. Then they'd curled up together beneath her blanket on the sofa and watched a movie while he'd caressed her with gentle hands as the adrenalin crash left her languid and soft in his arms.

Chapter 24: Bulletproof Vests

Over the next three months, the trepidation Chloe experienced after Cillian had forced her promise eventually eased. As the weather turned colder and the days got shorter, they seemed to find a rhythm together. They talked a lot more because she began answering his questions with more than one-word answers. She also asked several of her own. As long as she avoided the topic of leaving him, they got along just fine. And the more they talked, she found him engaging and even amusing.

He was also affectionate. Which was so at odds with his intimidating, domineering presence. He held her hand at every opportunity, even during meals. He kissed her often and always found reasons to touch her. She couldn't stop him in front of anyone without breaking the rules, and she knew he did it on purpose. He wanted her to get used to it. And she was, so much that most of time when they were alone, she'd forget to pull away.

She had to remind herself constantly not to be taken in by his charm. And he was very charming. But he was still Cillian. She'd seen first-hand how dangerous he was. And he didn't hide his true nature from her. He got what he wanted, always. And he reminded her of it often.

She tried not to think about her parents. It helped to ease the tension between them. Not that she completely forgave him, but apparently time heals old wounds, or at least fades them a little.

She still went to the beach every morning after breakfast and wrote her message in the sand. She didn't linger too long now, though, because of the icy wind and freezing temperatures. But she still made the trip. Only now she did it out of habit more than anything. She'd been on the island for five months and as days turned into weeks, she'd given up hope of being rescued.

She still hadn't gone back to her studio, and she wasn't sure she ever would. As long as she was being held here, she didn't want to open up that part of herself again.

Her training continued. She went with Cillian and Finn to the field after lunch each day. But lately the intensity of her training had increased dramatically. Both men pushed her harder, honing her skills. She was getting stronger and faster. Her aim was true when she fired her weapon, even on the move through the course they'd set up for her. She had to admit; it was exhilarating, and she enjoyed every minute of it.

She'd been introduced to all the members in Cillian's Team One. She already knew Terrance and Jacob, and of course Patrick and Rourke, but had never met Donavon "Van", Andrew "Drew", Micha, Felix or Zane until recently. They'd all been together in the dining room when she and Cillian came down to breakfast one morning. There was an underlying tension in the room as Cillian explained that it was time she became familiar with the men he trusted most. She had a feeling something was brewing, but had no idea what it was. Even Patrick and Rourke seemed tense lately. More vigilant when she left the castle.

Then a week ago, the men started jumping her at unexpected times throughout the day, testing her skills. She'd freaked out when Patrick did it the first time on their morning walk to the beach. But after she'd landed on her ass, he'd hovered over her with that boyish twinkle in his eyes as he told her she fought like a girl.

Now, she never knew when one of them would jump out at her from around a corner or from behind a door. So, she stayed vigilant and happily anticipated the next attack. It was a strange game, but it helped with her reaction time. She was pretty sure that was their intension. After each attack, they'd point out what she did right and what she needed to improve on. It made her train harder because her goal was to put one of them on their ass.

Cillian sat across from Chloe, admiring the sway of her beautiful breasts while they ate dinner. She was slowly getting used to being naked around him. He no longer allowed her to wear the robe. His jaw twitched slightly at the remembered battle from three months ago. She'd fought viciously for that robe. He'd nearly ripped the fucking thing to shreds. But it had been worth it. Now she was sitting across from him with that 'fresh, fucked' look he was becoming so addicted to, wearing nothing but her collar. Her delicate skin still flushed. Her hair in a tumbled disarray and her plump lips still swollen from his kisses. His dick got hard again just looking at her.

His angel was slowly blossoming here on the island. She'd needed a challenge. Something to take her mind off of the circumstances that brought her here, and the training had helped a lot. It gave her a sense of control. It also helped prepare her if they were ever attacked. In his line of work, it was imperative that she know how to defend herself. And the back of his neck itched. That was never a good sign. Something was coming. He just couldn't put his finger on it yet.

Her laughter brought his attention back to their conversation. She was telling him how she'd defeated Micha's latest attack. She'd resorted to kicking his men in the nuts if she couldn't take them down any other way. He grinned as he listened to her tale. His men had complained that she was a vicious little thing, but her laughter was music to his ears.

Oh, his little hellion still fought him at every turn, but he was convinced that was her way of coping with her situation. He enjoyed their tussles, so he saw no harm in it. But just once, he wanted her to embrace the desire she felt for him. And whether she wanted to admit it or not, she felt it. Her nipples peaked, and her tight little pussy creamed for him every time.

Just thinking about her had his dick as hard as a rock, and that frustrated the hell out of him. He wanted to fuck her again, now. But he had to leave after dinner to meet with buyers for GhostStorm47. They'd been planning the demonstration for weeks. Very powerful people were coming together to see what his weapon was capable of and to place their bids. He couldn't put it off. His bag was already sitting next to the door, ready and waiting for the text from Finn. But all he wanted to do was pull his angel onto his lap and kiss her.

When his phone chimed, she stopped talking. He picked it up and read the screen. "That's Finn, they're ready to go."

"When will you be back?"

"In about a week if all goes well." He smiled cheekily. "Will you miss me angel?"

Chloe eyed him warily. "No."

He stood up and bent over her. He put his finger under her chin and lifted her face to meet his. "I suppose I asked for that." He gave her a quick kiss before she could pull away. "Behave yourself. Remember the rules."

She rolled her eyes and pulled her face away from his hold.

She roused his dominant side so easily. He fisted her hair aggressively and pulled her face back to his. "Disrespectful little thing." He kissed her forehead then moved to her ear where he whispered, "remind me to spank your pretty little ass when I get back." Then he bit her earlobe. Abruptly he released her, then picked up his bag and walked out the door. He had a lot to do in order to get back to her.

With Cillian gone, Chloe tossed and turned restlessly every night. Apparently, she'd gotten used to being held by him during the night, and now that he wasn't here, she couldn't sleep. She cringed at the thought that she might miss him. He'd only been gone for a week so far this time, but Patrick and Rourke weren't able to tell her when he'd be back.

She was disgusted with herself when she realized she was curled up with her nose buried in his pillow. "Jesus!" She shoved it away and flopped onto her back. Staring at the ceiling in the dark, she tried to think of anything but him. It wasn't fair that he consumed most of her thoughts during the day, but at night? Oh God! At night she dreamed of him; his wicked smiles and his sexy taunts. More than once, she'd awakened in the middle of the night, edgy and needy. Reaching for him. Now she was exhausted from lack of sleep, and it was making her crazy. She had to stop! She willed herself to focus on something else. Anything else.

Thoughts of Storm helped. Her Storm. Well, not really hers, but she liked to think of him that way. Over the past week, she'd been spending a lot of time in the afternoons watching Frank work with him. Since coming to the island, she'd been visiting him nearly every morning for a few minutes during her run. He was used to her and let her pet him. He seemed much calmer now too. Not nearly as skittish, as if he was getting acclimated to his environment. Frank was convinced it was her influence. Even though he often complained in his ornery way that she was distracting the horse, he kept encouraging her to come back.

To Peters dismay, yesterday, she'd stepped into the corral. She'd stood calmly and waited for Storm to approach her. He'd been timid at first, but eventually his curiosity had gotten the better of him. He'd come looking for the apple she'd brought and allowed her to pet him while he ate the treat. It had been exhilarating. She hoped one day he'd let her ride him. Of course, that was not in her near future. He was still wild and had never held a rider. But she was convinced that eventually he'd allow her on his back.

She turned over onto her side and punched her pillow into shape, then closed her eyes. It was nearly 3am, and she needed to sleep. Her eyes were just drifting closed when the outer door of the suite burst open.

Chloe jumped out of bed, taking the blanket with her. She peered into the other room and through the light shining in from the outer hall, watched in horror as Finn and Terrance practically carried Cillian through the den. Yes, carried him!

Finn flipped on the bedroom light as he and Terrance half carried, half dragged Cillian into the bedroom.

"What happened?" She dropped the blanket in her rush to get to him.

Cillian lifted his head and met her beautiful, worried gaze. His shirt was soaked in blood and he was exhausted from pain and blood loss, but seeing her eased a tightness in his chest. He'd wanted to change into something else before coming to her, but hadn't had time. Fortunately, Drew, the medic on his team, had already removed the bullet from his side during the plane ride home.

"Hello, angel." He flashed her a wicked smile, hoping to ease the worry in her eyes.

His gaze traveled insolently over her, and a wave of possessiveness briefly overshadowed the pain. Her hair was tousled like spun silk falling around her shoulders. Her beautiful face, as usual, was bare of cosmetics and she was wearing another one of his T-shirts. The enormous shirt dwarfed her tiny frame. The hem falling nearly to her knees.

"We need the doctor!" She rushed to the house phone beside the bed and lifted the receiver.

"He's already on his way." Finn reported as he and Terrance eased Cillian down on the side of the bed.

Chloe dropped the receiver and went to stand in front of him. He reached out and pulled her between his thighs.

She went willingly and reached out to unbutton his bloody shirt. She opened it to see the bandage on his lower left side soaked with blood.

She eyed it, assessing the damage, then slowly lifted her gaze to his. "Bullet or knife?" She tried, but wasn't able to hide the anger in her voice.

He watched her carefully before calmly answering. "Bullet." He waited for her condemnation. He didn't deserve to touch her with so much blood on his hands. Now he'd brought the blood and violence right to her.

She finished removing the shirt and stepped back to take in the rest of him, searching for more injuries. Other than a weird pattern of dark bruises the size of marbles on his chest and abdomen above his wound, and dried blood on his side, there were no other injuries that she could see. Chloe tilted her head to the side and evaluated the wary look on his face. He was in pain, but hiding it well. He was also waiting for some kind of response from her. Maybe he thought she'd freak out or get hysterical. Instead, she turned and stomped into the bathroom and wet a few washcloths with cold water. She couldn't say why she was angry, but the sight of the blood coating his skin and the pain he was trying so hard to hide in those mesmerizing green eyes infuriated her.

She stomped back into the room and stepped between his thighs again. She gently cleaned the excess blood from his skin around the bandage.

"Baby don't." He tried to take the cloth from her. "You'll get blood on your hands."

"Stop." She pulled her hand away and glared at him. "Let me." Not even trying to hide her anger, she stared him down and waited for him to relent.

Cillian sighed heavily as he nodded and dropped his hand, letting her finish. He didn't want her to touch the blood, didn't want it to touch any part of her. But seeing her like this, he had to work hard to hide the grin that wanted to spread across his face. She was such a fiery little thing. And she was mad. Really mad. At him or on his behalf, he didn't know, but she was definitely angry. And her little hands, so gentle and warm, felt amazing. This was the first time she'd ever touched him voluntarily. And it frustrated him that this first time was to clean away the bloody proof of the violent life he'd forced her into.

Chloe didn't notice Finn and Terrance quietly leave the room. She was focused on her task and trying to figure out the best way to get him to lie down without hurting him further. She didn't ask how or why he was shot. He wouldn't tell her, anyway.

She finished cleaning the dried blood from his skin, then dropped the washcloths on the floor next to his shirt. She went to her knees at his feet and started working on the laces of his boots. When she had them both untied, she looked up and met his heated gaze. He'd been watching her the entire time.

She swallowed audibly. The desire burning in those green orbs was intense. She took a deep breath to clear the knot in her throat before asking, "is it going to hurt if I pull them off?" He would have to shift to help her remove them. She didn't want to hurt him further, but he needed to lie down. He was trying to act tough, but he was so pale she was afraid he'd pass out.

"Probably, but do it anyway." He couldn't help but smile at her. The site of her on her knees at his feet had his cock throbbing with need and completely distracted him from the pain in his side.

"Ok." She sighed. "Get ready."

He braced the arm on his uninjured side behind him to steady himself, then nodded at her.

She nodded back in silent communication, then pulled the first boot off. As expected, the movement caused his side to strain and pain seared through him. But he was very careful not to make a sound. When she looked up to assess him, he nodded again. "Go ahead. Get it over with."

He was so pale; he was nearly gray now. Chloe nodded again, then quickly removed the other boot. She'd tried to be careful, but there was no way to do it without his help. Once the boots were off, she turned and called out the bedroom door. "Finn, Terrance, I need your help."

"Alright, Chloe." Finn replied as they came back into the bedroom.

"Help me get him settled." She climbed onto the bed behind him and moved the covers out of the way, then fluffed and stacked the pillows.

Cillian looked up at his men and stood. "Help me around to the other side."

Terrance took his good arm and bore the brunt of his weight as he and Finn guided him around the bed.

Chloe scowled at him, but moved to push the blankets on her side of the bed out of the way.

He grinned in response to the little frown on her face. His little kitten was definitely furious. Before he sat again, he paused and looked down at the blood on his cargo pants, then back up at her.

Her eyes narrowed as she scowled again and climbed off the bed. While Terrance and Finn supported his weight, she removed his pants. There was no way to hide the evidence of his arousal, so he didn't try.

Chloe helped the men get him settled. When he was finally resting against the pillows, she realized this position was better because his wounded side would be to the outside edge of the bed.

When Doc came through the bedroom door, Cillian looked over at Chloe kneeling beside him and reached out and pulled the blanket up to cover her legs. She frowned at him again. But he didn't care.

She was sitting on her knees under the blanket beside him while Doc examined his wound. She looked tense as she watched every move Doc made. This wasn't the first time he'd been shot and probably wouldn't be the last. But he hadn't wanted her to see this side of his life. Hadn't wanted the violence that surrounded him to touch her. He reached out and took her hand, and to his surprise, she let him.

"It doesn't look like any major organs were hit. You got lucky again." Doc poked and prodded at the wound.

"Hump." Cillian grunted at him.

"I'll need to irrigate it to make sure there're no fragments still in there."

"Do it."

Chloe resisted the urge to smooth his hair away from his pale face. She fought her instinct to sooth him. That she felt the need to do it, pissed her off. She was afraid she was beginning to care for the asshole. She assured herself that she would feel compassion for anyone who'd been shot, and the fact that it was Cillian didn't matter. She was a compassionate person. She cared if others were hurt. That's all it was. She did not care for him. She didn't. She cringed internally because she knew she was lying to herself. How or when it happened, she didn't know. But God help her, she'd cared for Cillian O'Donnell.

Cillian stroked the back of her hand with his thumb and watched her expressive face while Doc inspected his wound for anything Drew may have missed. It hurt like hell, so he focused on the rhythm of his thumb, the angles and planes of her delicate face, her skin, soft and warm under his. This was what he wanted, what he was missing. Her focus on him. Her concern for him.

Chloe moved her attention from the wound to his face. He was staring at her again. He did that all the time. His face tightened briefly at whatever the doctor was doing, but other than that, he gave no indication that he was in pain. But she knew better.

"You look tired, angel." He hadn't missed the dark circles under her eyes.

"Ha! I look better than you." She smirked at him hoping to keep his mind off the pain.

He squeezed her hand in response to her impudence. "I haven't forgotten that I still owe you a spanking. Are you trying to add more licks?"

"You're in no condition to do it." She scoffed.

"Don't bet on it." He eyed her wickedly.

"Humph". She turned her nose up at him.

"What've you been doing while I've been gone?"

She couldn't resist any longer. She reached out and smoothed his hair back. "I've been spending a lot of time with Frank and Storm."

"What do you see in that crazy horse?" He scoffed.

"He's beautiful. But he's sad. He doesn't like to be caged in." She lowered her eyes to his chin. She didn't want to point out that she and the horse were a lot alike in that regard. Not while he was in so much pain.

"Like you." He said softly. He knew what she was thinking.

"Like me." She agreed. "He's getting better. He lets me pet him all the time now."

He gripped her hand tighter. "Chloe, he's dangerous."

"Not to me." She countered.

"Chloe."

"Cillian." She lowered her voice, imitating his foreboding tone. She grinned when his lip twitched before adding in her normal voice, "I didn't say I was riding him, just petting him."

"Humph." It was his turn to grunt as he tried not to smile at her attempt to imitate his voice.

"But I am going to ride him someday." She felt the need to add.

"No, you are not."

She leaned forward and put her face close to his and glared at him. "Oh yes, I am."

He searched her eyes. They were glittering with challenge, daring him. She looked so fierce, and all he wanted to do was kiss her. Instead, he met her challenge with one of his own. "Baby, if you get on that horse, I'll spank your pretty little ass so hard you won't be able to sit for a week." He whispered it so only she could hear him.

"You wouldn't dare."

"Try me."

She scowled at him. "Don't threaten me, Cillian."

"It's not a threat, baby. It's a promise."

They glared back at each other for long, tense moments. His stare moved to her lips. He broke the silence first.

"Kiss me, Chloe." He whispered softly in a wicked velvet voice that he knew made her shiver.

She bit her bottom lip and she cut her eyes toward Doc. She could feel the blush heat her face. But Doc had his head lowered to his task and wasn't paying any attention to them. She met his gaze again and hesitated.

"Kiss me." He dared.

She stared at him thoughtfully for a moment longer, then tentatively touched her lips to his. When he didn't take over like he usually did, she leaned back slightly and met his gaze. He didn't move or say anything, he simply waited. She contemplated her next move, then gently touched her lips to his again, only this time, she kissed him. She kissed his full bottom lip, then nibbled on it. When he opened for her, she slipped her tongue inside his warm mouth and met his.

For the first time in her life, she wasn't being kissed; she was doing the kissing. Her tongue dance against his then she suckled on it. She nipped his lip before kissing the sting away, and all the while he let her. It was exhilarating.

"Ok, that should do it." Doc interrupted.

Chloe pulled away from him so abruptly he wanted to shoot the fucking doctor. Instead, he inspected the bandage at his side.

"You know the drill. Take the antibiotics for ten days and rest. Two weeks at least. No strenuous activities."

"Yea, I know." Cillian grunted. He'd been shot several times before, so he knew the drill. But Doc didn't need to say that shit in front of her.

"I had to use sutures instead of liquid stitches because it's so deep, so don't tear them. I'll be back to check on it in a few days." He ignored the scowl on his boss's face and gathered his things. He placed a bottle of pills on the nightstand, then quietly left the room.

When the outer door closed, he watched as Chloe climbed off the bed and went out to the bar and brought back a glass of water. She handed it to him, along with a pill. "Are you going to play nursemaid?" He grinned when she frowned at him.

"Shut up and take the pill." She was aggravated with him and herself. She wasn't supposed to care about him. He was her captor, nothing more. She had to keep reminding herself of that fact. But the lines were slowly blurring and that could be very dangerous.

Cillian could see the turmoil in her eyes. She was fighting her feelings for him. It was a battle he wasn't about to let her win. He slowly swallowed the pill, then handed her back the water glass.

Chloe turned off the lamp and climbed into bed beside him. Before she could settle in, he snaked his arm around her and pulled her against his side. When she attempted to pull away, he tightened his hold. "Just lay next to me, angel. I'm tired, but I want to feel you against me."

She sighed loudly, but relaxed in his hold. When she lay her head on his chest and settled against him, he added in a teasing tone, "Can I talk you into taking off that shirt."

"No."

"You still mad?"

"Yes. You should wear a bullet-proof vest." He suddenly stiffened beneath her so she asked, "what?"

He was silent for long moments before answering, "I did."

Chloe lifted her head and found his menacing gaze in the dark. He watched her like a stalking panther would its prey. Very slowly she slid her finger over the strange round bruises she remembered seeing on his chest and abdomen. Her chest tightened as realization dawned. "These are from bullets hitting the vest." Pulse pounding, she moved to put space between them.

His glittering green gaze pierced hers, but he didn't respond. What was there to say? Instead, he tightened his hold when she tried to move away.

"Oh my God!" Frantic now, she pushed against him. Her heart was pounding so hard she was afraid it would explode. Fear was a sour taste in her mouth. "Let me up."

"Calm down, Chloe." He squeezed her tighter against him. When she continued to struggle, he added, "You're going to bust open my sutures if you keep doing that."

She instantly stopped and stared at him for long moments before giving in and laying back down. She pressed her forehead into his chest. He could have died. That thought kept running through her head like the credits from a movie. The realization hit her like a lead weight, settling heavily on her heart. She couldn't explain the fear and anxiety she felt at the thought of losing him. She shouldn't feel it. But the overwhelming sense of loss tore at her soul. She tried hard to fight the tears falling unchecked from her eyes. Silent tears dripping onto his chest beneath her.

Tears of frustration at herself for being so stupid, tears of anger toward him for making her care and tears of fear for him. She could have lost him.

Cillian cradled her head to his chest. His large palm rubbing her scalp softly, trying to sooth her. She was crying. His little angel was crying for him. "Chloe."

She didn't reply. There in the dark, he held her and soothed her as she cried herself to sleep.

Chapter 25: Closing the Deal

Cillian rested in bed against a stack of pillows, his laptop open, reviewing the video footage from the meeting the day before at the warehouse. Finn had shown up right before Chloe left for her run. She'd been hesitant to leave and that pleased him, but they had work to do, so Finn had teased her and she'd bolted out the door.

Watching the screen, he froze the frame every few seconds to examine the scene. They'd selected the location well before scheduling the meeting to give Titan's team time to set up surveillance. Once he could determine where the shots came from, he zoomed into the image. It was grainy and difficult to make out, but not impossible. He cut the piece of footage and imported it into an app Titan had created and waited while the clarity was restored.

Oden Aliachbar's partial profile materialized on the screen. His head bent to the rifle scope. Cold fury slowly settled over Cillian. "It appears Abdul wasn't happy about not being invited to the party."

"The question is, how did he know when and where the party was going to be?" Finn replied, while gazing at the image.

"Go through the files on all those who attended. Have Titan help you. Find the connection." He thought back over what he knew about the six men who'd been thoroughly vetted and approved to attend the demonstration. The sheik from Dubai had serious connections and a false air of respectability. He would see Abdul as beneath his notice. Same with the Russian Prince. The Chinese Mogul didn't fit the bill either. On the surface, not one of the six men invited would stoop to an alliance with a man like Abdul. But someone had.

"It'll take a few days, but we'll pull everything we can find." Finn assured. He crossed his arms over his chest and assessed his cousin. "How's Chloe doing?"

"She's fine." Cillian smiled to himself. "She's strong."

"She is. She handled the situation last night much better than we expected."

"Yes, she did." He paused then added, "you seem surprised."

"Not really. But you never know how someone will react under pressure until they're put to the test."

"I knew how she'd react. You could say I've been putting her to the test for months now."

"Yea, you have. And she's handled herself with grace and courage." He continued to stare at Cillian expectantly.

"And?"

"And now it's time to close the deal cousin."

"I intend to."

"She'll fight you."

"I wouldn't want it any other way. But I intend to play dirty."

"Yea?" Finn arched his brow in question.

Cillian placed his hand on the bandage at his side and grinned at his cousin. "Oh, Yea."

"You're an ass." Finn chuckled.

"True." Cillian smiled, then his expression became serious. "But I'll get the prize."

Chloe wanted to scream! Cillian was the devil himself. Here she was; hiding in the library. Her one refuge in this crazy place. The morning after Cillian had shown up with a bullet hole in his side, she hadn't been able to stop herself from fussing over him. She'd helped him to the bathroom because he seemed incredibly weak. And his huge frame had leaned so heavily on her that she knew he had to be in terrible pain. Once she had him settled back in bed, she'd brought him a piece of fruit to eat so he could take his pill. Then Finn had shown up. When he'd smirked at the way she was catering to Cillian, she'd escaped as fast as she could.

During her run that morning, she'd been able to shore up her defenses, but they'd slowly crumbled over the next few days. He'd been in so much pain that she'd called Doc back in to check his wound. After he'd examined Cillian, the two men had glared at each other for long moments before the doctor assured her it was just the healing process and the pain was expected.

Now, nearly two weeks later, he was driving her insane! She couldn't prove it, but she was sure he was milking the injury. He insisted he still needed her help for everything. She bathed him, helped him get dressed every morning and undressed every evening. The evenings were the worst. The heat simmering in his eyes when she knelt at his feet to remove his boots was unnerving. She'd even suggested that he should go bare-foot for the time being, but he'd refused.

To make matters worse, for the past week, she had awakened several times a night, *every night*, with fire burning through her blood. So wet and needy and close to orgasm, only to find him sound asleep. It didn't make sense. She knew he was doing something to cause it. He had to be. But she hadn't been able to catch him.

Now she walked around in a constant state of arousal and having to bathe him and dress him wasn't helping. And he watched her. Constantly watched her while he played the innocent. Never touching her intimately. At this point, she'd welcome his touch. She was close to begging for it. And no way in hell was she going to do that. So here she was, hiding in the damn library just to get a break!

Cillian sat at his desk, and only half listened as Father Shamus sputtered something about rules. He tuned him out as his thoughts circled back to Chloe, and a wicked grin spread across his face. He was an evil bastard. He knew it. Everyone did.

This delicious game of cat and mouse he'd been playing with her over the past week was about to end. And he'd win. He always won. He should feel some sense of remorse, but being the fucked-up bastard that he was, he didn't. He'd been toying with her. Preying on her emotions during the day and playing with her body at night while she slept. Softly suckling on her sweet nipples. Gently circling her little clit and fingering her pussy until she was hot and slick, only to pull away when she stirred. That had been the hardest part. Where he'd had to exercise the most restraint. But soon, soon, he'd have his reward.

"Cillian, are you even listening? You can't do this!" Father Shamus finally said in frustration when no amount of reasoning seemed to work. He'd heard about the girl. Everyone on the island and throughout the territory knew Cillian had taken her.

Cillian's focus came back to the priest. "I can do anything I want."

"But she has to be willing!" The priest insisted.

"She will be." He assured the ornery old man.

"Not coerced!"

"She'll be willing. The details are not your concern. Or have you forgotten who you work for?"

"Of course not." Father Shamus backed down immediately. What else could he do? He'd stated his case, but Cillian O'Donnell was not an enemy anyone wanted. The boy he'd ministered to, had offered communion to, no longer existed. That boy died with his parents a long time ago. The dangerous man sitting here now could crush him with one blow.

Chloe was anxious as she knocked on Cillian's office door. She hadn't done anything wrong, so she couldn't figure out why he'd summoned her to his office. And he had summoned her. She'd been doing an excellent job of avoiding him today. At least until Finn had stuck his head into the library where she'd been reading and told her Cillian wanted to see her in his office.

"Come in, Chloe." Cillian pushed his chair back from his desk and swiveled it around to face her.

When she stepped into the room, there was a man she didn't recognize sitting in the chair in front of Cillian's desk. From the white collar around his neck, she assumed he was a priest. He immediately jumped to his feet as soon as she walked in. Wringing his hands nervously in front of himself he looked between her and Cillian.

Cillian glanced at Father Shamus and nodded his head. "If you'll excuse us, please?"

"Of course." He whispered and hurried out of the room, shutting the door quietly behind him.

Chloe watched him leave, then turned her attention back to Cillian. She raised her eyebrow in question.

"Hello, angel." His gazed roamed possessively over her. He was extremely pleased with himself when her nipples pebbled to tight peaks under the ice blue dress he'd selected for her today. The matching three-inch-high heels on her dainty feet did amazing things to her legs and her ass.

When his beautifully cruel mouth formed a slightly expectant smile, Chloe nervously wet her lips. "You wanted to see me?" She stayed by the door, hoping to get this over with quickly. If she got too close to him, she might jump him.

"Come here, Chloe." He kicked his legs out, spreading his thighs, and extended his hand toward her.

She didn't move. No way was she getting any closer. "Finn said you wanted to talk to me."

"I do."

"About what?" She hid her trembling hands behind her back.

"Come here."

"Cillian."

"Are you going to make me come and get you?"

"I didn't break a rule or anything."

"Chloe, come here!"

She gave an exasperated sigh and balled her hands into tight fists and slowly walked to him. When she got close enough, he reached out and snagged her wrist and pulled her in close. He slid his hands up the back of her legs under the hem of her dress to hold her bare thighs just below the cheeks of her ass.

"That's more like it."

"You're obviously feeling better today."

"I am. Thanks to you, I've completely recovered." He smiled teasingly at her then added, "and cleared for any and all activity." He slid his palms further up to cup the bare cheeks of her ass.

"What do you want, Cillian?" His hands felt so good on her ass. She tried very hard not the push into them.

He kneaded the warm smooth cheeks. His fingers resting under the silk in the cleft between them. His angel had a luscious ass. And thanks to the thong she wore, he had full access.

Her breath caught in her throat as she stifled the moan that threatened to break free. "What are you doing?"

"We're just talking, baby." He slid his finger further down to circle the opening of her pussy. At the feel of her wet heat on his finger, he leaned in and touched his forehead to hers to whisper; "you're wet for me Chloe."

"Cillian." She whispered back; she was already on fire.

"So wet." He whispered softly as he pushed a thick finger deep inside of her.

"Oh, God." Her breath hitched and she flexed her hips automatically, trying for a deeper penetration when he started sliding that diabolical finger in and out of her. Her trembling hands settled on his shoulders to steady herself.

"Mm, so wet. Do you miss me, baby?" When her breath hitched, he grinned. "Yea, you do."

"Cillian," she groaned deep in her throat.

He kissed her forehead lightly, kissing a path down to her neck, where he suckled gently. "Chloe, do you want to video chat with your parents?" He breathed warm air against her heated skin.

"What?" Her eyes widened with shock. She was so close to orgasm; had she heard him correctly?

"Do you?" He persisted and moved his kisses to her bottom lip, her chin, then suckled that sensitive spot between her neck and shoulder.

"You know I do." She tried to focus on the conversation. It was important.

"Ok."

"Ok?" Her heart pounding loudly in her ears.

"Yes, Ok. I think you've earned a reward. Don't you?"

She groaned when he pushed his finger deeper inside of her.

"Don't you?" He persisted, his lips warm and wet against her skin.

"Yes, please." She didn't know if she was begging for more of his touch or the chance to speak with her parents.

"Ok".

"Really?"

"Yes baby, but let's talk about the rules."

"Of, of course." She breathed through the desperate heat racing through her veins and rolled her eyes at him. He always had rules.

He bit her shoulder and smacked her ass with his free hand in retaliation. "My disrespectful little hellion."

She moaned when the fiery sting sent a sizzle of heat to her core. "What…. What are the rules?"

"Take off your dress and I'll tell you."

When she didn't immediately move to do it, he pulled his fingers from her.

"No, no, don't!" She'd been so close.

"Do it." He lightly circled her swollen clit and waited.

With trembling hands, Chloe captured the hem of her dress and pulled it over her head.

He grinned triumphantly. "You're so beautiful." He yanked on her panties, then dropped the torn silk to the floor at her feet. He pulled her closer, sliding his finger deep again. "I'll be in the room with you the entire time." He suckled on the tip of her breast trough the lace.

"O. O. Ok." She gasped and lifted closer, pushing her breast further into the heat of his mouth.

"You can't tell them where you are or who has you." He licked at her other nipple. "No reference to the island, Ireland, or even the ocean. Not one." He scraped his teeth across the tip and her breath hitched again. "And you can't use my name or the names of my men. No using last names when discussing your new friends either."

"Alright." She ground her hips against his hand, trying to get the angle just right.

"Now to the terms."

"Terms?" God, she needed to come. His free hand moved from her ass to the jeweled collar at her throat. He lifted it and ran his finger under the warm gold and titanium while he watched her closely. "There are three."

She pressed down when he added a second finger inside her.

"First, from now on, you'll come to me willingly." He watched her closely, sliding his fingers deep and moved his thumb to circle her clit.

"What do you mean?" She gasped and leaned away to look at him. She tried desperately to rise above the fire raging through her. He dropped her collar when she moved and slid his finger down to circle her damp nipple, rubbing the sheer fabric of her bra against it, abrading it.

He bit her chin again as he continued to whisper against her skin. "You show affection without me having to force it. You come to me as my lover, ready and willing to fuck me anywhere and anyway I want." He sucked her pebbled nipple deep into his mouth, suckling sharply through the sheer lace of her bra.

"Oh, God! Wait...What?!"

He captured her thigh and lifted it over his own, opening her further. "Second, you're going to marry me."

"What?!" She gasped and tried to push away from him. "Are you insane?! I'm not marrying you!" No way! She was not tying herself to him permanently. She tried desperately to back away, but his hand on her thigh prevented it and her orgasm was so close her body was taking over.

"Third," he continued, as if she hadn't spoken. "We'll get married in an intimate ceremony here, today."

When she gasped, he added firmly, "today. But we'll have a large formal wedding in a month to celebrate so my people can attend."

"Today!" She closed her eyes and took a fortifying breath, trying desperately to compose herself. Then she looked into his blazing eyes and, voice trembling, stated calmly; "Cillian, I am not marrying you."

He tightened his grip, adding a third finger inside of her as his gaze turned menacing. His voice reflected it when he spoke. "There's no way you're speaking to your parents unless you are completely, legally," he emphasized the word then bit her lip, "mine."

"No." Her chin lifted instinctively.

"Then no call." He watched her closely before going in for the kill. "Such a shame though," he sighed heavily. "Leaving your parents to wonder what's become of you. Your poor mother, she must be so sad, so worried. She might even think you're dead." Anticipation was a rush of adrenalin hitting his system. He was such an evil fucker.

Her breath caught in her throat before she exploded. "You asshole!" The sound of her mother's screams echoed through her head. Her father's anguished demands breaking her heart all over again and helping her to find calm in the sensual storm he'd created.

"Those are the terms, Chloe." His pulse leapt when her beautiful blue eyes fired with rage. Sparkled with fury. He fought the urge to tie her up and fuck her right there on his desk. As it was, his cock was diamond hard.

Her trembles instantly turn from need to rage. She wanted to kill him. The thought of her mother's face, her screams, still haunted her. She lifted her hands to her head, squeezing in frustration. "You can't do this!"

He snagged her collar again and pulled her face back to his. "I can. Decide. Now." His expression had gone dark and fierce. His words menacing. He hadn't realized how much he wanted this until now. He had no intention of giving her time to think it through. His thumb pressed tightly against her clit.

Her mouth opened on a groan that she tried hard to suppress while she stared at him in disbelief. He expected her to decide right this second. In desperation she whispered in a ragged breath; "Why are you doing this to me?"

"Decide."

"But, Cillian,"

Unreasonably furious at her hesitation, he cut her off. "Married or not, I'm going to fuck this hot little pussy every day for the rest of your life." He growled and tightened his grip on her collar, pulling her closer. His fingers plunging deeper inside her, his thumb pressed tightly against her clit. "You're eventually going to have my children. And like it or not, you're going to be able to tell them that we were married when they were conceived." He sucked her nipple back into his mouth and lashed at it violently.

She gaped at his bent head as her mind went blank with shock. Slowly, her eyes focused back on his when he finally released her breast and lifted his head. In a tortured voice that was barely audible, she asked, "you're never going to let me go, are you?"

Still working his fingers deep inside her, he leaned in and kissed her trembling bottom lip softly before meeting her gaze again. "Never." He kissed her again. "This is us, baby." He kissed her. "We fit." He kissed her. "We belong together, you and me." He kissed her one last time, then leaned back and met her gaze.

Chloe stared into blazing green eyes. Was this really going to be her life? She swallowed past the knot in her throat. "Cillian." She whispered desperately and cupped his cheeks with trembling hands.

"Chloe." Cillian held her gaze and kissed her. When he released her mouth, he made his demand. "Decide. Now." She would give him this.

Chloe looked into those determined green eyes and made her choice. She refused to be a victim. "All this for one video call? No." She stated calmly. "Four one hour calls every week."

"One call a week for ten minutes." Slowly circling her clit, he waited for her to counter. He fought to hide his triumph. He had her.

She breathed through the sensations battering her. "Three calls a week; forty-five minutes each."

"One call a week for twenty minutes."

"No! Two thirty-minute calls a week."

"Done." Before she could react, he pulled her onto his lap and kissed her again. He kissed her long and hard. Fingers of his free hand buried in her hair, holding her to him, his other continuing to stroke deep inside her wet heat. When she pushed against his chest, he lifted his head and glared at her. "Willingly baby."

She met his blazing eyes for a moment then slowly, knowing she'd lost, understanding that with him, there was no going back, she leaned in and kissed him, and sealed fate.

Chapter 26: I Do! What?

Chloe was wearing one of the most beautiful dresses she'd ever seen. She didn't know where he'd gotten it on a moment's notice. But it had been lying on the bed along with a sheer white thong and matching thigh-high stockings when Cillian had carried her to their room. A winter white wool with a silk lining, the sheath was tailored to fit her perfectly. So perfect there was no need for a bra. It fell to just above the knees, with a small slit above each one. The wide-open scooped neck collar left the tops of her shoulders, neck and much of her chest bare, causing the jewels in her collar to stand out brilliantly against her skin.

She turned to regard Cillian's satisfied smile anxiously. Then her gaze dropped to the huge princess cut diamond on her finger. It had to be at least 5 carats, encrusted with tiny diamonds and set in a white gold band. She wiggled her finger slightly to get accustomed to the weight.

How could two little words change someone's life so drastically? But she'd done it. She'd said the words that now tied her to one of the most dangerous men in the world. What a terrifying thought.

"When did you get this?" She hadn't wanted to ask in front of Finn and Imogen, who'd both stood as witnesses to this disaster. So, she was glad they hadn't lingered.

"About five months ago."

Her gaze jerked back up to his and watched him smile. "And the dress?"

"Around the same time."

Cillian grinned at her surprised expression. She was so beautiful. The dress fit like a glove. He'd known it would. And he couldn't wait to peel it off of her. Her hair was up in the same sleek ponytail she'd worn the first night he'd seen her. She'd taken the time to apply a little makeup, and she looked amazing. "Come on angel, let's go up to our room."

She hesitated when he tried to guide her out of the little chapel. "Cillian, I want to call my mom and dad now."

"Ok. We'll do it from the den in our suite."

"Ok?" She frowned slightly. Was it really that simple?

"Chloe, I told you, I'll never lie to you."

When they stepped off the elevator, Cillian scooped her up into his arms.

"What are you doing?" Chloe gasped.

He grinned as he carried her across the little foyer, between the elevator and the door to their suite where Patrick stood guard, an amused grin on his face. He turned and opened the door for them.

Cillian stepped across the threshold and into the suite, kicking the door shut behind him. He placed her on the sofa in front of the coffee table. A sleek laptop was sitting on the table in front of her. He reached over and lifted the screen, and it came to life.

"Wait! I want to change first." She couldn't wait to speak to her parents, but not dressed like this. The beautiful dress was over the top! The sapphire collar was on display, and she was hoping to remove the enormous diamond from her finger when he wasn't looking.

"Angel, I've been waiting over an hour to peel you out of that dress." His eyes drilled into hers. "If you want to speak to your parents today, you'd better leave it on."

The look he gave her caused her pulse to speed up. Those gorgeous green eyes focused solely on her always had that effect. "Alright."

"Remember the rules, Chloe." He reminded as he reached over and hit a few buttons on the keyboard. The screen changed and the sound of ringing came through the speakers. He moved behind the screen and sat in the chair across from her. She watched him put the ankle of one leg on the knee of the other and rest his chin in his palm as he prepared to listen to her call.

The sound of her mother's voice brought her attention back to the screen. "Chloe! Oh, sweetheart!" Her mother cried as hers and her father's faces came into view.

Tears blurred her vision when she saw them. "Mom, dad!"

"Oh, thank God! Oh sweetie, are you alright?!" Angela Guidry cried.

"I'm fine mom. Please don't cry." Chloe slid her hands under her thighs to hide the wedding ring on her finger.

"Chloe." Her dad called.

"Dad." She whispered, devastated by the worry and the anger she could see in his eyes.

"Baby girl, where are you?"

Chloe took a deep, cleansing breath before answering. "I can't tell you."

"What? Why?" Before she could respond he added, "is he listening?"

"Dad, I can't tell you where I am or who I'm with, but I can tell you that I'm fine."

"But sweetheart," Angela cried out.

"Mom." She cut her off. "If I tell you, I won't be able to talk to you anymore."

The silence stretched for a few long seconds before her father spoke up. "Ok kiddo, how are you?"

"Dad." She tried to stop the tears. "I'm so sorry."

"Don't you dare apologize."

"It's my fault! I should've followed the plan and left with Sidney!"

"Chloe, honey," her mother interrupted. "You're a grown woman. You have the right to change your plans without consulting us. This is not your fault!"

"But dad! They beat you up!" She cried.

"Honey, that was nothing. I'm pretty sure I did more damage to them than they did to me. Don't you worry about that. Your mother's right. Now, no more tears." David's stern, fatherly voice echoed through the speakers. His eyes scanned her from the top of her head to her waist, which was all he could see through the camera. "Has he hurt you?"

"No."

"You look beautiful." Her mother chimed in.

"Mom, I'm so sorry you were put through all this. I'm sure you thought I was dead and it broke my heart not to be able to reassure you."

"What?" Angela looked confused. "Chloe, we knew you were alive."

"What? But... How?"

"From the first week you were taken, we've been getting emails every couple of days, telling us how you're doing and there have been pictures."

"What!?" Chloe glanced over the top of the laptop screen to find Cillian watching her.

"They've been coming to your mother's personal email account." Her father added. "This morning we got a message that you would call later today. We've been waiting all morning."

Chloe was speechless for a few seconds as she glared into Cillian's smoldering eyes. She thought back to her first night on the island when they were on the balcony. She's told him her parents needed to know she was ok. She'd said they wouldn't be able to handle not knowing. He'd listened and had been sending them updates, even pictures to reassure them. But he should've told her. It would've eased her mind so much. But then, he wouldn't have had anything to hold over her head. Her gazed moved back to the screen when her mother spoke again.

"You look stunning Chloe. That's a beautiful necklace."

She was still so shell-shocked she touched the collar absently with her left hand. At her mother's gasp, she realized what she'd done.

"Oh my God!" Her mother screeched.

"Chloe, what have you done?" Her dad cut in, fury blazing in his eyes.

"I needed to be able to talk to you." She pleaded; her voice was shaking as she tried to fight her tears.

"Chloe?" Her mother's stern voice came through the speaker. Angela made herself calm down. She knew her daughter well. "Look at me."

When Chloe met her mother's loving gaze, her anxiety eased.

"You're a smart girl. You do whatever you need to do to survive this. No apologies, no regrets. I'm so proud that you've made it this far in such horrible situation." She paused for a moment, then added, "Sweetheart, I'm so proud." She stared into her daughter's beautiful eyes. Eyes that matched her own and tried to communicate silently with her. Then she hesitantly and quietly asked the question burning in her soul. "Did he hurt you?"

Chloe couldn't lie. Cillian had never physically hurt her. Even that first night, when he'd taken her virginity. She blushed bright red at the meaning in her mother's solemn question, but she answered her anyway. "No, he didn't."

When her mother nodded in understanding, she felt the tightness in her chest release.

"Can he hear me?" Her father questioned.

"Yes."

David raised his voice to be heard clearly. "I may not know your identity yet, but I will find you. You stole the most precious thing in our world. She had better be whole when we get her back. If not, I don't care who the fuck you are, I'll kill you."

At her father's threat, Chloe looked over the top of the screen at Cillian again. He didn't react to it in any way. He just continued to watch her with those gorgeous green eyes.

Angela's loud, angry voice suddenly came through the speakers, adding to David's threat. "Don't you hurt my girl!"

Chloe couldn't help but grin at her mother's vehement demand. "I love you mom."

"Sweetheart,"

"How's Juneau? Can I see him?" She needed to change the subject quickly. Her parents were angry, and rightly so. She didn't want to give Cillian any reason to hurt them.

Cillian watched Chloe light up as she talked with her family. He wasn't concerned about David Guidry's threat. He didn't begrudge him either. If someone took Chloe from him, he'd do more than threaten her abductor, he'd destroy everything in his path until he found her. But David was never getting her back. Choe was his now. His wife. Nothing would ever change that.

Watching her now, he knew he'd made the right decision. She needed this. He hadn't realized she felt responsible for her own abduction. That she felt the need to apologize to her parents as if she'd done something wrong.

Long minutes later, he checked his watch. He'd been mentally pacing, waiting for the call to be over. He was already tired of sharing her. He wanted his wife beneath him. At exactly the thirty-minute mark, he stood.

When Cillian stood up, Chloe hastily said goodbye to her parents. They set a time for the next call that fit with the agreement before disconnecting the call.

Cillian flipped the top of the laptop closed and lifted her into his arms and carried her to their bed. He sat on the edge with her standing between his knees. "Did you enjoy your call?"

"Yes"

"Turn around."

She turned and presented him with her back. He slowly lowered her zipper, gently kissing her skin as it was revealed. He turned her back around to face him and, taking his time, peeled the dress down her torso revealing her beautiful breast. He stopped, leaving the dress at her waist, her arms still in the sleeves, pinned at her sides. Leaning in, he suckling her nipple deep into his mouth. Running his palms up the back of her thighs under the hem, he cupped her ass and held her in place.

When her nipple was a stiff, hard peak, he moved to the other one. Slowly, he pushed the dress to the floor. "Step out." When she lifted her feet, one at a time, he kicked the dress away, leaving her in only the sheer thong, stockings and her high heels. He smoothed his hands up her legs, over her ass, around to cup her breasts before moving up to her shoulders. Holding her gaze, he added pressure, gently pushing her to her knees between his thighs. "Take out my cock."

Chloe couldn't look away from those glittering eyes. Her hands trembled slightly as she fumbled with his zipper. As soon as his slacks were open, his heavy erection fell into her palm.

Cillian pulled the ponytail out of her hair, then fisted handfuls at her scalp. "Put me in your mouth."

Her breath caught in her throat. She'd never done this before and wasn't sure what to do. And Cillian was a large man, everywhere. His cock was huge. "I don't,"

"Shh, I'm going to teach you." He whispered wickedly to her. "I'll teach you how to bring me to my knees." He put pressure on the back of her head to move her closer to him. "Now open your mouth."

Chloe took her time learning the taste and feel of him against her tongue. His skin was warm and clean. He tasted tangy and a little salty.

Her innocent little licks were driving him mad. He groaned when she closed her lips around him. It felt so fucking good. "Suck hard." His breathing increased in short pants.

Her lips were stretched wide to take him. When her teeth accidentally grazed him, his grip on her hair tightened.

"Yea, baby." He hissed. "Harder."

Chloe was a little shocked at his reaction. He groaned loudly, and his entire body was vibrating. The harder she sucked, the more he trembled. Every few strokes, she'd let her teeth graze his shaft. When she did, she was rewarded with his sharp intake of breath and more of the salty essence seeped from the tip. It took her a few minutes to realize that she had control. The idea of controlling him, of driving him to the point of madness, was exhilarating.

"Take me to the back of your throat and swallow." His head fell back at the amazing sensations. "Oh fuck!"

Emboldened by his response, she sucked harder. Bringing him to the back of her throat and swallowing, then licking along the heavy vein that ran up his shaft. She repeated the path, changing the rhythm and pressure every so often. She paid close attention to what he liked by the sounds he made.

Cillian grasped her head tighter. He was in heaven. It felt fucking amazing. "Now take a deep breath. I'm going to push into your throat. You'll feel like you're going to choke. You won't. I won't let you, so don't panic. Relax now." He couldn't resist pushing her boundaries. He loved corrupting her, tarnishing that innocence.

Chloe took a deep breath and did as he said. When she felt him push into her throat, she gagged.

He immediately pulled back. "Relax, concentrate on how I feel. Take a breath now. Come on baby, take me." He whispered to her in that wicked brogue that teased her senses.

Slowly, he pushed into her throat again. This time, she concentrated on staying relaxed. She focused on the smooth, warm feel of his skin.

"That feels so good baby." He continued to pull out, letting her take a breath, then push back in as she adjusted to the pressure in the back of her throat.

Chloe cupped his balls in one hand, rolling them gently as she grasped the base of his cock with the other.

When she used her hands on him, he gave her a few minutes to see if she would take control. His pleasure amplified when she did.

Power. It was a high. It pulsed. Vibrated through her. She was making him come apart, and it was amazing. Her core caught fire, and the desire to push him further had her wet with need. She wanted more. She took him deeper and reveled in the sound of his voice as he hissed in pleasure. She increased the pressure and speed, wanting to see how far she could drive him insane.

Jesus, she was going to kill him! She was fucking amazing. He was going to come. His spine flexed. His balls tightened in her palm. "Chloe!"

He was getting harder, bigger. Swelling so much more. Stretching her lips tighter. His thrusts were almost violent now. She took him, relaxing into him. Learning how his body reacted when he was about to come. It was amazing, this intimate knowledge. She wasn't so innocent that she didn't know what was about to happen. Sucking him deeper into her throat again, she prepared herself for the explosion.

"Chloe! Oh fuck!" Cillian threw his head back and roared as he came.

When his cock stopped jerking as his release subsided, she eased off him. Instinct had her lapping at him softly. She looked up into blazing green eyes.

It took him a minute to catch his breath, for his brain to come back online. When he finally met her beautiful eyes, he grinned at the triumph he could see shining there. She was most definitely going to kill him. "Come here," he nearly growled.

He hauled her onto his lap and kissed her swollen lips. He slipped his hand between her thighs and pulled back from the kiss when he felt the wet heat touch his fingers. At the look in her glazed eyes, satisfaction pulsing through him. Sucking him off had excited her. She was so hot and wet. "Do you need me, angel?"

She bravely met his gaze and answered honestly. "Yes."

"Good girl." He praised her, then took her mouth again. He pushed her heels from her feet and turning, he dropped her on the bed on her back and came down over her. Slithering down her body, he yanked the sheer silk of her thong away and pushed her thighs wide. The glistening lips of her pussy called to him. He licked from her ass to her clit in a slow, firm stoke that caused her back to arch in response.

Chloe was on fire. She reached for his head. Gripping his hair tightly, she held him to her and thrust against his tongue.

Cillian chuckled at her aggression. "Yea, you need me baby." Then proceeded to take her to paradise.

He woke her an hour later to feed her, then he took her again on the dining room table. Afterward, she lay limp in his arms as he held her in the warm bath he'd prepared. He bathed her carefully and stayed in the warm water for a long time, letting it sooth her before he carried her back to bed.

Chloe woke hours later in the dark to Cillian sliding deep into her. She didn't think it was possible, but he rode her exhausted body to orgasm again. She barely remembered him slipping out of her as she passed out.

Chapter 27: Little Box of Chocolates

Cillian rocked back in his chair while he listened to Titan's report. There was no connection between Abdul and the six men he was negotiating with for GhostStorm47. None.

"Boss, I've checked and re-checked every connection. I've traced all six back to childhood, and I didn't miss a colleague or a lover. Not even a distant cousin. It has to be someone on the island." Titan's voice said through the speaker.

Cillian looked over at Finn, who was sitting in the chair across from his desk. "Go through the files of very man on my payroll."

"We'll start today." Finn assured.

"Titan, work with Finn. I want every one of them researched, including Team One."

"We did that before hiring them."

"Well, do it again."

"Alright Boss. I have the files. Finn, I'll send them to you. We'll go over them together to ensure we don't miss anything."

"Send them now." Finn met Cillian's hard eyes. "We'll find him."

"You better."

Chloe spent the weeks following her marriage preparing for the formal wedding ceremony Cillian wanted. She'd woken up the morning after their wedding night and went for her run. She'd been exhausted, her body was screaming at her to stay in bed, but Cillian was getting up, so she would too.

She ran with him and her security detail that morning, hoping to keep to her normal routine. However, that was where normal stopped. Cillian and Finn were spending long hours in his office, and she was busy with wedding preparations. Imogen threw herself into helping her plan an extravagant wedding. One fit for someone of Cillian's station in his territory.

In addition to the planning, scheduling and invitations, there was also a change in her normal, everyday attire. The closet Cillian had initially purchased for her was certainly getting used. Leaders from the other territories were coming in droves to meet her. With them came their wives. There were teas and brunches. Showers and dinners. She'd met so many people. Some she liked a lot, others not so much.

This morning marked exactly one week before the wedding. She and Imogen were going through the latest shipment of gifts. There were stacks of presents everywhere. They were busy working diligently to catalogue each gift and prepare a thank-you card.

She knew she needed help. And while she loved Imogen, she really wanted her mom. Whether she liked it or not, it was her wedding. And it was going to be huge! Her mom was supposed to be here. Her dad was supposed to walk her down the aisle. She'd been trying not to think about it too much, but as the day drew closer, her thoughts turned more and more to them. And then there was Sid. Her best friend should be standing by her side, her Maid of Honor. That was how it was always supposed to be. But nothing was as it should be, and she felt like she was drowning.

To keep functioning, she was simply going through the motions. That's what she was thinking when Imogen called her name for what must have been the second or third time.

"Chloe. Are you ok?" Imogen had been so busy trying to sort out the latest gifts that it had taken her a few minutes to realize Chloe wasn't listening to her.

"Oh, um yes. I'm fine. I'm sorry Imogen." She hadn't realized her melancholy was evident until she saw the concerned frown on the woman's face.

"Do you need a break? We've been at this for several hours."

Chloe gave a heavy sign. "No, let's finish it." She looked at the sea of gifts in front of her. There were colorfully wrapped boxes and bows everywhere. The thank you cards would get backed up if they didn't keep going.

"Alright, but let me just get you something to drink before we continue." Imogen jumped to her feet and went into the kitchen.

Determined to keep going, Chloe lifted the small robin's egg blue box next to her. It was another gift from Tiffany's. When she untied the white silk bow, she immediately smelled the delicious scent of chocolate. She hadn't eaten in several hours, and her mouth watered. She lifted the lid off the box and smiled at the six perfectly placed chocolate truffles. Now this is a gift! She immediately popped one of the candies into her mouth.

Chloe rolled her eyes in pleasure as the dark, rich chocolate melted on her tongue. The creamy truffle was divine. She was reaching for another when Imogen came back in with a glass of water.

"Chloe, no!" Imogen rushed over and snatched the box from her hand.

Chloe looked at her in surprise. "What?" She frowned at the box Imogen now clutched to her chest.

"Where did you get these?" Imogen was looking around the floor frantically.

"The box was sitting right there with the others. Why?"

Imogen watched her closely for a few moments. When nothing happened, she thought maybe she'd overreacted. She was just starting to relax and went to put the box of candy and the water on the table when she saw Chloe's expression suddenly change from confusion to surprise then to pain.

"Imogen? I, I don't feel well." Her skin became clammy and hot. She was getting dizzy and a sharp burning sensation attacked her stomach. It felt like someone had taken a blowtorch to her insides.

"Oh my God! Chloe, hang on!" Imogen ran to the bedside table and lifted the telephone and started screaming at whoever was on the other end of the line.

Chloe wasn't sure who she was yelling at, and she didn't care. The excruciating pain in her stomach took all of her attention. "I think I need to lie down." She stood up from her chair, only to find herself on her knees on the floor. Her hands barely caught her before her face hit the floor. The cramp tightening her abdomen was so fierce she screamed.

Imogen raced back to Chloe and pulled her up. "Chloe! Chloe, look at me!" Imogen pushed her into a sitting position. When Chloe tried to lie down again, she forced her head up. Tears burned her eyes when Chloe cried out in pain. Relentlessly, she grabbed Chloe's jaw and forced her mouth open.

"Imogen, stop!" Chloe was panting, trying to breathe through the horrible cramps. "I need to lie down."

"Chloe, please!" Imogen begged as she shoved two fingers into Chloe's mouth all the way to the back of her throat.

Chloe fought to back away from the intrusion. The pain was so fierce; it was paralyzing.

"Chloe, focus!" Imogen screamed in her face. "You've been poisoned! You have to vomit! Now!"

Through her terror and pain, she tried to listen. She did. But the buzzing in her ears and her own screams of pain were louder than the words coming at her.

Imogen shoved her fingers down Chloe's throat again, only this time she ignored the teeth biting down on her hand. Finally, it worked. Chloe gagged violently, then vomited. As soon as she stopped, Imogen shoved her fingers into her throat again, forcing her to vomit a second time.

Chloe heard pounding footsteps, but she couldn't turn her head because Imogen was holding her by her hair. She vaguely comprehended what was happening and attempted to cooperate, but the fire in her stomach was excruciating.

Through the disgusting gagging sounds she was making and Imogen's harsh breathing, she heard an ear-piercing roar. The sound, like a wounded animal, echoing through the room. Her gaze shifted toward the god-awful sound and met the blazing fury in her husband's eyes. She understood his fury. He probably thought he was about to lose one of his possessions. But what confused her most was the fear she recognized in those green depths. That was her last thought before everything went black.

Cillian's hands shook with rage as he gently lifted his unconscious wife into his arms. He turned and nearly ran into Doc when he charged into the room.

"Where did it come from?" Doc barked, all business as he followed Cillian over to the bed.

"A box of chocolates! They're over there." Imogen pointed at the offending box she'd dropped on the floor, with the remaining chocolates scattered haphazardly around it.

"Get them." The doctor instructed. "I'll need to know what's in them."

While he went to work examining Chloe, Imogen gathered what was left of the chocolates and put them back in their box. She handed it to Finn, who'd come in behind Cillian. She looked over at Chloe and, seeing her pale face, Imogen rushed into the bathroom. Wetting a washcloth with cold water, she brought it back to Chloe.

Cillian took the cold cloth from Imogen and carefully cleaned the vomit from her face. "Wake up, angel." His voice shook with fear and rage. "Come on Chloe, wake up."

"It's better that she's out." The doctor informed him.

"Why?"

"Less pain that way." Doc cringed at the terrifying look of retribution burning in his boss's eyes. He needed to focus on Chloe and not on his own fear. "Im, how long after she ate the candy, did she get sick?"

"It couldn't have been more than a minute. I went to get her some water because she seemed so overwhelmed by our task today. Her thoughts kept wandering, and she looked so sad that I thought she might need a break. She didn't have the box when I left. When I came back in, she'd already eaten one. She was sick almost instantly. It took about another minute for me to get her to vomit."

"Humph." Doc grunted as he continued his examination. "She's lucky you were here and reacted so quickly. You probably saved her life. I'm going to start an IV and push fluids through her system."

Cillian looked over at Finn, still holding the small box. "Lock it in my office and have Jacob guard the fucking door!"

"Consider it done." Finn snarled.

"I'll need the candy. Or at least a few pieces. I need to run some tests to find out exactly what she ingested."

Cillian watched Chloe for any sign that she might wake up. "Double her goddamned security detail. And Finn?"

Finn looked up from his phone to meet Cillian's menacing gaze.

"Find out how something edible made it in here without us knowing. Our fucking security protocols are in place for a goddamned reason."

"I'm already pulling the video feeds."

Hours later, Cillian sat propped up against the headboard of his bed with his legs stretched out in front of him. Thanks to the sedative laced with a heavy painkiller Doc had given her, Chloe was still sleeping. He watched the video feeds for what felt like the hundredth time. The intake area in the warehouse next to the airstrip was now playing in slow motion on his screen.

The signature robin's egg blue box should stand out, but they'd received several of them in all different shapes and sizes over the last few days. They'd been sorted and stacked with all the other gifts that were in line to be run through the scanner. He watched each blue box as it was loaded onto the belt. He didn't see one that matched the size he was looking for going into the machine.

Every package addressed to the castle went through that scanner. Then they were loaded onto a truck that brought them to the castle. When he viewed the tapes of the workers unloading them, he still didn't see the one he was looking for.

With a sinking feeling, he glanced over at Finn, who was sitting in a chair next to the bed by the IV pole on Chloe's side. "You're right. It's not here."

Eyes fixed on Chloe's pale face; Finn's jaw clinched tightly at Cillian's confirmation. He'd hoped he'd missed something. It suggested that someone here, one of their own, was involved. "We'll need to look into everyone coming and going from the castle over the last week."

"Make it the last month. And I want the tapes reviewed of every single person coming onto the island from the airstrip and the docks. If it's one of ours, they could've brought it in from either direction."

"Ok."

"I want Titan on it." Cillian added.

"He is. He already looked over the footage you just saw, but he didn't see anything either."

Cillian snapped his laptop closed and reached out to take Chloe's hand. He stroked his thumb over the back of it, then looked over at Finn again. "Find them."

"We will."

"Finn?" Fear was a dangerous emotion for a man like him.

"I know, cousin." Finn assured him.

Cillian placed the laptop on the table by the bed, then he laid down on his side, facing Chloe. He put his arm around her still form and kissed her forehead before resting his head next to hers.

Finn got up and went to look out the balcony doors to give his cousin some privacy. He wasn't leaving the room. Not that he thought anyone would get through the teams and come at her. No, they were cowards hiding in the shadows. He called Titan and gave him instructions while he watched the waves come in from the ocean off in the distance.

This had been a close call. If Chloe died, there would be no redemption for Cillian. He would be lost to them all. She was the one thing standing between him and total destruction. Everything the O'Donnell name represented throughout the centuries would be lost. Chloe didn't realize it yet, but he did. He knew his cousin too well. He hadn't displayed an ounce of tenderness, not one. Nor had he laughed, really laughed, since he'd lost his family. Other than anger and determination, there had been no emotion. Nothing. Until Chloe.

They faced an unknown enemy who's deadly intent was focused on her. They all had to be vigilant. Because he and his team knew that above all else, Chloe had to survive.

Chloe woke abruptly to a sharp pain in her stomach and pressure on her bladder. When she opened her eyes, Cillian's face was next to hers on the pillow. Her head was spinning, and she felt like she was drunk. More than drunk; totally wasted. There was a dull throb and an unusual weight on her hand. When she tried to move it, Cillian placed his hand on her arm to stop her.

"Careful, you'll pull out the IV."

She looked down at her hand to see what he was talking about. She stared at it for a moment in drunken wonder. She was seeing double. And her tongue felt really thick, so it was hard to talk around it. "Whad happened?" She slurred.

"You broke a rule today, angel." Cillian's hardened gaze met her glazed one.

"Oh, no I di'ent." She said in a singsong voice and wagged a finger from her other hand in his face. "I woulna do that, else I don get ta talk to my momma." She denied.

Cillian eyed her carefully, wondering how much morphine Doc was pumping through her IV. "Yes angel, you did."

"Nope, nope, nope." She said drunkenly and popped her lips loudly on each 'p'. Then her eyes turned serious. "I have ta pee Ci-lelelean."

Cillian stopped her when she tried to roll off the bed. She was fucking adorable, but he persevered. This was important. "You broke a rule. You ate candy that hadn't been checked out first."

"I like candy. Do you like candy?" She asked curiously. She tapped his chin playfully with the finger she'd been pointing at him.

"You're supposed to have it checked out before you eat it."

"Well, ya di'ent tell me that was a rule. So, shame on you." She tapped her finger against his nose.

"What were you thinking?" He captured her finger in his hand and held it to his chest when she went to pull it away.

"I was thinkin bout tha show."

"What show?" Cillian looked up at movement by the door and watched his men file into the room. They'd been waiting in the other room for any sign that Chloe was going to be alright.

Chloe looked up at the faces swimming before her and smiled delightedly. "Hi guys!"

When his men turned their concerned gazes to him, Cillian looked back at Chloe in surprise. "What show, Chloe?"

"You know."

"Tell me."

"The wedding. I don even have ta rehersh any lines. I just have ta say whad that man tells me to."

"You mean the priest?"

"Nope, nope, nope. He's not a priest. If he was, he would help me. But he di'ent, so nope, he's no priest."

His gaze roamed her face before he replied softly. "Our wedding is not a show, Chloe."

"Oh yes, it is. It's not real Ci-lelelean."

"Why do you think that?"

"I have ta pee." She turned to get off the bed again.

He held her still when she tried to move. "Chloe, why do you think the wedding isn't real?" He knew it wasn't fair to ask her right now. She was obviously drugged out of her mind, but she never told him what she was thinking. So, he ruthlessly pushed her for answers.

"Because silly, Sid isn't here." She looked up at all the people surrounding her, searching the crowd. "Is she here?"

"No, she's not here." He answered softly.

"Nope. She is not." She pulled her finger away from his hold and wagged it at him again. "See. I told ya so. It can't be a real wedding, else Sid would be here, cause she's gonna be my maid of honor. That's how it's spost ta be. An, an, my momma would be here ta help with tha dress cause mommas are spost ta do that. Oh an, an, my daddy would walk me down tha aisle. See Ci-lelelean, it can't be real." She pulled her hand from his hold and lifted both up and shrugged her shoulders.

At the sound of a grumbled curse, she looked up at Patrick and Rourke's concerned faces. "Hi Padreck! You an Rourkee, hey ya know that sounds like yorkie, ya know like that little dog. Only you're not little." She giggled. "But ya know what? You could be Thing One an Thing Two! But now there are four of you! Like that Dr. Suess rhyme." She laughed at her joke. "Thad's whad Sid would call ya. She's funny. She's, my friend. She's my BFFFFFFF." She got lost in the "F's" for a few seconds before she continued. "She is my friend. She is. But you're not my friends. I want ya to be, but you're not."

"Chloe lass, we are your friends." Patrick soothed. Rourke just scowled at Cillian again.

"Nope." Her lips popped the 'P,' again. "Ya have ta keep me here with your guns. Cause you got guns. Sid is my friend. Do ya know she's a badass?" She asked the group of men. When no one responded, she continued. "And she's butiful. And smart. You would like her. But she can't come here. Nope! Cause I'm a prisoner. I'm in a butiful prison. And I di'ent even do anything wrong."

Cillian sighed softly. "Angel?" Turning her face to his he kissed her forehead. He ignored his men, who were all glaring at him now.

She smiled sweetly as if suddenly noticing him and whispered as her drug glazed eyes met his. "Hi."

"Hi baby." He whispered back.

"Ya know thad thing they use ta burn sugar on top of Crème Brulelele? Thad fire thingy thad makes the sugar hard so ya can crack it with a spoon?"

Cillian's gaze turned to confusion. "A torch?"

"Yeah." She moaned softly. "Thad thing. It's burning my belly Ci-lelelean."

"I know, baby." Cillian closed his eyes, hoping to hide his fury from her. "I'm so sorry."

"I have ta pee really bad." She whispered again.

"Ok angel, hang on." Cillian got off the bed and went around to her side while his men filed out of the room. He disconnected the IV bag and placed it on her lap. "Hold this." Then he carried her into the bathroom.

Several minutes later with her bladder empty, her teeth brushed and her face washed, he had her tucked back in bed. She'd drifted off to sleep almost immediately. Cillian ran his thumb gently across her cheek as he watched her sleep. Every so often, she'd flinch, as if the pain followed her into her dreams.

This was his fault. The pain she was experiencing rested solely on his shoulders. If he hadn't taken her, she wouldn't have been poisoned. He tried to temper his rage for her sake. But the fact that someone was trying to get to him through her was making him insane with the need for vengeance.

In an effort to stay calm, he turned his mind to their earlier conversation. Her drug induced ramblings gave him incredible insight into her thoughts. No matter how often she smiled now, she wasn't happy. He should've known because she still wasn't painting. She'd yet to go back to her studio. He needed to figure out how to change

rocked back in his chair while he listened to Titan's report. There was no connection between Abdul and the six men he was negotiating with for GhostStorm47. None.

"Boss, I've checked and re-checked every connection. I've traced all six back to childhood, and I didn't miss a colleague or a lover. Not even a distant cousin. It has to be someone on the island." Titan's voice said through the speaker.

Cillian looked over at Finn, who was sitting in the chair across from his desk. "Go through the files of very man on my payroll."

"We'll start today." Finn assured.

"Titan, work with Finn. I want every one of them, including Team One researched."

"We did that before hiring them."

"Well, do it again."

"Alright Boss. I have the files. Finn, I'll send them to you. We'll go over them together to make sure one of us doesn't miss anything."

"Send them now." Finn met Cillian's hard eyes. "We'll find him."

"You better."

Chloe spent the weeks following her marriage preparing for the formal wedding Cillian was insisting on. She'd woken up the morning after their official wedding night to go for her run. She was so exhausted her body was screaming at her to stay in bed. But Cillian was getting up, so she would too.

She ran with him and her security detail that morning, hoping to keep to her normal routine. However, that was where normal stopped. Cillian and Finn were spending long hours in his office, and she was busy with wedding preparations. Imogen threw herself into helping her plan a wedding that was expected for someone of Cillian's station in his territory.

In addition to the planning, scheduling and invitations, there was also a change in her normal, everyday attire. The closet Cillian had initially purchased for her was certainly getting used. Leaders from the other territories were coming in droves to be introduced to her. With them came their wives. There were teas and brunches. Showers and dinners. She'd met a lot of people. Some of the wives she liked a lot, others not so much.

This morning marked exactly one week before the wedding. She and Imogen were going through the latest shipment of gifts that had already arrived. There were stacks of presents everywhere. They were busy working diligently to catalogue each gift and prepare a thank-you card.

She knew she needed help. And while she loved Imogen, she really wanted her mom. Whether she liked it or not, it was her wedding. And it was going to be huge! Her mom was supposed to be here. Her dad was supposed to walk her down the aisle. She'd been trying not to think about it too much, but as the day drew closer, her thoughts turned more and more to them. And then there was Sid. Her Bestie was supposed to be standing by her side, her Maid of Honor. That was how it was always supposed to be. But nothing was as it should be, and she felt like she was drowning.

To keep functioning, she was simply going through the motions. That's what she was thinking when Imogen called her name for what must have been the second or third time.

"Chloe. Are you ok?" Imogen had been so busy trying to sort out the latest gifts that it had taken her a few minutes to realize Chloe wasn't listening to her.

"Oh, um yes. I'm fine. I'm sorry Imogen." She hadn't realized her melancholy was evident until she saw the concerned frown on her friend's face.

"Do you need a break? We've been at this for several hours."

Chloe gave a heavy sign. "No, let's finish it." She looked at the sea of gifts in front of her. There were colorfully wrapped boxes and bows everywhere. The thank you cards would get backed up if they didn't keep going.

"Alright, but let me just get you something to drink before we continue." Imogen jumped to her feet and went into the kitchen.

Determined to keep going, Chloe lifted the small robin's egg blue box next to her. It was another gift from Tiffany's. When she untied the white silk bow, she immediately smelled the delicious scent of chocolate. She hadn't eaten in several hours, and her mouth watered. She lifted the lid off the box and smiled at the six perfectly placed chocolate truffles. Now this is a gift! She immediately popped one of the candies into her mouth.

Chloe rolled her eyes in pleasure as the dark, rich chocolate melted on her tongue. The creamy truffle was divine. She was reaching for another when Imogen came back in with a glass of water.

"Chloe, no!" Imogen rushed over and snatched the box from her hand.

Chloe looked at her in surprise. "What?" She frowned at the box Imogen now clutched to her chest.

"Where did you get these?" Imogen was looking around the floor frantically.

"The box was sitting right there with the others. Why?"

Imogen watched her closely for a few moments. When nothing happened, she thought maybe she'd overreacted. She was just starting to relax and went to put the box of candy and the water on the table when she saw Chloe's expression suddenly change from confusion to surprise then to pain.

"Imogen? I, I don't feel well." Her skin became clammy and hot. She was getting dizzy and a sharp burning sensation attacked her stomach. It felt like someone had taken a blowtorch to her insides.

"Oh my God! Chloe, hang on!" Imogen ran to the bedside table and lifted the telephone and started screaming at whoever was on the other end of the line.

Chloe wasn't sure who she was yelling at, and she didn't care. The excruciating pain in her stomach took all of her attention. "I think I need to lie down." She stood up from her chair, only to find herself on her knees on the floor. Her hands barely caught her before her face hit the floor. The cramp tightening her abdomen was so fierce she screamed.

Imogen raced back to Chloe and pulled her up. "Chloe! Chloe, look at me!" Imogen pushed her into a sitting position. When Chloe tried to lie down again, she forced her head up. Tears burned her eyes when Chloe cried out in pain. Relentlessly, she grabbed Chloe's jaw and forced her mouth open.

"Imogen, stop!" Chloe was panting, trying to breathe through the horrible cramps. "I need to lie down."

"Chloe, please!" Imogen begged as she shoved two fingers into Chloe's mouth all the way to the back of her throat.

Chloe fought to back away from the intrusion. The pain was so fierce; it was paralyzing.

"Chloe, focus!" Imogen screamed in her face. "You've been poisoned! You have to throw up! Now!"

Through her terror and pain, she tried to listen. She did. But the buzzing in her ears and her own screams of pain were louder than the words coming at her.

Imogen shoved her fingers down Chloe's throat again, only this time she ignored the teeth biting down on her hand. Finally, it worked. Chloe gagged violently, then vomited. As soon as she stopped, Imogen shoved her fingers into her throat again, forcing her to vomit a second time.

Chloe heard pounding footsteps, but she couldn't turn her head because Imogen was holding her by her hair. She vaguely comprehended what was happening and attempted to cooperate, but the fire in her stomach was excruciating.

Through the disgusting gagging sounds she was making and Imogen's harsh breathing, she heard an ear-piercing roar, that sounded a lot like a wild animal, echo through the room. Her eyes shifted toward the god-awful sound and met the blazing fury in her husband's eyes. She understood his fury. He probably thought he was about to lose one of his possessions. But what confused her most was the fear she recognized in those green depths. That was her last thought before everything went black.

Cillian's hands shook with rage as he gently lifted his unconscious wife into his arms. He turned and nearly ran into Doc when he charged into the room.

"Where did it come from?" Bronson barked, all business as he followed Cillian over to the bed.

"A box of chocolates! They're over there." Imogen pointed at the offending box she'd dropped on the floor, with the remaining chocolates scattered haphazardly around it.

"Get them." The doctor instructed. "I'll need to know what's in them."

While he went to work examining Chloe, Imogen gathered what was left of the chocolates and put them back in their box. She handed it to Finn, who'd come in behind Cillian. She looked over at Chloe and, seeing her pale face, Imogen rushed into the bathroom. Wetting a washcloth with cold water, she brought it back to Chloe.

Cillian took the cold cloth from Imogen and carefully cleaned the vomit from her face. "Wake up, angel." His voice shook with fear and rage. "Come on Chloe, wake up."

"It's better that she's out." The doctor informed him.

"Why?"

"Less pain that way." Bronson cringed at the terrifying look of retribution burning in his boss's eyes. He needed to focus on Chloe and not on his own fear. "Im, how long after she ate the candy did she get sick?"

"It couldn't have been more than a minute. I went to get her some water because she seemed so overwhelmed by our task today. Her thoughts kept wandering, and she looked so sad that I thought she might need a break. She didn't have the box when I left. When I came back in, she'd already eaten one. She was sick almost instantly. It took about another minute for me to get her to vomit."

"Humph." Doc grunted as he continued his examination. "She's lucky you were here and reacted so quickly. You probably saved her life. I'm going to start an IV and push fluids through her system."

Cillian looked over at Finn, who was still holding the small box. "Lock it in my office and have Jacob guard the fucking door!"

"Consider it done." Finn snarled.

"I'll need the candy. Or at least a few pieces. I need to run some tests to find out exactly what she ingested."

Cillian watched Chloe for any sign that she might wake up. "Double her goddamned security detail. And Finn?"

Finn looked up from his phone to meet Cillian's menacing gaze.

"Find out how something edible made it in here without us knowing. Our fucking security protocols are in place for a goddamned reason."

"I'm already pulling the video feeds."

Hours later, Cillian sat propped up against the headboard of his bed with his legs stretched out in front of him. Thanks to the sedative laced with a heavy painkiller Doc had given her, Chloe was still sleeping. He watched the video feeds for what felt like the hundredth time. The intake area in the warehouse next to the airstrip was now playing in slow motion on his screen.

The signature robin's egg blue box should stand out, but they'd received several of them in all different shapes and sizes over the last few days. They'd been sorted and stacked with all the other gifts that were in line to be run through the scanner. He watched each blue box as it was loaded onto the belt. He didn't see one that matched the size he was looking for going into the machine.

Every package addressed to the castle went through that scanner. Then they were loaded onto a truck that brought them to the castle. When he viewed the tapes of the workers unloading them, he still didn't see the one he was looking for.

With a sinking feeling, he glanced over at Finn, who was sitting in a chair next to the bed by the IV pole on Chloe's side. "You're right. It's not here."

Eyes fixed on Chloe's pale face; Finn's jaw clinched tightly at Cillian's confirmation. He'd hoped he'd missed something. It suggested that someone here, one of their own, was involved. "We'll need to look into everyone coming and going from the castle over the last week."

"Make it the last month. And I want the tapes reviewed of every single person coming onto the island from the airstrip and the docks. If it's one of ours, they could've brought it in from either direction."

"Ok."

"I want Titan on it." Cillian added.

"He is. He already looked over the footage you just saw, but he didn't see anything either."

Cillian snapped his laptop closed and reached out to take Chloe's hand. He stroked his thumb over the back of it, then looked over at Finn again. "Find them."

"We will."

"Finn?" Fear was a dangerous emotion for a man like him.

"I know, Cillian." Finn assured him.

Cillian placed the laptop on the table by the bed, then he laid down on his side, facing Chloe. He put his arm around her still form and kissed her forehead before resting his head next to hers.

Finn got up and went to look out the balcony doors to give his cousin some privacy. He wasn't leaving the room. Not that he thought anyone would get through the teams and come at her. No, they were cowards hiding in the shadows. He called Titan and gave him instructions while he watched the waves come in from the ocean off in the distance.

This had been a close call. If Chloe died, there would be no redemption for Cillian. He would be lost to them all. She was the one thing standing between him and total destruction. Everything the O'Donnell name represented throughout the centuries would be lost. Chloe didn't realize it yet, but he did. He knew his cousin too well. He hadn't displayed an ounce of tenderness, not one. Nor had he laughed, really laughed, since he'd lost his family. Other than anger and determination, there had been no emotion. Nothing. Until Chloe.

They faced an unknown enemy who's deadly intent was focused on her. They all had to be vigilant. Because he and his team knew that above all else, Chloe had to survive.

Chloe woke abruptly to a sharp pain in her stomach and pressure on her bladder. When she opened her eyes, Cillian's face was next to hers on the pillow. Her head was spinning, and she felt like she was drunk. More than drunk; totally wasted. There was a dull throb and an unusual weight on her hand. When she tried to move it, Cillian placed his hand on her arm to stop her.

"Careful, you'll pull out the IV."

She looked down at her hand to see what he was talking about. She stared at it for a moment in drunken wonder. She was seeing double. And her tongue felt really thick, so it was hard to talk around it. "Whad happened?" She slurred.

"You broke a rule today, angel." Cillian's hardened gaze met her glazed one.

"Oh, no I di'ent." She said in a singsong voice and wagged a finger from her other hand in his face. "I woulna do that, else I don get ta talk to my momma." She denied.

Cillian eyed her carefully, wondering how much morphine Doc was pumping through her IV. "Yes angel, you did."

"Nope, nope, nope." She said drunkenly and popped her lips loudly on each 'p'. Then her eyes turned serious. "I have ta pee Ki-lelelean."

Cillian stopped her when she tried to roll off the bed. She was fucking adorable, but he persevered. This was important. "You broke a rule. You ate candy that hadn't been checked out first."

"I like candy. Do you like candy?" She asked curiously. She tapped his chin playfully with the finger she'd been pointing at him.

"You're supposed to have it checked out before you eat it."

"Well, ya di'ent tell me that was rule. So, shame on you." She tapped her finger against his nose.

"What were you thinking?" He captured her finger in his hand and held it to his chest when she went to pull it away.

"I was thinkin bout tha big play."

"What play?" Cillian looked up at movement by the door and watched his men file into the room. They'd been waiting in the other room for any sign that Chloe was going to be alright.

Chloe looked up at the faces swimming before her and smiled delightedly. "Hi guys!"

When his men turned their concerned gazes to him, Cillian looked back at Chloe in surprise. "What play, Chloe?"

"You know."

"Tell me."

"The wedding play. I don even have ta rehersh any lines. I just have ta say whad that man tells me to."

"You mean the priest?"

"Nope, nope, nope. He's not a priest. If he was, he would help me. But he di'ent, so nope."

His gaze roamed her face before he replied softly. "Our wedding is not a play, Chloe."

"Oh yes, it is. It's not real Ki-lelelean."

"Why do you think that?"

"I have ta pee." She turned to get off the bed again.

He held her still when she tried to move. "Chloe, why do you think the wedding isn't real?" He knew it wasn't fair to ask her right now. She was obviously drugged out of her mind, but she never told him what she was thinking. So, he ruthlessly pushed her for answers.

"Because silly, Sid isn't here." She looked up at all the people surrounding her, searching the crowd. "Is she here?"

"No, she's not here." He answered softly.

"Nope. She is not." She pulled her finger away from his hold and wagged it at him again. "See. I told ya so. It can't be a real wedding, else Sid would be here, cause she's gonna be my maid of honor. That's how it's spost ta be. An, an, my momma would be here ta help with tha dress cause momma's are spost ta do that. Oh an, an, my daddy would walk me down tha aisle. So, see Ki-lelelean it can't be real." She pulled her hand from his hold and lifted both up and shrugged her shoulders.

At the sound of a grumbled curse, she looked up at Patrick and Rourke's concerned faces. "Hi Padreck! You an Rourkee, hey ya know that sounds like yorkie, ya know like that little dog. Only you're not little."

She giggled. "But ya know what? You could be Thing One an Thing Two! Cause now there are four of you! Like that Dr. Suess rhyme." She laughed at her joke. "Thad's whad Sid would call ya. She's funny. She's, my friend. She's my BFFFFFFF." She got lost in the "F's" for a few seconds before she continued. "She is my friend. She is. But you're not my friends. I want ya to be, but you're not."

"Chloe lass, we are your friends." Patrick soothed. Rourke just scowled at Cillian again.

"Nope." Her lips popped the 'P,' again. "Ya have ta keep me here with your guns. Cause you got guns. Sid is my friend. Do ya know she's a badass?" She asked the group of men. When no one responded, she continued. "And she's butiful. And smart. You would like her. But she can't come here. Nope! Cause I'm a prisoner. I'm in a butiful jail. And I di'ent even do anything wrong."

Cillian sighed softly. "Angel?" Turning her face to his he kissed her forehead. He ignored his men, who were all glaring at him now.

She smiled as if suddenly noticing him and whispered as her drug glazed eyes met his. "Hi."

"Hi baby." He whispered back.

"Ya know thad thing they use ta burn sugar on top of Crème Brulelele? Thad fire thingy thad makes the sugar hard so ya can crack it with a spoon?"

Cillian's gaze turned to confusion. "A torch?"

"Yeah." She moaned softly. "Thad thing. It's burning my belly Ki-lelelean."

"I know, baby." Cillian closed his eyes, hoping to hide his fury from her. "I'm so sorry."

"I have ta pee really bad." She whispered again.

"Ok angel, hang on." Cillian got off the bed and went around to her side while his men filed out of the room. He disconnected the IV bag and placed it on her lap. "Hold this." Then he carried her into the bathroom.

Several minutes later with her bladder empty, her teeth brushed and her face washed, he had her tucked back in bed. She'd drifted off to sleep almost immediately. Cillian ran his thumb gently across her cheek as he watched her sleep. Every so often, she'd flinch, as if the pain followed her into her dreams.

This was his fault. The pain she was experiencing rested solely on his shoulders. If he hadn't taken her, she wouldn't have been poisoned. He tried to temper his fury for her sake. But the fact that someone was trying to get to him through her was making him insane with the need for revenge.

269

In an effort to stay calm, he turned his mind to their earlier conversation. Her drug induced ramblings gave him incredible insight into her thoughts. No matter how often she smiled now, she wasn't happy. He should've known because she still wasn't painting. She'd yet to go back to her studio. He needed to figure out how to change that.

Chapter 28: Chocolate is a Girl's Best Friend

Cillian watched Chloe sleep while he contemplated his next move. He'd come to a decision in the early morning hours. It wasn't one he was happy about, but he'd do it. He looked over at Finn when he stepped quietly into the room.

Finn gave Chloe a once over as if making sure she was asleep before he asked, "you really want to do this?"

Cillian looked back at her and gently ran his knuckle down her cheek. "No, but I will."

"It's going to be a logistical nightmare." Finn warned.

"I know, but do it anyway." What was the point of having this much power if he couldn't use it?

"I'll take Team Two. At this point, I'd be hard pressed to get Alpha One to leave the castle."

When Cillian didn't reply, Finn slipped quietly back out of the room.

Cillian rested his head on his hand as he continued to watch her sleep. She'd woken up several times during the night to sharp pains in her stomach. Around 2am he'd called Doc to come back and increase the dose of morphine to help her rest more comfortably.

Doc had assured him she would recover. That she'd be up and around in a day or two. The question was, how was she going to react once she was feeling better?

He knew he'd have to make amends. She'd almost died because of him. So maybe he owed her this one concession. But that was all. Only this one. He'd changed her life irrevocably, but he didn't give a shit. She was going to have to live with it, and him.

He scowled as he ran his fingertip across her cheek again. They were in dangerous territory now. The power she had over him was staggering. He didn't like it. Not one fucking bit. It was supposed to be the other way around. And it would be when he was finished. She would be so fucking tied to him she'd never be able to imagine her life without him again. "You won't be able to fucking breathe without me, angel." He promised in a harsh whisper.

Chloe woke up without pain for the first time in three days. She turned her head to find Cillian asleep beside her. She stared at him for a few quiet minutes. He was a beautiful man. Oh, he was seriously intimidating, but he was also absolutely gorgeous. Actually, his entire team could all pose for one of those firefighter calendars Sidney had hung on the back of her bedroom door as a teen. She smiled to herself at the thought. They would all be mortified if she told them that.

Asleep, she thought he looked like a fallen angel. It was so unfair that he looked so perfect. But, upon closer inspection, she noted the dark circles under those incredibly long lashes. He also wore several days' worth of scruff on the lower half of his face. It made him look even more sinister than usual.

While she watched him sleep, she thought back over the last couple of days. The pain she'd experienced had been terrible. But she also saw flashes of images as they played through her mind like the reel of an old black and white movie. Shadowed scenes of Cillian caressing her face, his gentle attempts to feed her little sips of broth. That soft Irish brogue encouraging her to take more.

She listened to his even breathing as the conflicting emotions bombarding her started to take shape, and she didn't like the picture they painted. She remembered the fury in his eyes before she's passed out, but she also remembered the fear. That's what kept tugging at her conscience now. Everything was so confusing. How could someone as dangerous and conniving as Cillian O'Donnell really care about her?

She couldn't forget that he'd been sending reassuring messages to her parents. He'd tried his best to keep them from worrying too much. Oh, they were worried, but at least they knew she was alive and, mostly, unharmed. Why would he do that?

Before she thought better of it, she reached out and stroked her fingers through the unfamiliar scruff covering his chin. The bristles tickling her fingertips were soothing. She slowly lifted her eyes from the soft bristles to meet the incredibly beautiful sage green eyes staring back at her.

"Hi," he whispered softly.

"Hi." She whispered back.

"You scared the shit out of me." He continued quietly, a scowl forming on his face.

"I scared the shit out of myself." She smiled slightly and continued to run her fingers over his scruff. "But I think I'm fine now."

"Don't do that shit again." His growl was nearly a hiss.

"Don't worry, I'm pretty sure I've learned my lesson."

He stared at her for a long moment. "I'm sorry."

It was her turn to scowl at him. "You didn't give me poisoned chocolate. Which is sacrilege, by the way." She added in a snarky voice, hoping to distract him.

"What do you mean?"

She widened her eyes playfully. "Chocolate is sacred. They say diamonds are a girl's best friend, but I disagree. It's chocolate."

He chuckled. "Chocolate, huh? I'll have to remember that."

She was glad he laughed. In her experience, an emotional Cillian could be dangerous. She rubbed the scruff on his face again and changed the subject. "You look so different with this beard."

"Really, how so?"

"You look like an old man." She chuckled at the look of outrage he gave her.

"Old man?! I'm not that old."

"Maybe not, but you're a lot older than me and the beard makes it worse."

"You want me to shave it?"

"I think you should." She looked him over carefully. "And you should probably get some rest, you look like crap."

"I'll get right on that. Anything else?" He grinned.

"Yes, call that grumpy doctor of yours to come remove this IV. Then you can help me to the bathroom before he shows up."

The castle seemed to sigh in relief when its "queen" was pronounced recovered. The buzz of activity in preparation for the wedding resumed. Imogen hovered, constantly trying to get Chloe to eat. Apparently, she'd lost more weight than the woman considered healthy. Fortunately, her appetite slowly came back and within a few days, she was back to normal.

Cillian, however, was a different story. He was seething with fury. Everyone was uneasy, terrified to make a misstep. He barked orders, snapped at anyone who questioned him, and his menacing demeanor terrified the staff. When he wasn't scaring the shit out of everyone, he was locked in his office. She knew he was trying to figure out how the poison made it into their suite.

To make matters worse, Finn was gone. She hadn't seen him since the day she'd been poisoned. If anyone could calm Cillian, it was Finn, but she didn't know where he was.

Also, her security detail had increased considerably. Even inside the castle, she had at least two guards with her at all times. They even tasted her food before she was allowed to eat it. When she'd questioned Cillian about it, he'd gripped her hair in a tight fist and forced her mouth up to his for a brutal kiss. When he'd finally released her lips, he'd growled at her, telling her he could do whatever in the fuck he wanted. Then he'd turned and stormed off.

They were eating lunch together and, after reading a message on his phone, Cillian abruptly hurled his glass of tea against the wall. Chloe jumped in surprise when it shattered. Before she could ask what was wrong, he reached out and slid his finger under her collar and tugged insistently until the pressure forced her to stand and move between his thighs.

The door behind them flew open at the sound of the glass shattering.

"Get out!" Cillian roared at whoever came rushing in. He didn't look up to see who it was. He didn't give a fuck. They'd reached another fucking dead end. He still didn't know who was trying to take her from him, and there was no outlet for his rage. He wanted to find them and cut them to pieces one slice at a time. He wanted to watch them fucking bleed.

Chloe heard the door slam shut as he slid his hands under her skirt, causing it to rise. Grabbing the fabric of her panties, he ripped the delicate silk to shreds. In one motion, he slid his fingers up her inner thigh and pushed two of them deep inside her.

She wasn't prepared for the intrusion and lifted onto her tiptoes to avoid it. "Cillian?" She gasped loudly.

"Take it." He growled. He gripped her hip and pushed her back down onto his thrusting fingers. He circled her clit, then pressed down tight when it hardened.

Her body came alive at the dangerous vibe pulsing through the room. She groaned at the onslaught of sensations beating at her. He leaned in and captured her groan with his lips. His tongue thrusting deep, matching the rhythm of his fingers. Her body, as always, responded to his sensual attack. Her wet heat coated his fingers.

When Cillian felt the liquid fire he craved, he released her lips. Their harsh breathing echoed through the room.

"Take out my cock." His menacing eyes met her slumberous gaze. When she didn't react quickly enough, he lost patience. "Fucking do it. Now."

Chloe fumbled with the snap and zipper of his slacks. Her fingers trembling, her breathing coming in gasps. This dominate side of Cillian was titillating. Her senses responded to it, even as her brain tried to warn her of the danger. It was like holding an angry tiger by the tail, knowing that when you released him, he was going to eat you. And God help her, she wanted to be his next meal.

When she finally released his cock, the engorged head was already seeping with the thick essence of him. She used her thumb to circle the tip before sliding it down the heavy vein, then cupping his balls, rolling them firmly. She knew how he liked to be touched, and she used that knowledge to drive him on.

Cillian's head was going to explode. After so many days, her small hand on his cock was almost more than he could bear. It had been too long. He needed her. Now. He grabbed the backs of her thighs and yanked her up to straddle his lap. When her knees hit the chair roughly, he had the passing thought that if it weren't padded, she'd wear bruises tomorrow. He aligned the head of his cock with her center and, using his grip on her hip, forced her down as he thrust up into her.

Chloe groaned as she took him deep. His thick length seated completed inside her. She tilted her pelvis to take him even deeper. He used his hand at her hip and one at her shoulder and forced her to ride him hard and fast. She tipped over the edge quicker that she'd ever done before. She threw her head back and screamed at the intensity as she shattered around him.

Cillian was relentless, driving her through a second orgasm. Thrusting powerfully into her as he ruthlessly forced her down, over and over. He couldn't get enough. He wanted to crawl inside of her. He needed reassurance that she was safe, that she was here. That she was his.

He bit down on her shoulder, holding her in place as he came hard, bursting inside her as she clamped down around him.

The next morning, Chloe was pulling her hair into a high ponytail when Cillian came striding into the bathroom. He'd showered and dressed in dark jeans and a black cashmere sweater in record time.

She looked up and met his gaze in the mirror over her head. "I need a haircut."

"No, you don't."

"Yes, I do. It's getting too long."

"I like it."

"Well, you don't have to carry this weight around all day. I do."

"No."

"I'm not saying I want to cut it all off, but it needs to be trimmed. It's below my waist now and it's heavy."

He tilted his head and assessed her beautiful hair for a minute while she waited. It had grown quite a bit while she'd been here. "I supposed an inch or two won't hurt."

She scoffed and rolled her eyes. "Well, gee, thanks."

He tugged on the end of her ponytail slightly. "Disrespectful little thing." His eyes heated as he held her gaze in the mirror. "My hand is itching to spank that luscious ass."

"Not happening." Even though she smirked at him, she couldn't hide her blush. He always threatened to spank her when she got snarky, and he always followed through on those threats.

"Oh, it's happening, baby." He leaned down and bit her shoulder, then kissed the sting away. "I need to talk to you about something."

"About what?" She turned on her stool.

"Let's go into the other room." Cillian took her hand and led her into the bedroom. He sat on the sofa and she immediately straddled his lap, facing him. This is where Cillian preferred her to be when they talked.

"What's going on?" She asked when he had her settled where he wanted her.

He rested his palms on her bare thighs before he started. "Chloe, you're my wife."

A frown creased her brow. "I know that Cillian."

"If you leave here, I have every right to bring you home." He continued as if she hadn't spoken.

"I haven't broken a rule, so what's this about?"

"I know. I just want you to understand that nothing will ever change that."

"Ok."

"I want to give you something as a wedding present, something that I know you want. Again, it won't change anything. And there will be serious consequences to everyone involved if this doesn't go exactly the way I want it to. Do you understand?"

"No, not at all."

"That's ok, you will soon enough. Just remember what I said." He watched her silently. Waiting.

She frowned, trying to figure out what was going on. When she came up blank, she shrugged her shoulders and replied, "ok?"

"Ok. Come on, get dressed." He'd laid out a beautiful beige, lightweight, wool, pencil skirt, a cream colored cashmere sweater and soft fawn knee-high boots made of supple leather. It was the end of November, and the weather in this part of Ireland was cold. But, here on the island, the wind coming in from the ocean made it downright freezing.

Chloe dressed in the clothes he'd selected for her. The tailored skirt fell about two inches above her knees. The elegant boots were buttery soft and the thin high heel made her legs look amazing. She had to admit, Cillian had excellent taste in clothes.

"Ready?"

She turned at his question. The menacing expression he'd been displaying for the past few days was back. She eyed him thoughtfully again, then carefully replied. "Yes."

Breakfast was unusually subdued. Finn apparently still wasn't back for wherever he went, so she and Cillian ate in unusual silence. Every time she looked over at him, he was watching her. She was halfway through her second piece of toast before she'd finally had enough.

"What's wrong?"

"Nothing." When she frowned at him, he added, "I'm just glad your appetite is back."

"So is Imogen. I swear she's been following me around with a plate of sandwiches or a tray of cookies everywhere I go." She giggled.

"You lost weight." He grumbled.

"I know. But it will come back."

"You haven't asked any questions or said anything about being poisoned."

"So?"

"Why is that?"

"What is there to say? I can't change my situation. You won't let me go home. But I didn't die, so I guess that's something."

"Don't joke about it. And you are home." He glowered.

"I'm not." She tossed the toast back onto her plate. "Cillian, no one has ever tried to kill me before. So, excuse me if I don't know exactly how to react. Besides, I just figured you'd find out who it is."

"I'm working on it!"

"I know you are. But I have enough to worry about, don't you think?"

"Like what?"

She narrowed her eyes at him. "Are you trying to pick a fight?" She put emphasis on the word 'trying'.

He glared back. "Finish your breakfast. I have something to show you."

"I'm done." Her narrowed eyes turned to a scowl.

Cillian pushed back from the table, but didn't get up. When she did, he reached out and pulled her over to stand between his thighs. It was the same move he'd made the day before. So, she tensed and prepared for a sensual attack.

He palmed her ass with both hands as he narrowed his eyes right back at her.

Chloe instinctively put her hands on his shoulders to steady herself. She assessed him carefully. He was brooding and Cillian never did that. "What's wrong with you?"

He leaned forward so his nose was nearly touching hers. "You're mine."

Chloe rolled her eyes at him and sighed dramatically. He was acting like a caveman.

Cillian watched her closely. She wasn't intimidated by him at all. Part of him wanted to grin at that revelation. But the vice tightening his chest kept him focused. "Say it."

Still assessing his mood, she tilted her head to the side and asked softly. "Cillian?"

"Fucking say it, Chloe."

She did not feel like dealing with an angry tyrant all day. She had things to do. So, she tilted her chin slightly, which brought her lips to his, and she kissed him. As she knew he would, he quickly took over the kiss with brutal efficiency.

Long minutes later, when he finally lifted his lips from hers, she gave him the response he was waiting for. "I'm yours, Cillian." Whether she wanted to be or not, there was no disputing the fact. She had the huge rock on her finger to prove it.

He slid his arms around her and hugged her to him in a tight embrace. Then he whispered harshly into her ear, "don't ever forget it."

She waited until he released her to respond. "As if you'd ever let me."

"Never." He took her hand and led her out of the dining room and down the hall toward the main library, with Jacob and Micha pacing beside them.

Chloe was surprised to see Drew and Felix standing guard in front of the library door. When she and Cillian stopped in front of it, he turned her to face him before she could open it. "Don't forget, angel."

He gave her one last warning before taking her hand and threading their fingers together. He kissed her knuckle, then reached behind her and opened the door.

When they stepped inside, the sound of her name being screeched hit her ears before her brain registered what she was seeing.

"Chloe!" Sidney screamed so loud she was sure the windows shook. Finally! She didn't think she was ever going to see her best friend again! She launched herself across the room.

"Oh Chloe! Honey!" Angela Guidry cried and raced to her daughter!

Chloe screamed and laughed at the same time as she shook off Cillian's hand and caught the two most important women in her life in a huge hug. It was fortunate that Cillian was standing behind her to catch her when they both collided with her.

Cillian watched the three women as they held on to each other and cried. The vice grip on his chest tightened further. He looked over their heads and met David Guidry's assessing eyes for an intense moment. They sized each other up quickly. Movement to his left had him glancing over at Finn.

Finn had been standing guard inside the library with Chloe's family to ensure they didn't leave the room until he was ready to bring her in. He was in charge of making sure they didn't escape with Chloe.

"Ok, let an old man hug his girl." David waded through the women and lifted Chloe into his arms. He hugged her tightly. "Chloe Bell." He whispered into her ear. "I'm so sorry it's taking so long, but we're working on it, Chloe Bell." His words were barely a sound in her ear.

"Dad!" She knew he was trying to tell her something important, but she was just too excited to see him. Plus, she knew Cillian a lot better than he did. There was no escaping. She squeezed him tightly, hoping to reassure him.

It took David several long minutes to release her. When he did, he looked her over carefully. "You've lost weight."

"I know. I was sick for a couple of days. Food poisoning. But I'm fine. It was more gross than anything." She played it off as if she'd eaten bad potato salad or something.

"Oh honey, are you sure?" Angela assessed her as well.

"Yes mom, I'm fine. Really."

"Chloe, girl, you look amazing!" Sidney cut in, eying her friend closely.

Chloe looked at her family and her friend, then slowly turned back to Cillian. He was standing, legs spread wide, with his thick arms across his massive chest, watching them. She glanced over at Finn, who mirrored his stance before turning back to Cillian again. "You did this for me?" She asked in an astonished voice.

He nodded his head slightly and reached out and snagged her hand again. She turned fully to him with a beautiful smile on her face. That smile was everything, and it eased the tension in his chest.

"Thank you, Cillian." She stepped forward and threw her arms around him, and hugged him. When she released him, she slid her hands up his chest to his face, cupping his cheeks. She pulled his face down to hers and kissed him, putting everything ounce of gratitude and delight into the kiss. When she finally came up for air, she rested her forehead against his.

"You're welcome, angel." Cillian gently smoothed his finger down her cheek.

She giggled softly at the tense set of his jaw, then kissed him again. Now she knew why he'd been so moody for the last few days. "Thank you." She whispered softly again.

"Introduce me, angel."

"Ok." She kissed him one last time before turning back to her family.

David Guidry watched in surprise as Chloe turn from her mother to embrace her kidnapper. He didn't miss the quiet, tender moment between his daughter and Cillian O'Donnell or the way he handled her so gently. It was something to think about.

"Are you sure you're alright?" Sidney asked Chloe for what seemed like the twentieth time. She hated to keep harping on it, but this whole situation was surreal. They'd left the library and headed straight up to Chloe's suite, where they were having a spa day with facials, manicures and pedicures. And now that all those big, gun carrying men weren't hovering so close, she needed to know how her friend was really doing.

"He is a rather large man, Chloe. You'd tell us if he's hurting you, wouldn't you?" Angela had been shocked at the size of Cillian O'Donnell. He was a mountain of a man! And next to Chloe's diminutive stature, he appeared even larger.

"Yes, I'm fine. Or, as well as to be expected."

"What does that mean?" Sidney turned from painting her toenails and frowned at the open doorway where Finn was standing guard. She'd been trying to ignore the jerk all day.

Chloe followed Sidney's gaze and sighed loudly when she realized her friend was shooting daggers at Finn. "It means, I'm married now, so I'm making the best of it."

Angela looked up from her own nails. "Sweetheart, if you were blackmailed the marriage can be annulled." She glanced over at David who was sitting beside her on the sofa, then back at Choe. "Or, well, there's always divorce."

"Mom, Cillian won't let me leave him. And, well." She blushed slightly as she tried to think of a way to change to subject.

"Oh, good God!" Sidney gasped. "You don't want to leave, do you?"

"No! Yes! I mean." She paused and chewed on her bottom lip when she realized she wasn't sure anymore. She immediately turned toward Sidney and using her eyes, pleaded with her friend to change the subject.

"Chloe, honey. Possession isn't love." Angela said softly.

"Don't worry mom, I know that." She sighed and looked over at her father, and before he could say anything, she reiterated, "I know."

"Well, who wouldn't want to live in a castle?" Sidney exclaimed loudly and went back to painting her toenails. "I mean, this place is awesome!"

"You should see it in the summer. The fields are covered in wild flowers." Chloe grasped on to the new topic desperately.

Finn interrupted their conversation when he stepped into the room. Patrick followed him in, pushing a cart that held a bottle of Champagne in an ice bucket, a tray of finger sandwiches and another of petit fours. The bottom shelf of the cart held a bowl of ice filled with bottles of water and beer.

"Chloe, Cillian thought you might need a snack. He said you didn't eat much at breakfast." Finn was talking to her, but he was looking directly at Sidney.

"How nice." Sidney cooed.

At Sidney's tone, Chloe immediately looked to her friend, then back at Finn. This wasn't good. Finn's jaw was clenched as he maintained eye contact with Sidney.

"Thanks, Finn." Chloe tried to grab his attention.

"Eat up Chloe lass." Patrick cut in. "You're skin and bones now."

"You be quiet Patrick Kelly or Imogen will start following me around with sandwiches again!" Chloe cried in mock outrage.

"Maybe she should runt. At this rate Ian could take you down."

Chloe gasped in shocked amusement and pointed her finger to him. "Shut it!"

Patrick grinned wickedly, then turned to her parents. In a show of mock disappointment, he shook his head. "Rude." Then he turned back to her and made a clucking sound with his tongue. "Just rude lass."

Chloe's parents were watching the byplay between her and Patrick.

"She has lost some weight." David confirmed while he watched the way they were bickering.

"See lass, eat up." Patrick grinned triumphantly.

"Don't encourage him, dad!" Chloe giggled.

"Just who are you?" David asked.

"I'm in charge of that runts security." He threw a thumb over his shoulder at Chloe.

"Security?"

"Yes sir. But she probably doesn't need it. She's as mean as a snake and she fights dirty."

"Patrick Kelly, don't tell him that!"

"Why not? It's the truth."

"My, oh my, are all the men in this place so handsome?" Sidney interrupted by purring in an exaggerated southern drawl. Her calculating gaze perused Patrick openly before turning back to Finn with a triumphant gleam in her eyes.

"Keep it up." Finn practically dared her.

"I've only just started, Sugar." She purred, completely unintimidated.

"That's my cue. See you later, runt." Patrick quickly escaped out the door.

Chloe watched Sidney and Finn. The tension was so thick between them, you could cut it with a knife.

"Um, thanks Finn. I'm a little hungry." Chloe tried to break the tension as she reached for a sandwich. But before she could bring it to her mouth, Finn deftly plucked it out of her hand. He watched her with meaningful intent as he bit into it.

Chloe rolled her eyes. He and the team had been doing that with everything she tried to eat or drink since she'd recovered. Instead of complaining like she normally did, she kept quiet, hoping not to draw attention to what he was doing.

Finn ignored the luscious beauty sitting across the room, trying to bait him, and focused instead on the food that had been prepared for Chloe. He carefully opened the champagne and took a sip from the glass and waited to see if anything happened before handing it and a sandwich to her. Next, he popped one of the tiny cakes into his mouth. The sweet confection tasted delicious, but he'd bet his entire fortune it wasn't nearly as delicious as Sidney's little pussy was going to taste.

When he didn't get sick, he nodded his approval to Chloe then without looking at the beauty staring daggers at him; he left them to their fun. He and the feisty little American would have their time soon enough.

Chloe had hoped that her father hadn't noticed Finn tasting her food. But by the concerned look on his face, she had no such luck.

"Do you want to tell me what that was all about?" David tried for calm, but his fear made it difficult.

"Not really."

"Chloe."

She bit her lip while trying to decide how much to tell him. Cillian hadn't told her what she could or couldn't say. But she didn't want them to worry about her, so she was hesitant to give them the full story.

"Chloe." He warned. "Spill it, kiddo."

"I told you I had food poisoning."

"You did. But something tells me there's more to the story."

"Well, it may have been intentional."

"What!" Her mother and Sidney both gasped at the same time.

"I was opening wedding presents and there was a small Tiffany's box of chocolates. I ate one and immediately got violently ill. I was sick for a few days."

"Who sent it?" David barked as his temper boiled over.

"We don't know yet. Cillian and his team are working to find out. But, until they do, my security detail has been increased and they taste everything I eat or drink. Which is stupid really. I mean, what if one of them gets sick? It would be my fault."

"No, it wouldn't." David barked. "If Cillian hadn't kidnapped you, it wouldn't have happened in the first place." He jumped to his feet and started pacing.

"Dad, we're supposed to be having fun." Chloe fought back tears of frustration. She had no idea how long they were going to get to stay, and she wanted to enjoy them while they were here.

"David." Angela said softly.

"Angela, this is not,"

"David". She cut him off. When he glanced over at her, she cut her eyes to Chloe. He followed her gaze, and his expression softened.

"Honey, cut your old man some slack. I'm supposed to take care of you."

"I know, but can't we just have fun today. Cillian doubled my security. He's taken steps to make sure I'm safe. Now that we know there's a possibility someone is trying to hurt me, he's taking all kinds of precautions."

David watched her for a long moment before slowly nodding his head. He hadn't been given the opportunity to speak with Cillian O'Donnell alone yet, but he had every intension of doing so before he left.

Chloe looked up when the door opened again. Patrick was back, and he was escorting in a woman she didn't recognize who was carrying a bright yellow bag.

"Chloe, this is Ava." He introduced.

"Hi?"

"Hello. I'm supposed to give you a haircut."

"Really?" Chloe smiled, delighted. He'd listened to her. "Ok!" Chloe jumped to her feet. "We can do it in the bathroom. There's a stool in there. Will that work?"

"Yes, that should work just fine."

Chloe led Ava into the bathroom and pulled out the stool. When she turned around, Patrick was leaning against the doorjamb.

Chloe frowned at him. "Did you need something?"

"No."

Chloe waited, but when he just stared at her intently, she frowned again. "What are you doing?"

Patrick didn't answer, but his expression said it all. He was here to make sure Ava didn't try anything. Instead of pressing him further, she turned her attention to Ava and her haircut.

Sidney came in and hopped up onto the counter and they chatted and giggled while Ava got to work.

After Patrick walked Ava out, Finn took her parents to their room. Because of the time difference between the US and Ireland, they were exhausted. But when she hugged her mom goodnight, she hadn't wanted to let her go.

Sidney had been searching through the refrigerator in the kitchen while she'd said goodnight to her parents. When the door closed behind them, she held up a bottle of wine and two glasses. "Now that we have the place to ourselves, tell me everything."

"First, you tell me what the heck is going on between you and Finn." Chloe wagged her finger in Sidney's face.

Sidney got to work opening the wine so she could avoid Chloe's gaze. "There's nothing going on."

"I call bullshit. Talk Chica."

"You mean besides the fact that he's a surly pain in the ass."

"Finn? He's not surly. Stoic maybe, but not surly."

"Asshole is more like it."

"Ok, what happened?"

Sidney sighed loudly as she poured two glasses of wine. "He showed up at my apartment in the middle of the night and acted like a jerk, that's what happened."

"Oh, crap."

"Oh, crap is right. He wanted me to go with him, but he wouldn't answer any of my questions. Then he tried to force me to go! He put his hand over my mouth, so I bit the shit out of it. When he jerked his hand away, I started screaming. Loud. Like really loud. Loud enough to wake up my neighbors."

"That sounds like Finn. What'd he do when you started screaming?"

"He pushed me down on the bed and sat on me then pulled off his shirt and stuffed it in my mouth."

"Well, it could've been worse." Chloe took the glass of wine Sidney handed her.

"Oh yea, how?"

"He could've pulled off his sock and stuffed that in your mouth." Chloe giggled.

"Ew! That's gross!" Sidney scrunched up her nose. "Anyway, I stopped screaming because I was so shocked that he'd do that. And, he has a body to die for, if you know what I mean. He knows it too, the jerk. That's why he did it. But anyway," she waved that aside with her now half empty wine glass and continued, "I calmed down when he finally pulled out his phone and showed me recent pictures of you here. Then he said I could call your dad to verify that he was taking me to see you. You'd think he would've done that in the first place."

"I think these guys are used to getting what they want without ever having to explain themselves."

"Well, it sucks to be him, because he thinks we're going to have sex and that is so NOT happening." She emphasized the word not.

Chloe gasped loudly. "Did he actually say that?"

"Yes. And he keeps whispering in my ear all the wicked things he's going to do to me when we do have sex. Like it's a foregone conclusion."

"Sidney." Chloe warned her friend.

"Don't worry." Sidney cut her off. "He's seriously hot and the things he says is just… um, wow. But sex with him would be way too complicated. I mean, look what happened to you."

Chloe looked down to inspect her new manicure. "I didn't do anything to cause Cillian to kidnap me."

"Oh Chloe, I'm sorry. I didn't mean it like that." Sidney got up from her seat and threw her arms around her BFF, nearly spilling wine everywhere. "I know you didn't. And that's not what I meant. Let's just stay I'm staying as far away from Finn as possible and leave it at that."

"Good luck with that." Chloe scoffed and hugged her back. "Irish men are persistent."

"Yea, well, this American woman is going to resist temptation. The only problem with my plan is that he has my laptop."

"Why does he have it?"

"He took it as soon as I got on the plane. Some guy named Titan loaded something onto it to track my movements on the Web. I'm guessing it's to keep you and I from planning some great escape."

"Most likely."

"We could though, you know?"

"Could what?"

"Plan a great escape. You and I together can do just about anything."

"Hmm I don't know about that this time." Chloe finished her wine and let Sidney refill her glass.

"Hmm, is right. I don't think you want to escape." Sidney wagged her eyebrows playfully.

"How are you going to get your laptop back?"

"Smooth, real smooth subject change there, Chlo lo." Sidney grinned around her glass as she sipped. "Anyway, he's supposed to bring it to me later tonight. I have a deadline, which with the time difference here, is late tonight. It just pisses me off that I have to ask his permission to use my own laptop, and he said he has to be in the room with me the entire time. Which is completely ridiculous."

"Um Sid, that's not staying away from him."

"I know, but I'm sure I can ignore him long enough to get my work done. So, tell me about that gorgeous husband of yours. You know, the two of you together are so beautiful, it's almost hard to look at you."

Chloe grinned at Sidney's dramatics. "He is gorgeous, isn't he? But, he's also an arrogant ass. And don't forget, he kidnapped me and forced me to marry him." She thought it best not to add that he was also very dangerous. That went without saying.

"How in the hell did he get you to do that, anyway?"

Chloe's expression turned serious, and she got up to refill both their glasses before she answered. "It was the only way he'd let me speak to mom and dad."

"Oh Chloe." Sidney assessed her friend carefully. "It's just me now. Tell me the truth. Does he hurt you?"

"No."

When Sidney looked skeptical, she chewed on her bottom lip and blushed as she continued; "He really doesn't Sid. But he has a way of um, well, he's very good at getting what he wants."

"I'll just bet he is." Sidney chuckled. "Leave it to you to get kidnapped by the most beautiful man I've ever seen."

Chloe grinned at that, and her face flushed. "I don't think he'd like being called beautiful."

Sidney grinned back. "Probably not. So, tell me, why this big production tomorrow? I mean, you're already married, right?" She wagged her eyebrows suggestively, then started giggling.

"It has something to do with his position here in the territory and the expectations of his people. There's going to be over five hundred people here tomorrow. And I'm only going to know about fifteen of them and that includes you and mom and dad."

"That's a lot of people."

"I know, right? Most of them live here on the island, but those who don't started arriving in the last twenty-four hours. The really important ones, like leaders of the other territories, are staying here in the castle."

"I've seen a few people milling around, but we weren't introduced to any of them. Finn, the 'dick"tator'. Sidney held up her fingers and made the quote sign when she stressed the word dick. "Escorted us to our rooms and told us to stay there. He brought a late dinner for us last night and breakfast this morning.

"Cillian thinks someone is trying to kill me so he's keeping us away from everyone. I think if he could've cancelled the wedding, he would've."

"I didn't think about that." Sidney's eyes got huge. "What if someone comes at you tomorrow?"

"I'm never alone anymore. So, if they do, at least we'll finally find out who it is."

"Jeez. Aren't you scared?"

"I'm more afraid of standing up there in front of all those people. What if I trip or something?"

"Yea right. Like that's going to happen. Chloe, I'm serious."

"I know. But to be honest with you, I'm not really that scared. Cillian's entire team is guarding me and it would be almost impossible for anyone to get past them. Plus, I've been training every day with him and the team in weapons, self-defense, and martial arts since I got here. I'm pretty sure I can take care of myself."

"Wait, a minute! You've been training and they let you use a gun?"

"Yes. They're pretty tough on me, too. But I give as good as I get." She smiled smugly, remembering kicking Micha in the nuts the last time they sparred.

"You know that's strange, right? You're a prisoner here, but they let you hold a gun?"

Chloe thought about that for a minute. "Sid, it's not really like that. Not really. It's um, well, I don't know, it's hard to explain."

"Chloe, you." Sidney stopped mid-sentence and looked toward the door when it opened. She watched Cillian lock eyes with Chloe and stalk across the room toward her. Holy hell, but the man oozed sex. Looking over at Chloe, she was shocked to see the fire in his eyes reflected in her friend's eyes as well. It was so hot she was afraid to move in case she got singed. Holy moly, these two could burn down the damned castle.

Cillian jerked Chloe up into his arms, thrust his fist into her hair and tugged her head back, then took her mouth in a brutally demanding kiss.

Chloe responded by accepting the forceful thrusts of his tongue, the sharp nips of his teeth, and the firm glide of his warm lips, submitting to his need to dominate. An angry Cillian could be dangerous and unpredictable. She'd been away from him for most of the day and she knew Cillian; he never allowed much distance between them. But he had today, for her. To give her time with her family. So, she wrapped her legs around his waist and fisted both hands in the soft, dark waves of his hair, holding him to her as she lost herself in him. In the feel of him surrounding her, his taste, his smell, everything that was Cillian. She knew by now that her response would sooth the jealous monster raging at him. And it did.

Long minutes later, Cillian broke the kiss and rested his forehead against hers. "Hello angel, you taste like wine." He used his voice to entice her. The Irish brogue that always made her shiver. He hadn't seen her since this morning and he didn't fucking like it.

"Hi." Chloe whispered breathlessly.

"HOLY crap!" Sidney's stunned gasp came from behind them.

Both their heads suddenly turned toward her as if they'd forgotten she was there.

Cillian tightened his hold on Chloe. He wasn't about to let her go. "Micha is waiting to take you to your room. I believe Imogen has prepared a delicious meal for you tonight."

"Oh, ok." Sidney looked at Chloe and smiled. "I'll see you tomorrow."

"I'll be here. I'm going for an early run, so let's meet up after breakfast."

"Alright." Sidney headed toward the door. "I'll see you tomorrow morning." She blew a kiss to her friend, then hurried out the door.

When the door closed, Cillian sat down on the sofa with Chloe on his lap. His gaze traveled over her, lingering for long moments on her hair before moving to her clothes. "Did you have a good day, angel?"

"Yes. Thank you for bringing them here." Chloe absently rubbed her fingers across the rough five o'clock shadow covering his jaw. She was a little tipsy from all the wine and champagne, but she always liked the way his bristles tickled her fingertips. "You have no idea how much it means to me."

"You changed your clothes."

She looked down at her leggings. "It's difficult to get a pedicure in a pencil skirt."

He ran his fingers through her hair, then gripped a handful and tugged. "You had Ava cut off more than we agreed on."

"It needed to be trimmed."

"That's a lot more than a trim."

"Not really." She scoffed and continued to rub her fingers on his face. She really, really liked the way it felt, but she liked how it felt on other parts of her body too. She grinned to herself at that thought.

"Yes, really." He tightened his hold and tugged a little harder. His voice a whiplash of reprimand. "Ava said you insisted she cut off four inches."

"Mm huh" She liked when he pulled her hair.

"You disobeyed me angel."

"She told you?"

"Of course. I'm informed of every detail that has anything to do with you."

"Well, isn't that just great?" Chloe replied with a healthy dose of sarcasm and rolled her eyes.

"That's the second time today you've rolled your eyes at me."

Chloe bit her bottom lip and waited. The fire in his eyes was sexy as hell.

"Four inches of hair and two eye rolls. Your tally for the day has added up to 6 licks."

He abruptly pushed her to her feet, between his thighs. "Take off your clothes." He whispered in that demanding voice she always found hard to deny. Hungry eyes filled with heat and possession drifted over her. What little tenderness he was capable of didn't come close to softening the menacing quality that was so much a part of him.

"But," her voice shook with excitement and trepidation. The longer she held him off, the more demanding she knew he was going to be. After their separation today, he needed it.

He leaned in and pulled the wide collar of her sweater away from her shoulder and suckled the sensitive spot between her neck and shoulder that drove her crazy. Then he kissed his way slowly up her neck to her ear, purposely rubbing his bristled chin against her delicate skin. "Fucking do it." He whispered harshly, just before biting down on her earlobe.

Chloe shivered as heat slithered slowly down her spine. She'd never been able to deny him. She grasped the bottom edges of her sweater and lifted the soft cashmere up over her head, dropping it on the floor behind her. Then she stepped willingly into him, toward the sensual temptation that was husband.

Chloe stared in awe at her reflection in the mirror. Sidney and Angela's expressions both matched hers. The only one not stunned was Imogen. She was smiling smugly while adjusting the hem of the wedding dress.

"Oh, my gosh!" Angela exclaimed after adjusting the pearl band with the attached veil onto Chloe's head. "That is the most beautiful gown I've ever seen."

"It is, isn't it?" Imogen replied in smug satisfaction. "Cillian had three dresses commissioned for her to choose from."

"Chloe, girl, you definitely picked the right one. It's gorgeous!" Sidney reached out hesitantly to touch the soft white fur that rimmed the top of the off the shoulder neckline.

"I didn't pick it. I didn't even look at them. I just told Imogen to select the one she liked best, and I'd wear it." Chloe looked down at Imogen in stunned disbelief.

"Well, you do like it, don't you?" Imogen asked hesitantly, stressing the word 'you'.

"Yes!" She looked back at her reflection and in a hushed tone added, "it's perfect."

The three-quarter length sleeved dress had a plunging V-neck with two tiny strands of pearls clipped between her breasts holding the cups together and a corset fitted bodice, which as a whole did amazing things for her breasts. It hugged her torso, then dropped to the floor in waves of brushed silk and narrow vertical strips of lace. The back was open down to the middle of her spine. A delicate layer of lace covered the corset and the lace around the top of the dress was edged all the way around with the softest white fur she'd ever felt.

Chloe ran her hand down the bodice and let the pearls stitched into it tickle her palm. "I love the pearl accents."

"Those are Australian South Sea pearls. They're very rare." Imogen smiled at the three women gaping at her.

Chloe's hand shook as she raised it slowly to the warm, soft fur at her shoulder. "Please tell me this isn't real too?" She practically chocked out.

"Oh no, dear. The designer actually argued with him about that." Imogen mused, "but he didn't think you'd appreciate wearing real animal fur. However, he wanted you to be warm, so the fur was necessary. It's attached with tiny pearl buttons underneath so we can remove it after the wedding."

"It's beautiful." She whispered at her reflection.

"Oh honey, you're breathtaking." Angela fussed with one of the curls of Chloe's hair that rested on her chest. There were three thin, evenly spaced braids on each side of her head resting on the outer layer of the rest of her hair that was all pulled up in a beautiful clip at the back of her head. Her long curls with the braids interlacing the thick mass were pulled over one shoulder. Tiny pearls were pinned into the braids on the sides of her head.

"Thanks mom."

"Now, you have something borrowed." Sidney pointed at the clip in her hair that she'd given her to use. "And the sapphires in your necklace are obviously your something blue. But what about something old and something new?"

"You can use my pearl bracelet." Angela held up her wrist. "It was your great grandmothers. It'll match perfectly."

They all turned toward the door at the sound of little feet hitting the floor at a fast clip. Annie skidded to a halt just inside the bedroom door. She took one look at Chloe and shrieked!

"Chloowee you wook soo pwetty!"

"Annie! I told you not to run." Molly scolded as she came in behind her daughter. She looked up at Chloe, and her breath caught in her throat. "Oh my God!"

Chloe giggled at Molly's reaction. "It's a little over the top, don't you think?"

"Absolutely not! It's perfect."

"Thanks."

"Wook at my pwetty new dwess!" Annie grabbed the hem of her little lace and tulle white dress and held it out proudly for Chloe to see. "Mommy said I get to be you'we fwower giwl."

"That's right. You get to walk in front of Sidney." Chloe pointed to her best friend. Sidney smiled and waved at the little girl.

"Who awe you?" Annie asked, and came toward the mirror.

"Annie, this is Sidney. She's my best friend. She's going to be in the wedding too."

Annie looked up at Sidney and smiled. "You'we vewy pwetty, but not wike Chlowee, you gots bwack haiew. Did you get a new dwess, too?"

"Yes, I did. Do you like it?" Sidney lifted the hem of her own dress and held it out exactly like Annie had with hers. The Antique gold silk was exquisite. The color matched her eyes perfectly. Even if Chloe hadn't picked her own dress, Sidney knew from the form fitted sexy style and the color that Chloe had picked this one specifically with her in mind. She was also amazed that she'd been able to get it here so quickly. Obviously, that powerful husband of hers could get things done.

"Yes!" Annie squealed and clapped her hands. Then she turned to her mother. "Mommy, can we go get mawwied now?"

"Not yet, sweetheart, but soon." She turned back to Chloe. "Thank you for asking her to do this. She's been so excited."

"I wouldn't have it any other way."

"Man on deck!" Rourke called from the outer room. "Is it safe to come in?"

"Yes, we're almost ready." Imogen called as she finished fluffing the hem of Chloe's dress.

"Good." Rourke walked in and stopped dead in his tracks when he saw Chloe. She was so beautiful; it took him a minute to catch his breath. He recovered quickly and held out a shoe box. "Special delivery."

"Hello again, Patrick". Angela said in her most motherly tone of disapproval and stepped forward.

"Mom, that's Rourke."

Angela frowned and looked from Rourke to Chloe, then back to Rourke. "I thought you said his name was Patrick."

"They're twins. What's that?" Chloe asked and pointed at the box in his hands.

Completely unaffected by Chloe's mother, he grinned sheepishly and thrust the box at her. "Open it and find out, runt."

She flipped off the top and froze. "Oh. My. God." She breathed out the words in a hushed voice. Inside the box nestled in blush pink velvet was a pair of gorgeous white leather ankle boots.

They were lined with white fur that extended over the top edges. The thin three-inch heel was a beautiful mother-of-pearl. They were amazing! "Where in the world did you get these?"

"Boss said all three of the dresses he had made for you had fur because it's so damn cold outside."

"Ooohhh, you said a bad wowd." Annie chimed in.

Molly put both hands on her hips and glared at him. "Language, Rourke Kelly!"

Rourke bent down and tapped Annie's nose. "Sorry princess." Then he looked back at Chloe. "Anyway, the guys thought you'd need something warm on your feet. So, um, there you go."

"Y'all bought me boots?" She asked, mystified.

"Well, yea." Before she could say anything else, Rourke tapped her nose affectionately, just like he'd done to Annie, then walked out.

Chloe turned around and held out the box for the women to see.

"Well, there's your something new." Sidney said in awe as she peered into the box. "And holy cow, they're something alright."

"Wow! Chloe, they're beautiful." Molly added. "To think, those obnoxious men not only came up with the idea, but they got it right, too. I'm impressed."

"You and me both." Chloe breathed.

Imogen beamed with pride and took the boots from Chloe and helped her slip them on.

"Knock, knock." Finn called from the outer room. "Is everybody decent?"

"Yes. You can come it." Chloe called over her shoulder.

Finn whistled when he saw her. Chloe met his eyes in the mirror and he smiled. "You look beautiful Chloe."

"Thanks. We're almost ready."

He held up a gift bag. "Cillian sent this up for you."

Chloe opened the bag, then glanced up at him. "Gloves?"

"It's freezing out there. He said you'd need them."

Chloe pulled out the fur-lined white silk gloves. She slid one on and the glove came to mid-forearm, nearly covering the bare skin of her arm where the three-quarter length sleeve stopped. Her mother stepped forward and helped her put the other one on.

"No gloves for me?" Sidney drawled; her voice full of sarcasm.

"I'd never forget you." Finn grinned and pulled out a second pair of gloves from his back pocket. They were also fur lined, but the silk was the color of antique gold and matched her dress perfectly. When he tossed them to her, she instinctively caught them in mid-air. He grinned again at her stunned expression, then blew her a kiss. "I'll see you later, gorgeous."

Before she could respond, he turned and walked out. She scowled at the door. "Jerk." She looked down at the gloves and fought her smile. She stroked the soft fur of the beautiful gloves. He was smooth, that was for sure, but she wasn't buying it. He wasn't sweet or charming. He wasn't. No, in her experience, Finnigan O'Donnell was anything but sweet.

"Alright ladies. It's time to go." Imogen said and clapped her hands.

When they finally emerged from the bedroom, it was to find Patrick and Rourke waiting for her. "What are you guys doing here?" Chloe looked around the room expectantly. "Where's my dad?"

Patrick stepped toward her with a tiny black box in his hand. "Relax Chloe, he's outside in the hall."

Rourke opened the door for the other women. "Imogen is going to take you ladies down and get you situated. Chloe will be down in a few minutes."

When the door closed behind them, Patrick opened the box and lifted out a tiny device.

"What's that?"

"Security."

"What do you mean?"

"It's a comm link. You're going to be mic'd up with the rest of us." Patrick replied and stepped close, showing her the communication device. "This way, if there's a problem, you'll know it immediately. It'll reduce your reaction time."

She scoffed at him. "You mean so you'll know what dad and I talk about while we're walking down the aisle."

"True. But you'll be able to hear us as well. And, no one would ever expect Cillian's wife to take part in her own protection. But he'd never leave anything to chance. The ceremony is in the sunroom, but all the doors are open to accommodate everyone. That makes you vulnerable."

"You think someone's really going to take a shot at me, don't you?" Her hands trembled slightly.

"No, but we're going to err on the side of caution and be prepared." Patrick fitted the tiny ear bud into her ear. "Now, check in with one of the team members to make sure the connection is clear."

Chloe sighed loudly. She couldn't believe this was going to be her life now. "Cillian, can you hear me?"

"Hello angel."

His deep Irish brogue whispered in her ear. The familiar sound sent shivers down her spine and helped to settle her nerves. "I didn't sign up for this."

"I know. Come down angel. Our guests are waiting."

Chloe looked from Rourke to Patrick, then nodded her assent. Rourke opened the door and her father stepped into the room.

"Chloe, you look so beautiful!" He stepped to her and took both her hands in his.

"Thanks dad." She squeezed his hands, then turned to her guards. "Guys, I need a minute with my dad."

"Chloe." Patrick's voice held a slight warning.

She hadn't been alone with her dad since he'd arrived and she needed a few moments with him. She wanted to assure him that she was ok. "Patrick Kelly, there is a mic in my ear. You all can hear every word we say, so don't give me that tone." She glared at him and insisted, "I need a minute!"

Patrick scowled at her. But Cillian's voice came through the mic. "Give her what she wants."

"Well, thank you very much, oh mighty king!" was her smart ass reply.

"You know that fiery little temper turns me on baby, but I'm counting every indiscretion for payment later."

Even through her frustration, the sexy voice in her ear caused her to shiver again.

Patrick and Rourke, the assholes, were snickering when they closed the door.

Chloe ignored the byplay in her ear and focused on her father. He still held both of her hands. "They can hear us."

"I figured as much. Don't worry, Chloe Bell." He winked at her and squeezed her hands tightly.

"Dad?" Her voice was a question. He'd never called her that until she'd been taken. She still hadn't figured out why.

"Sweetheart." He cut her off before she could question him further. "I know they can hear us, but I want you to know that I'm doing everything I can to bring you home. He may have connections at the executive level in our government, but so do I. I'll find a way." David promised. He needed her to know he would always fight for her. But after finally meeting with Cillian O'Donnell earlier in his office, he didn't know what to think.

From what he'd seen, Chloe and Cillian were circling around each other. It was obvious to everyone else that there was something there. He wasn't sure what it was, but it was something. It didn't matter though because Chloe hadn't had a choice. If she had, would she have chosen him?

"Dad, don't do anything that'll get you and mom hurt. I won't be able to live with myself if something happens to you."

"Chloe"

"No, I'm serious."

"Don't you worry about us. We're going to be fine. And Chloe Bell, so are you."

"I know. I've survived so far." She assured him.

"Of course, you have. But I'll figure out a way to free you. I'm working on it. Do you trust me?"

"Yes."

"Good, now let's get this over with."

"Alright."

"You really do look lovely. I've always looked forward to walking you down the aisle, I just never envisioned it would be under these circumstances."

"Me either. I'm just glad you're here with me."

"So am I Sweetheart." He took a deep breath. "Are you ready to go?"

"Yes, I suppose I can't put it off any longer."

"No angel, you can't." Cillian's ominous voice came through the mic.

Cillian was seething. The longer he'd listened to Chloe and her father talk, the angrier he'd become. If she thought she was going to leave him, she was dead wrong. And David, the fucker. He'd thought they'd come to an understanding. He'd asked him earlier if he'd met his Angela for the first time and only had a few moments with her then knew he'd never see her again; what would he do? David hadn't answered the question, but he'd given him something to think about.

No, his angel wasn't leaving him. He'd never allow it. Her security was already tight, but he could tighten it further if he had to. His expression must have mirrored his thoughts because Finn, who was standing as his best man, nudged him slightly. At the interruption of his thoughts, he looked up the aisle. And there she was.

She was the most beautiful thing he'd ever seen. Head held high, back straight, she walked toward him through a sea of strangers and a potential threat to her life with a confident, polite smile, as if daring someone to take their best shot. She didn't cower. Not Chloe. No, his angel was strength and confidence wrapped up in a beautiful little package. And watching her come to him, he forgot his anger.

Chloe was fine and holding her own as long as she maintained eye contact with Cillian. But halfway down the aisle, her mother's sniffles captured her attention, causing her to look away momentarily. In that fleeting moment, she hesitated. Looking around at all people watching her with mixed expressions, she wondered what the hell she was doing. How had her life come to this?

"Angel." His soft voice in her ear brought her gaze back to his.

"Cillian?" There was no hiding her anxiety when her voice shook. Her father squeezed her hand slightly to reassure her. But it was the expression in Cillian's eyes that captured her attention.

The anxiety in her voice tore at him. She looked so tiny standing there. She wasn't timid by nature, but she seemed so now. His instinct was to go get her. But she had to come to him. And he knew her well enough to know that when she was unsure, his girl needed to be challenged. So, he tilted his head, lifted an arrogant brow, and smirked at her as he taunted, "Are you backing out on your word?"

At the sound of his taunting voice in her ear, Chloe lifted her chin. The asshole. "Of course not," she hissed back. Then she held his gaze as she straightened her spine and pasted a polite smile on her face again and continued down the aisle.

Cillian wanted to grin, but he dared not. She was magnificent. She came to him like the queen she was meant to be. The territories held their own hierarchy and as he was currently the reigning king; she was most definitely his queen.

When he took her hand in his, he continued to hold her gaze as he bowed slightly to her bravery and kissed her hand. Then he turned her toward the priest and the rest of the crowd fell away.

Chapter 31: Oh, Bless Your Heart!

The receiving line into the ballroom was a nightmare. Chloe stood next to Cillian and faced a never-ending line of people she didn't know. She'd been instructed not to let on that she was mic'd or that the team was listening to everyone and everything. She was introduced to so many people, she would never remember their names. Patrick and Rourke stood guard close to her and Cillian the entire time while Finn and Van stood by her family at the head table.

The wives of the other territory leaders were the only ones she recognized. And she'd only met them once or twice when they'd visited the castle in the last week. Because of tradition, they were at the head of the line and had already passed through. Now she was facing the next wave of leaders in succession. These particular men hadn't been invited to the castle previously, and she was beginning to understand why.

Their hard eyes and obvious fake smiles were a little intimidating. But they were nothing compared to her husband, so she didn't flinch as she shook their hands and tolerated their insolent perusal. Patrick had moved closer to her and Cillian's arm was now wrapped securely around her waist, both of which gave her a sense of security.

"O'Donnell, it's about time you fulfilled your duties and took yourself out of the game." Martin Bohannon smirked as he shook Cillian's hand.

"Martin, welcome." Cillian greeted coldly. "Chloe, meet Martin Bohannon. He's head of one of the smaller territories to the North. Martin, my wife, Chloe."

"Hello." She took her cue from Cillian and greeted him with a polite smile. She was glad she hadn't removed her gloves yet. She was sure his hand would be as greasy as his smile.

"Well now, aren't you a pretty little thing?"

When Chloe didn't reply, he arched a brow and turned back to Cillian. "I believe you know my guest, Natasha." He turned to indicate the beautiful woman beside him. The inappropriate white dress she wore was so tight it appeared to be painted on as it hugged her curves. The neckline was scooped so low, if she sneezed, her breasts would pop out. Her thick black curls lay strategically around her chest to bring attention to the already obnoxious display. And the fire engine red nail polish on her fingertips matched her lipstick.

Martin's oily smile made Chloe's stomach turn.

"She remembers you fondly." Martin sneered and cut his eyes at her slyly.

If he was waiting for a reaction from her, he would be sadly disappointed. The first thought that popped into her head was, boy oh boy, Natasha had put a whole lot of effort into making this statement. Then she had to fight to keep from giggling at the absurdity of it. She was glad Sidney wasn't standing next to her. If so, they'd both be in hysterics. Instead, she watched quietly as Cillian shook the beautiful woman's hand and waited to see what would happen next.

"Natasha." Cillian greeted and tried not to sneer as he said her name. She was one of the many women he'd played with in the underground clubs years ago. He'd never played with the same woman twice, her included. So, he wasn't sure what Martin's end game was in bringing her here, but he had no intention of playing.

"Always such a *pleasure* to see you Cillian." She leaned in too close, giving him an excellent view, and emphasized the word 'pleasure' through her pouty lips.

He ignored the innuendo and turned to greet the next guest in line.

Natasha's temper ignited when she was so casually dismissed. How dare he! Cillian O'Donnell was supposed to have been HER white whale! Livid, she turned her focus to the little bitch standing next to him.

Several years back, she'd spent a few delicious hours in the dungeon with him. Of course, she'd played coy at first while he went through most of the female members in the club. She'd even had a bet with two of them that she'd eventually catch him in her web. That when she was finished with him, she'd own him. After all, she was the most beautiful woman in the club, and everyone knew it. So, she'd bided her time, playing hard to get and waited for him to come to her, reeling him in slowly. When she finally gave in to his invitation, she'd followed his every command with exacting perfection in that dungeon. And he'd been masterful. A delicious experience she couldn't wait to repeat. But afterward, the arrogant son of a bitch never looked her way again. Not once. It had been humiliating! Not only had she been laughed at by the other women, but she'd lost a fucking fortune on that bet.

Luckily, she and Martin had been friends for years. They'd been fucking for just as long. Plus, she knew Martin had always been jealous of

Cillian and his position. He hated him. So, when she'd seen the invitation to this farce of a wedding on his dresser, she'd insisted on being his plus one. Now, Cillian would get to see what he'd given up for this stupid little girl.

"Natasha." Martin warned in her ear. He was beginning to think this little scheme of hers was a terrible idea. He knew her temper. And taunting Cillian with an ex-lover was one thing, but allowing Natasha to direct her venom toward Cillian's new bride was completely another. The way her guards were hovering, if Natasha hurt Chloe in any way, he might be the one to pay the price. And he wasn't about to die so his piece of ass could get even for a perceived slight that happened years ago.

Natasha ignored Martin's warning. This was her chance and she was going to take it. She doubted the little innocent could handle a man like Cillian O'Donnell anyway. So, she painted a devilish smile on her face as she leaned in close and whispered to the little bride. "If you need any pointers on how to fuck him, you just let me know, Precious."

Chloe felt Cillian's arm around her waist tense instantly, and Patrick stepped closer. Unfortunately for Natasha, they'd both heard the whispered insult clearly through the mic.

"Get the" Cillian's furious voice cut through the chatter of those close by.

But Chloe was ready. She expected it. After all, Natasha hadn't gone to all that trouble with her appearance for nothing. Really? That dress was ridiculous. She'd come looking for a scene, now she'd get one.

Chloe had cut her teeth on the vitriol one encountered as a member of the New Orleans elite. As the daughter of an exceedingly wealthy businessman, with a mother who'd been one of the most sought-after debutants of her day, Chloe had experienced her fair share of it before she was even old enough to drive. Hell, she'd attended the most prestigious private school in the city with some of the most vicious girls ever born. From sitting at the king's table during the many Mardi gras balls she'd attended to being dragged to brunches and afternoon teas given by society's top matrons, all of which were fraught with scandal; she could handle this. She'd been taught to handle anything that might be thrown her way in polite society, anything. The question was, could Natasha handle her?

Channeling her best impression of Clairee Belcher, Chloe looked up at Cillian as if appalled. She cut him off mid-sentence and using the most arrogant southern drawl ever uttered, she stated; "Cillian darlin, I *must* apologize. I didn't realize it was customary here in Ireland for the 'Madams' to attend social gatherings so openly."

"What?" His stunned gaze met hers, his browed furrowed in question.

"I'm mean, really! At least in N'awlins, they're secreted off in a back room somewhere for the single men to visit discreetly. You know, with a door leading to a back entrance or an alleyway. Such vulgarity is never allowed so openly in polite society." She had to bite down hard on the inside of her lip to keep from laughing at the totally shocked expression on his face.

"Madams?" Cillian nearly chocked.

"Oh, I'm sorry!" She gasped innocently. "What do y'all call high-class hookers here in Ireland?" The roar of laughter in her ear nearly made her lose it.

"I'm not a whore!" Natasha's wickedly smug expression turned to enraged fury.

"Oh dear, I must have misunderstood. But didn't you just say you'd give me pointers on how to have sex with my husband?" Chloe asked innocently, but loudly. "Of course, you used a much more *vulgar* term." She dragged out the word vulgar, which in her southern drawl, really brought home her point. "One should neva hear such *vulgarity* in polite company." She raised her hands to her chest and shivered delicately, as if the mere thought of the word might send her into hysterics. She could win an academy award for this scene.

"You bitch!" Natasha hissed.

"See, such language." Chloe clucked her tongue and shook her head as if disappointed, then looked back at Cillian. "Please don't be angry darlin, she simply can't help it. But she has to make a livin now, doesn't she? Shall I ask Imogen to prepare a room for her in the servant's quarters so she can conduct her business in private during the reception?" She tried to keep a straight face as she watched Cillian's stunned expression change to sheer delight. She also had the team laughing like hyenas in her ear, which wasn't helping either.

For the first time in his life, Cillian was at a complete loss for words. She was magnificent. He was about to kiss her when Martin spoke.

"Natasha, I believe it's time for us to move on." He'd never seen Natasha turn that shade of red before. He took her arm and attempted to guide her away.

"Fuck you!" Natasha shrieked and reared back her hand. But before she could deliver the slap to Chloe's face, three things happened at once.

"Natasha, no!" Martin yelled and grabbed her hand.

Chloe braced her weight on her back foot and lifted her hands to defend the attack, and Patrick jumped in front of her. When Chloe peeked up over his shoulder, she realized the Team had completely surrounded them. Apparently, they'd been working their way toward her while they'd listened to the conversation through the mic.

Martin's horrified gaze met Cillian's furious one. "Cillian, I had no idea. Please believe I would never," he tried to cover his own ass. Having Cillian as an enemy was not only dangerous, but would be disastrous financially. But Natasha, the stupid bitch, wouldn't shut her fucking mouth.

"Get your hands off me, asshole!" Natasha's scream cut off Martin's attempt at an apology as the Team hustled them out a side door.

Chloe didn't ask where they were taking them. She didn't care. She turned back to Cillian and smiled, then acknowledged the stunned couple who were next in line as if nothing had happened. "Hello, I'm Chloe."

Cillian cleared his throat so he could speak and followed her lead. "Chloe, this is Anton White, a colleague of mine and his daughter Haven." He wanted to roar with laughter like the men were doing in his ear. Instead, he held it in as best he could to make the next introduction. But one thing was for certain. His wife was fucking perfect!

The beautiful young woman had a gigantic smile on her face, and her eyes were sparkling with laughter as she took Chloe's hand. "Hi, I'm Haven and that was awesome!"

"Hi Haven. It's nice to meet you." Chloe couldn't stop herself from giggling with Haven.

"I want to be you when I grow up!" Haven continued.

Haven appeared to be Chloe's age, or maybe even a little older, but Chloe appreciated the comradery. She turned and pointed at the main table where her mother was sitting. "I learned from the best. Stop by our table later, Haven. I'll introduce you to the queen."

"Thank you, I will." She suddenly looked over Chloe's shoulder, and her expression changed. Her smile turned from open and happy to guarded. "Hello Patrick."

"Haven." Was Patrick's only response.

Haven nodded slightly and turned back to Chloe with a forced smile. "I'll be sure to stop by. Thank you, Chloe." Then she turned and walked away without looking back.

Chloe looked over her shoulder at Patrick. He was watching Haven's retreat with a scowl on his face. "What was that about?"

"Nothing." He replied as he continued to stare at Haven.

She assessed him for a moment. There was definitely a story there. She couldn't wait to talk to Haven later and find out. When she turned back to Cillian, he was watching her with the oddest expression on his face.

"Is something wrong?"

"No. No angel, everything is exactly right." He grinned and winked at her, then turned to the next guest in line.

Ten minutes later, they were nearly done. Chloe could finally see the end of the line, and her mind turned to the huge glass of wine she was going to reward herself with when this was over. She glanced longingly at Sidney, and they made eye contact from across the ballroom. She watched as her friend nodded slightly and stood up with two glasses in her hands and headed her way. She'd obviously read her mind. From the distance, it looked like Finn tried to stop her, but she was ignoring him. Now he was following her with a scowl on his face.

"Cillian, darling! You must introduce me to your little bride. She's simply adorable."

The woman's shrill voice startled Chloe and brought her attention back to the last couple in line. The woman's appearance matched her voice. Her sharp pointy face was covered in thick, heavy makeup and the red dress she wore was way too tight, showing off her scrawny, model thin frame. Her overly large breast enhancements made her look sort of like a Pez candy dispenser. Chloe bit her lip to keep from giggling as that image popped into her head.

The woman threw herself into Cillian's arms and hugged him tightly, lingering for an uncomfortably long moment. Then she turned to her husband and gushed. "Isn't she darling Richard? She looks just like a little china doll!"

"Chloe, this is Richard Buchannan and his wife Margo." Cillian's expression said it all.

Chloe sighed softly to herself. Here we go again. She smiled politely at the rude woman and extended her hand. "Hello."

"Hello darling." Margo's voice sounded as if she were speaking to a small child. Her smile was overly bright as she turned to her husband. "Richard dear, didn't you want to ask Cillian about that program you're working on?"

Richard immediately engaged Cillian in a brief, quiet conversation, leaving Margo to eye Chloe speculatively. "Cillian and I go *way* back."

"Do you?" Chloe wanted to smirk. She didn't, but she wanted to.

"Yes, we do." She replied in a decidedly condescending voice. Then she tilted her head, assessing Chloe before lifting her hand and giving a dismissive wave as she leaned in close to whisper, "You can't tell at all."

"Tell what?"

"There might be a tiny bump, but nothing large enough to be noticeable."

"Bump?"

"Oh, come now. Really? You don't honestly expect everyone to believe that *you* caught the most eligible bachelor in Ireland, do you? Surely, you're pregnant, or," she raised her brow, "oh, you clever girl," she cooed, "did you trick him?" Margo winked at her. "Don't worry, your secret's safe with me." She giggled maliciously, then pursed her lips and put her finger up to them in a sign of a conspirator's whispered secret.

Cillian stopped talking to Richard and turned toward Margo. He hated that bitch. He still didn't know what Richard saw in the woman. She'd been throwing herself at him for years before she'd finally married Richard. But even now, she continued to do it right under his nose.

Undeterred, Chloe leaned into Margo and, using her most concerned southern drawl, whispered back loud enough for those around them to clearly hear, "oh, bless your heart! You must've eaten some of the canapé's while waiting in line." Then she clucked her tongue sadly. "You might want to find the powder room dear. You, um, well" she clucked again "there's no delicate way to say this but," she pointed to her own mouth and tapped her bottom lip, "you have something green stuck in your front teeth."

Margo's smug expression quickly changed to one of shock, then anger, then mortification as she tried to decide if the little bitch was lying to her. She ran her tongue across her teeth to determine if it was true. Not knowing for certain, she turned and without another word, rushed toward the ladies' room, leaving her husband to follow in her wake.

Sidney burst out laughing from behind her. "Girl, that was classic!" She reached around and handed her a glass of wine. "Here, you earned this."

Chloe ignored the men, laughing hysterically in her ear as she and Sidney giggled uncontrollably. When she finally stopped long enough to catch her breath, she looked pointedly at Cillian, who was trying hard not to laugh himself. "Those women are hideous! You surround yourself with some pretty awful people Cillian O'Donnell." Before he could respond, she continued. "I believe I'm finished here. I'm going to get something to eat."

She turned abruptly and arm in arm, she and Sidney walked through the crowd together toward Imogen who was waiting to take them to a little parlor set up specifically to remove her veil and the fur from her dress. On the way, neither woman paid any attention to the two men following close behind them so they didn't see the amused grin of one or the satisfied but possessive smile of the other. But David and Angela Guidry did.

When her empty plate was taken away, Chloe sipped her third glass of wine and looked out over the crowded ballroom. Almost everyone was dancing and having a good time. Most of those were the people who lived on the island. However, there were a few stoic faces in the crowd who remained at their tables. Several in small groups whispering in hushed voices.

She switched her attention to the beautiful décor. The room had come together beautifully. Each table held a tall crystal vase overflowing with gorgeous white, cream and dusty pink orchids with antique gold and champagne colored silk ribbon woven through them. Pearl strands shown brilliantly against the gold and completed the elegant creations. Candles floating in strategically sized vases surrounded each centerpiece, all resting on white tablecloths with champagne colored silk runners.

Cillian suddenly lifted Chloe out of her seat and settled her onto his lap. He took her full wineglass from her and handed it to a passing server.

"What are you doing?"

He flashed her a wicked grin, but didn't answer her. Instead, he slid his hand along the bare skin of her back, then tucked his fingers into the opening at the bottom of the dress and turned back to Finn and continued their conversation.

Sidney wiggled her eyebrows at Chloe suggestively, then moved Chloe's abandoned chair out of the way and scooted hers over so they could talk.

Chloe shook her head at her husband's possessive display. He'd been touching her all evening. When they'd posed for the pictures, he'd insisted on, he'd whispered wicked things in her ear causing her to blush terribly.

When they'd danced the first dance of the evening in front of everyone, his suggestive whispers had gotten worse. It was a good thing he was such an accomplished dancer, because she'd nearly stumbled several times. And each time, he'd chuckled softly and nibbled on her neck. She'd never been so glad for the music to stop in her life.

She caught site of Ian walking past and when he glanced her way; she waved him over.

"Hey." Ian said from the other side of the head table.

"Hey dude. You look handsome." And he did. Ian had grown at least four inches in the last few months, so he towered over her now. He was dressed in a tailored black suit and his hair was combed. It was probably the first time she'd ever seen it that way. Normally it was a mass of loose curls around his head.

"Thanks. Gram said if I wanted to come, I had to wear this." He pulled at his collar.

"I'm glad you did."

"I picked my own shoes though." He grinned and lifted his foot.

Chloe stood up from Cillian's lap and leaned over the table to get a better look. Then she laughed at the white sneakers on his feet. "You'd better not let her see those. She'll probably have a stroke."

"Na, she'll cut me some slack."

"I wish I could've gotten away with wearing sneakers." Sidney chimed in as she smiled at the handsome kid. He was tall and gangly, and his voice cracked a little when he talked.

Ian blushed slightly when the beautiful woman spoke to him. "I don't think they would match your dress."

"You're probably right. I'm Chloe's friend, Sidney." Sidney stuck her hand out to greet him.

"I'm Ian." He blushed again when he shook her hand. "Are you from America too?"

"Yes."

"Ian is Imogen's grandson. He lives here with us." Cillian added.

"You get to live in a castle?" Sidney smiled brightly. "That must be a lot of fun."

"I guess."

"How'd you do on your math test yesterday?" Chloe asked.

Ian smiled at Cillian as he answered Chloe. "I aced it, thanks to Cillian."

"What do you mean?" She frowned slightly and looked from Ian to Cillian.

"Cillian helped me study for it." Ian said proudly. Cillian had been helping him with his math a lot lately.

"You did?"

"I didn't do much. Ian's a bright guy. I'm glad to hear you did well. Have you eaten yet?" Cillian quickly changed the subject.

"Yes. I liked the lamb with that cherry glaze stuff the best. It was really good." Before he could continue, a group of boys rushed over and grabbed his arm, pulling him away, chattering excitedly about video games and chocolate cake.

Cillian chuckled as he watched him hurry away with his friends. Then he turned back to find Chloe watching him.

She narrowed her eyes at him. "You are full of surprises, aren't you?"

"Yes." He answered simply.

"Well, this is fun, but it's time to hit the dance floor. Come on Chloe." Sidney grabbed her friend's hand to pull her away from the table.

Chloe turned to Cillian. "I'll be back."

He reached out and pulled her out of Sidney's hold and back onto his lap.

"What are you doing? We want to go dance."

"Kissing my wife." Then he did just that.

She was breathless by the time he ended the kiss. He nibbled on her neck, then kissed her jaw before giving her another soft kiss on her lips. He whispered against them, "go. Have fun with your friend angel."

Sidney dragged a dazed Chloe away from the table and snagged a glass of wine from their server. She handed it to her as they headed for the packed dance floor. "Holy shit Chlo lo, that was hot!" She fanned her own face to make her point.

Chloe sighed heavily. "I know. He does that all the time." She sipped the cold wine, hoping to cool herself down a little.

The music was fabulous and perfect for dancing. The pulsing beat of the latest hits blasted through the speakers. They danced, they sipped their wine, and they yelled to each other over the music, just as they'd done so many times before in the clubs in New Orleans. When the song switched, Haven danced by. Chloe reached out and grabbed her hand and pulled her into their circle.

"Hey Haven!"

"Hello Chloe! I was wonderin if you were goin to venture out onto the floor." Haven smiled and reached out and clinked her glass to Chloe's.

"That husband of hers doesn't let her wander too far." Sidney added and lifted her glass as she twirled around to the music.

"I saw that. He scowls at anyone who gets too close. Da and I both noticed it. It's amusin to watch." Haven giggled.

"Haven, this is my friend Sidney. Sidney, this is Haven!"

"Hey Haven. That's an awesome name and I love your accent! It's beautiful." Sidney commented.

"Thank you on both accounts. It was my grandmother's name. I can't help the accent though. When I drink it gets worse. Da says it means my Irish is showin." She threw her head back and laughed.

"That's a great way to put it." Sidney clinked Haven's glass, and they shook their asses and started bumping hips to the beat.

"You and Chloe have beautiful accents, too!" Haven added.

"Well, you could say our southern is showing." Chloe added as she shook her ass and raised her glass.

"Your dress is beautiful." Sidney yelled over the music to Haven. And it was. The hunter green dress hugged Haven's curves, stopping at mid-thigh where a lighter shade of green chiffon pleated three-inch ruffle swayed softly.

"Thanks. Yours is gorgeous. I love that color. It matches your eyes perfectly."

"So does yours." Sidney replied. Haven's dress matched her beautiful green eyes. It also set off the fire in her thick auburn hair.

"You know you two are completely surrounded, don't ya?" Haven made a point to look around at Chloe's security.

Chloe knew they were there. She could hear them in her ear. "Yes. Just ignore them. I do." She grinned at Micha and Terrance, who'd followed them onto the dance floor along with most of Team One.

"Do you live on the island?" Sidney asked as she made a sexy turn, using her swaying hips to lead into it. She glanced up and met Finn's heated gaze off in the distance as she did it. He winked at her, but she didn't acknowledge it.

"No, I moved back onto my father's estate after I finished at University. It's on the mainland."

"What's your degree in?" Chloe asked.

"I have a master's in finance. But I don't really use it."

"Then what do you do?" Chloe asked as she moved her hips and slid into a sensual turn to match Sidney's.

"I blow stuff up."

"What!" Came Chloe's shocked response.

"Did you just say you blow stuff up?" Sidney asked with a surprised giggle; not sure she'd heard correctly.

They both stopped dancing and stared at Haven in shock. Haven busted out laughing at their stunned expressions.

"Yes. My father is a demolitions expert. I've trained under him for years and now I work for him. He has a very lucrative business. He's even trained a few of Cillian's men." Haven said proudly.

They started dancing again as they stared at her in wonder. Chloe spoke first.

"So, let me get this straight. You have a degree in finance, but you work for your father's demolition business?

"Yes."

"And you blow stuff up for a living?" Sidney asked before Chloe could.

"Yes." Haven grinned wickedly.

"Ok, I think that's the coolest thing I've ever heard!" Sidney laughed wildly.

"I wanna blow stuff up!" Chloe yelled and looked over at Sidney, then back to Haven. "Haven, you've gotta teach us how to blow stuff up!"

"Sure, I can do that." Haven laughed delightedly.

All three women toasted and drank as they turned in the middle of the crowd.

The music changed again to a slow, pulsing beat of erotic notes. Chloe felt him before he even touched her. Cillian's strong arms slide around her waist and turned her into him. In one smooth move, he took the nearly empty wineglass from her and passed it to Micha behind him.

"Hello wife." Cillian held her close as they danced to the sensual rhythm. Watching her dance with her friends had been torture. Her fluid moves screamed sex.

Chloe rested her hands on his chest. "Hello husband." She giggled. "I wasn't finished with that wine."

"Baby, when you start talking about wanting to blow shit up, I think it's a sign that you're probably done." His warm, soft lips nuzzled her neck on the opposite side from where the mic was located.

"You heard that?" She leaned into the tingling sensation.

"The entire team heard that." He bit her neck, then ran his tongue up to her ear.

"Ah well. I'm going to learn how. Haven's gonna teach me." She shivered.

"Let's go upstairs baby." He whispered and kissed a trail back to her shoulder, pulling her closer, he pressed his aching cock against her as they moved.

"But my family,"

"They'll still be here tomorrow. I promise." He turned her as the music pulsed through them.

Chloe looked over at her girls; Sidney was dancing with Finn and Haven with Patrick.

Sidney was looking at Finn's wicked smile suspiciously while he moved her slowly around the dance floor. Chloe was surprised at how well Finn moved.

But Haven was a different situation all together. She'd closed down. She wasn't smiling anymore, and she was avoiding eye contact with Patrick while they danced. And it was obviously pissing him off. Oh yea, there was definitely a story there.

"Angel." Cillian's patience ran out. He lifted her into his arms and headed for the door. Most of Team One fell in behind him.

Chapter 32: No More Dancing

Cillian sat on the edge of the bed with Chloe standing between his knees. She looked stunning in the dress he'd commissioned for her. One of the top designers in the world had made it specifically for her. But he couldn't wait to get her out of it. "Turn around baby."

She turned and presented him her back. "Don't rip my dress." She warned in a snippy tone when he tugged harder on the lace than she thought necessary.

He leaned in and nipped her shoulder with the sharp edges of his teeth. "I'll rip it if I want to."

"Don't you dare!"

He kissed the bare skin of her back, his hands working steadily at the delicate buttons. "Why?"

She sighed dramatically, as if it killed her to admit. "Because it's beautiful."

"I'll buy you all the beautiful dresses you could ever want."

"I want this one."

"Why this one, baby?" He whispered against her skin.

"Because it's my wedding dress."

"And?" He coaxed.

"You said I'm going to have children. I don't know if that's true or not, but if I do, one might be a daughter and she just might want to wear it one day. So, you can't rip it."

"Ok, angel." He chuckled softly. Then it was his turn to sigh, letting her know he felt put out about it. But he went to work gently unbuttoning the tiny pearl buttons.

When he released the last button, he pushed the snug fitting dress to the floor. She bent down to pick it up, giving him a beautiful view of her rounded ass. He palmed it with both hands and held her still while he leaned in and bit her cheek.

Chloe squeaked, then giggled at herself as she glanced over her shoulder. "You're a very tactile man." Did she really just giggle? Oh crap! How much wine did she drink?

"Yes, I am." He slid his hands down her legs to her ankles and unzipped her boots. After she kicked them off, he spun her around to face him. "Slide those stockings off, baby," he demanded. His hushed Irish brogue, thick with need.

Chloe boldly lifted her foot and placed it on the bed between his thighs, then slowly slid the stocking off. She dropped it on the floor and repeated the process with her other foot. Only this time, her toes brushed his heavy erection gently before settling into place.

A gleam of amusement and heated arousal simmered in his green eyes. She'd definitely had a lot to drink. "You're playing with fire, angel. Be very careful or you might get burned."

Chloe put her foot back onto the floor. "I've survived the heat before." Standing in only her white lace thong, she shivered with anticipation and held out her hands to him; palms up, fingers curled and wrist together, indicating she was ready to be bound. He tied her up nearly every day, and she'd come to not only expect it, but to crave it.

His eyes blazed at her in response. Holding her gaze, he let her see the fire she ignited inside him. "Yes, you have little one. And beautifully so." His angel relied on his ropes to allow herself the freedom to enjoy his touch. She'd convinced herself that if restrained, she couldn't fight the passion they shared. While he loved seeing her bound for his pleasure, he was determined that tonight would be different.

Cillian took Chloe's offered hands in his and pulled her onto his lap. Once she was straddling him, he placed her hands behind his neck. He slid his palms down her torso and tucked his thumbs under the lace thong at her hips and yanked, snapping the delicate material and pulling it from her.

"You should probably buy stock in silk and lace." She giggled when the tattered remains of her panties floated to the floor.

"Who says I haven't."

Chloe rested her weight on his thighs and slid her hands from around his neck and held them out again so he could tie her up. She frowned in confusion when he took them and put them behind his neck again.

Settling his palms at her hips, Cillian smiled at her confused expression and pulled her closer into him. Her naked breasts rubbed against the material of his jacket, and her heated core pressed tight against his erection. It was decadent, having her naked in his arms, wearing only her collar while he was fully clothed. The image of them in the mirror across the room would be burned into his memory forever.

He leaned in and nibbled at her neck. "You handled yourself very well tonight angel." The deep Irish brogue whispered against her skin, making her tremble.

"Hmm." She shivered as his lips moved down her neck to her shoulder. "Thank you."

"It just proves that you were born to be mine." He sank his teeth into her.

She gasped, and her head fell back to give him better access. "No, I wasn't."

"Yes, little one, you were." He kissed the bite mark to sooth the sting. "You fill the role perfectly."

"Well, those women are awful."

"They are." He agreed. "That's why I need you."

"You don't need me necessarily; you just need better friends."

"I don't have friends. Well, other than Finn. I have acquaintances."

"That's very sad."

"Not really."

"Oh yes, it is. Everyone needs friends. They have your back. They tell you if your lip gloss is smeared. They call you when they find the perfect dress in your size on sale. And they stand there holding on to it, daring anyone else to touch it until you show up. If for some strange reason you're not there shopping with them in the first place."

"You hardly ever wear lip gloss." He kissed her shoulder. "And you don't need to worry about sales. You'll have every dress you'll ever want."

"Ugh". She grunted. "That's not the same thing at all. Spending the day shopping and finding that perfect buried treasure is fun. Then going to lunch with the girls and having wine while you talk about what you've found and what shoes you're going to wear with it."

"Shopping, huh?"

"Yes shopping. Or playing tennis or going dancing at a club. You need your friends. Who's going to go to the ladies' room with you?"

"The ladies' room?"

"There are long lines for the ladies' room. The men's room; not so much. But the ladies' room? Always a line. Who's going to stand in line and keep you company while you wait? Your friends, that's who."

"And when you go dancing?"

"Yes, when you go dancing. I love to dance."

"I'm glad you brought that up angel."

"What friends?"

"No dancing. After tonight, I have a new rule."

She signed heavily. "Of course, you do. What now?"

He chuckled at her disgruntled question and ran his teeth along the edge of her chin. "You're never allowed to dance again unless I'm with you."

"What?" She tried to pull back to meet his gaze, but he held her to him.

"You heard me. You're too fuckin sexy when you move like that."

"Humph. You're being ridiculous."

"I don't believe I've ever been called ridiculous."

"Well, you are." Then she puffed out a breath. "But it doesn't matter. I'm not allowed to go anywhere without you, anyway."

"True. And you never will." His palms slid down to cup the rounded cheeks of her ass, his fingers settling into the crevice between them.

She slid her fingers into his hair and pulled sharply. "Be nice Cillian."

He turned abruptly and placed her on her back on the bed then settled between her thighs. "I'm always nice to you."

Chloe burst out laughing. "Oh, no you're not!"

"Baby." He pushed the bulge behind his zipper tight against her core. "You're the only person I'm ever nice to." Before she could respond, he moved her hands to his face and held them there, and kissed her. When she cupped his face, holding him to her for the kiss, he released her hands and removed his jacket, all the while never breaking the kiss.

Cillian kept kissing her, one drugging kiss after another as he undressed, then settled back between her thighs. He wedged the thick head of his cock at her slick entrance and slowly slid inside her. Satisfaction settled deep at the proof that his kisses alone had her slick and wet for him. He set a languid rhythm as he stroked into her.

Chloe wrapped her legs around his waist, allowing him to go even deeper. Using her hips, she tried to urge him on. "Faster!"

He ignored her demand and kept up the leisurely pace. He pulled her arms around him and wrapped his around her, holding her close while he took his time. Over and over, slow, deep, gentle thrusts designed to seduce.

Long moments later, Chloe couldn't take it anymore. "Please!" This slow, tender possession frightened her. She needed to be bound and taken hard and fast. Needed to burn in the fire so she didn't have to think, only feel. That she could handle. This, this was something else. This gentleness was terrifying, so intense it had the power to steal her heart.

Cillian rested his forehead against hers and met her pleading gaze with his determined one. He slowly slid deep and softly swiveled his hips, making her gasp. Her pussy tightened around him. "You like that, baby?"

"Cillian." She was desperate. She put her feet on the bed and thrust her hips against him.

Ignoring her attempt to entice him, he kissed her next plea away with more of those soft, deep, drugging kisses. Pumping into her gently, over and over, slowly leading her where he wanted her to go. "There, baby." he teased softly. "Your sweet little pussy is so hot and wet for me." He was determined to prove to her once and for all that the passion they shared was not one sided. Had never been one sided. That she craved his touch as much as he did hers.

He continued to whisper to her about how good she felt around him and how pleased he was with the way she responded to him. When she tipped over the edge, he held himself deep inside of her and let her ride it out. When she came down the other side, he continued with the tender possession until she peaked again. Then and only then did he allow himself the freedom to thrust hard and deep shoving high up into her as he came.

Cillian woke Chloe repeatedly throughout the night, taking her again and again in that slow determined pace, only allowing her brief naps in between. He was immensely pleased when the time for her run came and went and she hadn't stirred. Even now, she lay draped across his chest, and he stroked her back as she slept.

He'd have to wake her soon. Her family was leaving later this afternoon. He knew their leaving was going to make her sad, but he couldn't wait to get them off his island.

She shifted in his arms, and her nipple brushed across his chest. He grinned to himself as his cock thickened at the sensation. At this rate, they'd never leave the bed. She was the drug to his addiction. He rolled over, taking her beneath him, and eased into her again.

Chloe groaned as she came awake to Cillian sliding deep inside of her again. She was swollen and sore from the many times he'd taken her throughout the night. But each time had been better than the one before. She'd come so many times, she'd lost count. But now she was raw. "Cillian." She groaned when he planted himself deep.

"Fuck baby, you feel so good." He groaned back into her ear. "Your pussy is swollen and tight around my cock. And still so wet, slick from my come inside you." He lost his will to go slow and thrust hard.

She groaned again at his words. "I'm sore." But she tilted her hips to meet his thrusts.

"I know, angel, but take me anyway. Wrap those pretty legs around me."

Chloe did as she was told and locked him tightly to her with her legs. Opening herself wider to accept him.

"Good girl. Such a good girl." He crooned softly. He kissed her, thrusting his tongue deep to mimic the thrust of his aching cock. He was probably as sore as she was, but he didn't care. He wanted her sore. He wanted her to remember this. When she said goodbye to her family later, he needed her to still feel him deep inside her. Needed her to remember that she belonged here with him. Belonged to him.

He rode her hard, thrusting powerfully. When she finally came, so did he. They peeked together in a kaleidoscope of sensations. Breathless and spent, he collapsed on top of her. She took his weight.

When he finally caught his breath, he raised up on his elbows to look down at her. "Good morning wife."

Chloe couldn't help it. She giggled at his serious expression. "I think you killed me!"

He grinned and kissed her nose. "I think you'll survive." He kissed her lips, then lifted off of her. "I'll be right back."

Cillian grabbed his phone and sent out a quick text, then went into the bathroom and started the water running to fill the tub. Once it was filled, he scooped Chloe up and carried her into the bathroom. He put her on her feet in front of the sink, then went to brush his teeth. When he finished, he turned on the shower and as soon as it was warm enough, stepped into it.

Chloe took a long look at herself in the mirror when she finished brushing her teeth. She was still flushed from her last orgasm. There were dark shadows under her eyes from lack of sleep and marks of possession from Cillian's mouth covering her neck, chest and her breasts. The pearl band that had held her veil was long since removed sometime during the night, but the little pearls in the braids were still there. She was too exhausted to take the time to remove them, so she pinned her hair up high on top of her head and followed Cillian into the shower. They washed quickly, then together, they eased down into the hot bath. She leaned back against his chest and let the hot water sooth her aching body.

"We missed breakfast." Chloe mused as she lazily played with the bubbles. She was trying desperately to keep her mind from going back to the way Cillian had acted last night. There'd been no urgency, no frenzied coming together in a whirlwind of heat. Instead, the long intense night of slow gentle touches seriously freaked her out.

"Imogen is making something for us now. She'll send it up as soon as it's ready." He smoothed his fingers around her nipples absently.

"What time is my family leaving today?"

"Later this afternoon." He heard the little catch in her voice so he kissed the top of her head.

"Will you let them come back sometime?"

"I don't know."

She glanced up sleepily and met his intense gaze for a moment, then looked back at her hands as she continued to play with the bubbles. "I'm your wife, that makes them your family now too."

"I don't know if they would agree with that, angel. We'll have to see how they react when they get back to the states."

They finished the bath in silence.

Chloe was seated next to Cillian at the table in their suite, working her way through a large stack of pancakes when a thought hit her. "Cillian, am I still a prisoner?"

He considered her carefully, wondering where this was going. "You're my wife."

"So, I'm no longer considered a prisoner?"

"That depends on how you look at it. You can't leave, if that's what you mean."

"I know. But other than you, no one ever really treated me like a prisoner, anyway. Well, the guys did for a while, but not really."

"What are you getting at Chloe?"

She looked him straight in the eyes and went for it. "I want a cell phone."

He frowned at her, but before he could reply, she continued; "I know I can't leave, but there's no reason I can't have a phone. That Titan guy can load whatever software is necessary to monitor it. I don't care. You'd do that, anyway. But I want to talk with Sidney and my parents."

"You agreed to the two video calls a week."

"That was before. Now everyone and their mother knows I'm your wife. You made sure of that yesterday. So, the rules have changed." She said with a smug smile. "I'd actually like my old cell phone back so I have all my contacts, but a new one will do."

He regarded her for long moments then his lips twitched slightly. His angel was taking her place as his queen. This was her first attempt to use her power, power she didn't fully comprehend yet, to demand what she wanted. She hadn't asked. She'd stated what she wanted and expected to get results. There was no way he was going to deny her. Hell, she was right in that Titan would monitor her use of the phone. So would he, closely. "Alright. I'll have it for you this afternoon."

Chloe tried really hard to hide her surprise. "Thank you." She smiled brilliantly.

"Now kiss me, baby. Your parents are on their way up and I have to go to work." He pushed his chair back from the table and spread his thighs and waited.

Chloe got out of her chair and stepped between his knees. From experience, she knew what he wanted, so she slid her hands round his neck and her knees up over his thighs, settling onto his lap. He always wanted her there when they talked. Once she was in the now familiar position, she kissed him.

Satisfaction sizzled through him when she placed herself in position without being told to do so. His arms encircled her and held her close as he accepted her kiss. She was no longer timid when she kissed him, either. She'd learned quickly what he liked and now willingly gave it to him.

Hours later, Chloe sat in her favorite chair in the library, sipping hot cocoa. Imogen had been ready with it when she and her family had come in from the stables. After being ill for so many days and planning the wedding, it had been a long while since she'd visited the stables. Unfortunately, Storm had been less than a perfect gentleman when she'd introduced him to her family.

"Honey, are you sure it's safe to be around Storm?" Angela asked for what must've been the 5th time.

"I don't ride him mom. Not yet, anyway." Chloe grinned when her mom's eyes nearly bulged out at her answer. Storm had misbehaved during the visit, so the idea of riding him would definitely make her mother nervous. It seemed that Storm didn't like sharing her, either. Frank had to take him in hand and lead him away. Of course, Frank had grumbled the entire time. But he was no match for Angela Guidry. Her mother had charmed the cantankerous old man and had him blushing by the time they'd decided to head back to the castle. She couldn't wait to tease him about it tomorrow.

David smiled at his wife. He appreciated Chloe's attempt to keep her mother's spirits up. The time to depart was approaching quickly, and Angela was anxious about leaving Chloe behind.

He looked around the cozy library and noted that the fireplace had already been lit and was blazing before they'd returned. He also noted that Imogen had obviously been waiting for them to come back. She'd had the hot cocoa ready. What surprised him most, though, was the peppermint stick that had already been placed in Chloe's cup. It seemed Imogen knew his girl well.

While the girls sipped their cocoa and talked about the horses, he turned and studied Patrick, who stood inconspicuously just inside the door. Micha and Zane were standing guard on the other side of it. It was apparent these men took Choe's security very seriously. They'd surrounded them during the walk out to the stables. Of course, they'd been friendly and engaging, but the steely eyed men were on guard and aware of their surroundings and knew exactly where Chloe was the entire time.

Patrick had asked Chloe to let him drive them, but she'd declined in favor of walking in the fresh air. To his surprise, Patrick hadn't argued with her. Instead, he'd teased her about having a red nose by the time she got to the stables, but he'd immediately called the team out to accompany them. With the friendly banter between her and the team, it wasn't hard to see that they really cared for her.

Even Cillian. And he'd paid attention. Close attention. He found the expression on the man's face when he looked at Chloe very interesting. Especially when he thought no one was watching.

David picked up one of the many books on art history that littered the coffee table. "You've ordered quite a few books, Choe. Do you have a lot of time to read?"

"I didn't order them. They were already here." She pointed at the many shelves full of books that surrounded them. "Imogen must be pulling them for me."

David doubted that. He casually flipped the book over and looked at the tag on the bottom. Just as he thought, someone had purchased it recently. He didn't correct her, but he found it interesting. "It's fortunate the library has plenty of books on your favorite subject."

"Yea, I never get tired of reading about the history of art and the artists themselves."

"It's not the same as painting, though, is it? Have you been able to paint at all since you've been here?" Angela asked.

"Um." Chloe took a sip of her cocoa to avoid answering the question immediately.

"Chloe, you should show your family your art studio." Patrick spoke up from across the room. Then he grinned when she scowled at him.

"You have a studio?!" Angela asked, delighted.

"Yes, well, um." She didn't want to show them, but she was at a loss at how to explain why. So, she sipped at her cocoa again, hoping the cup hid her expression.

"Oh Sweetheart, that's wonderful. I'd love to see it."

"Me too." Sidney chimed in softly while eyeing Chloe carefully. There was a story there, and she wanted to know what it was before she had to leave.

When Chloe didn't immediately answer, David added; "Chloe honey, we'd really love to see it."

Her chest tightened at the thought of going back in there. But from the expectant looks on their faces, they weren't going to let it go. "Alright." Anxiety riding her hard, she stood and headed toward the door, leaving her family to follow her. She glared at Patrick when he continued to grin while he opened to door for her.

Stepping to the side, Chloe leaned against the wall, purposely not going further into the room. She hadn't been back in here since that awful day. The canvases she'd covered in black were no longer scattered on the floor. Imogen must've come in and picked them up because they were now leaning against the back wall.

"My goodness!" Angela gasped when she followed Chloe through the door of the studio and walked straight into the center of the room. She turned in a slow circle, taking in the magnitude of the art supplies displayed perfectly in organized bins and canisters. The easels set up strategically to capture the light and the view from the windows. It was perfect for Chloe. "This is amazing!"

Sidney walked around the room inspecting the supplies, opening boxes and running her finger across the handles of the brushes resting in bins, waiting to be used. "Chloe, this is just…. Wow." She turned and frowned at Chloe when she realized she was still leaning against the wall and she looked pale. "What?"

Chloe didn't answer, and she kept her hands on the wall behind her so they couldn't see how badly they were shaking. Her eyes were focused on the floor instead of the room. She didn't want the reminder of the one thing she loved most in the world, but was refusing to allow herself.

When Chloe didn't answer, Angela and Sidney shared a concerned look.

"Chloe, honey?" David watched his girl, trying to figure out what she wasn't telling them.

But Angela's motherly instincts kicked in, and she took a closer look at the studio. It was then that she saw the canvases covered in thick black paint leaning against the wall. She considered them for a long moment, then turned and did the same with the easels. The black canvases were significant. And there were none of the colorful projects, half completed, that you'd expect to see sitting on the easels. Taking it all in, her heart broke. She walked over to Chloe and gently took her hands from behind her back and held them in her own. "Sweetheart." She whispered gently. "Tell me."

Chloe shook her head as tears trickle down her face.

Aching for her, Angela pulled Chloe into her arms and held her tightly. She rubbed her hand soothingly up and down Chloe's back like she'd done so many times before when she was a child. "Tell me." She repeated.

"He hurt dad." Chloe's sobbed into her mother's shoulder.

Angela held her while she cried. When David would have interjected, she shook her head slightly at him, letting him know to let her cry. He never could stand to see Chloe cry, but she needed to get it out. When she finally settled and just held on, Angela whispered softly, tears of her own evident in her voice. "Sweetheart, are you punishing him, or yourself?"

"I don't know."

"Yes, you do."

Chloe sniffled. "I'm not sure anymore. I just know that I don't want him to have this piece of me."

"Sweetheart, you can't suppress who you are. You'll only hurt yourself in the long run."

"But mom,"

"Chloe, honey,"

"No! I don't want to give this to him." She insisted almost petulantly. "He doesn't deserve it. He's already taken so much!"

"You're not giving it to him. You're giving it to yourself. Painting is such an important part of who you are. Please honey, don't do this to yourself just to spite him."

"It's the one thing he can't take from me."

"But he is taking it. And sweetheart," Angela pulled Chloe's face from her shoulder and lifted her chin so their eyes met, "you're letting him."

"Mom, you don't understand."

"Sweetheart, listen to me. Until we can get you out of here, you still have to live. Not just survive Chloe, live. Which means you have to be who you were meant to be. You're an artist. You paint. Don't let anyone take that from you. Especially him."

Chloe glanced over at her father, then toward Sidney. They both nodded at her.

"Your mother's right, kiddo."

She sighed heavily and wiped her face. She hated to admit it, but she knew her mother was right. In a way, she was letting him take this from her, too. Until now, she hadn't thought of it that way. Resigned, she nodded to let her mother know she understood. "Ok."

"Ok." Angela kissed her forehead and said a silent prayer.

Cillian gripped Chloe's hand tightly while they stood on the small runway and watched his jet take off. He had the feeling if her father thought he'd get away with it, he would've jerked her onto the plane with them at the last minute.

She'd said her goodbyes, hugging them and clinging to each one tightly and crying as if her heart was breaking. She was still crying. Deep, agonized sobs that shook her entire body.

The site of those tears rolling unchecked down her face lessened his anger, but only slightly. He'd watched the monitor and listened to the conversation in the studio earlier. He'd watched her collapse in tears in her mother's arms. He'd heard her say she was purposely keeping her talent from him. Purposely not painting to spite him. He already knew that, but after last night, it pissed him off to hear her say it.

He'd struggled to hold his temper at bay during lunch, knowing her parents were leaving soon. But he'd wanted to turn her over his knee and spank that sweet little ass. He still itched to do it, but those tears held him in check. Instead, he lifted her into his arms and carried her back to the waiting SUV.

His team, tense and on alert, surround them as he carried her to the waiting car. Cillian held her on his lap, his arms holding her close, with her face pressed to his chest as they traveled back to the castle. He rested his chin on top of her head and let her cry. It was the only sound on the otherwise silent ride. There was nothing to say. He would not make a promise he wouldn't keep.

When they pulled up to the front door of the castle, he tilted his head slightly, indicating to his team to leave them alone. As soon as the last door shut, he pulled Chloe away from his body and cupped her face. He couldn't help but think how beautiful she looked with tears in her eyes. They made the cornflower blue sparkle like the gems in her collar. The site made his dick hard. Yea, he knew he was fucked up. "Are you finished?"

Chloe tried to suppress the uncontrollable quakes and sniffles so she could answer. She'd cried so hard she was having trouble catching her breath. There was no trace of compassion in Cillian's eyes, only restrained patience as he waited for her to stop.

"Get it under control angel." Never taking his eyes from hers, he leaned in and kissed her trembling mouth hard. Then he lifted his head and, with a razor-sharp voice, he continued. "I know you're upset, but you're not walking through the castle with your heart on your sleeve and tears in your eyes. You Americans have a saying." He paused to make sure she was paying attention before he continued. "Never let them see you sweat. That holds true here as well. You're my wife. You. Are. Mrs. Cillian O'Donnell. And as my wife, you will never, ever let an outsider see you in a vulnerable state. That includes the main floor staff and the castle guards." He waited a beat to let that sink in. "Do you understand me?"

Chloe closed her eyes to shut him out while she tried to get control of her emotions.

"No, look at me."

She took a shuddering breath, then reluctantly opened her eyes and met his fierce gaze. She could tell from the look in his eyes that he was angry. She didn't know what he had to be angry about. She was the one who'd just said goodbye to her family, not knowing when or if she'd ever see them again.

"Say you understand."

As she listened to him dictate to her, her sadness quickly morphed into anger. She jerked her head from his hands and glared at him as she wiped her face. "You're being an ass."

"Say it." He growled and shook her slightly for emphasis.

"I understand." She hissed back in a furious voice.

"Good, now let's go."

When they emerged from the SUV, Cillian took her hand and threaded his fingers through hers. She wanted to pull away, but didn't dare with the team surrounding them. Instead, they walked through the main floor of the castle together in stony silence. As they passed through the spacious rooms heading toward the elevator, she noticed that the staff and the guards were indeed watching them. She supposed they always watched, but she'd never paid attention before.

After the elevator doors closed behind them and their security detail, she turned to meet Cillian's steely gaze. He lifted an arrogant eyebrow at her in a gesture of 'I told you so.' She hated that smug expression. He'd known the staff would be watching. He also knew she wouldn't have wanted them to see her in such a state. She'd never in a million years admit he was right. So, she turned her nose up and faced forward, ignoring his amused chuckle.

Cillian led Chloe to the sofa in their bedroom. As soon as she sat down, he handed her the small gift that had been sitting on the coffee table. The box was wrapped in lavender paper with white roses and was the size of a cell phone box. She grinned at him and quickly opened the top and pulled out the phone.

"Thank you, Cillian!"

"Sidney's and your parent's numbers are already programed into it as well as mine and the rest of the team's."

Chloe turned the phone on and began scrolling through the numbers.

"They won't land for another six hours, but if you text them now, they'll get it as soon as Finn gives them back their phones."

Chloe looked up at him again. He was watching her intently, and there was no way to miss the tension in his eyes. "I assume there's a program on here to monitor my texts?"

"Both text and phone conversations, so you and Sidney can't plan some great escape." The corner of his mouth twitched at the memory of listening to them through the security camera two days before.

"Well, we could," she giggled, "it just wouldn't be successful."

"Brat." Cillian leaned in and kissed her.

When he ended the kiss, she reached up out of habit and rubbed at the scruff on his shadowed chin. "Thank you."

He pushed his jaw into her hand, enjoying her touch. "You're welcome. Oh, I almost forgot." He pulled an envelope from his back pocket and handed it to her.

"What's this?" She took it, but was more interested in her new phone.

"Your new Identification card, bankcard and your credit card."

She looked up at him like he was crazy. "My what?" She ripped open the envelope and three cards fell into her lap. The ID had her picture and her new name on it. The gold bankcard and the black American Express card both also had her new name on them. "Oh my God!" She looked up at him in stunned disbelief. "Cillian?"

"You have an account set up with funds to cover anything you want."

"Really?" She was a little skeptical, but who could blame her.

"Yes, but Titan will monitor your spending in case you try to buy a plane or a yacht for your great escape plan." He chuckled. "Now why don't you get some rest. You didn't get much sleep last night." He grinned wickedly at the reminder and turned on the gas fireplace for her.

"Where are you going?" Chloe kicked off her boots and laid down on the sofa, pulling her blanket over herself. He was right. She was exhausted.

"I'll be in my office. I have some work that needs my attention." He left before he gave into the urge to fuck her. At this rate, they were probably going to kill each other. But what a way to go? And that tender gesture she'd just displayed soothed the anger that had been pulsing through him since watching her in the studio.

Chloe sent a quick text to Sidney and her parents, letting them know her new number, and asked them to text her back when they landed. She was beyond happy that she'd be able to talk to them whenever she wanted now. She snuggled down into the warm blanket and closed her eyes. Within minutes, she was asleep.

Chloe stood in the center of her studio. After her nap, she'd put the credit cards and new ID Cillian had given her into the jewelry box in her closet. Then she'd changed out of her black cashmere sweater and the white corded skinny jeans in favor of black leggings and one of the oversized shirts she wore when she painted.

She stared at the blank canvas sitting on the easel for a long time. Her mother was right. If she didn't paint, she was letting Cillian take it from her. She couldn't let that happen. So, she took a deep breath and for the first time in nearly five months, lifted her brush and put paint to canvas.

Soon she was lost in the familiar feel of the brush in her hand and the acrid smell of paint. The sound of the brush stroke as it made contact with the canvass was pronounced in the otherwise silent room. Lines and shades took shape, transferring the image in her head onto the canvass. And suddenly, her world opened up again, welcoming her back with open arms and something deep inside of her settled. Calmed.

Chapter 33: Tennis Shoes Make the Best Weapons

Cillian sat in the living room with Chloe on his lap. It was two days after her family left, and it was time to show her the tunnel. Finn would be here as soon as he ensured team two was on duty.

"How are your parents today?"

"Dad went back to work this morning. Mom says he doesn't think anyone can run the business without him."

"I can see that. He's an ex-soldier. He's used to being in charge."

"True, but moms in charge at home." Chloe laughed. "I didn't keep her on the phone long. She had a lot of errands to run."

Chloe assessed Cillian carefully. Small talk was not his thing. "Is something wrong?"

"No. I just have something to show you."

"What?"

"Let's wait for Finn."

"Finn? What's going on?" She turned her head when someone knocked on the door.

Cillian lifted her off of him and let Finn into the suite.

"Ready?" Finn looked from Cillian to Chloe, then back to Cillian.

"Ready for what?" Chloe asked.

Finn gave her a crooked grin. "Your tour of the secret escape tunnel."

"The what?" She giggled at the idea.

"We need to show you the tunnel." Cillian reached for her hand.

"No way! A secret tunnel? Really?" They had to be teasing her.

"Really." Finn confirmed.

"By all means, let's see this tunnel." She thought they were full of crap, but she followed Cillian into the bathroom, then frowned when he opened the closet door.

The narrow closet was a galley style walk in. There were shelves on both side walls stacked with towels, linens, and toiletries. Cillian had her crouch down so she could see under the second to last shelf from the bottom on the left. There was a pad under it and when he put her hand on it, the back wall pushed back and slide open.

"Wow! Now that's cool." She gasped in surprise. Then she smiled. "How very 'James Bond' like."

Cillian chuckled at her reference, then took her hand and led her through the door.

On the other side was a landing about 10 feet by 10 feet. Cillian showed her the lever that made the door slide back into place. As soon as it closed completely, dim lighting lit the space.

On the wall to the right, were several coats hanging on hooks. He'd pointed out two that were her size. One was white with a gray camo pattern; the other was a green camo pattern. Both coats were made of Gore Tex with removable interior liners. There were also two pairs of boots that matched the coats and a small bullet-proof vest.

"Always put the vest on first. Here, let me show you." Cillian helped her into the heavy vest and showed her how to secure it. "Never forget to wear the vest. Now, you select the coat based on the weather." He said, "If it's snowing outside when you go into the tunnel which even though it's been snowing lately, it's very unusual here, you wear the white one. I want you covered in white today. You'll need it when you come out the other end." He held out the coat for her. "Now put this on."

"Ok."

"There're gloves and a ski mask in the pockets of each coat. Use them, no matter how hot it is outside. Do you understand?" Finn added.

"I guess."

"Chloe, this is important. Don't guess." Finn barked at her like he did when they were on the practice field.

"Ok, yes. I understand." Jeez! The idea of a hidden tunnel had been an exciting adventure until Finn's demeanor had turned serious. Then when Cillian pulled down two nine-millimeter Nano's from a shelf above her coats, it got real.

"You'll take these with you. Don't forget the extra clips." Cillian pointed to the extra clips sitting next to the guns, then put the guns back in place on the shelf.

"Is this really necessary?"

"Yes. If you ever have to enter the tunnel, it will be because your life depends on it. If that's the case, you'll need the weapons. No one knows about this tunnel other than Team One, Imogen and now you. Never tell anyone it's here, under any circumstances." Finn added. He'd been protecting Cillian his entire life. Now Chloe was a part of that protection, so she needed to follow his instructions exactly.

"Now you're starting to freak me out." Chloe rubbed her hands up and down her thighs nervously.

"There's no need to freak out. This is just a precaution." Cillian assured.

"You probably won't ever need the tunnel, but it's important for you to know it's here and how to navigate it if something happens." Finn added.

"Something like what?"

Finn sighed heavily in frustration. "Chloe"

"Angel," Cillian interrupted in a soothing voice. He took her trembling hands into his. "Don't be afraid. If there's a security breech or we're attacked, this is your route to safety. But that hasn't happened in over one hundred years. Like I said, we're just taking precautions here."

"Oh. Ok." She bit her lip to keep from asking more questions.

"Now, this is your 'go bag.'" Cillian lifted the backpack from a hook and unzipped it to show her the contents. "It has a first aid kit, two flashlights, extra batteries, a knife, a disposable phone, water bottles and a few granola bars. I also added a pair of jeans and a sweater for you. If you have to escape, I don't want you to delay going into the tunnel for any reason. You can change on the landing, but do it fast. And don't forget to take the bag with you."

"Ok."

"Chloe, don't go into the tunnel by yourself without it."

"Ok, got it."

Cillian and Finn put on the other white coats that had been hanging on hooks on the wall next to hers.

"Alright angel, let's go." Cillian took her hand in his and held a flashlight in the other. He led her off the landing and down the steep stairs. As soon as Finn stepped off the landing behind them, the lights went out.

"What happened?" Chloe clutched Cillian's hand in a death grip.

"The light automatically turns off when you step off the landing. That's why you'll need the flashlight."

"Why does it turn off?" If it weren't for the flashlight, it would be pitch black in here. The walls were already closing in on her, and she felt like she was suffocating. She took several deep breaths.

"Focus Chloe. The light goes off to keep any glimmer of it from shining through cracks in the walls on the other side. You'll also need to be very quiet while you're in the tunnel. We're going to pass rooms that may be occupied and they'll hear you."

"Ok Cillian." She whispered. She tried to focus on her breathing and follow his directions.

"These stairs go down two flights. You'll end up on the second floor. At the bottom of the steps, turn right. The tunnel will slope down as you walk because it's going to take you down under the ground."

"Has there ever been a cave-in?" The thought of being underground was making the feeling of being suffocated worse.

"No angel. We keep it repaired and inspect it every six months."

"I inspect it myself, Chloe." Finn added softly. "You'll be safe." He felt like shit for scaring her. He hadn't realized how this must appear to her.

"Once it slopes you know you're heading in the right direction. It goes on for a little over a mile and a half. You'll come out by the last line of caves on the other side of the apple orchard."

"What happens if I go left instead?" If she was scared enough to come in here alone, would she be able to remember which direction to go?

"It will take you to a locked closet in the basement. But you'll know you've gone the wrong way because the floor won't slope downward."

"Why wouldn't I just go to the basement and hide?"

"Never do that Chloe. Ever." Cillian insisted.

"Chloe, if we're attacked, they're going to search the basement. It's the most likely place to hide. Plus, they'll probably try to set the place on fire. If that happens, you could get caught in there." Finn said. "Always go right."

She started breathing heavier as they descended further down the steps. She wasn't claustrophobic normally, but she was feeling it now.

Cillian squeezed her hand slightly, wanting to comfort her, then changed tactics. His angel always met any challenge head on. "Don't tell me you're afraid of the dark?" He scoffed. "I was four when my father brought me into the tunnel the first time. I wasn't scared at all."

"Shut up Cillian."

"Disrespectful little thing." He squeezed her hand again. "I'm going to spank you for that later."

Chloe was glad it was dark, so Finn wouldn't see her blush. "I didn't say I was scared; you jerk! And I've been in tunnels before. Heck, back home you have to drive through the tunnel in Mobile to get to the beach. I've been through it lots of times."

"Jerk, huh? Your tally is getting higher, baby." He teased.

"Stop it!" She hissed. But it was too late. She could hear Finn chuckling softly behind them.

"This way." Cillian said softly. They'd reached the bottom of the steps, so he guided her to the right. "It was built for men to travel through quickly so there's plenty of headroom."

Chloe felt the floor slope as they progressed through the dark. "Why are we still talking so low?"

"Because we're still inside the castle walls. Remember, we've only gone down two levels. Our suite is on the fourth. This wall," he tapped the wall on his right softly, "is the back wall of powder rooms by the ballroom on the second floor."

"When will I know I'm outside the castle?"

"You'll know. The temperature will change drastically."

Chloe walked with Cillian and Finn down the tunnel. About ten minutes later, she felt the air get much colder, and she knew she was out of the castle. "We're out now." She said out loud to herself.

"Yes, we are." Finn confirmed.

She was glad to have the coat. Out in the sunshine, it was cold, but it not miserably so. Down here in the dark, the cold was bone chilling. They walked at a brisk pace, and it still took about twenty minutes to get to the end.

Cillian shined the flashlight on the wall in front of them. "You see this panel?"

"Yes."

"Put you hand flat on it and hold it there for at least ten seconds."

Chloe removed her glove and did as he instructed. A green light flashed around her hand, then the wall in front of them moved. As soon as the door opened, sunshine bathed the area and a cold wind hit her face. When she moved to step out, Cillian took her arm to stop her.

"Always check before you leave the tunnel. You never want anyone to see you."

She turned and watched him and Finn scope out the area before he nodded slightly.

"You see, the cave directly in front of you about ten yards away? The one with two boulders in front of it?"

Chloe looked to where he was pointing. "Yes."

"Look to the left. Do you see the smaller one? The one with four shorter boulders?" He pointed in that direction.

"Yes, I see it."

"That's your destination. When you come out of the tunnel, there could be enemies crawling all over this place. You'll need to get behind those boulders as fast as possible. Got it?"

"Got it."

Before she could move, the rest of Team One suddenly surrounded her. They'd materialized out of nowhere, all dressed in white to match the snow banks surrounding them. Terrance smiled at Chloe as he slid into the opening, where they remained concealed by the tunnel. "You ready Chloe?"

She looked at all the men surrounding her in confusion. "We're not under attack right now, are we?"

"Would I be smiling if we were?" Terrance asked.

"Knowing you, yes." Chloe rolled her eyes and smiled at the huge man.

Terrance chuckled. "You're probably right, runt."

"Chloe, remember. No one can know about the escape tunnel, not even those you consider friends here on the island. So even though we're just showing you the way, you still have to remain hidden from prying eyes." Cillian reminded.

"I remember." She nodded toward the boulders. "I'm ready."

"Ok, when you get behind the boulders, stay low, but stop and wait for me."

Chloe took a long look around but didn't see anyone through the trees. Once she was sure she wouldn't be seen, she bent low and took off running. She slid around the edge of the boulders and crouched down. She looked at the wall of the cave while she waited on the others, but she didn't see an opening anywhere.

When the men joined her, Cillian pointed to a cluster of small rocks on the ground by the cave wall. He crab-walked over to them and lifted the fourth one on the right, then motioned her over.

She moved like he did, then crouched beside him.

"Put your hand down here."

Chloe looked closer, and sure enough, there was a pad imbedded in the ground, just like the one on the inside of the tunnel door. As soon as she placed her hand on the pad, she heard a scraping noise, but saw nothing.

Cillian covered the security pad with the rock again, then motioned her to the side of the wall. It was then that she realized the wall was another boulder, not the cave itself. It was as tall as the cave, so it was very deceiving. She slipped behind it and that's when she saw the opening.

She following Cillian into the cave and waited for the rest of the men to come inside. When the last one stepped through the door, Cillian took her hand and placed it on the panel in the wall by the door and it closed. As soon as it closed, lights came on and there was a humming sound.

"That's the generator. When the door is closed from the inside, the lights and the generator are activated. You're locked in now. Only those who's prints are programmed in the security system can open the door. You're sealed in and you're safe."

Chloe turned and looked around the large space. It looked like a living room or maybe a man cave. A black leather sectional sofa that looked brand new was in the middle of the room. A dark gray long square coffee table had been placed on a thick light grey rug on the floor in front of it. Beyond the sofa on the right was a small kitchenette with a small refrigerator, a sink, and a little microwave. On the left was a glass enclosed room.

"The bathroom is through that door." Cillian pointed at the door next to the refrigerator.

He took her hand and led her into the glass room that was equipped with computer screens on the back wall, a long desk, and several rolling chairs. He took her hand and pressed it to another pad, and the computers came to life.

"This is the surveillance room. You'll be able to see what's happening outside from here. That can be a blessing and a curse."

"Why?"

"Because, once you're in here, you are not to open the door again under any circumstances."

"What if someone has a gun on you, or Imogen, or even Ian?"

"Doesn't matter. You don't open the door."

"You can't be serious. I won't leave them out there to be killed!"

"Yes, you will. Your job is to survive."

"Cillian!"

"Chloe, once you open the door, they'll more than likely kill them, anyway."

"I don't,"

"Chloe!" He barked. "Your job is to survive."

She glared at him. She'd just see about that.

As November rolled into December, Chloe settled into a routine. Missing Thanksgiving at home had been tough, but at least she'd been able to video chat with her parents. She'd stayed on the call with them for over an hour.

To Cillian's frustration, she still went to the beach and sat on her rock every morning. It was freezing outside, and he didn't like her being out in the cold weather, but she'd insisted. She no longer wrote her message in the sand, but being out there allowed her time away from him to just breathe.

As Christmas approached, the castle buzzed with anticipation. She was helping with the decorations and spending a lot of time in the kitchen baking. Now that she was Cillian's wife, Imogen consulted her on everything. Chloe finally had to tell her to just do things the way she'd always done them, so she could learn how it worked. Who knew decorating a castle could be such an enormous task? It was overwhelming. Between that, training and painting, she was really busy, which aggravated Cillian when he had to search for her.

She spent hours in her studio painting. She escaped every morning after breakfast. She'd visit the beach to clear her head, then close herself up in her studio until Cillian came in each day to bring her down to lunch. On those occasions, when she wasn't at a stopping point, he'd sit and wait until she was. Every time he had to wait; he'd spank her for it, which led to even more pleasurable, naughty things. She found that she craved those moments and often made him wait on purpose.

They'd had sex in practically every room in the castle. And each time, Cillian took her like a man possessed. He was relentless. He'd come out of his office tense and frustrated and reach for her. She knew he was angry that he hadn't been able to find out where the poison she'd ingested came from, and he took out that frustration on her body. He was solely focused on bringing her so much pleasure it left her weak and trembling.

Cillian also practiced his rope art on her all the time. She'd been tied up in so many positions, but what he called the butterfly was her favorite. The feel of his ropes sliding across her skin and his hands moving over her gently gave her the strangest sense of being cherished. His intense need to control her, to dominate her, was incredibly wicked and so damn hot she'd burn with need. He was taking her over, molding her into someone she didn't recognize, and she was helpless to resist him.

She hated to admit she was as addicted to him as he was to her. She craved his touch and couldn't wait for him to emerge from his office, anticipation strumming through her veins along with the fiery heat of arousal.

Cillian read the report again before passing it off to Finn. Titan waited patiently on the line for them to review the information he'd just sent over. When Finn finished reading, he tossed the document onto the desk.

"I'll pull in the team."

"Be ready to leave in an hour." Oden Aliachbar had been spotted in Paris visiting his lover. He was gay, but he kept his sexuality and his relationship a secret from Omar. Titan had discovered the lover during his investigation and they'd staked out his home. Oden had been spotted slipping in the back door twenty minutes ago. Finally. Tonight, he'd settle the fucking score.

"You're going with us?"

"We'll take Micha, Zane and Drew. The rest of the team stays on Chloe."

"Cousin, let me take care of it."

Cillian ignored the concerned look in Finn's eyes and got to his feet. "One hour." He left Finn and Titan to handle the details and went to find Chloe. Anticipation sizzled through him; his cock rock hard with it. It was always like this before a mission.

He found her on a ladder in the main foyer, hanging garland. His anger at seeing her on that ladder only added to the intense sensations coursing through his blood. Heads would roll when he found out who'd let her climb the fucking thing. He came up behind her, reached over his head and plucked her off of it, and flipped her over his shoulder.

"Hey!" Chloe screeched when she was suddenly lifted into the air. Then she found herself thrown over Cillian's shoulder. She hung upside down as he made his way to the elevator. "Put me down!"

He swatted her ass, hard. "Quiet."

"Ouch! What do you think you're doing?" She grabbed handfuls of his shirt and used it as leverage to lift herself up enough to see if anyone was watching them. She had to blow hard to get her hair out of her face so she could see.

"I said be quiet." He smacked her ass again, harder this time.

In retaliation, she reached back and pulled his hair.

"Keep it up angel and you won't be able to sit for a week." Cillian stormed into the elevator, scanned his print, then jabbed at the button that would take them to their floor. "Do you want to tell me why you were standing on a fuckin' ladder nearly ten feet off the ground?"

"I would've thought that was obvious." She knew her snarky response would drive him on.

"We have staff for that."

"I can do it just as well as they can."

"No, you can't. My wife is not climbing a ladder when I pay a fuckin' army to take care of shit around here."

Anticipation pulsed through her. He was angry, seething with it. He'd never hurt her, but he'd take out that aggression on her. She pulled his hair again, egging him on. "I'll climb it if I want to."

"Try it." His menacing voice was harsh in the otherwise silent elevator. "Whoever brings you another ladder or is in the vicinity when you climb one will be fired." He flipped her up and back against the wall in the small space. His hand fisting in her hair, pulling her mouth to his.

She instinctively wrapped her legs around his trim waist, her hands sliding up his massive chest to circle his neck. When he came up for air, she bit his lip.

"Fuck!" He ground his thick cock against her center. "Oh baby, you'll pay for that."

When the elevator door opened, Cillian marched across the foyer and stepped through the door of their suite. He kicked it shut behind them so hard it was a wonder it didn't splinter. He didn't stop until he was in the bedroom, where he tossed her on the bed.

"Strip." He barked as his hands went to work on his belt.

"Cillian." She warned.

"Chloe fuckin strip. Now! Or I'll rip those clothes to shreds." He yanked his shirt off over his head, then started pushing his jeans down his thighs.

She jerked her sweater over her head, then slipped her thumbs into the band of her leggings. She caught her panties and slid them both down and off. Scorching heat flooded her veins as she watched him undress. He was so beautiful she got distracted for a moment. But when he lifted his foot to step out of his jeans, she reacted. She flipped over onto the other side of the bed and took off running.

"Fuck!" Her running triggered his hunting instincts every time. He lunged across the room, and caught her around the waist. He jerked her up and around so her back hit the wall. The need to control her, to make her submit firing his blood.

Chloe immediately wrapped her legs around his waist and canted her hips. Her hands gripped fistfuls of his hair and pulled him to her breast. She was on fire. This heated insanity nearly driving her insane.

"Fuck baby! Be ready. Please be ready for me." He sucked her breast deep into his mouth, pulling hard on her delicate flesh.

"I am"!

He couldn't wait a second longer. When the head of his cock met her slick center, he gloried in her response to him and surged deep.

When Cillian slammed into her, going all the way to the hilt in one motion, she screamed and nearly came.

"Good girl. Such a good girl." He breathed against her breast as he pulled almost all the way out, then violently thrust again. "Lock those pretty legs tight, baby."

Chloe did as she was told and locked her ankles at his lower back. He was so hot and hard inside her. In this position, he could go higher, bumping against her cervix. Each time he pulled back, he hit the spot deep inside her that sent her soaring.

"This pussy is so good." With one hand cupping her ass and the other fisting her hair, he hammered into her.

Chloe flexed her hips and met his brutal thrusts, matching his intensity. Lightening raced through her, zapping at never endings, firing her senses. Heat ignited in her core. Her body took over; her hips flexing, her back arching, pushing into his thrust as she came hard, screaming his name.

"Yea, that's it, baby. Come for me." His harsh, sinful words tempting her, urging her on. He surged deep and held, letting her lock down on him and ride out her orgasm. "You're so fuckin beautiful takin my cock."

Chloe leaned in and bit his chest hard, then sucked the skin deep into her mouth, marking him as her orgasm rolled through her.

Her bite triggered his own orgasm. He squeezed her tightly and pumped deep, over and over as he flew apart and emptied into her. When the last pulsing wave subsided, he rested his head on the wall above hers.

"Chloe, baby." He groaned. "Are you alright? Did I hurt you?" He was afraid the adrenalin spike had clouded his judgement. He tried to temper his aggression where she was concerned, but it never worked.

Chloe was limp in his arms, her head nestled against his chest as he held her. His hands suddenly gentling on her skin.

"I'm fine." She felt like a wet noodle, but she wasn't hurt. She wiggled for him to let her down when his cock slipped from her.

Instead of releasing her, Cillian carried her into the bathroom and placed her on the counter. He wet a cloth with warm water and held it between her legs to sooth her before cleaning her thoroughly then himself.

He tossed the cloth into the hamper, then helped her down from the counter. "I'm leaving for a few days."

"When?"

"As soon as the plane is ready."

"Where are you going?" She knew he wouldn't answer, but she couldn't stop herself from asking. The last time he left, he'd been shot.

He gave her a deadpanned look, then turned and headed toward the closet.

Chloe hurried after him. "The last time you left, you came back with a bullet hole in your side."

Cillian turned back toward her at her furious tone. "Chloe,"

She cut him off by jabbing her finger in his chest and yelled, "don't let that shit happen again!" Then she stomped past him to her own closet to get dressed.

Cillian dressed quickly in black cargo pants and a black T-shirt. He put on his boots, then threw a few days' worth of clothes into his go bag. He always kept toiletries in the bag, so he left it on the floor and stepped into the doorway of Chloe's closet.

He leaned against the doorframe and watched her as she yanked a sweater over her head. It was obvious she was pissed off. "I don't intend to get shot again."

She put her hands on her hips and scowled at him. "So, you're saying you intended to get shot the last time?"

Yep, his little angel was furious. His lip twitched, and he tried hard not to smile in satisfaction. "You're working up to a serious spanking."

"So, what!? You're not going to be here to give it to me!" She yelled.

Yep, seriously pissed. "I'm keeping track." He smirked and walked toward her. "We'll settle up when I get back." Before she could respond, he lifted her up and kissed the fuck out of her. When he had his fill, he dropped her back onto her feet and turned to leave.

"Jerk!" Chloe yelled and threw a tennis shoe at him.

When the shoe hit his back, he glanced over his shoulder and laughed. "Keep it up baby. I can't wait to settle your debt on that gorgeous ass." Then he walked out.

Cillian watched as Oden Alliachbar, right-hand man to a known terrorist, the man who'd tried to kill him, screamed in fury. He was covered in tiny precise cuts from the top of his head to the bottom of his feet. Not an inch had been missed. He'd stoically endured each cut to his body with no reaction, refusing to engage. He hadn't started screaming until they'd moved on to his lover. Paul Fisher hung naked from chains beside him, bleeding and unconscious.

A pulley system suspended both men two feet off the ground with their hands bound by chains above their heads. The chains on their ankles passed through rings embedded in the floor and connected to a pulley system. There was enough slack for both men to lift their legs parallel to their body. Oden had tried to use that slack to his advantage, but it hadn't worked. Each time he tried to kick out, Cillian jerked on the chain attached to the pulley that would yank his feet down and his arms up.

They'd caught the lovers sleeping peacefully in bed together two nights ago. Upon waking, Oden had immediately reached for the gun that was no longer under his pillow. When he opened his mouth on a curse, Cillian had shoved the barrel of his nine-millimeter to the back of his throat. Once he had his attention, things had gone smoothly from there.

Finn had injected them both with a sedative that knocked them out within seconds. Then the team had made quick work of binding their hands and feet and carrying them out. The drive to the club on the outskirts of Paris at three in the morning had been quick. During the flight over, Cillian had reached out to one of his contacts here in the city to secure the place. The nightclub upstairs had closed an hour before they'd arrived, and the basement was a perfect place for the interrogation to come. His contact used the soundproof room regularly for just this purpose.

Cillian sighed heavily. "Now let's start again, shall we?" He leaned forward in the chair he was straddling and rested his elbows on his knees.

The steel chain dangling from his fingers. "How did you know about the meeting?"

There was no compassion in him for this man. Oden helped Omar Abdul terrorize his own people. They'd detonated bombs in populated cities, killing hundreds for no other reason than to keep attention off of their seedier activities. They were heavy into trafficking; kidnapping girls as young as eight years old. Taking them to training camps in the desert to be conditioned through pain and degradation, then selling them to the highest bidder. Paul Fisher was one of the negotiators they used for those transactions. Oden was a disgusting piece of shit, as was his lover. The world would be a much better place without them.

Oden glared at his enemy with hatred in his eyes. He was just thankful that Paul had finally passed out. Hearing his love scream in pain was almost more than he could bear. He could tolerate the cuts and having his nails ripped away. Even loosing fingers and toes. The freezing cold from hanging there for so many hours was child's play. He'd been trained to withstand torture from his father's own hand. This was nothing to him. But Paul was a different story. Paul had not been trained to withstand this kind of treatment. Paul with his beautiful skin and delicate body. He would not last much longer.

"What? Nothing to say?" When Oden still didn't reply, Cillian nodded at Finn to proceed. "Let's see if we can change your mind." They'd been working these two over for nearly forty-eight hours and Oden hadn't broken. Not once. It was time to step up the game.

Using heavy steel mesh gloves, Zane and Drew each grabbed and held Oden's legs out wide. He struggled violently in their hold as Finn approached. Finn hummed to himself while he wrapped razor wire tightly around the tops of Oden's bare thighs, securing it just below his knees. All while Oden cursed and struggled. After Finn clipped the last piece of wire in place, Zane and Drew let go of his legs and Cillian yanked on the chain, forcing his legs down.

"Fuck!" Oden screamed as the wire sliced deep into his balls. He immediately jerked his legs apart to keep the wire from further slicing into his tender flesh. But as he moved, his muscles flexed and the wire cut deep into every inch it covered. The excruciating pain from the cuts caused him to drop his legs, which resulted in more slices to his balls. He screamed in agony at every move as he forced his legs apart.

Finn lifted a wooden baseball bat, tossing it back and forth from one hand to the other while he waited. He'd drilled a hole through the center of the barrel and poured melted steel into it for added weight. It was one of his favorite toys.

"Oden?" Cillian called in his soft Irish brogue as he handed the chain to Zane. "How did you find out about the meeting?"

Oden refused to answer while he eyed the man called Finn as he tossed the bat. The muscles in his legs ached from holding them out, and the wire was cutting deeper into his skin. The blood making it slick so that it shifted, finding new areas to slice.

Cillian shook his head. "So, the hard way, then?" He nodded at Finn and released the demon. "Batter up."

Finn smiled in anticipation then stepped in front of Oden. He cocked the bat back, then swung with all his might, striking him in the stomach. As ribs broke and he lost his breath, Oden instinctively brought his knees up on impact, curling into a ball, then shrieked as the razor wire sliced into his balls and his cock. He immediately vomited what little contents were left in his stomach.

Zane jerked the slack from the chains attached to his ankles, yanking his legs down, causing more slices, but opening him up for another blow. Finn delivered the second blow with equal power and Zane instantly release the chain. Their timing perfect. Oden's ear-piercing screams echoed off the walls as his body curled in on itself again.

Zane didn't give him time to catch his breath or to stop screaming. He quickly yanked his legs down again and Finn delivered the third blow and watched dispassionately as the involuntary reaction happened again and he curled up, slicing the lower half of his body to shreds.

Oden's screams stirred Paul to consciousness. He groaned weakly and turned his head as much as his arms would allow toward his lover. When he saw Oden's mutilated body, the thick jagged cuts sliced deep into his cock, his balls nearly severed, he shrieked!

Cillian casually lifted his hand to signal Finn to stop. He waited patiently while Oden's agonized screams turned to moans, and Paul stopped shrieking before he spoke again. "Oden, you were going to tell me how you knew about the meeting?"

Oden's gasps of pain shook his body so hard the slick razor wire shifted constantly, continuing to cut deep. He tried desperately to speak, anything to make it stop. Never in his life had he experienced such agony. He'd heard rumors whispered in back rooms about Cillian O'Donnell. He just hadn't believed them.

"Oden, one more swing of that bat and your balls are going to detach and fall to the floor." He nodded at Finn, who lifted the bat again. "I believe it's in your best interest to answer my question."

"A woman." He rasped in a shredded voice before Finn could swing. He hoped these men would kill him now. He preferred death to this. His father had not prepared him for this.

"What woman?"

"Please! I do not know her name." He hissed through clenched teeth.

"You expect me to believe that?"

"I swear! I do not know!" He cried out earnestly. "She only speaks with Omar. He refuses to say who she is."

"Then how do you know it's a woman?"

"Please!" He gasped. He never imagined there would be a time in his life when he would pray for death. "I heard her voice when they were on the phone! They were on the speaker."

"It is a woman!" Paul gasped out in a painful plea. "We both heard her voice."

"Tell me about her voice. Is she Middle Eastern, British, Asian, American? What does she sound like?"

"She is Irish." Oden's shaky voice replied. "One of yours." Tears fell as he waited for death.

Cillian willed himself not to look toward Finn. Not to display his rage. "How do you know she's one of mine?"

"There were too many details for her not to be."

"How does she contact Omar?"

"She calls his private cell phone. No one has that number, but somehow, she does." This had to end soon. He prayed to Allah that they would not leave him here to bleed out.

"How did they meet?" The demon in him raised its head.

"He knows her family!" Oden gasped desperately. Death needed to come soon. Hell had to be better than this.

"Who are they?"

"I do not know, I tell you! I do not know!" He tasted blood in his mouth. It hurt to breathe, so he was sure his internal injuries were severe.

Finn raised the bat again.

"Please! I do not! They are connected to the business, but there are so many there is no way to know."

"Do they meet in person?"

"She has never come to the dessert. They only speak by phone. They were discussing an acquisition when I heard her voice."

"What kind of acquisition?"

"I do not know. I only heard parts of the conversation. She has something of value to sell. A treasure Omar wants!"

"What else can you tell me?"

"I've told you all I know. Please! There is nothing else."

Cillian looked over at Finn. Along with the fury burning in his belly, his neck itched like a bitch. "We're done here." He nodded once, then pulled his gun from its holster and shot Oden in the head. Finn simultaneously did the same to Paul.

He pulled the burner phone from his back pocket. He dialed the number quickly with fingers that shook with rage. "Patrick," he barked when the man answered. "No one goes into the family wing other than the members of Team One and Imogen."

"Boss?"

"No one, not even the fucking maid. Understood?" His instincts were screaming at him.

"Got it. Rourke and Terrance are on duty right now. I'll let them know."

"We'll be back in a few hours."

Cillian slid into bed and pulled Chloe against him. Having his arms around her, his hands touching her, helped to sooth the furious beast raging inside him. It had taken longer than it should've to clean up after the interrogation. Either that, or he was just overly eager to get back to her. But, to add to his frustration, when her body came into contact with his, she was wearing a T-shirt and panties. He'd intended to roll her under him and thrust deep into her tight little pussy, but now he'd have to undress her first. He fuckin hated that shit. He wanted her naked and ready for him.

"You're back." Chloe whispered in the dark as she came awake to Cillian's familiar hands sliding over her skin under her T-shirt.

"Hmph." He grunted and pulled the shirt over her head. He didn't want to talk. He wanted to fuck. His cock ached to be buried inside her. Unwilling to wait any longer, he abruptly sucked her breast deep into his mouth. He lashed at her nipple with rapid flicks of his tongue as he slid his hand down the center of her body and straight into her panties. He pushed two thick fingers into her and settled his thumb over her clit in a quick, sensual assault.

"Jeezus!" Her back arched, pushing her breast further into the heat of his mouth as fiery sparks of arousal assaulted her. She reached down and grasped his thick forearm to halt his movement so she could catch her breath.

"Don't." He barked viciously into the darkness against her nipple then immediately sucked it back into his mouth as he ruthlessly shook her hand off and thrust his fingers deep again. "Spread your legs." He commanded in a harsh voice against her breast. His other hand moved to rip her panties away.

"Wait!" she gasped. But there was no waiting. He didn't even pause before ripping the delicate lace away. As soon as it was gone, he shoved her knees wide and settled between her thighs.

When the head of his cock slid against her slick opening, Cillian groaned. He was both pleased and relieved that she was already wet for him. If she hadn't been, he wasn't sure he would've cared. He needed this too much. After the past few days, he needed her. It was his only thought as he plunged to the hilt. Her tight, wet heat surrounding his cock felt like coming home.

"Oh my God!" She gasped at the sudden intrusion, her fingernails digging into his back.

He pulled back and thrust deep again, powering into her. His dominance and aggression igniting the fire that always blazed out of control when he took her like this.

It was wild, frantic. Her nails clawed his back, her hands buried in his hair, his in hers. They came together in a violent explosion. He was insatiable, taking her up fast, shoving her brutally over the edge. Her orgasm sent her flying apart so quickly she cried out at the intensity of it. She clamped down on him as she came, her tight heat strangling his cock. And she felt him explode deep inside her. He groaned against her shoulder as thick jets of his release bathed her womb.

But Cillian didn't stop. He couldn't. This, this was what he needed. He continued to thrust into her even after his own orgasm, his cock never losing its hardened strength.

He needed more, so much more. He cupped the back of her head in one hand and her ass in the other, holding her to him as he plunged deep and set a brutal pace. Her luscious ass fitting perfectly in his palm. His fingers slid into the slick crevice between her cheeks; slick from their combined releases. He rubbed persistently against the forbidden little rosette until it relaxed for him. Then, pushing inside, he buried his finger deep and used his cock like a weapon, thrusting repeatedly against the sensitive bundle of nerves in her hot little pussy. And yea! Fuck yea! His angel screamed and exploded again for him. Gripping his ass tightly, her feet planted on the bed, she shoved up against him, taking his thrusts.

His hand left her head and reached for the headboard. He used it for leverage and thrust up high into her, letting her ride him. His eyes blazing as he watched her work his cock. He felt the walls of her pussy ripple and clutch at him. Then his beautiful girl surged up and bite his chest, clamping down with her teeth as her pussy clamped down on his cock. It was glorious; it was amazing. His balls tightened, his cock swelled further, but it still wasn't enough. She had to know she was his.

She came down the other side, breathless and spent beneath him. "Again!" He commanded and captured her sensitive nipple between his teeth, licking the tip with hard strikes of his tongue, needing her to fly again. Aching for her to stay with him.

Exhausted, Chloe arched into the relentless sensation on her oversensitive nipple. She clutched his head to her breast, where he continued to suckle strongly. She knew she'd wear his marks for days. But he'd never been like this before. Almost rabid. Oh, he was always rough and aggressive. His dominant nature wouldn't have it any other way. But he wasn't talking to her like he usually did. He wasn't whispering wicked things in her ear, enticing her with naughty suggestions. Cillian wouldn't hurt her; she knew that now. But this was different, as if he were someone else. As if that frightening part of him, the one she'd only ever seen glimpses of was in control now. Whatever happened during his trip must've been terrible.

She needed to bring him back somehow. So, Chloe did the only thing she could think of in the heat of the moment to soothe him. She locked her ankles at his lower back, opening herself completely to his thrusts. She grabbed his face and lifted it away from her breast. His fierce, menacing gaze pierced hers in the moonlight. Daring her to defy him. Before he could lower his head again, she gently smoothed her hands over the scruff on his face and smiled at him. Then she slowly brought his mouth down to hers and she kissed him.

She gave herself over to the kiss, nipping and suckling gently at his mouth. He tried to take over, his tongue thrusting deep, but she didn't follow. Instead, she set a soft course to lead him where she wanted him to go. She continued to hold his cheek in one hand as she ran her other palm gently down his broad chest, over his tight flexing abs and around to his hip where she griped him to her. She tilted her hips and met his thrusts, matching his rhythm. Then, pushing back against him softly, holding him closer each time, she gradually, slowly, guided him to a calmer pace.

When she finally had his attention, she released his mouth and met his fierce gaze head on. "Come back to me." She whispered softly, breathlessly. Then she leaned up, wrapping her arms around him, holding him tightly to her, and placed a gentle kiss on that sensitive spot where his neck and shoulder met.

"Baby," he groaned helplessly. His angel with her beautiful blue eyes shining in the moonlight. She was so fearless as she held his gaze, but so gentle. Her tender caresses, her soft kisses. He hadn't known that was what he'd needed. What he'd craved. And it was more than enough.

Chloe's internal clock woke her early the next morning. She turned slightly to get a look at Cillian in the predawn glow streaming in through the windows. He was still sound asleep, which was unusual for him at this hour. His arm was wrapped around her waist and his leg was thrown over hers, with his face buried in her hair.

She could see dark smudges under his thick lashes, indicating he hadn't had much sleep in the last few days. There was no damage to his gorgeous face that she could see. And from the strength he'd exhibited last night, she was pretty sure he didn't have any fresh injuries, but she'd have to check that out later. Her stomach was turning again.

She had a touch of the stomach flu the last few days. It wasn't anything serious, just sniffles and a sore throat, but she'd never run a fever. The nausea came and went at different times throughout the day, but she'd only vomited a few times.

Since being poisoned, everyone overacted when it came to her health, so she hadn't mentioned it. The last thing she needed was for them to freak out and start coddling her. Or to have Imogen following her around, watching her every move. There was too much to do.

Tomorrow was Christmas Eve, and everyone was hustling to finish up last-minute preparations. She was too. And as long as she didn't eat anything too heavy and drank warm tea, she was fine. She'd told a little white lie to Imogen, saying she wanted the hot tea because of the cold weather. But really, it soothed her throat. She was exhausted too, but she'd been spending long hours in her studio working on a project. She was trying to get it finished in time for Christmas.

She eased out of Cillian's hold and slipped from the bed. Treading lightly, but quickly, she made her way to the bathroom just in time. It would've been awful to vomit on the floor.

She was brushing her teeth when he walked into the room and came to stand behind her. He obviously hadn't shaved in days because he had a beard and his hair was sticking up all over his head. She was sure that was from her hands the night before. He looked like a rumpled mess. She met his gaze in the mirror and grinned around her toothbrush.

Cillian smiled back and slid his arm around her waist, pulling her back against him. "Good morning angel." He kissed the top of her head, then moved to his own sink.

"Good morning. You look like crap." She giggled, then rinsed her mouth. It was weird to be so happy that he was back.

"You look beautiful." He countered.

When Chloe finished brushing her teeth, she leaned against the counter and watched while he shaved. "No bullet holes this time?"

"Not this time." His gaze slid over her, taking in the sight of the marks he'd left on her the night before.

"Good." She nodded her head in approval, then turned to leave.

"Where are you going?" He asked into the mirror while he watched her gorgeous ass walk away.

She didn't turn around, but answered over her shoulder. "I don't want to be late for my run. I have a lot to do today."

"Wait for me."

"You don't have to come with me." He still looked tired to her.

"Chloe." His sharp voice made her pause and look back at him. "You're running with the team this morning."

She signed heavily. Not this again. So much for a peaceful start to her day. "Alright."

She walked out the door and headed straight for the kitchen. She only had a few minutes to spare while he finished shaving. She hurried to the counter and grabbed a handful of the crackers she'd been keeping there. She ate them slowly while she got dressed, hoping they would settle her stomach.

Cillian tied his running shoes while he stared at the Christmas tree in the corner. He'd noticed the colorful lights twinkling in the dark last night, but hadn't thought much about it. Getting to Chloe had been his singular focus. Now that he had time to look, he was pleased to see it. There hadn't been a Christmas tree in this suite since the Christmas before his parents died.

He was just wondering if it had been Chloe's idea or Imogen's when Chloe walked in. He assessed her outfit, trying to decide if she was going to be warm enough. "You should probably where a heavier jacket. It snowed last night, and the temperature dropped again."

"This is fine." She tossed her wool cap onto the table and selected a banana. "This jacket is fleece lined and so are the running pants. Anything heavier will be too hot once we get moving. I'm practically sweating now." She peeled the banana and took a slow bite. Bananas seemed to help with the nausea too, but only if she ate it slowly.

Cillian picked up her wool cap and took her free hand. "Alright, let's go."

Chloe looked around in surprise at all the men standing outside their door when Cillian opened it. Finn, Patrick, Drew and Jacob were all waiting, dressed in running clothes, with their guns as usual, strapped to their chests.

"Hey guys." She was glad to see that they didn't have any apparent injuries, either.

"Hey runt. You ready to run?" Finn asked.

"Yep." They all surrounded her as they stepped onto the elevator.

346

When they reached the back patio, every member of the team was there, except for Rourke and Terrance. She looked up at Cillian and waited until he met her gaze. "What's wrong?"

The men shifted uncomfortably. But Cillian simply met her question with a silent, emotionless expression.

She put her hands on her hips and waited. He wouldn't lie to her. Instead, he just simply didn't answer. She hated it when he did that.

"Do you want to run or not?" His voice was a whip of disapproval.

She waited; nope, he wasn't going to say a damned thing. "Yes."

Chloe was used to running with the men surrounding her, but not practically the entire team. So, it took longer today than it should've to get in the zone. But by the first mile, she could turn her focus away from them. Heading into the second mile, adrenalin heated her muscles and her endorphins kicked in. The cold wind on her face was exhilarating, and exactly what she needed to clear away the exhaustion. She ran faster, her arms and legs pumping into a familiar rhythm as she flew over the grassy terrain.

Imogen was waiting for them with cold water when they returned. She'd obviously known the entire team was going to be there because she had glasses for them all. Chloe took her glass with her and left to go shower. When she reached the elevator, Cillian's thick muscular arm reach around her to hit the button before she could. Surprised, she turned to find all the men behind her.

"What are y'all doing?" This was ridiculous. She was just going upstairs to shower.

"What's your hurry angel?"

"I'm starving and I have a ton of work to finish in my studio."

Cillian smiled at her snippy tone. "We're all pretty hungry too."

Thankfully, the elevator wasn't big enough for all of them, but more than half the men piled in. When it stopped at their floor, Cillian caught her arm and held her in place before she could step out.

Finn stepped around her, and he and Drew both entered the suite alone while they waited outside.

Chloe eyed Cillian accusingly, but remained silent. As soon as Finn and Drew came back out and held the door for them, she stomped inside. She went straight to the shower and abruptly flipped it on. She ignored Cillian and undressed while the water heated.

When she moved to step into the warm shower, he caught her arm. She yanked out of his hold and stepped under the spray.

Cillian crowded her against the shower wall. "Angel, you're going to get that spanking you've been steadily working up to." He smoothed his palms over her ass, then swatted it sharply.

She glared at the jerk. "Is there a new threat? Is someone else trying to kill me?"

When his teasing expression turned serious and he didn't answer her question, she had enough. She stomped her foot in frustration. "Tell me!"

"Angel." He warned.

"Cillian, tell me."

Using his chest, he pushed her further back against the wall. He shoved his hand into her hair, fisting a handful of it to pull her face toward his as he leaned in. His expression turned ominous. "You do not give the orders here."

His menacing voice sent a shiver down her spine. But she didn't care. She scowled up at him and slapped her hands on his chest to push him back. "Stop doing that!" She snapped. "Stop trying to intimidate me, Cillian. How am I supposed to protect myself if I don't even know what or where the threat is coming from?"

"You're not. The team will protect you. I'll protect you."

"I don't doubt that. But what if the unexpected happens? I need to know what's going on so I can be prepared. I'm not some delicate flower. I can handle it. Besides, what the heck have y'all been training me for over the last seven months?"

Her little show of defiance was hot as hell. No woman had ever stood up to him the way she did. But he did not explain himself to anyone. Ever. When he gave an order, it was fucking followed. No questions asked. But shit! She was right. And he fuckin hated it. The filth that he waded through was never supposed to touch her.

He captured her hand at his chest and held it there as he slid his other from her hair and around to cradle her throat with his palm. He lifted her chin further with his thumb. His tiny little wife was so brave, glaring up at him while she stood her ground. Not a delicate flower? His ass. That described her perfectly. Only add a spine of steel to go along with it. He fought a smile as he brought his mouth to hers and whispered against her lips. "Alright."

"Alright?"

"Yes, alright, we'll talk at breakfast." Then he kissed her.

Chapter 35: Cry at Christmas

Cillian massaged Chloe's scalp as she dozed on his chest. Her hair was soft as silk between his fingers. She was draped across him, with her legs straddling his hips. His softened cock had slipped from her wet heat only moments ago.

Earlier, he'd thought he was having the most erotic dream he'd ever had. His little angel was kneeling between his thighs, sucking his cock deep into her throat. His hand was fisted in her hair as he guided her, urging her on. He'd woken abruptly at the need to come and had been captured by blue eyes glittering with excitement as she watched him while she worked his cock.

As soon as she'd realized he was awake, she'd crawled up his body and straddled him. Bringing the head of his cock to her slick entrance, she'd plunged down. Watching her ride him had been a beautiful site.

Chloe had never initiated sex before. Not once in nearly eight months. So, he'd tried hard not to take over. To let her take the lead. But it simply wasn't in his nature. All too quickly, watching her fuck him had him so desperate, he'd lifted to her. With one hand behind her neck, the other at her hip, he'd captured her nipple with his teeth and thrust up hard and took control.

She'd hugged him close, holding him at her breast, and followed him. Working her hips in sync with his, catching his rhythm and plunging down on his thrusts. They'd come together in a whirlwind of pleasure. It had been fast, desperate; an insatiable hunger that was quenched in what felt like mere seconds.

And now; now she was sleeping. Breathing softly against his chest. He'd pulled the blanket back up over them to keep her warm, and she'd snuggled into him like a little kitten and fallen back to sleep.

As he lay there, staring up at the ceiling, his thoughts centered on her. He'd never met a woman like Chloe before. She didn't seem to care about what he could give her. Nor did she try to play head games with him. Of course, initially she'd had no idea who he was or the power she'd have as his wife. But he didn't think it would've made a difference. It was telling that she hadn't even touched the outrageously expensive jewelry in the case in her closet.

He looked down and smiled at her blonde head when she shifted in her sleep, rubbing against his chest and grumbling something inarticulate. He smiled. He'd been doing that a lot since meeting her.

He'd been so tired of the conniving games women played in an effort to secure their place at his side. So, for nearly a year, he'd avoided them. But the instant he'd seen Chloe standing in that gallery, such a contradiction of sweet innocence and self-assured confidence had sealed her fate. She was tiny, delicate, but also strong and confident as she stood her ground and went head-to-head with him. He'd been incapable of resisting her.

She was settling into her new role perfectly. And she was painting again. It soothed him that she was back in her studio. She was also baking in the kitchen with Imogen and Ian. He'd walked in on them yesterday and had stepped into a flour battle between her and Ian. They were both covered in white from head to toe and giggling hysterically. Imogen couldn't stop laughing while she tried to corral them. Terrance and Rourke had been standing in the corner trying to dodge the white cloud.

She also continued to visit Storm. Coaxing him to her with treats. He was going to have to do something about that horse. He had a feeling she was working her way up to riding him, and there was no way he was going to let that happen. That damned horse was a devil to everyone but her. He smiled again in the early dawn. His angel had a way of charming devils.

Yesterday at breakfast, she'd listened carefully when he and Finn updated her on what they'd learned about the possible threat. When they'd finished explaining all they knew, she'd taken a deep breath, looked at him and she'd thanked him for telling her. Afterward, she'd been quiet for about ten minutes, as if contemplating her fate. Then she'd quietly asked what they wanted her to do. She'd been shaken, but she told them she trusted them to handle it.

Chloe woke up, with her face planted in Cillian's chest. She wiped the sleep from her eyes and looked up to see if he was awake. "What are you smiling at?"

"Good morning angel."

"Merry Christmas Cillian." She reached up and rubbed the scruff on his chin.

His smile got bigger. "Merry Christmas."

She started squirming to get out from under the blanket he'd secured around them. "Where are you going?"

"Let me up. I'm starving. And, I want to give you your present."

"You got me a present?"

"Of course. It's Christmas." She looked at him like he was being silly.

Cillian released her and let her climb out of bed. He grinned while he watched as she suddenly raced to the bathroom. He waited until he heard the water running, then followed her.

Chloe popped the last bite of her second helping of spinach and mushroom quiche into her mouth. Delicious! Because it was Christmas morning, they were having a quiet breakfast in their suite. Imogen left the food on the table for them and went to spend her morning with Ian.

Cillian waited for her to finish before taking her hand and guiding her to the Christmas tree. He threw a blanket and some cushions on the floor. "Sit here, I'll get your presents."

"But I want to give you yours."

"Ladies first." He was already digging through the gifts he'd purchased for her. He pulled out the first of many and handed it to her.

The heavy box was wrapped in red foil paper with a white bow. Chloe unwrapped it carefully. She gasped when she pulled the last of the paper off. "A laptop?" She looked down at the image on the box depicting the newest model, then back up at him and repeated. "You got me a laptop?" She couldn't hide her excitement as the grin spread across her face.

"You'll need it for this." He handed her a large white envelope with a red bow taped to the front.

Her forehead crinkled. "What's this?"

"Just open it."

Confused, she opened it and pulled out the document inside. When she saw the letterhead from her art school, her breath caught in her throat. After she read the first line of the letter, re-instating her for the new semester, she gasped. Slowly, she looked back up at him. "You did this? How?"

"Do you like it?"

"Yes! Oh my God, yes!" She jumped up and launched herself into his arms.

He laughed at her reaction as he caught her. "Your schedule is in there, too. The semester starts after the first of the year. You'll attend via the video courses they've created for you."

Chloe pulled back and stared at him for a moment, still in shock. "Thank you, Cillian."

"You're welcome angel."

"I never thought." her voice caught.

"I told you, I didn't steel your future, I just changed it. You worked hard to get accepted into the Master's program at that school, there's no way you're not going to finished."

"Cillian O'Donnell, you're going to make me cry at Christmas!" She yelled and laughed at the same time while she wiped at the stupid tears on her face.

"That wasn't my intention." He chuckled. "Why don't you give me my present instead?"

Chloe smiled through her sniffles. "Alright, but remember, it's ok if you don't like it." She wiggled for him to put her down. Then she carefully pulled out the wrapped gift she'd leaned against the wall yesterday.

Just as carefully, he took it from her and met her excited gaze. "I'm sure I'll like it." Then he began to slowly peel the paper back.

She was bouncing on her toes with excitement while she waited. He was taking way too long.

When the last of the paper was torn away, Cillian turned the canvass in his hand around to see the front. Then he stared at it in silence for a long time.

As the silence stretched, so did her anxiety. "I can paint something else for you if you'd prefer."

Cillian stared at the beautiful painting of his family home. She'd recreated the image of the sun setting behind the castle. The white washed stones meticulously depicted in shades of sandstone, beige and grey, shadowed corners darkened from the sun's disappearance behind the mountain. She'd even included the deep blue waves rippling among the turquoise and lighter blues as they crashed on the sandy shore, sending up the spray it caused in bubbles of silver and white.

His favorite part was the waves crashing around the jetty of rocks where she sat looking out at the ocean. Her white blonde hair was blowing in the breeze. She was smiling, stretching her foot down to dip her toe into the water. And above her was the image of him standing on their balcony with his hands braced on the railing as he looked down at her.

It was absolutely stunning. She'd been spending long hours in her studio. But he'd never dreamed it was to create something so beautiful for him.

He looked up from the painting at her standing in front of him. She was chewing on her bottom lip and one bare foot was moving over the other anxiously. He smiled at his girl. "This is beautiful Chloe. Thank you."

Her smile lit up her face as she exhaled audibly. "You're welcome."

Cillian carefully placed the painting against the wall out of the way, then turned and scooped her up into his arms and carried her back to bed.

Cillian's phone ringing woke him from a deep sleep. He and Chloe had spent most of Christmas Day in their suite. Only emerging to have a late lunch with Imogen, Ian and those of his staff who had nowhere else to go for the holiday. It was the O'Donnell tradition. But afterward, he'd brought Chloe back here. They'd worked out in the gym then, after their shower, watched the Christmas movies that were a part of her family's tradition and eaten leftovers on the couch.

He untangled himself from Chloe to answer the phone. He glanced at the screen and frowned in the dark. It was 2:30 in the morning, and Gregory was calling. This could not be good news. Gregory was one of the men assigned to Chloe's parents in the States.

"What happened?" He asked immediately upon answering.

"We have a problem." Gregory stated harshly. "The Guidry's were in an accident." He continued without being prompted. "Their vehicle was pushed over the railing of the Causeway bridge on their way back from David's father's farm."

"Are they alive?" Cillian held his breath as he waited for the response that could crush Chloe. He felt her stir and glanced over to see her perched on her knees beside him. Her long hair tangled around her like a cloak.

"Yes." Jude and I went over the side after them while Nathan called for help. We got them out. They're in the hospital. Both are pretty banged up. David's in surgery now."

He exhaled softly while still holding Chloe's gaze. "The driver of the other car?"

"We have a license plate. It's a rental. And Boss?"

"Yes?"

"It was deliberate."

"Fuck!" Chloe jumped, startled at his bark, so he reached out and ran his hand over her cheek to soothe her.

"I'm texting you the details of where we are and what we've found so far. I'm watching Angela's room. Jude and Nathan are posted outside the operating room. The staff here are not appreciative of our presence, so if you could do something about that, it would be helpful."

"I'll make the calls. We're on our way."

Cillian disconnected the phone, then looked over at Chloe. "Get dressed, baby, hurry. And pack a bag for a few days."

"What happened?" She asked. Her heart was in her throat.

"I'll explain everything on the plane. Right now, I need you to hurry." He turned back to his phone and started dialing.

Chloe jumped off the bed and ran to the bathroom. Cillian was still on the phone as he passed her going in on her way out. She dressed in dark blue skinny jeans and a tank, then added a soft pink sweater over it. She pulled on a pair of boots, then threw a bunch of stuff in a bag in record time. She grabbed the bag and a heavy coat and rushed back into the bedroom.

Cillian was waiting by the door, already dressed with his bag over his shoulder. He was holding his phone in his hand with ear buds in place, barking orders to whoever was on the other end of the line. He opened the door, then reached out with his free hand and threaded their fingers together.

Chloe stayed quiet while he talked on the phone. When they stepped out of the suite, she wasn't surprised to see Patrick and Rourke waiting on them. Both were dressed in warm clothes, bags over their shoulders, and weapons strapped in place.

When they came out of the elevator on the first floor, they were met by the rest of the members of Team One, all except for Van and Finn. They were rushed out to a line of SUV's waiting to take them to the airstrip.

Cillian continued to make calls, barking orders. Chloe had to bite her tongue to keep from screaming at him to tell her what was happening. He'd said her parent's names more than once. And from the one-sided conversation, she was able to determine that they were at a hospital. She was quietly freaking out, but he seemed to be helping them as best he could at the moment. That was all that kept her from interrupting him.

As they emerged from the warm SUV out into the freezing wind, Chloe was surrounded and escorted, her hand secured in Cillian's, up the steps into a luxurious jet. Cillian, still talking on his phone, helped her out of her coat, then seated her next to him in a plush black leather captain's chair. Rourke took her bag and Patrick handed her a bottle of cold water.

"Buckle up runt." He instructed, then he and Rourke buckled into the seats behind her.

As Chloe waited patiently for Cillian to finish his call and tell her what happened, she studied the way the men moved together like cogs of a well-oiled machine. It was obvious they'd worked as a team for a very long time.

Cillian glanced at Terrance, who was seated closest to the cockpit door. "Let's go." Terrance reached up and knocked twice against the door. Immediately, the plane started moving.

He pulled the earbuds from his ears as he disconnected his last call. The hospital administrator had been roused from his bed and given specific instructions to have the staff allow his men to protect the Guidry's. They were also to be given the best care his money could provide. He wanted the very best physicians flown in if necessary. And he'd demanded that they be put in one of the private suites set aside for elite, confidential visitors.

When the administrator had balked, his next call was to one of the US government officials he worked with regularly. Moments later, the CEO of the hospital had called to assure him that his orders would be followed. He also reported that Angela had a laceration on her head that had been stitched. She had a concussion that they were monitoring closely and her arm was broken but had been set and casted. She'd been sedated and was resting comfortably.

David hadn't fared so well. He'd come in unconscious with a head injury. He'd had an MRI and the neurosurgeon would be in soon to look at it. He was currently in surgery to set his broken leg, which had been broken in two places. One being a compound fracture. He had a collapsed lung; three broken ribs and the air bag had broken his nose.

The CEO assured Cillian that he would be there to provide an update when they arrived.

He'd also called Titan and had him working to find out who rented the black SUV that had been used to run the Guidry's off the road.

Now he had to break the news to Chloe. He turned and took her trembling hand in his, brought it to his mouth and kissed her knuckle. He was proud of her. She'd been so patient, waiting silently while he'd handled the details. But taking her home had never been a part of his plan, and he didn't like it.

"Tell me." Her voice quivered.

"First, you need to know that we're heading to the states. I'm taking you to see your parents."

"What happened?"

"You will return home with me afterward. You're not going to fight me. You're going to get back on this plane of your own free will and come home. Do you understand?" His voice was a whip of demand.

Chloe didn't care. "What happened Cillian!?"

"Say you understand Chloe or we'll turn the fuck around right now." When she didn't answer, he demanded, "say it!"

"Yes! Ok. I understand! Just tell me!"

"Your parents were in a car accident."

"Oh my God!" She felt like someone had punched her in the stomach.

"They're both alive Chloe." He assured. "Your mother is in a room, resting. Your father is in surgery." He listed the multiple injuries to both her parents. He didn't leave out a single one.

Tears streaked down her face. Fear tightened her chest, and she suddenly felt very nauseated.

"Angel." He leaned over and kissed her forehead. "We'll be there soon."

Chloe took a small sip of her water and turned to stare out the window. The jet had taken off so swiftly they were already leveling out. Lack of sleep, stress and the quick movements of the plane weren't sitting well and her stomach was turning. "How long will it take to get there?"

"About seven hours."

She looked down at her trembling hands. "Cillian, I um, I don't feel well." Her stomach was churning. "I think I'm going to be sick."

"Hold on angel." He quickly unbuckled his seatbelt, then hers. He lifted her into his arms and rushed into the bedroom in the back of the plane.

Terrance got up and followed them, bringing her water and a box of crackers. Once Cillian placed her on the bed, Terrance handed him the water, and put the crackers on the bed beside them, then disappeared.

"Baby, do you need to use the lavatory or do you want to try eating a cracker?" Cillian ripped open the box and handed her one. She looked a little green.

"I'm not sure. I'll try the cracker." She took a small bite and when it didn't come back up, she took another bite. She relaxed against the pillows and slowly ate another one.

Cillian propped himself against the pillows next to her and rested his head on his hand as he watched her. "Better?"

"I'm sorry. It's just nerves. Are you sure mom and dad are going to be ok?"

"Don't apologize, just rest. And yes, the CEO of the hospital said that baring no unforeseen complications, they should both be fine."

Chloe cuddled into him, so he slowly eased onto his back. She rested her head on his chest, and he curled his arms around her. "I can't lose them." She whispered sadly.

"I know baby." He kissed the top of her head and ran his hand in soothing circles over her back, massaging gently until she finally drifted off into a restless sleep.

Hours later, he watched the expressions on the faces of his team as Cillian listened to Titan's report. They were gathered around a table in the conference room just down the hall from Angela Guidry's hospital room. Terrance had volunteered to stand guard at the door to watch over her and Chloe, so Nathan could be a part of the meeting. They needed every detail he could provide.

After landing in New Orleans, they'd come straight here. He'd left Chloe sitting with her mother. He hadn't wanted to leave her, but he also didn't want her worrying about her parent's safety or her own. She had enough on her plate at the moment and didn't need to be involved in this discussion.

They'd been trying for the last twenty minutes to figure out what was going on. Titan's research showed that the SUV was rented under a bogus company name. The license given for the rental was fake. Neither Gregory, Jude nor Nathan got a good look at the driver. The windows were tinted black and since it was dark outside when the accident happened; it had been impossible to see inside the vehicle.

So far, the evidence suggested the accident was a deliberate attempt to kill the Guidry's. But there was also the possibility that it was orchestrated to bring either him or Chloe to the States. The question was, who was the target?

Terrance smiled at the pretty blonde nurse as she approached. He'd been introduced to her when they'd first arrived. He preferred her to the surly nurse who'd been by earlier. "Hi Nadine."

"Hi Terrance. I'm just checking on Mrs. Guidry. Because of her concussion, I need to wake her up and it's past the time for her next pill."

Terrance frowned at her in confusion. "But that other nurse was here about fifteen minutes ago to do the same thing."

Nadine frown back in her own confusion. "What other nurse? It's just me and Charlotte on duty tonight."

Terrance's senses came alive. "Maybe it was Charlotte?"

Nadine became alarmed and hurried toward the door. "Terrance, Charlotte's been with me at the desk all night."

Terrance rushed into Angela's room. She was in her bed, sleeping, but Chloe was nowhere to be seen. He hurried to the bathroom and knocked, but when no answer came, he pushed open the door. She wasn't there. "Fuck!" He glanced over at Angela. She hadn't stirred. "Check her vitals." He barked the order at Nadine while pulling out his phone.

He hit the button to make the call while he continued searching the room. When he looked up at the ceiling, he froze. "Son of a bitch!" One of the ceiling tiles had been moved, but whoever moved it hadn't put it back in place completely.

"What?" Cillian answered on the first ring. He was already out of his chair and rushing down the hall. There was only one reason Terrance would interrupt the meeting.

"Boss, Chloe's gone."

"What the fuck do you mean she's gone!"

Chloe screamed as she came awake to a searing pain across her thighs. The whip whistled through the air a second time, striking her across her abdomen, then a third time slicing the skin below her breast. She screamed in agony again!

"Oh look, the little whore is finally awake." Roisin Murphy sneered at the stupid cunt and waited for her to shut the fuck up.

Screaming! The sound hurt her ears and shredded her throat. Sheer agony! She was drowning in it. She'd never hurt so much. She couldn't breathe! She was wading through a quicksand. Terror, so sharp, so intense, it was suffocating. What was happening? What the hell was happening!?

Roisin giggled. "Awe, did that hurt?"

She had to think! Oh God, it hurt! Chloe squinted to see through the darkness. Was that really Roisin's voice? And Jesus! What the hell was she hitting her with?

"What? Nothing to say now, you little whore?" Roisin taunted. Then she walked around behind Chloe and swung the whip again, striking her across her bare back.

Chloe screamed again as the whip sliced her open. Holy shit! It was hard to concentrate as fire seared her back. If Roisin was here, that couldn't be good.

She breathed deep and opened her eyes again. Whatever this place was, it was dirty, cold, and damp. She tried to move her arms, but she was hanging by her wrists from a thick, rough rope that was tied way too tight. So tight it was cutting off her circulation and cutting into her skin. She flexed her fingers, but she couldn't feel them. And, oh God! She was naked! No! No! No!

The cuts from the whip burned like fire. Her scalp behind her left ear was stinging. So was a spot behind her left knee and her right ankle. They must've cut her because she could feel wetness sliding from each spot. She had to assume it was blood. And she was naked! Oh God, she was naked! There was a light over her head spotlighting her while leaving the rest of the room in total darkness. And the room smelled like the swamp. Wet mud and moldy decay. She could feel the splintered floor under her bare feet. Nail heads protruding from old weathered boards were digging into her heels.

"Careful Rosie. I know you hate the bitch, but you said the buyer didn't want her damaged." Arnold Crump reminded her. He wanted his money and this little bitch was worth a fuckin fortune. But she was also beautiful, and he was gonna fuck her before they sold her. He couldn't wait. When they'd undressed her, he'd sucked on those plump titties. Now his cock was as hard as a rock.

Chloe gasped! Oh, God! Who was that? Shit!

"Shut up Arnie! He said not to damage her face. That's just so he can verify her identity." Roisin laughed, then turned to Chloe. "That's right, little whore. I sold you to the highest bidder. You know the old saying; the enemy of my enemy is my friend. Cillian has a lot of enemies." Roisin laughed hysterically. "And they can't wait to get a piece of you."

Where the hell was Cillian!? Breathe Chloe. Think! Think goddamned it, think! Focus! You can do it. Slow your breathing down. Focus. That's it, ok, ok. You can do this. What the hell happened? She'd been sitting next to her mother's bed. She remembered that. There was a nurse. She remembered the nurse! The nurse was too close. She didn't like her so close, too close... The sting at her neck. Nothing. And now Roisin. Roisin!

Roisin swung the whip, and it struck the floor next to Chloe's foot, making her jump and cry out. "You know," she mused in a playful voice, "you should've just eaten the chocolates and died like a good little whore." She swung the whip with all her might, this time catching Chloe across her abdomen again.

Chloe screamed loud and long.

"Hold up Rosie. You said we could fuck her before he gets here. I don't mind a little blood, but shit. Don't fuck up those titties. They tasted so good, didn't they, Arnie?"

"Oh yea. And so plump I couldn't get the whole thing in my mouth. But I sure tried, didn't I Tom." Arnie snickered. "And look at that pussy, all bare and pretty. I bet it's gonna be tight."

Oh, God! No! This couldn't be happening! Where the hell was Chillan?!

"You here that whore, you're going to be the bell of the ball." Roisin smiled delightedly. "I think I'll video them fucking you. Send it to Cillian as a belated Christmas present. What do you think?"

"That's right." Arnie added. "I'll make you a star, baby." He got tired of waiting and approached the girl out of the darkness. "Let me taste those sweet titties again." He taunted her while he rubbed his dick.

Chloe only thought she'd felt terror before. This new horror was nearly debilitating. Oh God! She tasted bile in her mouth as she shuddered uncontrollably. She recognized his mean eyes. She'd seen him on the island when she'd first arrived. When he reached for her, she flinched away from his rough hands.

Arnie laughed. "Where you goin pretty girl? We're gonna have a real nice time." He plumped her breast, then pinched her nipple hard in a bruising grip.

Chloe screamed as fury suddenly overshadowed her terror. She closed her eyes so she didn't have to see the excitement in his eyes. She had to think fast. She had to do something. Then she remembered the nail heads in the floor. They hadn't suspended her or tied her feet. She could use her legs. At least that was something. Ever so slightly, she adjusted her weight on her left foot. It hurt like hell when a nail head cut into her heel, but she held the position and waited. She was probably only going to get one shot, but she wasn't going down without a fight. If she timed it perfectly, at least she might be able to put this guy out of commission. She had years of training. She could do this.

Arnie laughed and squeezed her nipple harder when she closed her eyes. "Awe, what's wrong?" He moved closer. "I'm not as pretty as your man?"

Chloe jerked her knee up as hard as she could between his legs.

Arnie screamed and fell to the floor, clutching his balls. "You fuckin bitch!" He gasped as he curled up and rolled around on the floor.

"She's a feisty one now, ain't she?" Tommy laughed and stepped out of the dark to take his shot. He stayed far enough away to ensure he didn't take a knee to the nuts, too. Poor Arnie was gonna have to ice his balls. But that worked in his favor. "Mmm," he moaned playfully and rubbed his dick. "I like a little fight."

"Step back." Roisin ordered as she prepared to swing the whip again. "I'm not done." This girl had humiliated her in the eyes of her grandfather. She'd been coached since birth for one purpose and one purpose only. To help aid her family in taking over the O'Donnell territory.

She was supposed to be the asshole's wife. Her job was to get him to marry her. But thanks to this little bitch, she'd failed. And she'd been cast out of her own home. She couldn't go back until she took care of the situation exactly like her grandfather instructed. She had to follow his instructions to the letter! But before she did, though, she wanted this bitch to hurt.

Tommy scowled. "You said we could fuck her!"

Roisin turned to the men, her accomplices. She'd been fucking these two brothers for years. It had taken her grandfather even longer to cultivate their backgrounds so they could get hired on to one of the O'Donnell crews. They'd been her eyes and ears on the island for so long, she supposed she owed them something.

"Oh alright. Fuck the little whore." She glared down at Arnie, still lying on the floor holding his nuts. "You probably won't be able to get it up, but if you can, go ahead." She reached out and grabbed a handful of Chloe's hair and yanked her head back. "Get used to it, slut. Consider this an initiation into your new life as a slave." She laughed again. "You'll spend the rest of your life on your back. I just wish we'd succeeded in killing those parents of yours. But don't worry, I'll finish the job before I go back home."

No! It was them? They'd tried to kill her mom and dad?

She shoved Chloe's head down, then just for spite, punched her in her breast as hard as she could. She loved hearing the little bitch scream.

Chloe struggled to breathe from the blow. These people were monsters. They were going to rape her and stupid Roisin was going to watch. She felt bile rise in her throat. Before she could swallow it back, she vomited.

"Ew. Such a nasty cunt!" Roisin laughed and jumped back out of the way of the spray.

When Tom moved forward, she stopped him. "First, go find some bolt cutters or something. I want that necklace before he gets here." They'd tried to find the clasp to open it and when that hadn't worked, they'd all yanked on it as hard as they could. The fucking thing wouldn't budge.

"Where the fuck are we supposed to find bolt cutters out here in the goddamned swamp?" Tom snapped. He wanted first shot at the girl. He'd earned it.

He was the one who had to fuck that ugly nurse's aide ever since they'd come to the States. And getting her hooked on heroin so he could blackmail her had taken a lot of his time. This was bullshit! He'd done all the fuckin work.

He'd been the one hiding in the fuckin crawl space of that hospital for hours waiting on his chance to snatch the girl. He's the one who'd hoisted her up and strapped her to his chest. The whole thing from the moment she'd been injected had taken ten minutes. They'd timed it perfectly, and it had been brilliant. He even had to remember to use the scanner to find the chips embedded under her skin and cut them out before they'd left the parking lot. Because fucking Arnie forgot. And who the fuck chipped their woman, anyway?

But shit! He'd taken all the risks, and he wanted the first shot! The little bitch was hot as hell!

"I don't give a shit where you find them." Roisin snapped. Her grandfather was going to kill these two morons if they didn't follow her instructions. "Just find them. She's not leaving here with that necklace. Those sapphires are real. That thing is worth over a million dollars."

Tom and Arnie both stared at her in shock. Then Arnie croaked out, "a million dollars?"

For the first time since waking up in this horrible place, Chloe felt a small since of relief. She'd forgotten about her collar. But now she could feel the weight of it around her throat. Oh, thank God! Cillian would come.

She knew he would. She just hoped he got here before whoever Roisin was planning on selling her to did.

"At least. Now go. Besides, we have plenty of time." Roisin turned and smiled smugly at Chloe. "Her new owner isn't due for another hour and no one knows where we are." Then her smile turned vicious. "Lets you and I have some fun while we wait, shall we?" Then she giggled loudly as she let the whip fly.

Chloe screamed so loud she was sure she'd done permanent damage to her vocal cords. She was exhausted, and it was difficult to stay on her feet. But the pressure on her wrists was excruciating. Blood dripped down her arms from where the ropes cut into her skin. She had to force her feet to bear her weight and took several deep breaths. He'd come, she knew he'd come. And he was going to kill this crazy bitch. She just had to hold on. She took another deep breath and braced for the next strike. This was going to hurt like hell. She just hoped she was strong enough to survive it.

"Still so smug." Roisin clucked her tongue in disdain. "You think Cillian's going to save you, don't you?" Then she laughed evilly. "You stupid whore, we cut out your tracking devices. He'll never find you now."

Tracking devices? She must be hallucinating. They say pain does that to a person.

Chapter 36: Who You Calling a Hag?

Cillian and his men crept silently through the swamp like ghosts in the fog as they surrounded the old, dilapidated cabin. This was the most important mission of his life. His total focus was centered on getting to Chloe. He forced himself to stay calm as the sound of her screams echoed through the darkness, shredding his soul.

"Easy." Finn whispered into the mic in his ear. They were almost in position. If Cillian lost control, they'd lose their element of surprise.

"Kill them all." Cillian hissed back. These fuckers were going to die. He would bathe in their blood. His fury, his rage, burned like molten lava as they were forced to listen to her scream.

Whoever took her, had her too long. The instant Terrance said she was missing; he'd opened the app on his phone that was connected to the chips under her skin. The chips weren't giving off a signal, which indicated they'd been destroyed. And the only way to do that was to cut them out. Furious, he'd switched over to the app linked to her collar and felt a tremendous sense of relief when the indicator light blipped across the screen. His relief was short lived because the signal was already speeding away from the hospital.

They'd raced to the SUV's and doggedly followed the signal deep into the Louisiana swamp. When they'd gotten to within a half a mile of where the signal had stalled, they'd parked the vehicles and came in on foot. Now they were silently moving into position, but the sounds of Chloe's screams had every one of them on edge.

His rage was eating him alive. He'd taken every precaution with her security. They'd trained her in hand to hand combat and weapons. She was guarded around the clock. Her food was tasted before she was allowed to eat it. He'd made sure she was comfortable with the escape tunnel. He'd taken her through it so many times now she could navigate it in her sleep. All that shit had been for nothing. Nothing!

Terrance eased into position beside the door. There were several cement blocks stacked up in front of it that were being used for steps to get inside. With his height, he wouldn't need the steps. He disappeared into the darkness against the wall beside the closed door and waited.

Micha, Patrick, and Rourke circled around to the back door to cut off any escape while Jacob and Felix crouched beneath the filthy windows on each side. The black SUV parked in front had a steel bumper on the front. No doubt the same SUV that ran the Guidry's off the bridge. Zane slid beneath it to work his magic and disable it.

Finn faded into the space on the other side of the steps. He was about to give the signal to go in when Terrance whispered softly into his comm. "Two men, coming out." Then he eased further into the shadows.

Cillian watched as the door to the cabin opened. The light from inside silhouetted two men as they stepped through it. Behind them, he caught a brief glimpse of Chloe hanging from a rope, naked and bleeding. Her screams so much louder than before. A woman with a whip in her hand was striking her repeatedly. Then the door closed, cutting off his view. He lost the grip he'd been holding on his rage and surged forward. But before he could attack, Finn and Terrance slipped up behind both men and slit their throats. Then dropped their dead bodies to the ground like the garbage they were.

Cillian flew past them and up the makeshift steps. He heard Finn curse as he sprinted past, but he didn't hesitate. He kicked the door completely off its rusty hinges. It flew into the room ahead of him as he dove to the floor and rolled, coming up on a knee, his gun aimed at the woman holding the whip. The shock and terror on her face offered no conciliation. It was nothing compared to the fury coursing through him when he realized who she was. He fired his gun before she could say a word. The bullet blowing out the back of her head.

Cillian didn't spare Roisin a glance. He surged to his feet and reached for Chloe. "Angel," his tortured voice growled as his arms encircled her as gently as possible and lifted her to take the weight off of her wrists. She was covered in blood from her breasts to her feet, with streaks of it sliding down her arms from her torn wrists.

"Knew you'd come." She gasped in a shredded voice that was barely audible.

"Always angel, always. I got you, baby." Before he could reach up to cut her down, Finn was there, doing it for him. "Drew, get in here!" He held her gently while Finn sliced the rope at her wrist and carefully removed it. She hissed audibly when the rope took some of her skin with it.

Finn rubbed Chloe's hands briskly to help with the fiery sensation of needles he knew would assault them once the blood started circulating again. He carefully inspected her hands to ensure the color was returning. Already seething with fury, his tight jaw clenched harder when he realized her wedding ring was missing.

He looked over his shoulder at what was left of his second cousin's head. His shock at seeing Roisin in this place, that whip in her hand, knowing that she was responsible for this made him murderous. The fucking bitch! He looked at her hands, and sure enough, Chloe's wedding ring was on her right pinky finger. He stomped over to her body, crouched down, and yanked the ring off. Before he moved back to Cillian and Chloe, he shifted and delivered a viscous kick to her chest. He was only mildly appeased when he heard her bones shatter beneath the blow. Then he gently slipped the ring back onto Chloe's finger, where it belonged.

Cillian held Chloe carefully. She was covered in blood and shivering violently in his arms. "Baby, I need to get you dressed. We have to get you out of here."

Holding her to him, he turned and faced his men. All but Drew lowered their gazes respectfully. He was too busy clinically assessing the whip marks on her lower back. Patrick stepped forward with her clothes. He'd found them in the corner on the floor.

"Wait." Drew eased her leg aside to see where the blood on the front of her body was coming from. "Fuck! You can't put those jeans on her. It'll hurt too much."

"Here." Zane walked through the door and carefully draped the blanket he'd found in the back of the SUV out front around her and Cillian.

With Finn's help, Cillian adjusted the blanket around her to keep her warm. She never took her face from his neck as she cried softly. "Let's go." He looked over at Felix. "Torch it."

Felix nodded, then he and Terrance went out and dragged the bodies of the two dead men into the cabin.

Cillian, with Chloe in his arms, surrounded by the rest of his team, disappeared into the night.

Cillian sat next to Chloe's hospital bed, watching her sleep. As soon as they'd settled her in the back of the SUV, he'd called the hospital CEO and told him they were on their way in. A team of clinical personnel had met them at the back service entrance and ushered then quickly into the elevator that took them back up to the presidential floor.

A doctor had been waiting to exam her. But when he'd laid her on the exam table, she'd cried out and reached for him. He'd leaned over her and forced her to maintain eye contact while he soothed her with his voice. Whispering quietly to her, telling her how strong and brave she was.

She'd been struck repeatedly with the whip. Most of the lash marks were surface cuts, but two were deep enough to require liquid sutures. One across her thigh and the other just under her left breast. The wounds where the chips had been cut out had to be stitched as well. As did the deep laceration on her heel. Her wrists were shredded, and she was covered in dark bruises, including a ring of them round her collar where they'd obviously tried to yank it off of her.

Cillian ran the tip of his finger across her soft cheek. She was finally sleeping. They'd given her a mild sedative with the pain medication so she could rest. Chloe hadn't responded when the doctor asked if she could tell him what had happened to her. She'd just held his gaze, ignoring the doctor's questions and silently withstood the exam, her hand squeezing his tightly the entire time. She hadn't spoken a word since he'd carried her out of that cabin.

When she'd finally drifted off, the doctor had assured him she hadn't been raped. He'd checked because the bruises on her breasts were obviously from hard fingers and marks from someone's mouth. Marks he hadn't left there.

Now, remembering each mark that covered her body, the bruises on her breasts, the cuts and scrapes, he wanted to kill the fuckers all over again.

"Cousin." Finn whispered from the chair next to the door.

"What?" Cillian answered without taking his eyes off of Chloe.

"I'm sorry." Finn said in a tortured voice.

"Don't."

"But,"

"You had nothing to do with it."

"I should've known. Roisin has been obsessed with you for years. I just thought it was a childhood crush and later, the wants of a selfish girl."

"We all did." Cillian turned and met Finn's gaze. "Not your fault."

"But it was my responsibility."

"Finn, this is not on you. I don't blame you and you know Chloe wouldn't either."

Finn's gaze shifted to Chloe. She looked like a tiny broken doll in that bed. "She looks so broken."

"She's not." He said fiercely, then leaned over and kissed her forehead. "Chloe is a lot stronger than you think."

"I know she is, but this,"

366

"She survived. That's all that matters. I'll get her through the rest." And he would. Probably kicking and screaming. But he'd pull her through whatever repercussions came from this day.

Finn blew out a breath on a harsh sigh. "She's going to need clothes that won't rub against the slashes."

"Call Sidney." Cillian instructed. "Tell her we'll need at least two long loose skirts, bulky sweaters that cover her neck and wrists easily and tell her about her heel. She'll know what shoes to bring that won't hurt her."

"Shoes?"

"Finn, you know Chloe. She's going to want to see David and Angela as soon as she wakes up. Which will help with her own recovery. But she won't want them to know she's been hurt."

"I'll call her. She's been texting me since we got here." Finn grinned slightly.

"Texting you?"

"Yes, well, Chloe texted her we were here to check on her parents. But Sidney hasn't been able to reach her since. And when you had them moved to this floor, their names were automatically changed to Confidential Patient so no one will give her any information. I won't give her access to this floor and she's pretty pissed about it."

"Why didn't you bring her up here?"

"Initially? Because, we didn't know who the target was. The team needed to focus on you, Chloe and the Guidry's."

"Makes sense."

"Yes, well, I'm afraid she doesn't see it that way. So, she's pissed. Really pissed." He chuckled. "And that woman has a mouth on her."

Cillian grinned. "Does she?"

Finn rubbed his jaw in anticipation. "Oh yea."

"Chloe baby, wake up!"

The dark cabin was freezing. She could smell the swamp. Ropes were cutting into her wrists. Burning like acid. The laughing. Her skin being sliced open. And the laughing! She could hear her laughing. Men leering at her, touching her.

She was screaming. It hurt so much! Where was he? When was he coming to get her? That voice. Was he here? It was his voice. Commanding her. The commands soothed her. She tried to focus on the sound of his voice through the chaos and terror. His voice, so demanding.

"Cillian!" Chloe's eyes flew open! And there he was. On the bed with her, holding her and stroking her hair, whispering to her.

"I got you, angel."

"Cillian." She whimpered. God, she sounded so pathetic!

"Shh, I've got you, baby." Chloe was trembling violently. He held onto her as gently as he could, hoping his body heat would soothe her. Her terrified screams shredded his blackened soul.

"They were going to rape me!" She cried out softly.

"But they didn't." He soothed. "You were so brave."

"It was horrible! I was so scared!"

"I know angel. I'm so sorry."

"Cillian!" She needed him to know.

"Shh baby."

"She tried to kill my parents." Tears fell steadily as she sobbed.

"Roisin?" That surprised him.

"Yes! She said she was going to finish the job after they sold me."

"Sold you?"

Chloe turned her head away, crying silently. Was it her fault her parents were pushed over the side of that bridge?

"Chloe?"

She stayed quiet while she considered that. Could it have really been her fault?

"Chloe?" He called again and reached out and gently pulled her face back to his. "Tell me everything they said."

"I don't want to talk about it anymore." She buried her face in his chest and cried as if her heart were breaking.

Cillian pushed his fingers through her hair and massaged her scalp. He tried to temper his voice, but his fury was a living, breathing thing. "I know you don't. But you will."

"Cillian."

"Tell me." He ordered. "I need the details while they're still fresh in your mind." He sounded like an asshole. He knew it. He wanted to hold her, soothe her, but that wasn't going to help her.

"I don't,"

"Chloe." He cut her off. "Use your training. You said so yourself; we've been training you for months. You're strong. Use that strength now and tell me what I want to know."

She continued to cry into his chest for a long time. He let her while he waited.

She was so tired; her eyes were closing on their own. But she didn't want to close her eyes. Every time she did, she was back in that cabin.

"They were going to sell me into slavery. They had a buyer and everything." She cringed visibly.

"What?" Cillian worked hard to keep his voice calm.

"She said he would be there in an hour. She couldn't hit me in the face because he wanted proof it was me. Like he knew me or something."

"Did she ever say a name?" He asked carefully.

"No, she just said he was coming, and that he was buying me." Chloe scowled against his chest. "They're disgusting."

He urged her head out of his chest, gently using the grip he had on her hair. He looked her right in the eyes. "They're dead."

She met that fierce gaze with one of her own. "Good."

"Who was the nurse that came into your mom's room?" If she wasn't already, he wanted that bitch dead too.

Chloe held his gaze while she thought about that. "I don't know. They never mentioned her."

"How did they get you out of the room?"

"She drugged me. She was leaning over me to check mom's pulse then she stuck me in the neck with a needle."

"You let her lean over you? You let her get that close to you?"

Angry at herself and him, she yelled, "this wasn't my fault, Cillian!"

"Shh." He put a finger up to her lips. If he wasn't so furious, he would think her little show of temper reassuring. He was very glad to see it. He'd rather she be angry than terrified. "No, it's not. At all." He stressed. "But in the future, I don't want you to ever let a stranger get that close to you. Not for any reason. Ever again, is that clear?"

She scowled at him for a few seconds. She hated to admit that he was right. She hated it. But she remembered being uncomfortable with how close the nurse was to her. God, she was so stupid! She blew out a frustrated breath. "Yes."

"Good." He kissed her lips softly, just a quick touch, then pulled back.

"How are my parents?"

"They're both recovering."

"I want to see them."

"You will. But first, I have a surprise for you?"

"Cillian, I need to see them."

"First the surprise." He gave her another quick kiss, then got out of the bed and went to open the door.

Sidney raced through it with Finn on her heels. "Chloe!" She went straight to the bed and practically threw herself into Chloe's arms. Only remembering her injuries at the last second.

"Sid!" Chloe whispered in shock. She couldn't help it. She burst into tears again. They hugged each other, holding on for forever while they cried.

Sidney tried to be as gentle as possible. She was afraid to touch her. Finn, the asshole, hadn't told her exactly how Chloe had been hurt, only that she had. She'd spent the last two hours terrified, envisioning the worst.

She leaned back to inspect her best friend's condition. She looked terrible. She was as pale as a ghost and her wrists were torn to shreds, as if she'd been tied up with a really tight rope. And she had bruises covering her neck around her necklace. She reached out and touched the edge of one wrist, tears sliding unchecked down her cheeks. "Oh, Chloe."

Chloe took Sidney's hand in hers and squeezed. She was about to say something, but she wasn't sure what when the door opened again.

A pretty blonde nurse came in carrying a tray of food. "Hello Mrs. O'Donnell. My name is Nadine. I'm the nurse in charge of your care."

Chloe pulled Sidney onto the bed beside her, then wiped her tears away. "Call me Chloe, please."

"Ok Chloe. I wanted to introduce myself and let you know Charlotte and I are the nurses on duty. If you need anything, please let us know."

"Thank you."

Nadine placed the tray on the mobile table over the bed then added, "we're also taking care of your parents."

"How are they?"

"They're recovering nicely. Your mother is resting. Your father hasn't woken up yet, but he's on a heavy sedative, so we don't expect him to for a while yet."

"Do they know I was hurt?"

"No Ma'am. Now, I need you to eat this. It's time for your next pain pill and you shouldn't take it on an empty stomach." Nadine said politely, then left.

Chloe pushed the tray aside, then looked up at Cillian. "I need to see them."

He crossed his arms over his chest and smiled. "After you eat."

"I'm not hungry."

"Too bad, eat."

"Cillian!"

"Chloe, the only way you're going to get to see them is if you eat something." She hadn't eaten anything in over twenty-four hours.

"But,"

"Fucking eat." He growled. His fury slipping its leash.

Her temper ignited. "Don't curse at me, Cillian!" Then she scowled when he stared back at her and lifted that arrogant brow. Her scowl deepened when Finn leaned over Sidney and lifted the cover off her plate. He took a bite of the steak, then the baked potato, and finally the green beans. After he nodded that it was safe for her to eat it, Sidney called him a few choice words under her breath. Chloe couldn't help it. She giggled at the wicked grin Finn gave her best friend.

"Keep it up Gorgeous."

Sidney just rolled her eyes at him, then reached over and took a green bean off of Chloe's plate and popped it into her mouth. "Not bad. It's no shrimp po-boy but it'll do for now."

Chloe belligerently picked up her knife and fork and took a small bite of the steak. She had no appetite and was sure she'd be sick if she tried to eat. But the filet was cooked to a perfect medium rare. It was so delicious, it melted on her tongue. She hadn't realized how hungry she was until that instant. She tried not the groan at how good it tasted, but didn't succeed.

She scowled again when Cillian chuckled.

After Chloe finished eating, she took the pain pill, then Cillian carried her into the bathroom. He placed her in the shower on a stool and gently washed the dirt and grime, remnants of her time in the cabin from her hair and skin. When he was finished, he wrapped her in a thick robe and carried her back to bed.

He placed her in the center of the bed, then turned toward Sidney. "Alright Sidney, you're up." Then he moved back out of the way.

"I'm on it." Sidney opened the bag that Finn had carried in with them earlier.

"On what?" Chloe glanced into the big bag.

"You can't go see your parents looking like a hag." Sidney scoffed, hoping to lighten the mood. "You'll scare the shit out of your mom."

"Who are you calling a hag, hag!" Chloe giggled tiredly. It felt so good to be with Sid again.

"Hold still and let me work my magic." Sidney tried to hide her worry. Chloe was so pale, and she looked exhausted. The rope burns on her wrists and the bruises on her neck were horrible. Whatever had happened to her friend had been awful. She wanted to ask. But the tension in the room was so thick, she knew it wasn't a good idea.

Cillian and Finn had moved to the chairs by the door and watched while she worked. She applied subtle makeup, covering the shadows under Chloe's eyes, and attempted to cover the bruises on her neck as best she could. She dried and styled her hair so it fell in waves around her neck and shoulders to better hide the clear bandage behind her ear.

"Alright. That's the best I can do. Here." Sidney pulled a mirror with a long handle out of the bag and handed it to her. "Take a look."

Chloe studied her reflection in the mirror. She looked so much better than she had earlier. She'd glanced at herself in the bathroom mirror and

Sid was right. She had looked like a hag. Now she looked a lot better than she felt. "Not bad."

"I brought you something to wear. That husband of yours was very specific, so if you don't like it, that's on him."

Finn and Sidney stepped out while Cillian carefully helped her into a long flowing sage green skirt with a cream-colored lace pattern stenciled into the material. The long-sleeved bulky cable-knit sweater was a muted shade of light grey. The turtleneck covered her throat, and the sleeves came down past her wrists to the center of her hands. It was comfortable and very pretty, but more importantly, it covered her wounds. Thankfully, Sidney had thought to bring a cotton tank to wear under it to try to contain her breasts. Wearing a bra was out of the question.

She was out of breath and exhausted by the time Cillian slid the buttery soft grey ballerina flats onto her feet. They were a half a size too big. And Sidney had inserted a gel sole into each to help cushion the wound on her heel.

Now she was nearly sweating from pain and shaking with exhaustion, but she was not going to let that stop her from seeing her parents. No matter what the nurse said, she needed to see them for herself.

"Sit for a few minutes and rest." Cillian lifted her back onto the center of the bed and laid her back against the pillows. She was trembling again.

"Don't let me fall asleep." She met his concerned gaze and pleaded, "please."

Cillian sat on the bed next to her and laced her fingers through his. "I won't."

Chloe sat in a plush warm leather chair between her parent's hospital beds. She had no idea where Cillian had found such a comfortable chair in a hospital, but it helped. It was electric with a heated seat and back cushion that kept her aching muscles from locking up. She really did hurt everywhere. The pain was so sharp it was difficult to breath. The medication helped, but she'd need to lie down soon.

"Honey, you look tired." Angela said as she watched Chloe closely.

"Jet lag I supposed." She kept her voice quiet on the pretense of not disturbing her father, but her throat was shredded.

"Maybe." Angela replied skeptically.

"I've been spending a lot of time in my studio." She deflected again. "You know how I get.

"Oh sweetheart! I'm so happy you're painting again."

Chloe smiled at her mother. "Thanks to you."

"Well, the job of a mother can be soo exhausting." Angela playfully swiped the back of her hand over her forehead.

Chloe giggled. "At least you haven't lost your sense of humor."

"Not likely." Angela giggled with her. Then she sobered and looked over in the corner of the dimly lit room to where Patrick sat reading then looked back at Chloe. In a quiet voice, she asked, "how are you really Chloe?"

Chloe thought about her question for a minute, her mind going back over the last few months, then she shrugged her shoulders. "I'm painting."

"You said that."

Chloe held her mother's gaze and tried to figure out how to explain her relationship. It was complicated, very complicated, but it was theirs. So, she continued softly. "For Christmas, Cillian gave me a laptop and he got me re-enrolled in school for the spring semester."

"Oh honey, I just." Angela paused, trying to decide what to say.

"Mom." Chloe interrupted softly. When Angela met her gaze again, she smiled. "It's hard to explain, but I'm fine."

"But honey"

"Mom" she said again determined to get her point across and keep her from worrying. "Really, I'm fine." Then she grinned to let her know that she truly was.

"How's a guy supposed to sleep with you two yacking so much." David Guidry called from his bed.

"Dad!" Chloe jumped from her chair and nearly yelped as her foot hit the ground abruptly. She hid the reaction with enthusiasm. "You're awake!"

David chucked softly then winced. "Don't yell sweetheart. My head's killing me."

Chloe took his hand in hers and squeezed. "Thank God you're awake. I was so worried."

"I'm fine." He assured her then turned toward his wife. "Angela love, are you ok?" David tried to assess her injuries from the distance.

"Yes. Mild concussion and a broken arm. Nothing to worry about." Angela smiled at the love of her life. "But you're a different story. You scared the hell out of me."

Chloe gasped and turned quickly toward her mother. She never cursed. Never.

But David smiled wickedly. "Now baby, you know I love it when you get saucy."

"David!"

"Dad!"

He chuckled at his girls. "Don't worry. I'm going to be fine." He gave Chloe a serious look. "Thanks to Cillian's men."

"What do you mean?" Chloe asked in confusion. She stared at him then turned to catch the knowing look her mother gave him. "What?"

"They pulled us out of the car. Out of the water." David said quietly.

"Who did?"

"Chloe, Cillian has had his men watching us. You know that. If they hadn't been there, we wouldn't have made it out."

"Cillian's men pulled you out?"

"Yes. I was trapped, my leg was broken and stuck between the dashboard and the console. They dove into the water after us and before I passed out, they were pulling us free of the car. They saved us baby."

"Cillian's men? The men who beat you? They saved you?" She looked over into the corner at Patrick. He had his head buried in the book he was pretending to read but he was grinning.

"They didn't hurt me honey. They pulled their punches; I told you that. But yes, they saved us." David assured.

Chloe looked from her father to her mother for confirmation.

"He's right." Her mother agreed.

"Huh." Chloe sat back in her chair then clenched her jaw to keep from crying out when her wounds came into contact with the cushion so abruptly.

"Now, enough about us. Tell me how you're doing?" David asked.

Cillian eased out of bed and carefully tucked the blanket around Chloe. She was so exhausted; she'd fallen asleep before they'd even pulled out of the hospital parking lot. She'd stirred briefly when he'd lifted her out of the car. But by the time he stepped into the elevator to the hotel's penthouse, she was out again.

Now, he left the bedroom door slightly ajar so he could hear if she stirred and stepped into the living room. His team were all there, waiting patiently.

"She asleep?" Patrick asked softly.

"Yes. For now." Cillian scanned the somber faces of his men. His gaze landed on Terrance, then moved to Felix. "Were you thorough?"

"Yes. There's nothing left. No traces." Felix answered. "We waited in the woods while it burned to see if anyone showed up. No one did."

"It was a large blaze." Terrance added. "Anyone going out there would've seen it from a mile away."

Cillian nodded. He pulled out a chair from the dining table behind him and flipped it around. He straddled it, his elbows resting on the top of the chair back and faced his men. "They were going to rape her then sell her into slavery."

"What the fuck!" Terrance swore.

"The fuck!" Patrick hissed at the same time while all the other men grumbled similar curses.

"They had a buyer lined up. The thing is," Cillian looked around at his men before he continued, "the buyer was buying Chloe specifically, not just any woman."

"You've got to be fucking kidding." Finn swore.

"That's why her face wasn't damaged. Apparently, the buyer demanded that concession so he could identify her."

"I'm surprised Roisin was able to show that kind of restraint." Finn scoffed.

"Money buys a lot of restraint." Jacob, who was usually the quiet one, added.

Cillian nodded at him. Jacob didn't talk much, but he was highly intelligent. "My gut says it's Abdul, but I don't have proof yet."

"I'll kill the fucker!" Terrance hissed through clenched teeth.

"I'll kill him." Cillian promised. "With my bare fucking hands. Just as soon as I can prove it. In the meantime," He looked back at Finn, "Silas is done."

"Agreed." Finn nodded. "Roisin couldn't have come up with that plan on her own. She wasn't that fucking smart."

"My thoughts exactly. I should've settled the score years go." He met each man's gaze somberly before he continued, "it's past time I took my revenge. Not just for my parents, but now for Chloe too."

"When do we leave?" Van asked as he stood up from the chair in the corner.

"Tomorrow morning after Chloe visits with her parents."

"Should we increase their security?" Zane, who was leaning with his elbows braced on the back of the sofa, asked quietly.

"No. The threat to them was eliminated tonight. Chloe said Roisin told her she was the one who tried to kill them. Those two assholes with her were driving the SUV that pushed their car over the edge.

"Arnold and Tommy Crump. Roisin's fuck buddies from the island. Obviously, her eyes and ears." Finn added from where he sat flipping his knife in his hand.

"That's right." Cillian glanced his way again. His eyes livid. "I want their entire team dismantled. Have them all off the island before day break."

"Consider it done."

"I also want to know how we missed their connection to the Murphy's. Titan has some explaining to do."

"I'll set up a call. We'll figure it out." Finn met Cillian's furious gaze head on. "I promise cousin."

The sound of Chloe's scream had the men instantly jerking their gazes to the partially closed door. Cillian bolted out of his chair and raced to the bedroom.

"Chloe! Goddammit wake up!" Her screams were eating him alive. He kissed her cheek, her nose, her eye lids, her forehead and finally her lips. Raining soft kisses over her entire face as he held her gently in his arms. "Come on angel. Wake up now, come back to me."

Chloe forced her eye lids open. She had to see that she was really with Cillian and not in that terrible place any longer. She met his blazing, furious gaze. "Cillian!" She cried out and threw herself into his arms, burying her face in his neck as tears streamed down her cheeks.

"I've got you, angel." He whispered. She was trembling violently. So much, he worried she'd accidentally open the liquid sutures. He held her for a few minutes, massaging her neck and scalp trying to calm her down while she cried.

When she settled, he glanced at his watch. She'd been asleep for less than an hour. She was exhausted, but the nightmares were keeping her from the rest she so desperately needed. He'd intended to feed her when they got here which was why he hadn't given her a pain pill on the drive over. But now it was way past time for her to take it. She flinched when he gently ran his hand over her back. She was definitely in pain. He shifted to place her on the pillow, but she cried out and clung to him.

"Angel, I'm not going anywhere. But you need to take a pill."

"No. It'll make me sleepy." She shook her head. "I don't want to sleep."

"You need to rest."

"No! I have to stay awake." She shook her head rapidly as fear began to overwhelm her again.

"Chloe, I'll be right here. I'm not going anywhere."

"No! Please, I don't,"

"Stop!" He gently fisted a handful of her hair at the nape of her neck to hold her head still. "You have to get some rest or you won't be in any shape to see your parents tomorrow. They'll be expecting you."

"I don't want to sleep." She whispered desperately.

"Doesn't matter. Your body needs it to heal, so you'll take the pill."

"I said no."

"Then you won't get to see your parents before we leave."

"What?" She pushed away from him and looked up in shock at his foreboding expression. "Why?"

"I told you; you need the rest."

She searched his face for any sign of tenderness and found none. "Why are you doing this to me?" Couldn't he see that she was afraid.

He tugged on her hair, lifting her chin higher, not allowing her to look away from his intense gaze. "You will take the fucking pill." He growled. "You will fucking sleep and you will not have nightmares about that fucking shit anymore."

She sucked in a huge breath then opened her mouth to speak, but he covered her lips with his palm.

"You will." He demanded then released her as he reached for the pill bottle on the nightstand by the bed. He shook out a pill then grabbed the bottle of water he'd put there earlier. He held out his hand to her. "Take it."

"No!" She practically yelled. Why was he being so hateful!

"Then let's go." He moved to get off the bed. "We can be in the air, headed back home in less than an hour."

"What? We can't leave! What about my parents?" She stared at him in disbelief.

"You want to see them; you take the fucking pill."

"Why!" She screamed in his face causing her sore throat to ache worse. Then she added almost hysterically; "why are you doing this to me?"

Cillian surged forward, his hands bracing on the bed next to her thighs, caging her in. He leaned over her menacingly, crowding her with his size. His face less than an inch from hers. "You're letting those fuckers control you with fear!" He growled his fury through clenched teeth. "I will not fucking allow it."

"You weren't there!" She screamed. Tears of frustration sliding down her cheeks.

"Take the pill or we leave now. Your choice baby." He held up his hand again.

"I hate you!" She hissed. The thought of going to sleep and sinking back into that place was terrifying.

"No, you don't. Now stop stalling and fucking take it or get ready to leave." He demanded harshly.

Chloe snatched the pill from his palm and tossed it to the back of her throat. She chugged the water to wash it down then put the cap back on the bottle. He leaned back on his knees careful to keep his weight off of her and watched her take it. Afterward, he gave her a smug smile.

At the sight of that stupid smile, she lost it. She hurled the bottle at his head. "Asshole!"

He laughed as he caught it. He expected no less from his little hellion. "As soon as your injuries are healed, I'm going to spank your pretty little ass for that."

Chloe flipped him off.

He lifted an arrogant brow. "Is that an invitation?"

She refused to dignify that with a response. Instead, she turned over to face the wall and laid her head back down on the pillow. She was so mad her adrenalin was pumping. She wanted to claw his stupid eyes out. But truthfully, she hurt everywhere. And the adrenalin spike only made it worse.

Cillian chuckled softly as he lifted away from her and quickly undressed. He slipped beneath the covers beside her. She tensed when his hand settled on her hip. It was one of the only places on her that wasn't injured. "Shh, just relax. You're in no shape to fight me tonight."

Chloe lay there dreading the darkness that was slowly creeping in. It didn't take long for the pill to do its job. Within minutes she was drifting off to sleep. Before she lost consciousness, she whispered, "if I wake up screaming again, it's gonna be your fault."

"I know baby," he whispered back softly. And he did. It was his fault. But he'd be damned if he'd let her continue to be afraid. Kicking and screaming, whatever it took to get her through this, he'd do it. Because his angel would not live in fear.

Chloe woke up screaming again several hours later. Cillian held her in the dark, whispering to her that she was safe and so brave. Eventually she cried herself back to sleep. She didn't stir again until he woke her an hour after sunrise.

Chloe sipped her Ginger Ale and nibbled on a cracker as she stared out the window of the plane. During take-off, she'd gotten nauseated again. She wasn't surprised. She had no appetite. And the pain and exhaustion were taking its toll.

The men were all huddled in the back of the plane talking quietly. But she was just too exhausted to care or to even try and listen in.

Surprisingly, she wasn't as upset about going back to Ireland as she'd first imagined. Her parents were going to be ok. And it was all thanks to Cillian. He'd hired a physical therapist to help them recover as quickly as possible and a nurse to stay with them until they did. And he'd done it without her having to ask. When he'd casually mentioned it this morning at breakfast, she'd been so shocked she'd nearly choked on her coffee. But he'd simply smiled and asked if she was ready to go see them. Now, because of his thoughtfulness, she had no choice but to forgive him for being such an ass last night.

Also, Gregory, Jude and Nathan were staying to continue watching over them. Of course, they were no longer designated to the shadows. Her mom saw to that. Angela Guidry was now on first name basis with all three of them whether they liked it or not. She'd stated firmly that it hadn't mattered why they were there initially, only that they'd saved hers and David's lives. That made them family. And the one thing you never did with Angela Guidry, was deny her what she wanted.

Her mom was amazing. Chloe smiled to herself at the thought. Then she eased her seat back into the reclined position and closed her eyes. She was too tired to fight sleep any longer. Exhaustion was a heavy fog settling over her. Her sore muscles and the deep bruises hurt just as bad as the cuts that covered her back, her stomach and her thighs. Cillian had insisted she take a pill to stay on top of the terrible pain racking her body. He'd placed two small pillows behind her at the sides of her body so they supported her, keeping her slash on her back from making direct contact with the seat cushion then he'd covered her with a soft blanket.

She wiggled her toes then adjusted her injured foot to keep pressure off her heel. The cut throbbed, but not as bad as it would've if not for Cillian. He'd carried her everywhere she went until she'd stepped into her parent's room this morning. He hadn't liked it, but she'd gritted her teeth and walked in as if nothing was wrong. The last thing they needed was to worry about her.

Now she was crashing. There was no keeping herself awake any longer. She listened to the comforting cadence of Cillian's voice behind her as she slowly drifted off.

Cillian sat in the back of the cabin surrounded by his men. They spoke quietly about strategy; placement and timing all the while, keeping an eye on Chloe. She was so pale and fighting hard to stay awake. But even if the nightmare haunted her, she needed rest. He just hoped this time, her exhaustion would keep it at bay long enough for her to get it.

It'd been remarkable to watch her walk into her parent's hospital room this morning. Her head held high, shoulder's back with a beautiful smile on her face. She showed no outward sign of the pain racking her body. She limped slightly, but you had to be really paying attention to notice it. He'd been so proud of her. And his men had all crowded into the room with them against her better judgement. But it had worked to distract her parents in case she faltered.

Sitting there while she visited with them had been a struggle. He'd been mentally pacing the entire time. His patience stretched to the point of breaking by the time they'd left for the airport. He had an overpowering urge to get her back on his island. He needed her tucked away where he knew she'd be safe.

With his men crowded into their suite last night, he hadn't been able to care for her the way he needed to. To touch her, inspect those injuries closely and ensure himself that she was whole. But there had been no asking them to leave. They were a group of very pissed off warriors on the edge. And Chloe's screams were like gasoline on their blazing tempers.

Cillian turned his attention back to the laptop in the middle of the table. He listened and watched while Finn showed them every entry point into the Murphy home. The residence was a mansion surrounded by a ten-foot electric wrought-iron fence. They noted the security camera's, the dogs and the images of the guards as they made their rounds.

He'd been planning his revenge on Silas Murphy for a long time. He'd written code that interrupted satellites, allowing him to control them for brief moments of time in order to record the inner workings behind that fence. They knew the path the guards took and when they changed shifts. They knew when the dogs were released, where they were kept and who fed them.

He'd also been using one of his programs to interrupt financial transactions and route those funds across several countries and depositing them into bogus accounts. Money had been disappearing from the Murphy coffers for years now.

Silas knew he was the one doing it. He'd known from the beginning that Cillian would be coming for him. That's why he'd spent so many years trying to take him out when he and Finn were younger.

It had been a game of cat and mouse designed to make Silas Murphy sweat. He'd enjoyed it too, but no longer. Had he taken the son of a bitch out years ago, Chloe wouldn't have been hurt. That was on him. Now it was time to finish the game.

Silas was a devious fucker who dealt in heroin and human trafficking. He'd made his fortune working with sleaze and filth, the dregs of society. It was even rumored he'd killed his own daughter in law after she realized the family she'd married into and made an attempt to take her daughter and run.

That daughter was Finn's mother. Silas had two sons. The youngest, Peter was Finn's grandfather. He was killed when Finn's mother Martha was five years old. Martha's mother was the one who disappeared mysteriously a few months later. Everyone knew Silas had something to do with her disappearance, but no one could ever prove it.

Not wanting to be bothered with a young girl, Silas shipped Martha off to a boarding school where she spent most of her young life. University followed, which was where she'd met Finn's father Jack, Cillian's uncle. They married against Silas' wishes and Jack brought his new bride home to O'Donnell Island.

Silas had been enraged when Martha ran off and married Jack O'Donnell. He'd had plans for her. Unbeknownst to Martha, her grandfather had promised to give her to a man thirty years her senior. The man was wealthy and powerful and fortunately for Silas, he wanted Martha. Silas had dangled her in front of him for years, while they waited for her to come of age. Silas wanted control of his enterprises. To take them over from the inside. His way in, was supposed to have been through the beautiful Martha.

When that didn't happen, he'd turned his sights toward the O'Donnell's. Using intimidation, he tried to scare Martha into providing information on them. He'd been jealous of Cillian O'Donnell Sr. all his life and covetous of his role as leader of the territory. Silas lived on the edge bordering it and felt he was better suited to lead. However, every attempt to usurp power from the O'Donnell's had failed. The brothers, Jack and Cillian's father were no strangers to Silas Murphy's schemes and protected Martha, keeping her out of her grandfather's reach.

His father saw Silas as a pest to be exterminated. So, he sent crews to intercept shipments and to save those poor souls when he heard of a new group coming in. He interrupted Silas' operation at every turn. Disrupting his cashflow and as the years passed, causing him to go deeper and deeper into dept.

Then one vile act turned the tide in his favor. As a last-ditch effort to keep from going under, Silas used his mansion as collateral to borrow money from one of the smaller territory leaders not aligned with the O'Donnell's. He paid off a pilot to plant the bomb on his father's jet. The pilot parachuted out, leaving them stranded. Minutes later, their plane exploded, taking the lives of both his and Finn's parents as well as their grandparents. Leaving both boys orphaned.

During the years Cillian and Finn were surviving in the underworld, Silas had been able to rebuild his fortune. Unfortunately for him, his every attempt to secretly take out Cillian and Finn had failed.

He never came at them directly. He wasn't that stupid. But when all other attempts failed, he obviously decided to use his only other weapon; his granddaughter, Roisin. Cillian and Finn both should have figured that had been his plan. But she'd been so young when she'd reached out to Finn on the pretense of getting to know her cousin. And as was their habit, they'd kept her out of the family wing when she was on the island. Never allowing her to get close to anything that might be important enough to bring back to Silas.

She was spoiled of course and obviously had a crush on him, but they thought it was a passing thing. When she went off to university, they figured she'd outgrow it. But on the rare occasions that she was allowed back on the island to visit Finn, her obsession with Cillian only grew. They hadn't thought of her as a threat. Had no idea she was as vile and vicious as her grandfather. And Chloe had paid the price for their mistake.

"Silas has a force of thirty men. He's not too bright because he has them on two twelve hour shifts. So, fifteen are on duty at a time. In all, we'll be outnumbered three to one." Finn explained.

"Don't forget your great uncle and his wife." Cillian added. "He's just a fucked up as Silas. And we know Roisin's mother is a piece of shit. Don't expect her to go down easily just because she's a woman." He glanced at Terrance who had a soft spot when it came to women.

Terrance grunted. "Anyone in that house is fair game."

"Good." Cillian nodded. "We go in three nights from tonight. There'll be no moon. I wanted to use GhostStorm47 to wipe out his finances first, let him sweat, but it'll warn him we're coming."

Finn chuckled. "You've been dreaming of letting Ghost loose on him for years. You'll have to control yourself."

Cillian raised an arrogant brow. "He's the reason I created it. And I plan to give him a show, right before I kill him."

Finn shook his head. "Of course, you do."

Chapter 38: Pretty Maids All in a Row

Cillian gently placed Chloe in the center of their bed. She'd taken the pain pill right after they'd eaten the meal Imogen had prepared. This time she hadn't argued about it. But she hadn't eaten much either, even with him bullying her. He'd tried tempting her with chocolate cake, but she'd just stared at him through tired eyes. So, he'd given up and taken her into the shower and carefully washed her hair and bathed her. Now she was dry, clean and beautifully naked.

Chloe reached to pull the covers over herself. She was covered in slash marks, cuts and bruises, not to mention those horrifying marks on her breasts. Marks Cillian hadn't left. Those disgusting men had put them there. Every time she looked at them, she started crying all over again. And, she didn't want him to see them.

"Don't." Cillian caught the blanket and tugged it out of her hand.

"I'm cold." She lied. She was shivering with anxiety, so she figured he'd buy it.

"No, you're not." He always kept the room at a comfortable temperature for her to be naked.

She met his burning gaze and tears threatened to fall again. "Please." She whispered.

"Baby." He whispered back. There were no words. Her delicate skin was so battered and bruised. He slowly leaned in and placed his mouth over the mark another man dared to put on her. He'd replace those marks with his own. Letting his lips travel gently from one mark to the next, he suckled sharply, making sure to cover each one, replacing them.

Chloe closed her eyes and focused on his mouth against her skin. It was strange to want this, to need it. Even stranger that he knew.

When he finished covering the marks, Cillian looked up from her breasts at his girl. Silent tears trickled down her pale cheeks. He reached out and gently touched the large black bruise on her right breast. Then kissed it softly. Next, he ran his finger down and over to the wound under her left one and kissed it too. "These are badges of courage." He explained quietly.

He moved his hand gently over the wound then down to the cuts on her belly and thighs, following each touch with a kiss. "We all carry them. But you were never meant to. I'm so sorry baby."

"It's not your fault." She whispered as she concentrated on the gentle touches and the sound of his voice.

"But it is."

"They saw me naked."

"They're dead."

"Not, them."

"Who?"

"The guys."

Surprised, Cillian looked up at her face, but her eyes were still closed. She'd been avoiding the team since her rescue, now he knew why. "Angel, look at me."

Chloe eased her heavy lids open and met his fierce warrior's gaze.

"They saw a team mate, tortured and bleeding, nothing more."

She stared into his eyes for long moments before she responded on a harsh whisper. "I was naked."

"Chloe, if Patrick had been taken instead. If he'd been naked and bleeding, hanging from that rope. And you were part of the mission. Would you be focused on his naked body or on saving him?"

"It's not the same."

"Yes, little one. It is."

"I wish,"

"Baby" he interrupted. "I think they see you as a little sister, but also as a member of the team. Why do you think you've been training with all of them instead of just me and Finn?"

Chloe broke eye contact and turned her head away. She hadn't thought of it that way. "I don't know."

"They needed to know your strengths and limitations and you needed to trust in theirs. You are to never purposely put yourself in danger. But you will be able to defend yourself if you need to."

"I didn't defend myself this time."

"You were drugged. It could've happened to anyone."

"No, it couldn't have. You said so yourself. I let that nurse get too close to me. No one on the team would've fallen for that."

"No, they wouldn't have. But you won't again either. And they have backgrounds and training that is very different from yours."

"I know." She met his gaze again and added, "But once I woke up, I defended myself."

"Did you?"

"Yes. One of them moved in close and started touching me. He was going to rape me." She shuddered at the memory. Then lifted her chin and added proudly, "so, I knee'd him in the nuts as hard as I could."

Cillian smiled at her smug look. "I'll just bet you did."

"I did. Dropped him like a stone." She yawned deeply.

Cillian chuckled. "Good girl. You bought us some time to get to you." He continued his exploration of her injuries, kissing every mark.

"Cillian?"

"Yes?"

"Roisin said 'the enemy of my enemy is my friend' and that you had a lot of enemies. She said one of those enemies was the person who was going to buy me."

Cillian closed his eyes briefly. When he opened them again, she was staring at him.

"It's not your fault." She said again.

"Yes, it is."

"She was a horrible person. She's the one who tried to poison me too."

"Did she say that?"

"Yes. Did you two go out or something?"

"No, never." He reached out and wiggled her toe. She was getting sleepy. "And I don't go out."

She smiled and moved her foot because it tickled. "I noticed."

Cillian raised an eyebrow at her. "Do you want to go out?"

"Most women like to get dressed up and go out." She mumbled. "I like to go dancing."

Cillian groaned dramatically and dropped his head, pounding his forehead on the bed. "I told you baby, no more dancing."

"You said I couldn't dance unless you were there, not that I couldn't dance." She countered sleepily.

"Hmph, I'll have to think about that." He slid his hands slowly up the sides of her legs to her hips. Her eyes were already closing. "Go to sleep angel."

"K." She mumbled.

Cillian watched her for a long time while she slept. The dark circles underneath her eyes were very telling. Imogen had been so upset when she'd seen her. And she hadn't even seen any of her injuries yet. She just looked so exhausted and she was moving slowly because the soreness was setting in.

He laid down beside her and pulled the blanket over them. He hoped that talking more about her kidnapping would ease the horror she'd experienced. If so, maybe it would keep the nightmares away.

She'd screamed in her sleep again on the plane ride home. They'd dimmed the lights and everyone had just settled in to rest for the remainder of the flight when her screams echoed through the darkened cabin. It was a heart-wrenching sound that had his men on edge.

He'd lifted her into his lap and kissed her awake. Trying anything to bring her out of it. As soon as she'd awakened, he'd carried her back to the bedroom. It had taken a long time to settle her down. She'd clung to him and cried for nearly an hour.

She'd refused to try to sleep again, so he'd turned on the TV. He was flipping through channels when he found an old John Wayne movie called El Dorado. She'd immediately stopped him and smiled saying it was one of hers and her mother's favorites. The tightness in his gut had relaxed slightly at her smile.

There was no popcorn on the plane, but he found potato chips in the galley. He'd brought them to her to snack on along with a cold Ginger Ale. She laid her head on his stomach and together they watched the old movie. By the end of it, she was asleep. Then and only then did he allow himself to doze off.

They were dressed all in black with their faces painted so they faded into the night. Alpha team one, and two members from team two moved through the trees like ghosts. The Kelly twins opting to stay back to guard Chloe. Each man aware of his surroundings and the danger they faced.

Zane stepped from behind a tree and crouched. He pulled a digital pad from his tactical bag and quickly linked into the video feed monitoring the estate. He patiently recorded five minutes of footage, then replayed it, watching closely for any unnecessary or sudden movements. When he found none, he looped the footage and uploaded it into the video server housed inside the security room. Once he hit play, the footage replaced the live feed. "Video up."

Finn slid across the ground out in the open as he approached the fence. He pulled a signal jammer from the side pocket of his own bag. Quickly turning it on, he waited while it searched out and connected to the current running through the fence. Once he locked onto the frequency, he shoved the jammer's pointed end into the ground then selected deactivate. Almost instantly, the faint hum of the electric current running through the fence ceased.

He reached into his pocket and pulled out the pebbles he planned to use and tossed them at the fence for confirmation. When nothing happened, he whispered into the comm in his ear. "Fence down."

"It's a go." Cillian hissed a response.

Immediately eight other men slithered across the lawn into position, encircling the perimeter of the estate. With synchronized movements, they scaled the ten-foot fence with ease. Each landing on silent feet in the soft grass on the other side. They had one hour before the guards' changed shifts. That meant the men on patrol had been on duty for eleven hours now. They'd be tired and getting careless during their rounds. The dogs wouldn't be brought back out until the new crew made their first round of the perimeter.

Cillian relied on his men to follow the plan as he raced on silent feet past the guard in his section, slicing his throat as he went. "One down." If they were lucky, the team would eliminate the guards before the first shot was fired. A quick and clean in and out.

He flattened himself against the wall, fading into the corner by the side door and counted off the seconds as he waited patiently. Two minutes later, the next guard to walk the perimeter stepped outside. Cillian surged forward, slicing a Z pattern, neck, belly, groin into the guard then caught him before he hit the ground. He pulled him behind a bush then moved back toward the door. "Two down."

He eased the door open and slide inside, his Glock leading the way. He quickly cleared the room and moved into the grand foyer and over to the stairs that led to the second floor. Hugging the wall, he made his way soundlessly to Silas Murphy's bedroom. At the door of the master, he waited while he listened as each of his men checked in. All fifteen guards had been eliminated. Finn was moving up behind him. Felix, Terrance and Zane were making their way to the son's bedroom. The rest of the team moved into position to guard their backs.

Cillian glanced over his shoulder and made eye contact with Finn. When he nodded his assent, Finn slipped in front of him then eased the door open. Finn went in low, crouching silently, gun ready for any threat. He followed him in. Silently, they made their way through the small sitting room to the bedroom.

Silas was asleep in the middle of the bed. A lamp on the nightstand illuminated the room in soft light. As Cillian made his way to Silas, he heard a chain rattle slightly then Finn inhale sharply. He adjusted his stance to keep Silas in his sights and see what had caused Finn's slip. What he saw enraged him. "Fuck!" He hissed in disbelief.

He leaned over Silas and shoved the barrel of his Glock into his partially opened mouth. "Wake the fuck up asshole." He growled in fury.

Silas' eyes flew open then nearly bulged out of his head when he saw Cillian O'Donnell hovering over him! He instinctively reached for the gun.

"I wouldn't do that if I were you. Touch my hand and I'll blow the back of your head off. You are one sick fuck!" Cillian growled. "Finn, get her out of there."

In the corner of the room was a small animal cage. Inside the cage was a young girl. She didn't look much older than eleven or twelve. She had leather cuffs on her wrists and ankles and all four of her limbs were connected together behind her back to an O ring. She was lying on her stomach and the chain Finn heard jingling attached the ring to the top of the cage, keeping her immobile. She had a ball gag in her mouth, a thick black leather collar around her throat and her tiny naked body was covered in bruises and whip marks.

The girl shook violently as Finn approached the cage. "Mother fucker!" He swore as he reached out and pulled the key off of a clip affixed to the cage right in front of her. "He put the goddamned key right in front of her face." Finn turned blazing eyes toward Silas Murphy. "Kill that fucker!"

"Oh, I intend to." Cillian shoved the barrel of the gun to the back of Silas' throat so hard the suppressor attached to the end of it broke several of his teeth.

"Easy now, we're not going to hurt you." Finn spoke softly to the terrified girl. "Terrance, master bedroom, now." Finn whispered into his comm. This was going to kill his friend. But he was the only one of them who had any experience with little girls. His little sister wasn't much older than this one when she'd been taken. So, this would bring back painful memories for him, but they didn't have a choice. The rest of them had no idea how to handle a little girl.

"I'm on my way. Brother and sister-in-law have been eliminated." Terrance reported as he made his way stealthily toward the master bedroom.

Finn unlocked the cage door and reached in to unhook the chain from her cuffs. Then he unbuckled the ball gag and eased the large red ball out of her mouth. "I have to slide you out so I can get the cuffs off, ok?"

She nodded weakly but continued to watch him through terrified eyes.

Finn considered the battered girl for a quick second. "Jesus, I don't know where to touch you that's not going to hurt."

"It's ok. Please just get me out." Her voice was so low he barely heard her.

"Alright, I'll try to be careful. Here we go." He reached into the small cage and gently lifted her slightly at her shoulders then slowly slid her out.

As soon as he had her out of the cage, he removed the collar then started working on the cuffs. When he released the last cuff, she skuttled away from him until she hit the wall behind her then curled into a protective ball.

Finn watched her carefully but didn't approach her. "Your arms and legs are going to tingle from the circulation coming back, so be ready. It's going to feel like fire ants stinging you. Try wiggling your fingers and toes. That should help."

"What the fuck?" Terrance hissed as he walked through the door and saw the tiny battered child on the floor.

She flinched and immediately shrank further into herself.

"Easy." Finn warned and raised his hands up so she could see them.

Terrance, realizing instantly that he'd frightened her, slowly crouched down in front of her, but far enough away that he hoped she didn't feel threatened. "I'm sorry, little one." He gentled his voice to a soft cadence. "I didn't mean to frighten you. I was just surprised to see you here."

"Please don't hu..hurt me!" Lilly stuttered. She was trembling uncontrollably and the other guy was right. Fiery needles of sensation were attacking her arms and legs. She'd never be able to run.

"Never." He said gently, making sure to maintain eye contact with her so she could see he was telling the truth.

Silas mumbled, trying to speak around the barrel in his mouth.

"Shut up, asshole." Cillian barked. "I want to blow your fuckin head off so bad right now."

"What's your name?" Terrance focused on the girl, ignoring the others in the room.

"L..Li...Lilly." Lilly Carmichael forced the words from her dry throat. He had kind eyes that sparkled like hammered gold, but that didn't mean he was kind. She knew better now.

"Lilly, I'm Terrance." He pointed at his chest with his thumb. Then he nodded toward Finn. "That's Finn and the guy by the bed is our boss, Cillian."

Lilly didn't reply. She just stared wide-eyed at the huge bald black man crouched in front of her. He was so big, he blocked out most of the light in the room. And he had a long, jagged scar on the left side of his face. But if she ignored the scar, he kind of looked like the youth minister at her church.

"Where are you from?"

"Ka.. Katy, Texas."

"How old are you, Lilly?"

"Fourteen." Her voice cracked on her reply.

Terrance wanted to tear this fucking place apart! How dare, these motherfuckers! Instead, he fought his rage and smiled softly. "Ok Lilly from Katy, Texas, I know I'm big and I'm scarred, but I won't hurt you. I give you my word. And while you're with me, I won't let anyone else hurt you either."

Lilly watched him skeptically. She'd been hurt enough already. They'd done terrible things to her and the other girls. Things her mind refused to dwell on right now. But none of those horrible men had kind eyes. None of them even tried to be nice. Could she really believe him?

"How did you get here?" Terrance asked.

Lilly took a deep breath to steady her voice. Her throat was so dry it was hard to talk. "Some men grabbed us outside of Starbucks. I think it was about a week ago, but I'm not sure." Her bottom lip quivered and tears trickled down her cheeks.

"Us?" Finn asked from across the room where he'd backed away to give her space. He was searching through a dresser for something for her to wear.

"Yes. My big sister Laura and me."

"Where's your sister now?" Terrance asked.

"Down in the basement with the others."

"The others?" Finn's startled gaze shifted to Cillian's then turned back to the girl. Slowly so as not the startle her, he handed Terrance a T-Shirt for her to wear.

"Put this on Lilly" Terrance carefully placed the shirt on the ground in front of her.

"There's twelve of us down there. Or there was until he brought me up here." She slipped the shirt over her head quickly. Her stomach recoiled at the through of wearing clothes that Silas had worn, but she was glad to be covered up for the first time in days.

"Jesus!" Cillian growled then turned his focus back on Silas. "I had big plans for you, asshole. But you're not worth my time, you disgusting motherfucker!" Before he could change his mind, he pulled the trigger five times. All those years. Patiently working to take this fucker down. The plans to make him suffer. He'd dreamed of ways to torture him. And it was over in an instant. He thought he'd be disappointed. But one look at that little girl was all he needed. "We have a problem," he called into his comm. "We're headed to the basement."

"Copy that." Came the multiple replies.

"Catch our six. We have a young girl with us. Priority one." Cillian walked over and stood behind Terrance. "Can you walk?"

"Are you here to save us?" She didn't trust them. They hadn't hurt her yet, but they had guns. And the "boss" just killed Silas like it was nothing.

"We are now." Finn answered. "Lilly, we're going to go down to the basement to get the others. You stay behind Cillian. Terrance is going to be right behind you. We need to move now."

Lilly wrapped her arms around herself again then glanced warily at Terrance.

"Ok Lilly, let's go." Terrance reached out his hand and waited.

She stared at his hand for a long moment. He didn't push, he just waited to see if she would take it. She didn't want to, but she wasn't sure she could stand without help yet. She'd been in that cage for hours and still had needles attacking her limbs. She looked up from his outstretched hand to meet his kind gaze again and spoke softly. "Your scars don't scare me." She thought he should know. Everything else about these men scared her, but not his scars. "My momma says scars add character. She said each one tells a story. Some have happy endings, some don't."

Terrance smiled sadly at the little girl when she slowly placed her tiny hand in his. "That's right little one, some don't." Looking at her, he could see why they'd taken her. Lilly was stunning with her alabaster skin and thick black hair full of soft curls. Her big blue-green eyes were surrounded by thick dark lashes too. Beautiful eyes that had unfortunately seen more than a child ever should.

Finn glanced over his shoulder as he moved toward the door. "Half of the guards are still alive, so we have to be quiet as we move. Can you do that Lilly?"

"Yes. But there are usually guards in the basement."

"How many?" Finn whispered right before he eased the door open.

"It's different every day. They come down there and, and, um" Her lip trembled as more tears fell.

"Don't think about it right now Lilly. Let's just go find your sister." Cillian whispered then motioned for her to follow him as he fell in behind Finn. They'd memorized the floor plans so they knew where they were going, but finding it in the dark would take time, time they didn't have.

As a group, they traveled silently down the stairs that led to the foyer. Zane and Felix whispered into their comm's making them aware of their positions before they appeared out of the dark. Zane stepped behind Terrance to better protect his six. He knew if things went to shit, Terrance would protect the girl before he'd protect himself. Felix took the lead with Finn as they made their way down to the basement while the rest of the team secured the house.

Cillian felt the monster inside him rear its head. He wanted to roar with fury. The girls were in cages. Fucking cages! They were all completely naked and covered in bruises and bloody whip marks. The site so reminiscent of the state he'd found Chloe in just days before.

Like Lilly, each girl had a leather collar at her throat and cuffs locked around each wrist and ankle. Some were shackled to cots, others hanging from rings embedded in the cement wall at the back of their cages.

When they'd initially approached the basement door, they'd heard screaming. He, Finn and Felix had left Terrance and Zane outside with Lilly while they'd quietly slipped into the dimly lit room. The scene they'd encountered had enraged them. Three guards were raping one of the girls on the floor in the center of the room while the others watched from their prisons.

He and his men had come in silently like demons out of the dark and attacked them from behind. In his rage, he'd sliced his target's throat so deep he'd nearly decapitated him. Felix and Finn simultaneously doing the same to the other two. Once they were down, Felix dragged the bodies away from the girl and Finn crouched beside her. She screamed again as he approached.

"Easy." He tried to sooth her. "I'm going to unhook you."

The girl stopped screaming but continued her desperate cries as Finn unhooked each cuff. As soon as she was free, she scuttled across the room to get away from him and curled in on herself.

"Find the fucking keys." Cillian barked the order at his men. He was going to burn this fucking place to the ground. He just wished these disgusting assholes were still alive so he could lock them in these goddamned cages. He wanted to burn them alive.

"On the hook by the door," came an exhausted voice from a cage in the back corner.

Finn searched out the voice in the dim light while Cillian rushed toward the door and the keys. His gaze locked onto blazing blue green eyes exactly like her sisters. Her disheveled black hair was a riot of curls around her head and shoulders. Her delicate alabaster skin, so like her sisters, was covered in blood and bruises. It was obvious that this is what little Lilly would look like as a young woman. "Laura, I presume?"

The beautiful girl lifted her chin, eyes narrowed in fury as she demanded, "where's my sister?"

Before he could answer, Cillian opened the door and Terrance stepped inside. Lilly shot around him like a rocket and raced to her sister's cage.

"Laura!" Lilly screamed. Tears of relief trickling down her cheeks as she gripped the metal of the cage that held her big sister.

"Lilly! Thank God! Baby, are you ok?" Laura yanked at the cuffs locking her to the rings in the wall. Every place on her abused body ached, every movement excruciating, but she didn't care. She needed to get to Lilly. She'd been going insane for two days, terrified of what they were doing to her baby sister.

Lilly avoided answering her question by looking over at the dead bodies in the corner. She was glad those monsters were dead. She just wished it was all of them instead of only three. Seeing them dead, she turned somber eyes to the man she'd just decided to trust. "Terrance, please get her down."

"I'm on it, Lilly." Terrance met Laura's furious eyes and nodded slightly in approval. She hadn't been broken yet and she'd need that anger to sustain her. He quickly worked to unlock the door of the little cell then moved into the cramped space and began working on her cuffs.

"Who are you?" Laura kept her eyes on Lilly while the big man removed her cuffs. For such a big guy, he was extremely gentle. But she was more concerned for Lilly. She was avoiding eye contact with her. This wasn't a good sign.

"My name is Terrance."

"How did you find us?"

"By accident. We would've come sooner had we known you were here." Terrance caught Laura when the last cuff was released and she began to fall. "I got you."

Laura cried out when his hands came in contact with her skin.

"I'm sorry." Terrance whispered.

"Iss..ok" she mumbled. He had huge hands. They were gentle, but there wasn't a place on her body that didn't hurt.

Once they'd freed all the girls, Cillian assessed their situation. They were way out of their element here. These young women had been brutalized. Most were so weak they could barely stand on their own. To make matters worse, one of them was Russian and didn't speak a word of English. Another was speaking in broken English but kept switching back to Spanish so fast Felix, his linguistics guy, was having trouble keeping up. And two refused to speak at all.

It was obvious they were all from different parts of the world. And they were all in need of serious medical care. Drew was attempting to give them aid. But every time he got too close; they'd scream in terror.

Cillian turned and met Finn's furious gaze. "We need to call Jupiter."

"I know, but first we have to figure out how we're going to get them out of here." He looked at the group of battered women who were now huddled together then back at Cillian. "They're in no shape to run."

"Mr. Cillian?"

"Yes Lilly?" Cillian looked over at Lilly who was standing with her sister out in front of the others. She was the youngest and from the injuries he'd seen on her little body, she'd been hurt just as badly as the rest of them. But she was clinging to her sister's hand and together they were out in front. The two sisters standing bravely between the men and the other girls.

"Please don't leave us here. We'll run if we have to. We won't slow you down. I promise."

"Lilly honey, we're not leaving you. We just have to figure out how to get all of you out of here safely. Ok?"

She blew out the breath she'd been holding. "Ok."

"Chloe, baby wake up." Cillian sat on the bed beside Chloe and shook her gently. They'd only been back home for a few days. She was healing, but still needed to rest.

"Hmm." Chloe squinted from the glare of the lamp light as she woke. Once her eyes adjusted, she took one look at Cillian's face and knew something terrible had happened. His face was covered in black paint but she could tell by the look in his eyes that something was very wrong. Forgetting her injuries, she sat up abruptly and nearly groaned when her aching body protested. "What's wrong?"

"We have a situation."

"Is someone hurt? Who?" She started to panic. His team were her guys. She cared about every single one of them.

"I need your help. Get dressed angel. Hurry." Cillian hated bringing her into this, but he didn't have a choice.

It had taken a lot longer than expected to get back to the island. The women were naked, beaten bloody and it was freezing outside. They'd needed clothes before he could move them.

He'd called over the comm link to have Jacob and Van find something for each girl. They'd silently avoided the rest of guards and searched until they found T-Shirts, socks and blankets. That was the best they could do under the circumstances.

He and his men left that basement with those terrified girls and made their way to the garage. They hadn't had a choice. The girls weren't strong enough to travel over the rough terrain in the cold. The rest of his men met them at the top of the stairs and as one, they'd moved quickly through the house.

They were almost at the door to the garage when they'd encountered the rest of the guards in the kitchen drinking coffee. One of the girls had cried out in terror, eliminating their element of surprise. As expected, the guards hadn't gone down easily. But they'd gone down. It just took longer than it should've.

Then they'd loaded the girls into the cars in the garage and driven out the front gate. After exchanging the cars for their own SUV's, they'd gone straight to the marina. It had taken even more time to delicately encourage the girls to board the yacht. They wanted to run. But with a lot of patience, Terrance had talked Lilly and her sister into it and the rest followed their lead.

He'd called and left a message for Jupiter from a burner phone once he had them secured on his yacht. Jupiter specialized in locating the lost. He recovered high profile kidnapped victims, going into places no one else dared. He claimed a high price for his services and used those funds, working behind the scenes to take down sex trafficking rings.

No one knew Jupiter's real identity or those of his team. They were ghosts. He'd met Jupiter years ago when he and Finn lived in the slums trying to avoid Silas. A few years later, Jupiter helped them recover Terrance's sister.

Within minutes of leaving the message, Jupiter returned the call and was already on his way to pick up the girls.

Now the women were huddled together in his foyer down stairs. They'd refused to go any further inside afraid they were exchanging one prison for another. He'd called Doc in to treat them, but they wouldn't let him get near them. And several of them really needed it. His team had turned to him with knowing looks. He'd scowled at them, but he knew they were right. He'd had no choice but to come and get Chloe. Hopefully, she could calm the girls enough to let Doc examine them.

Chloe dressed as quickly as possible in a bulky sweater that covered her still bruised throat and wrists and a long flowing skirt.

"You'll need shoes baby." Cillian knelt at her feet with fuzzy socks.

"Tell me what happened." Chloe eased down onto the bed while Cillian helped her with her shoes.

"There were girls, Chloe. Twelve of them."

"What do you mean, girls?" Her gut clenched.

"In the basement of the house where we were. They were in fuckin cages!"

"Cages?"

"Baby, they're a mess. Doc needs to treat them, but they won't let him."

"You've got to be kidding me." Chloe's mind instantly flashed back to that horrible cabin.

"Angel, we need you." He hated fucking doing this to her, but he had no choice.

At the sound of his voice, her thoughts came back to the here and now. She stared into his anguished eyes for long moments before she blew out a sad breath. "Then let's go."

Cillian stepped out of the elevator with Chloe in his arms, Patrick on his heels. He carried her into the foyer and set her gently on her feet.

Chloe took one look at the disheveled group and nearly gasped in horror. They looked hopeless and terrified. She wanted to cry for them, but she knew they didn't need her tears. Not now. No, right now, they needed her help. So, she straightened her shoulders and looked over at Patrick who'd cursed under his breath the minute he'd seen them too.

"Patrick, go back up to my closet. In the bottom two drawers of the center island, you'll find leggings and sweat pants. In the drawers above them, you'll find sweatshirts and sweaters. Bring them all please. Oh, and in the top drawer on the opposite side, you'll find socks. They need clean socks." She'd find shoes for them later.

"Ok Chloe." Patrick turned and jogged back toward the elevator.

"I'll go help him." Rourke followed him out of the room.

Chloe turned back to Cillian. "You need to have someone go wake up Imogen."

"I'll do it." Finn stepped forward.

"Tell her we need hot chocolate." Chloe assessed the group of women quickly. "Lots of hot chocolate. And soup. She made some for me earlier."

"Got it."

"Oh, and Finn?

"Yes?" He paused at the door to look back at her.

"Wash that stuff off of your face." She turned to the rest of the team. All of them had black paint covering their faces. "All of you, wash that stuff off. You're probably scaring the crap out of them."

Finn grinned slightly at the sound of her snippy voice then he nodded his approval that she'd taken her place here and walked out.

"Chloe, baby. They need medical care first." Cillian insisted.

"Chloe, I need to treat them." Doc added.

Chloe turned and met Cillian's gaze. "Trust me."

He lifted his hands wide, palms out to indicate she had the lead. She nodded approvingly at him then turned to address the women. "Ladies, my name is Chloe. I'm Cillian's wife." It was the first time she'd ever referred to herself that way and surprisingly, it felt right. She wanted to look over at him to see his reaction, but didn't. She was worried that if she did, the women might think she was lying. Instead, she continued, "I know you're all very frightened and none of you have any reason to trust us. But I promise, we're going to take care of you and get you home." She'd make sure of it. "Now, who wants to come upstairs and take a hot shower?"

Lilly peeked up at the tiny beautiful woman then shifted her gaze to Terrance. He smiled and winked at her. She quickly averted her gaze back down to her feet. They were filthy. But so was every inch of her body; filthy and disgusting. She knew she would never be able to wash away the filth. She could still feel Silas' hands touching her, feel him inside of her, tearing her apart. She shivered in revulsion and slowly raised her hand. She was so tired and scared out of her mind but oh God, she desperately wanted a shower.

Surprisingly, all but two raised their hands. Chloe smiled when one of the young women stepped forward holding the hand of a much smaller replica of herself. The woman was about her age, but the little girl with her was just that, a little girl. Chloe's heart broke all over again when she saw her.

"You're not Irish." The woman stated skeptically. Fury and hatred burned deep into Laura's soul. She wasn't certain she'd feel this overwhelming need for revenge if those monsters had only taken her. But they'd taken Lilly too. And they'd hurt her. Now she had to stay vigilant to make sure nobody hurt her again and she had to get her baby sister home.

"No, I'm an American." Chloe answered. "And from your accent, I'd say you are too. Texas maybe?"

"Yes. Katy Texas. I've heard your accent before. When I went to New Orleans for Mardi Gras last February."

"That's right. I'm from New Orleans. What's your name?" Chloe carefully navigated the conversation. It was evident the other women were looking to this one as their leader. And she didn't trust them one bit. If she could reassure her then the others might be as well.

"I'm Laura." Laura looked down at the top of Lilly's head. She wanted a hot shower so badly. But more than anything at this moment, she wanted it for Lilly. "This is my sister, Lilly."

"Hello Lilly." Chloe met the little girl's big blue-green eyes when she peeked out at her through a curtain of black curls just before she averted them back down to her feet. "Would you like a hot shower and some clean clothes?"

"Yes." Lilly didn't lift her gaze from her feet again, but she nodded her head decisively.

"Alright." Chloe looked back to Laura for confirmation. "What about you Laura? Are you in?"

Laura let out the breath she'd been holding. Was this real? Were they really going home? If this was a trick, it was a cruel one. She looked down at the top of Lilly's head then back at Chloe. "Yes, I'm in."

"Alright ladies, follow me."

"Chloe." Cillian warned when she moved to the steps. He didn't want her walking on her injured foot, he'd rather carry her. And he also didn't want her up there by herself with the women.

"I'm fine." She assured him. And to her surprise, every one of the women followed her up the stairs to the guest wing.

Cillian nodded toward Jacob and Zane. Both men fell into step behind them, making sure to keep a comfortable distance away.

The group didn't want to split up. Chloe tried to encourage them to each take a room, but she supposed they figured there was safety in numbers. However, by the time Patrick and Rourke brought the clothes, some of them were rethinking that decision.

Chloe considered each woman, trying to decide what was going to fit who. "I'm kind of short, so this stuff is going to be too small for most of you. But it's clean and it's yours."

She held onto a pair of leggings that came to just above her ankles and a sweater that had three-quarter length sleeves then put the rest of the clothes on the bed. "Lilly, this is the closest I've got to fitting you."

Lilly was drooping with exhaustion. She wished Sasha would hurry up and finish her shower. She fought the tears that wanted to fall when Chloe offered her the clothes. Clothes that she'd picked just for her. She looked toward Laura to see what she wanted her to do.

"Go ahead honey, take them." Laura wanted to wrap Lilly up in her arms and take away the horror of what they'd been through. She couldn't do that, but there was one thing she could do. And she would; for Lilly. So, she turned toward Chloe. "If the offer to use another room is still open, I'd like to take you up on that."

"Of course. There are rooms for all of you. Come on, I'll show you."

Laura took Lilly's hand and followed Chloe to the next room. Just like the first one, this room was beautiful. She was afraid her filthy socks would ruin the rug. When she stopped to remove them before going in, Chloe waved her through.

"Don't worry about that. Let's just get you situated."

Laura stared at Chloe for a long moment. "Thank you, Chloe."

Chloe smiled. "Let me know if you need anything. I'm going to go see if the other women want rooms of their own now too. Take your time. I'll be waiting at the end of the hall by the stairs. When you're finished, we'll get you something to eat."

Chloe and Imogen watched as the women ate hot soup and crusty grilled cheese sandwiches. Imogen had been beside herself when she'd seen them. But when she'd met little Lilly, she hadn't been able to keep the tears from falling. Chloe had taken her back into the kitchen on the pretense of getting them water and iced tea so she could calm her down.

After their showers, Doc treated the open wounds on the few women who'd allow him near them. They couldn't force the others to accept the help, so Chloe led them into the dining room instead.

Now the women had eaten and were quietly sipping hot chocolate. Cillian and his team were all leaning against the walls surrounding them. He cleared his throat to get everyone's attention.

"I called a contact of mine to help you. His name is Jupiter."

"Jupiter?" Chloe asked, puzzled by the odd name.

"Yes. He specializes in finding the lost and bringing them home." Cillian turned from Chloe to address the women. "We don't think yours were random kidnappings. Because you're all from different parts of the world, it symbolizes a pipeline."

"If it is, Jupiter will shut it down so this doesn't happen to another woman." Finn added.

"His plane lands in an hour. He's coming to take you all home." Cillian held up his hand when some of the women panicked and started crying.

"You expect us to trust him?" Laura asked in angry disbelief as she reached over and took Lilly's hand.

"After what you've been through? No. But I trust him. He's helped us in this area before." Cillian answered.

"Terrance?" Lilly's voice quivered as she turned terrified eyes toward him.

Terrance had been leaning against the wall directly behind her. At her call, he stepped forward and crouched beside her chair. "Little one," he addressed her softly. "I know it's difficult, but I trust him or you wouldn't be leaving with him."

"But, I'm afraid." She whispered.

Her frightened little whisper broke his heart. She'd been incredibly brave so far. "Lilly." He whispered gently. "Didn't I say I wouldn't let anyone hurt you while you're with me?"

"Yes, I know you said that, but I'm still scared."

"I know you are. I would be surprised if you weren't. But Jupiter is the perfect guy for this." He turned to include Laura in his next statement. "He helped me when my own little sister was taken away from us. What happened to you, happened to her too. But he found her for me and brought her home. He'll do the same for you."

Laura sighed sadly and met those sincere golden brown eyes. In his eyes she saw the same anguish she felt in her heart reflected there. She nodded to let him know she understood. Then she did something she hadn't know she was capable of anymore, she trusted him. "Lilly, if Terrance says it's going to be ok, it will be."

The women were all huddled together around Chloe in the hanger when Jupiter's plane landed. Cillian was uneasy about Jupiter being on his island. He couldn't put his finger on why, but his senses were screaming at him.

Moments later, Finn escorted Jupiter and his men inside. Cillian wasn't surprised when they all came in wearing disguises. He'd never seen Jupiter's face before. In order to protect his identity, he never went out in public without one.

He wore a ball cap pulled down low over his eyes. His hair was covered in a black bandana tied at the back of his neck beneath the cap. He wore thick rimmed glasses and Cillian knew better than to trust that those brown eyes were his. His face was covered in a dark beard that looked real. His nose had a sharp beak and was crooked like it'd been broken. The last time he'd seen Jupiter, he hadn't had a beak nose, so that wasn't real either.

"Thank you for coming."

Jupiter shook Cillian O'Donnell's hand then surveyed the group before moving his gaze back to Cillian. He was a man of few words, but he needed details. "I have a medic on my team. How serious are their injuries?"

"Some have deep cuts that need stitching, but they won't let us get close enough to do it. Obvious signs of rape and torture, but none have been examined."

"That's not unusual. We'll take care of it. Tell me what you know about where you found them and how they got there."

Chloe watched from her position in the center of the women as the group of men came in. They were really big and looked rough and mean. But she figured they'd have to be considering what they did. Several of the women whimpered, so she assumed they thought the same.

Chloe squeezed Laura's hand to give her reassurance then did the same to Lilly. "I'm going to go ask how soon they'll be ready to leave. I'll be right back." She wanted to get a closer look.

Both men turned as she approached them. Cillian reached out and took her hand as soon as she was within reach.

"Angel, this is Jupiter. Jupiter, this is my wife." Cillian pressed their joined hands to his thigh.

"Hello, I'm Chloe."

"Jupiter." Jupiter considered her for a long moment before he spoke again. "Are they ready to go?" He nodded toward the women.

"They're afraid, but yes, they want to go home. It just may take some convincing to get them on the plane with you."

"Do you think you can get them on board and settled while we finish up here?"

"Maybe. I'll try." Chloe glanced up at Cillian when he squeezed her hand tightly.

"No."

She reached up and touched his chest with her free hand. "You know they need me."

"No." His neck was itching so she was not getting on that fuckin plane.

"Cillian, little Lilly needs reassurance. All of them do."

"Chloe."

"Please," she cut off his next words, "let me do this for them."

"It's not unusual for victims to resist rescue efforts. Their terror keeps them for thinking rationally. If they trust her, they'll need her." Jupiter added.

Cillian knew that, but he didn't like it. He looked over at the terrified group all desperately clinging to each other then met his wife's beautiful pleading blue eyes. He sighed heavily because for some fucked up reason, he couldn't deny her. "Alright, but make it quick."

Chloe handed Laura the last blanket to tuck around herself. She'd chosen the front two seats for herself and Lilly. A man named Jericho stood a few feet away at the front of the plane by the door and had directed them to the seats. Other than Jupiter, the rest of his team were already on board and unfortunately, their presence was scaring the women.

Lilly was trembling uncontrollably, so Laura curled her body around her and hugged her close. She spoke softly over Lilly's head to Chloe. "Do you know where they're taking us?"

"No, but I'll ask Jupiter when he gets here if you'd like."

"Please. I think it'll reassure everyone. If we know the plan, then we'll know what to expect."

"Ok. Hang tight a minute." Chloe approached Jericho. "Do you have a pen and paper?"

The stoic man opened a cabinet and pulled out a pencil and a sheet of paper then handed it to her.

"Thank you." Chloe smiled slightly at his silent demeanor. None of the men had spoken a word since they'd boarded. She quickly wrote down her cell phone number on the paper then gave the pencil back to him.

"Here." She pushed the paper into Laura's hand. "This is my number. You call me when you get home."

"Ok." Laura tightened her fist around it. "Thank you, Chloe."

Before Chloe could reply, both of their gazes suddenly shifted to the door of the plane as Jupiter rushed in, leaping over the last few steps and landing abruptly inside. The door was already lifting as the stairs collapsed and it closed behind him.

"Go!" Jupiter yelled out the order and the plane suddenly started moving.

"Wait!" Chloe surged toward him. "You can't leave yet. I have to get off first."

"You're coming with us." Jupiter stared at her intently.

"What?!" Chloe looked at the man like he was crazy. Cillian was going to lose his mind.

"Chloe Bell." David Brock Guidry, Jr., aka Jupiter, pulled off the glasses then removed the hat and bandana as he said his little sister's name. The sister who had basically disappeared from the face of the earth nearly a year ago. He'd been tearing the world apart looking for her. Now it made sense why he couldn't find her. He always found his target, always. He had contacts everywhere. But Cillian O'Donnell had very important connections too. Even in the US. That explained why the most important target he'd ever searched for had disappeared into thin air. His baby sister, Chloe.

Chloe stared at Jupiter in disbelief. It couldn't be. He was dead. She'd gone to his funeral. She'd grieved enough for a lifetime. But as she watched him slowly peel the rubber disfigured nose away to reveal his own beneath, she could see it. Take away the beard and the scars and oh my God, she could see it! He looked just like her dad. "Brock?"

Chapter 40: Definitely a Man Thing

The plane came to an abrupt stop before it had even built-up speed which caused Chloe to lose her balance. Brock caught her when she stumbled before she hit the floor. She hissed when his hands came into contact with the slashes hidden under her bulky sweater.

"Son of a bitch!" Justice stormed out of the cockpit. "That motherfucker's playin chicken with a goddamned plane!"

Brock tried to hold onto Chloe, but she jerked out of his arms.

"Let go!" Chloe yelled and yanked away from him. She was still in shock and royally pissed off. How was this even possible?

"Chloe Bell," Brock reached for her again.

"Don't you touch me!" She stepped further away from him as she yelled, "how could you do this! They said you were dead!" She was screaming. She could hear her own voice ringing in her ears. She had been devastated when she'd lost him. And her mother, oh God! Her mother still hadn't recovered completely.

"Chloe, calm down!"

"Don't you tell me to calm down! Are you crazy?!" She was getting more hysterical by the minute. This was going to kill her mom and dad. The ringing continued. It took her a second to realize the ringing was a phone. And it was coming from Jupiter, Brock or whoever the hell he was.

"Chloe, I can explain everything, all of it. But you have to calm down so we can get out of here." Brock figured she'd be surprised, but he hadn't expected her to react quite like this. She was furious.

"I'm not going anywhere with you. Open the door!" Chloe snapped. Who the hell did he think he was? She could not believe this shit. She was so angry and hurt she wanted to cry.

"No, now calm down so we can talk." He looked at Justice, "what do you mean he's playing chicken."

"Dude, the second that door closed, two SUVs pulled out in front of the plane. We're blocked in. Jagger almost hit them. He says until they move, we can't take off. It's as if he knew what we'd planned."

"Chloe?" Laura called over their conversation. You could clearly hear the anxiety in her voice. "What's happening?"

Chloe tried to pull herself together enough to reassure the women. In her shock, she'd completely forgotten they were there. "Don't worry Laura," she glanced over Laura's head to include the rest of the women, "this is my brother." She glanced back at him and hissed, "my dead brother!"

Brock hit the button on his phone to send the call to voicemail and stop the annoying ringing. "Chloe, dad called and told me what happened. We've been searching for you for months."

"Dad! Dad called you?"

"Yes."

"Dad knew you were alive? All this time?"

"Yes, he's known from practically the beginning. He never bought the Navy's story and kept digging. We had no choice, for his own safety, we had to tell him."

"What? Tell him what? And what about mom?" She demanded.

"Um Jupiter," Jericho interrupted. "There are a lot of guns pointed at us right now. And some crazy asshole is under the plane fucking with the access panel."

"Fuck! How did that son of a bitch know?"

"Brock!" Chloe yelled to bring his attention back to their conversation.

Brock blew out a frustrated breath then bowed his head and rubbed the back of his neck. "Chloe Bell, it's kind of a long story."

"Start talking." She was so angry she wanted to smack him!

Brock glanced over at the frightened faces of the girls on his plane then to his men who to his frustration appeared amused. He scowled at them then turned back to Chloe. "Alright, I'll tell you. But it's not pretty."

"Look around you, Brock." Chloe waved her hand toward the girls who were all staring wide eyed at them. "Life isn't pretty."

"That's very true. And it's a shame. What I have to tell you may upset them." He pointed his thumb toward the girls just as she had.

"Nothing you say can be worse than what we've been through," Laura chimed in from her seat in the front row. "Tell her."

Brock wanted to snap at the beautiful girl and tell her to mind her own business, but he wouldn't. She was right, she'd been through hell. They all had. And to make matters worse, he couldn't keep his eyes from constantly wanting to shift in her direction. Even in her battered state, she was fucking beautiful. And if he'd met her somewhere else, anywhere else, he'd be all over her.

Instead, he looked down when his phone started ringing again. "He is persistent, I'll give him that." He hit the button the send the call to voicemail again.

"Yes, he is." Chloe agreed gravely. "Start talking."

Brock stared at his sister for a long moment. She'd grown into a beautiful woman. She was as strong and confident as his dad said she was. And God, he'd missed her.

"Brock!"

"Ok," he couldn't help but smile at her demand. "To answer your first question, no, mom doesn't know. It was too risky."

"I can't believe dad kept this from her; from me."

"Chloe, it was the only way to ensure you both stayed safe."

She gave him a skeptical look. "Explain."

Brock looked at his men again to make sure they were still on board with this. They'd talked about it at length while they'd searched for her, but he needed to know they were still ok with it. After all, it wasn't just his story to tell.

"Do it." Jericho and Justice who were both standing by the door to the cockpit said at the same time.

Brock returned the nod the rest of his team gave him then leaned back against the wall and started talking. Thanks to Cillian O'Donnell, it didn't appear that they were going to be able to leave at this point anyway.

"It was my sixth year with the Seals. My team took a mission to retrieve a very important government official who'd been kidnapped while traveling on business. We'd located the target and were in the middle of extraction when we stumbled upon something the military didn't want us to find. They called them pleasure palaces. They were houses where women were kept hostage. It was a brothel really."

"What?" Chloe gasped in shock. This was not at all what she'd expected him to say.

"They were brought in from all over the world." Brock continued. "These women were of all ages, some as young as fourteen and fifteen. Their handlers would shoot heroin into their veins as soon as they arrived and quickly got them hooked. That's how they controlled them. Once they were addicted, they'd do anything for it. The bastards didn't even have to lock the fucking door to keep them there. The men used them for entertainment. Entertaining dignitaries and influential officers. Their handlers were paid top dollar for this service. It was disgusting."

"Oh my God." Chloe whispered.

"Oh Chloe, it was awful. We couldn't leave them." Brock looked over at his men. Rage blazed in their eyes at the memory.

Chloe followed his gaze and her breath caught at the looks on their faces. She turned her attention back to her brother when he continued.

"Harris, the guy we rescued was badly wounded and didn't have a lot of time, but he agreed with us. You see, he has daughters. Four of them. And like us, he couldn't stomach leaving them. So, we went off the grid for a few weeks and he used his resources and we were able to get them out of there. We had to kill the entire crew in charge to do it."

When he paused, Chloe looked confused. "But that would make you a hero, wouldn't it?"

"No honey." Brock sighed sadly.

"Why not?"

"Some of the handlers as well as those influential officials were our guys. They were part of the network. They were using the girls for their own entertainment."

"And they were making a fortune." Jericho added.

Chloe turned at the sound of his voice to look at him. "You were there?"

"We all were." Jericho waved his hand toward where the other men were sitting.

Chloe looked back at Brock. "So, what happened next?"

"Our CO lost his shit. He wanted us all dishonorably discharged and charged with murder."

"But why?" Chloe was so confused.

"Because we deviated from the mission and as a result, American soldiers died."

"But,"

"Chloe, he didn't care why they were killed. Only that they were."

Chloe stared at him for long moments trying to decide what to say next. Brock's phone started ringing again. She walked up to him and took it out of his hand then sent the call to voicemail herself.

"So, you were all dishonorably discharged?" She turned to include Jericho and the other men. She had to assume they were part of the original Seal team.

"No." Brock looked to his men. When they all nodded in agreement again, he turned back to her and continued. "Like I said before, Harris is a very important man." He stressed the word 'very'. "And Harris is not his real name. I used it to keep his identity secret. He pulled some strings and had the entire incident completely removed from our records as if it never happened. Then he faked our deaths."

Brock's gaze shifted to his team again then back to Chloe. "We all had to make a choice. And I know it hurt you, but I still think it was the right one. Harris formed a task force; code named JUPITER. That's us. We rescue the lost, those who need us. We aren't government employees, we're independent contractors. Sometimes we take contracts for the government when they really need us. But in order for this to work, we had to be ghosts. If not, we'd always have to fear for the lives of our families."

"Why JUPITER?"

"It stands for Justice, Unrelenting Protection, Innocent Trust, Every Rescue. It's our creed. This is my team." He waved his hand at his men then indicated the women and added, "this is what we do."

Chloe moved her gaze from one man's serious face to another. "You all follow him?" She pointed at Brock.

They all nodded, but it was Jericho who spoke up. "Always."

Just then Brock's phone started ringing again. Chloe met Brock's gaze then glanced down at the phone in her hand. She deliberately hit the button to answer it and brought it to her ear.

"Hey." She said into the phone while maintaining eye contact with her brother. God, she'd missed him so much.

"Are you alright baby?"

"Yes."

"Open the door, angel." Cillian ordered into the phone.

"We're kind of in the middle of something Cillian."

"Chloe, open that fuckin door!" He barked loud enough for everyone on the plane to hear him.

Chloe had enough of arrogant men. Seriously! She was on an emotional rollercoaster and certainly didn't need him yelling at her. "Don't curse at me Cillian O'Donnell! I love you, but you're getting on my nerves!" Chloe barked right back.

There was a long strained paused before he exploded. "Don't you dare tell me you love me for the first time over the goddamned phone! God damn it, Chloe! You get your ass out here where you fucking belong and tell me to my face!"

She hadn't meant for that to come out, but Jeezus, she had a lot going on at the moment! She rolled her eyes at his angry command and replied in a snarky voice she knew would probably earn her a spanking later. "I'm busy talking to my brother right now." She frowned at Brock's team when they cursed under their breaths.

There was another long pause before he continued in a strained voice, "angel, there are a lot of guns out here and in there, a lot of hostility and you're in the center of it. That's not a good place for you to be in your delicate condition."

"Cillian, I'm mostly just really sore and stiff now, the cuts are healing. I'm fine." She assured him.

"That's not what I'm talking about and you know it."

Chloe frowned in confusion. "Then what are you talking about?"

"Chloe," Cillian hissed into the phone. "I have an IQ that's off the charts, but it doesn't take a genius to count weeks?"

"Weeks? What the heck do you mean, weeks?" She glanced around at her audience. Everyone was watching her closely now. Battered women, smug men and her brother, all of them were watching her with avid interest. And Cillian was so furious, his voice so loud, they could all hear him clearly through the phone.

"You want to do this now? Fine! You're exhausted all the fucking time. You're nauseated more often than not and you spent weeks vomiting in the mornings and several times during the day."

When she gasped, he continued. "Yes, I know about that. I have cameras everywhere remember?" His voice was rising with his frustration. "And, you haven't had a period since the last week of October!"

Chloe sucked in a sharp breath as realization of what he meant dawned on her. Then she snapped just as loudly, "I am not pregnant Cillian!"

Cillian closed his eyes in frustration. He squeezed the phone in one hand and the bridge of his nose with the other. He'd waited weeks for her to tell him. He couldn't figure out why she hadn't. Was this it? Did she really not know? Was that even possible? "Chloe,"

"I'm not" she gasped in desperation. Her hands trembled so much she nearly dropped the phone. Oh God, was she? She tried to think back to her last period. True, it had been a while, but who could blame her for not paying attention. She'd been pretty freaking busy lately, what with getting married, being poisoned, a huge ass wedding, Christmas, her parent's accident then being kidnapped, AGAIN... really, who could keep up?

"Chloe, baby please open the door." Cillian whispered softly.

She wanted to cry. Was it possible? "Cillian," her whispered voice trembled.

He heard the fear and uncertainty in her voice. His little hellion was always so brave, so sure of herself, but this had obviously blindsided her. "Angel, it's going to be ok." He whispered to her using his Irish brogue shamelessly, knowing it soothed her.

"I, um." She didn't know what to say. A baby! Oh my God, a baby!

"Angel, it'll be ok. You and me, we got this." He reassured her gently.

"You promise?" Her voice was shaking so badly, but she needed to hear him say it. In that exact moment, she needed the sound of his voice reassuring her. She wanted to climb through the phone to get to him and she was clinging to it for dear life.

"Yes baby, I promise. And angel, you know I never lie to you."

"I know." Her whisper was barely audible. She thought about it for a second and he waited. He was right. He never did. Even when it served him, Cillian never lied to her. She took a deep fortifying breath. Her nerves settled; the trembling stopped. "Please don't hurt my brother."

"I won't as long as you come out of this unscathed."

"Cillian, please."

"Trust me angel."

She looked up and met Brocks troubled gaze. "I already did." She whispered. And she had. She'd given him Brock's identity knowing in her heart that he'd never do anything to endanger him. "I need to talk to my brother."

"I know baby." He knew she had to be devastated at the news that he was still alive and had been all this time. "You tell my brother-in-law to take those girls home then come back here so you can visit with him."

"Ok," Chloe whispered then absently dropped the hand holding the phone to her side, forgetting to disconnect the call. She looked at her brother with pleading eyes. "Brock, please open the door."

"Chloe no." Brock groaned his answer. He'd just found her. How could she expect him to let her go? He'd heard their conversation. He knew she was pregnant. But that didn't change anything. She needed to go home.

"Please. I love him." As soon as she said it again, she knew she was right.

"Chloe, have you ever heard of Stockholm syndrome? It's"

"Yes," she interrupted. "But trust me, that's not what this is. I love my husband, Brock." Then she smiled, unexpectedly delighted as she added, "I love him. And, I'm going to have his baby."

"Chloe?" He pleaded.

"Open the door, Brock." Chloe ordered softly.

"Open the door Jupiter." Laura chimed in.

All eyes turned to Laura who was staring daggers at Brock.

"Stay out of this, beautiful." Brock snapped.

Laura's chin lifted stubbornly and she glared at him. "For God's sake, just open the damned door. Why is it so hard for men to believe that a woman is capable of knowing her own mind?"

Chloe couldn't help it, she giggled. Laura's words and her fearless response to her huge, intimidating brother was just plain crazy under the circumstances. "That's definitely a man thing."

"Definitely." Laura agreed and smiled back. A real smile. The first one in a very long time.

Chloe turned back to her brother who was staring at Laura with an odd look on his face. "Make things easier for everyone and just open the door. Because trust me, this plane is not taking off with me on it." She smiled brightly again when she added, "my husband would never allow it."

"For fucks sake Jupiter! Open the goddamned door and let that little runt out of here before her husband loses his shit!" Jericho laughed.

Brock signed dramatically then walked over and hit the button to open the door. "We'll be back when we're finished with them." He nodded his head toward the women.

Chloe's gaze followed his nod and she looked back at the girls. "It's going to be alright. He'll take very good care of you." She assured them because now, she truly believed it.

"I know." Laura answered. And for the first time since she and Lilly had been snatched out of the Starbucks parking lot, she did. She looked from Chloe to Jupiter who was watching her closely and smiled again. "We know that now. Thank you, Chloe."

Chloe smiled sadly. She wasn't sure about all of the other women, but Laura? Laura was going to make it. "Remember to call me when you get settled back at home. Let me know how you're doing."

"I will. Good bye Chloe."

"Bye Laura. Bye Lilly." Chloe added when she spotted little Lilly peeking out from under her blanket. Lilly didn't reply, but the little girl smiled softly before ducking her head again.

Chloe stepped onto the landing of the stairs and looked out at the tarmac. The members of Team One, her guys, were all standing there with guns pointed at the plane. The minute they spotted her, they immediately lifted the barrels into the air and away from her. She searched the dark for Cillian; and there he was. Standing with his strong arms across his massive chest, his narrowed hips and long legs spread wide looking powerful and as arrogant as ever.

She met his steely gaze from across the tarmac and he slowly lifted an arrogant brow at her. Taunting her. It was so like him. She held his gaze as she walked slowly down the steps. Once she was on solid ground, she headed toward him. He smiled that sexy smile she loved so much and she couldn't stop her own smile from spreading across her face.

He opened his arms wide and she stepped into him, throwing hers around his neck. He lifted her gently into his arms and she wrapped her legs around his waist. He held her to him, resting his head on top of hers. "Angel." He whispered against her ear. "Tell me."

"I love you, Cillian." She whispered into his neck.

"I know. It's about damned time you admitted it." He chuckled when she gasped in outrage. "And angel?"

Chloe lifted her face from his neck to meet his gaze "What?"

"I love you."

She smiled softly. "Checkmate Cillian."

Cillian O'Donnell threw his head back and roared with laughter.

Keep reading for a sneak peak of my sizzling Irish King; Finn.

Irish Kings

Finn

Sidney Bourdonnay woke instantly when a broad hand covered her mouth. The large palm muffled her scream. Her eyes flew open on contact, meeting the furious gaze of the one man she feared most. Beautiful green eyes, glittering with fury, bore into hers. "Hey, gorgeous. Remember me?"

Shit! Shit! Shit! This is bad! Really bad! She'd been avoiding his calls and texts for the last two weeks! She had to. She was a freaking train wreck waiting to happen; impulsive and reckless. If you didn't believe her, just ask her mother. She was nothing like her best friend Chloe; she wasn't dependable or responsible. No, not Sidney. She always ended up throwing caution to the wind and diving in headfirst. Consequences be damned. But in this, with him, she'd promised herself she wouldn't. He was the one temptation she couldn't allow herself. Oh, she'd always been drawn to dark, moody, bad boys. But him? He wasn't a boy. And he wasn't just dark, he was dangerous. Viciously so. And he scared the crap out of her.

The night of Chloe and Cillian's wedding was the first time in a long while that she'd let herself go and acted on impulse. She'd done exactly what her mom always accused her of. She'd thrown caution to the wind. But in her defense, he was sexy as hell with his wicked taunts, whispering in her ear, touching her, enticing her. And the night they'd had together was seared into her brain forever. And holy shit! The passion was so hot, they'd nearly burned down that beautiful castle. Amazing, frightening, sizzling. All fell short of describing him and what he'd done to her that night. She shivered every time she thought about it. But then she'd gone home. Back to the real world. She hadn't come to her senses until she'd stepped off the plane in New Orleans. That's when reality hit, and she realized what she'd done. And the long drive back to Baton Rouge for class was full of recriminations.

Finn O'Donnell was livid. She'd been putting him off for months. Then two weeks ago, when her time was up, she stopped returning his texts. Avoided his calls. She was naïve if she thought she could hide from him. He respected her desire to graduate. He got it. He knew it was important to her, so he'd waited, and waited. Now he was done. "You think you can give me a little taste of that sweet pussy, then run away and never look back. Oh gorgeous, you don't know who you're dealing with. But you're about to find out."

Sidney mumbled into his hand. Her eyes shooting daggers at the beautiful Irishman. Damn him!

Finn glared into the sparkling, whiskey-colored eyes of the most beautiful women he'd ever seen. His woman. He slowly moved his hand away from her mouth, but before she could scream, he replaced his hand with his lips, covering hers, driving his tongue deep. Relishing her taste, taking what he wanted. He'd waited months to feel her lips under his again. And it was like coming home. She opened for him like a beautiful flower, welcoming him in.

Sidney savored the warm, firm lips against hers, the power he harnessed, the restraint he showed only for her. He could take her over so easily.

He ended the kiss, then covered her mouth with his hand again. This was his show, not hers. She was his weakness, his kryptonite. "You asked for time to finish school. I gave it to you." He hissed against her ear. "I've been patient, Sid, and I'm not a patient man. Ask anyone. But no more. This ones on you."

Jesus, he was hot; he tasted amazing. Spicy and warm. She craved just another taste. Had since the first kiss. He was an addiction burning through her blood. One that could make her reckless soul take flight. She couldn't allow herself this pleasure. This longing scared the shit out of her. Even now, her toes were curled, her core was damp, her senses on fire from just his kiss.

Finn settled his large frame over her smaller one and groaned as he nestled into her soft curves. He leaned in close, suckling the tender skin of her neck tightly, leaving his mark before glaring into those whiskey eyes again. "I'm done waiting, gorgeous."

Still lost in the heat from his kiss and his lips at her neck, it took her a second to process what he'd said; too long. The sharp sting at her neck came out of nowhere. Her eyes flew open in stunned accusation when she realized what he'd done. "Finn, no!" She mumbled into his palm.

"Yes!" He snapped, as his temper ignited. "And just remember, this is on you, Sid." He rested his forehead against hers. "Shh gorgeous girl. Just relax."

His whispered words were the last thing she heard, his warm lips on hers, the last thing she felt before her world went black.

Check Out My New Series. Coming soon:

Wild Orchids

What does it take to make a difference in someone's life? To change it for the better? While some are natural bystanders, others are not. That's the case here. But it's a well-kept secret. One that has been passed down from mother to daughter, generation to generation, since around the late 1800's.

I'm talking about a group of women you'd never suspect. They are the upper echelons of the New Orleans elite. The women behind the running to the city. Old money. High society. Sophisticated southern women who long ago decided, enough is enough.

There's a war raging across this country. It is a war against violence. It's victims? Women and children. Their Hero's? The unexpected, the diverse, a compassionate group who have come together for one goal. To rescue these victims from their living nightmare and set them free.

These heroes are backed by powerful women driven by a mission to right the wrongs committed against those less fortunate. Using their wealth and station in life, they fight for those who can't fight for themselves. And in doing so, have formed a private club for women by women. This club is called the Wild Orchids Garden Club.

Welcome to the new generation of Wild Orchids.

Friday

"Are we really having this conversation again?" I slam my glass onto the little bistro table nearly spilling iced tea everywhere.

"Yes, we are." Cecilia Wakefield, affectionately known as CiCi, also my best bud in the world says and tosses a balled up napkin at my head. I expertly bat it right back at her.

"Just once! One time, I'd like to have lunch without discussing it!" I sound like I'm whining because I am.

"You bring it on yourself. If you'd just do it already, we could move on." CiCi growls then takes an exaggerated bite of her chicken salad on toasted croissant to make her point.

That's so CiCi. She thinks everyone should be happily married like her or at least in a committed relationship. Or in my case, any relationship will do. But I supposed that's not really fair. She knows me better than anyone and she loves me. She just wants me to be happy. And I really do want to be in a relationship. But it's complicated.

I'm Alexandria Monroe. Alex to my friends. I'm an attorney like my dad. Well, not exactly. He's a corporate attorney while I prefer to be in the trenches. I work for the DA's office. My Godfather Beauregard Delaneuville, try saying that five times really fast, is the District Attorney and my boss. I call him Uncle Beau, which he loves by the way. I'm his favorite little soldier in an army of attorneys working in his "bullpen".

I'm twenty seven years old, successful, I live in a beautiful apartment overlooking the city, I have a loving family and wonderful friends. My life is great. Oh wait, did I forget to mention one critical flaw? I'm still a virgin. Yes, you heard me. A twenty seven year old virgin! And unfortunately for me, the status of my unbreeched Va-JJ has been a topic of our lunch conversation for way too long.

Too long as in years! And lunch? Nearly every Friday at this cool little place called La Cafe Petite.

I spend my days between the DA's office and the New Orleans criminal courthouse a few blocks down from here. Sawyer Bennet, CiCi's younger sister by two years, is an ER doctor at Tulane Medical Center which is only one block away. Her schedule is really hectic so this location is better for her. CiCi's schedule is a lot more flexible because she works for both of our fathers at their prestigious corporate law firm across town. She makes the big bucks, so we make her schlep across town to come visit the little people.

La Cafe Petite is just what the name says. The Little Cafe. It's on the corner of South Liberty and Gravier Street tucked back behind a garden of roses. Yep, roses in New Orleans, the concrete jungle. Tasha Carter owns the cafe, but her husband Donny takes care of the roses. He's a horticulturist and runs a very successful gardening business uptown.

We love it here. We have our usual table right in the front window overlooking the rose garden. The walls inside the cafe are painted a soft sage green and the floors have tile that looks like birch wood. Kind of like the real birch hardwood on the floor in my apartment. The bistro tables are covered with white table cloths that have calla lilies stenciled in sage green. It's light, airy and beautiful.

The menu isn't the usual New Orleans fare either. Thank goodness. You won't find shrimp po'boys or red beans and rice on Tasha's menu. Don't get me wrong, I love the traditional New Orleans food, but I can't eat it every day.

"Just do it already? Is that really what you just said? It's not that simple and you know it."

"It really is." My best friend assures.

"It REALLY isn't?" I stress the word really just to be a smart elec. "Imagine this. Say I meet a guy. Say we hit it off and date for a while. Now we want to take it to the next level. He finds out I'm a virgin at almost 30 and"

"You're not almost 30." CiCi scoffs.

"Let me finish. He's going to think one of two things." I hold up two fingers to count off. "Either I'm a prude or... and this is the big one. He's going to get the idea that I've saved myself just for him! He'll think I'm a psycho. It's a no win situation at this point."

"CiCi, leave her alone. If she wants to be a thirty year old virgin like that guy in that movie, then who are we to stop her." Sawyer, my other bestie points out.

I stare at her in horror at the idea. My eyes so wide they might pop right out of my head. "You take that back twerp! Right this minute!"

Sawyer sticks her tongue out at me then in her little sing song voice sings, "sticks and stone Alexandria Grace Monroe may break my bones."

Like the mature adult I am, I stick my tongue out right back at her.

"Ladies!" CiCi sighs. "Enough!"

Then she turns serious mother hen eyes my way.

"Alex, you won't even consider a serious relationship because you think being a virgin makes you a freak or something. It's ridiculous! And it's holding you back. Every time a guy even hints at getting serious, you bail."

"I do not." I defend myself. I'm always defending myself. But I'm lying through my teeth and they both know it.

"Yes, you do!" Sawyer accuses stabbing at a tomato in her salad. "Just last month I set you up with Terry Edwards, that sexy orthopedist. You wouldn't even go on a second date with him. I know, because he told me you gave him the "let's be friends" spiel."

I can't help but scowl at them both. "He was too nice. I'd end up walking all over him."

"Who cares, you idiot!" Sawyer rolls her eyes at me. "You weren't supposed to marry him, you were supposed to bang him!"

"Are you nuts! I'd end up seeing him again at some fundraiser or somewhere else like that and you know it! I'd be humiliated!" God! Didn't they get it? What successful, confident woman is still a virgin at twenty seven years old! So, I was busy getting through law school and starting my career. And yes, Wild Orchids takes up a lot of my time, but no one knows that and it's not like I can explain it to them. It's a secret.

CiCi reached over and grabbed my hand. "Alex, honey. Being a virgin is not something to be humiliated about."

"Says the happily married wife and mother of our beautiful Able Graham." I scoff then grin at the smile CiCi can't help spreading across her face at the mention of her son.

"So," Sawyer gets this evil gleam in her eyes. "What you're saying is," she pauses for affect. "That a nice guy is out and anyone you might see again is a no go."

"Exactly!" I nod my head to make my point.

"Well, now we're getting somewhere." CiCi folds her arms on the table and leans in.

"What do you mean?" I have a bad feeling in my gut.

The two sisters grin at each other then they turn those evil grins toward me.

"We have the perfect guy for the job." CiCi tells me and gives me a smug smile.

"What are you talking about?" I look from one smug face to the other. I see knowledge in their eyes. "You guys are evil!"

"Don't be so dramatic." Sawyer scoffs.

"Who's the guy?" This is such a bad idea.

"Let's get business out of the way first, then we'll tell you about," CiCi uses her fingers for air quotes, "the guy."

I don't think I want to know about "the guy", so I grab onto the new topic like a life line. I quickly take a look around us to see how close the other occupied tables are before I begin. "Diana Bradford is up next. I'm having lunch with her on Sunday to check out her "greenhouse". It's perfect for an Orchid. She's housed several for us in the past."

"She has. She really looks forward to it and keeps reminding me not to skip her in the rotation. Just make sure and remind her that it may be last minute." Sawyer adds, all business now.

"Do you have a lead?" The majority of the Orchids come from Sawyer's connections with ER physicians across the country. Sawyer was a child prodigy. She's two years younger than CiCi and I, but graduated high school with us. She could've graduated well before that but her mother was concerned about her social skills so she held her back to graduate with CiCi. As it was, she was close to having her bachelor's degree in pre-med by then. This chick is seriously smart.

"Not yet, but that could change tonight for all we know." Sawyer pushed her plate aside. "I'm supposed to call a colleague of mine on the east coast later this afternoon. He left a message on the Orchid line earlier to call him after hours. So, I'll let you know what I find out."

"We'll be ready." I assure her.

"Oh, and when you're at Diana's, ask her if she's taking her blood pressure medication. Your Mom's worried. She said Diana keeps forgetting to take it." Sawyer adds.

"Diana Bradford is not forgetting to take anything and you know it." CiCi declares. "She doesn't think she should have to take any medication. She says she has a strong constitution."

"Olivia mentioned that. But apparently, she had a 'come-to-Jesus' meeting with Diana earlier this week. And you know your mother." Sawyer raises an eyebrow at me.

I roll my eyes. "I'll just bet she did. I would've liked to have been a fly on the wall for that conversation."

My mother, Dr. Olivia Monroe, is a pediatric neurosurgeon. There are very few in the state so she's crazy busy. However, she makes time to check in with the elderly members of the Garden Club on a regular basis. Especially those who are alone. She's also a take no prisoners kind of woman. She holds nothing back when it comes to someone's health. And knowing my mother, Diana Bradford didn't stand a chance.

"Me too." CiCi agreed.

"Ok, I'll meet with Diana, check on her meds and her "greenhouse" and report back next week unless we need it sooner." I push my plate aside and drink the last of my tea.

CiCi does the same and signals our waitress for the check.

Sawyer, ever the preceptive one watched her sister closely. Her smiles have been mostly forced today. "How are you holding up?"

CiCi's smile falters slightly. "Not as well as I'd like. He's been gone ten days now with no word."

"What does Baron say?" Baron is my older brother. He and Thomas, CiCi's husband have been best friends all their lives. They joined the Marines together right out of high school. After finishing their first tour, they got out and opened a security company. Recently, Thomas took an assignment to rescue a kidnapped son of some dignitary in France, but went off the grid ten days ago.

Sawyer and I have been trying to keep CiCi occupied and help out with Able as much as possible. But I can tell, it's taking its toll on her.

CiCi shakes her head. "As of yesterday, there's still no word."

She's not crying, but I can see she wants to. I reach across the table and take her hand and give it a squeeze. Sawyer places her hand on top of mine in a show of solidarity.

"Thomas is as tough as they come. You know if he's gone radio silent, there's a good reason." I assure her.

"Baron said the same thing. He reported in that the rescue was successful. Now he's trying to lose a tail."

"Well, that explains it. You know he would've called in for backup if he needed it. Thomas would never take unnecessary risks now that he has you and Able." Sawyer adds quietly.

"I know. And you're right." CiCi blows out an exasperated breath. "I'm just being silly. Let's talk about something else." She smiles at us to reassure us, but we're not fooled.

"Alright. Let's tell Alex about the guy." Sawyer says and gives me   a   big   smile,   all   teeth.

Author's Note

I would love to hear from my readers. Your reviews give me wonderful insight into your thoughts and how my stories are received. Please leave a review. Good, bad, or indifferent, I would appreciate the feedback.

KATIE BROUSSARD

I was born and raised in Louisiana so my sassy southern attitude comes naturally.

For twenty-eight years now, I've been blessed to be married to the best guy I know. He is the love of my life, my best friend, and my rock. And while our two sons may be the apple of their father's eye, they hold their mother's heart in the palms of their hands.

I'm also very lucky to have the coolest friends a girl could ever wish for. Together, we're mostly a 'hot mess'! And I wouldn't have it any other way.

I enjoy a great read. Whether it's a steamy romance, a nail biting thriller, or a well written cook book, I simply love to read.

At the moment, I'm opening a new chapter in my life. I spent the first half making mistakes, burdened by responsibilities, and always doing what was expected. I intend to spend the second half enjoying new experiences and living by my own terms. So, I'm excited to see what the future holds and what new experiences await!

Follow the Author:

Follow Katie Broussard at:

Twitter: @KatieBroussard3
Facebook: Kate.broussard
TikTok: @kbroussard22